NORA'S ARMY

Denis Collins

Helena
who shook the hand of
the Great MAC Arthure!.

Denis Collins

10/0 7

Washington Writers' Publishing House
Washington, DC

D0111421

This book is a work of fiction. Names, characters, places and incidents are products of the author's imagination, or are indeed historical figures and events used in a fictional situation.

Copyright © 2006 by Denis Collins
All rights reserved

COVER PHOTOGRAPH by Bert Katz
AUTHOR'S PHOTOGRAPH by Riley Collins
COVER DESIGN by Denis Collins
TYPESETTING by Barbara Shaw
PRINTING by McNaughton & Gunn

LIBRARY OF CONGRESS CATALOGUING-IN-PUBLICATION DATA
Collins, Denis, 1949-
    Nora's army / Denis Collins.
        p. cm.
    ISBN 0-931846-83-8 (alk. paper)
    ISBN 0-931846-82-X (pbk : alk. paper)

    1. World War, 1914-1918—Veterans—Fiction. 2. Sevareid, Eric, 1912-1992—Fiction. 3. African American journalists—Fiction. 4. African Americans—Fiction. 5. Indians of North America—Fiction. 6. Race relations—Fiction. 7. Nineteen thirties—Fiction. 8. Washington (D.C.)—History—20th century—Fiction. I. Title. I. Title.
    PS3603.O4542N67 2006
    813'.6—dc22
                                                2006027639

Printed in the United States of America

WASHINGTON WRITERS' PUBLISHING HOUSE
P. O. Box 15271
Washington, D.C. 20003

DEDICATED TO
Fireproof Pam

ACKNOWLEDGMENTS

I'd like to thank the members of Washington Writer's Publishing House, in particular Laura Brylawski-Miller, Catherine Kimrey, Elisavietta Ritchie and Barbara Shaw, for shepherding the book through production stages; the members of the writers' group; Eli Flam and Elisavietta Ritchie for editing various drafts; Phil Woods for punching me at exactly the right moment; and the *Washington Post, New York Times,* the *Washington Times,* Associated Press and the District of Columbia Library.

DRAMATIS PERSONAE

The Lovers:
Randolph Walker, 18: Lived his first 13 years rich and white, the next five poor and Negro.
Nora O'Sullivan, 17: Irish farm girl who sailed to America in search of a thief.
*Eric Sevareid, 19: Found his first big story in an East St. Louis rail yard.
Jenny Broom, 21: Prostitute on floating Lighthouse.

The Law:
*Pelham Glassford: Washington DC Police Superintendent.
*General Douglas A. MacArthur: Army Chief of Staff District
*Major George S. Patton Jr.: Executive officer of the 3rd Cavalry.
*Major Dwight D. Eisenhower: Principal aide to General MacArthur.
Ned Tobin: District Police officer.

Bonus Veterans:
*Walt Waters: Leader of the Bonus Expeditionary Force.
Dennis Diamond: Nora's Bonus Camp protector.
Tom Halloran: Machine gun musician.
*Joe Angelo: Saved MacArthur's life in WWI.

The Mystics:
Virni Tabak: 15-year-old Perfect Master.
Madame Blisky: Mighty My Mistress.
*Sweet Daddy Grace: Minister of United House of Prayer.

Gangsters:
Fat Carlos
Juan Williams

Supporting Cast:
Will Cutler, 17: Leader of Outcasts gang,
Tommy Baker, 18: Walker's first and best friend in Washington.
Henry, 21: Kemunkey Indian.
James Kemper: Thief who stole Nora's silver cup.
Neil Gold: Owner of Criers Club.
Ken Cord: Party Chief, Washington Communist Society.
Jack Allman: Nora's former school teacher.
Frank Briley: Owner of Briley's General Store.
Catherine Briley: Frank's niece.
Mr. Luke: Randolph Walker's grandfather.
*Herbert C. Hoover: President of the United States.
Richard Drury: Staff at Smithsonian Institution.
Max Berga: Newspaper reporter.
*Beulah Limerick, 17: Whoopee girl. Murdered.
*Evalyn MacLean: Owner of the *Washington Post* newspaper and
   Hope Diamond.

*Real characters, fictionalized.

April 30, 1932

WALKER

I thought she was a boy at first, skinny and chalk white, without sense enough to stay out of the Stead. The only white people who went there were police or social workers, and this one, dressed in wool pants and a snap brim cap, wasn't either, just a tall, skinny kid, lost or stupid and probably both. Then she took off the cap and let her hair get away.

She was maybe a quarter of the way into the tacked-together shacks and laundry lines, standing between a bare-chested man shaving above a metal bowl and a little boy who dropped his ball when her hair came free. I might have dropped something too, the way her hair stood out against the sheets, not because it was so pretty but because it looked like it might catch fire any second.

She looked at me and I looked back and since my mouth was open I figured to say something.

"What do you want here?" It sounded rougher than I meant, especially since I was feeling good that morning, better than I had in months. But there it was, my first words to Nora O'Sullivan offered up like a mouse turd.

"I've never met Negro people before," she said in a soft Irish but with a look straight as a punch. Close like that, her hair down and yellow specks blazing in her green eyes, I guessed she was about 17 and tall for a girl. Negro people. The way she said it.

"So you're just off the boat and you want to see some genuine colored folk?"

"I do." Her smile wasn't clever or challenging, more like a kid hoping for circus elephants, which was too bad because there was no way I was giving her a sightseeing tour, not on this day.

I turned to walk away and heard myself say *follow me*, and she did, past the shacks and sheets that crisscrossed the Stead like sails. Through the smell of boiled cabbage, messed diapers and whatever scent my own recklessness was giving off. I wondered what she was thinking, but she didn't look to be thinking at all, just watching everything and breathing deep like it all smelled sweet, and for the first time I noticed her eyebrows, and that even in chunky men's clothes she was almost beautiful.

"What are they doing?" She was pointing at a crooked line of kids standing at one corner of the Stead's four cobblestone alleys.

"Waiting for Aunt Jane to take them to church."

"Is she your aunt?"

I could have explained but didn't know if she'd understand, being from so far away. "No. She's just…Aunt Jane."

I knew most of the people in the Stead from my days selling numbers and was surprised nobody had anything to say about me walking this unlit match of a girl through their Sunday morning. But all the church people were hurrying to get dressed and everybody else was either sleeping or too hung over to care. When we got back to where we'd started, by the boy with his ball, she shoved her hair under her cap and introduced herself.

"My name is Nora O'Sullivan. I've come to America to get something that was stolen from me." She stuck out her chin as she said it, like daring me to contradict her. When I told her I was about that same business myself, she nodded as if she understood completely, which was at least half more than I did.

We stood for a while, her back to 17th Street and mine to the Stead. Finally I said, "The Bonus Army is coming today. You want to see them?"

She didn't ask what the Bonus Army was, or how far we'd go to find them, just said sure, wherever I wanted to take her. That told me something about Nora O'Sullivan, but it would be three months and a few people dead before I figured what.

～

DID I MENTION I'm colored? But you'd have guessed that. A lot of people don't like the word colored, like it better than nigger or jigaboo, but still think it's more disrespectful and uncapitalized than Negro. And lazy too since everybody except The Invisible Man is some kind of color. But colored works best for me.

A genuine Negro knows at least half of what every other Negro knows about a universe of things, beginning with their mama's list of shit you don't say or do around white folk. But since I spent my first thirteen years as a white boy, not passing for one but actually believing I was the real deal, and the next few playing hermit in the woods beside the Potomac River, I'd only been colored for three years when I met Nora. Trust me, that's a little late to get into the game.

What I did know, what you only have to be colored for half-an-hour to know, is you don't walk beside a white girl in downtown Washington, D.C., even if she is dressed in men's clothes with her hair tucked under a farmer's cap. So when we got to where the alley meets 16th Street, I told Nora to keep a step or two behind.

That's when she gave me her look, which is damn impressive the first time you receive it, a look that goes from curious to steamed in two heartbeats.

"I won't be trailing you like a servant or a dog," she says.

I smiled at her like you'd smile at a young and not very bright child. "I don't know what it's like in Ireland, but in every one of the United States of America a white woman doesn't walk next to... me."

"Who's to stop us?"

I should have gotten mad at that, like all I needed to make the world a slice of cherry pie was a little courage, but I figured to let her see for herself.

"Step up, but put some rocks in your pocket in case we have to fight our way out of trouble." She could see I wasn't kidding.

The day was sunny and dry and not yet hot enough to melt tar, one of the fifteen or twenty perfect days we get each year in D.C. Walking south on 16th Street, I noticed what Nora was noticing— the embassies of France and Great Britain with their hanging flags and black touring cars; the smell of flowers being sold from little carts mixing with the stink of horse shit; old women selling nickel apples from curbside wicker baskets as trolleys clanged down K Street.

"Did you just steal that apple?"

I looked where Nora was looking, at the green apple in my right hand and knew I must have snatched it from the last apple cart. I didn't remember doing it, stealing being as unconscious a habit with me as nail biting.

"That woman is a friend of mine," I joked, "She gives me apples and I give her stock tips."

Nora took the apple and bit into it, chewing slowly, like it was too good to swallow.

"This country is mad for stealing," she said. "When I got off the train from New York, a pack of boys on bicycles stole my satchel."

"I bet you stopped to hear a boy singing from a church tower."

Nora's eyes popped wide. "*Pennies from Heaven!*"

"A beautiful voice, huh?"

"A group of us stopped to listen when of a sudden, these boys with scarves over their faces came on bicycles, howling and grabbing."

"I can get it back for you," I said and waited for her to be impressed.

"No need," smiled Nora. "I already have. I pulled a bicycle from one of them and followed the rest to their hideout."

For the second time in less than an hour my mouth was left hanging open.

"There was no trouble in it at all," she explained sweetly. "I traded the gang leader the bike for my satchel and that was the end of it."

"And what about the boy whose bike you took?"

Nora lowered her eyes. "The crowd got hold of him and beat him fierce."

I couldn't get my brain around the idea that this girl had sailed across the Atlantic in search of one thief and then, before she had time to take a deep breath, chased another bunch into their hideout. Not that Will Cutler's gang of 12-and-13-year-olds was exactly cutthroat but Nora had no way of knowing that. I snuck another look at her, at the freckles on the bridge of her nose, her fuzzy pink earlobes and those eyebrows! Every other woman in sight, at least the ones who cared enough to work at it, had eyebrows like Carole Lombard or Joan Crawford, plucked thin as though hard times couldn't support even that luxury of hair. Nora's eyebrows were thickets that climbed her forehead like wild vines.

"I know that building." She was pointing at the White House. "There's one like it in Dublin's Phoenix Park."

"That's where President Hoover lives."

"I heard a song on the train. About Hoover and a whistle."

"'Mellon pulled the whistle, Hoover rang the bell, Wall Street gave the signal and the country went to...'"

The last lyric was smothered by an elbow to my ribs, thrown by a white guy going the other way. It didn't hurt so much as surprise the hell out of me. Walking down 16th Street with a white girl and didn't see it coming! Nora turned like she might go after him. I'd have laughed if I had the breath.

"Leave it," I grunted. "That was my fault."

In Lafayette Park a hundred men wearing pieces of old military uniforms stood talking in small groups while kids played hide-and-seek behind statues and trees. A circle of women sat under a massive oak with roots that knuckled above ground. Hanging from the door of a car parked by the curb was a sign that read "**Bonus Or Bust.**" On the other side of Pennsylvania Avenue, about forty uniformed cops stood with their backs to the White House.

"What is this?" It was the first question she'd asked about the Bonus Army.

"These guys are veterans of the war. They were voted a bonus by Congress to be paid in 1945 but they need it now."

"It's a small enough army."

"This is just a few locals. The army's coming from everywhere else."

As I watched the scene play across Nora's face—the kids, their mothers, the cops across the street—a feeling came over me, so old and buried it took me some time to remember where it came from. Centerfield. Even the clouds overhead could have sailed directly from that old sky above Westchester.

I took Nora to meet my Party chief, Ken Cord. He was talking with men I recognized from the Tuesday night meetings.

"Comrade Cord, this is Nora O'Sullivan. She's just come from Ireland on a quest."

Cord was wearing carpenter overalls, thick buckled boots and an Army cap. He hadn't worked as a carpenter for ten years, but liked to say you couldn't win converts to Marxism wearing a $30 suit.

"Anybody who's not on a quest of some kind isn't living," said Cord with a slight bow to Nora. "Are you here to see history made today?"

Nora bent her knees and for a second I thought she might curtsy, but being a few inches taller she was only trying to get under his straw boater and look him in the eye. She said, "I'm here to see whatever there is to see."

A shout came from the east end of the park and everyone pushed forward. An open-backed truck carrying thirty men appeared, half of them waving American flags. That first truck was followed by a second and then a third. The veterans were singing, "It's a long way to Tipperary," which I figured Nora knew well. (She'd tell me later that she'd only heard it twice before and both times sung by Americans.) When the last of the sixteen trucks passed, we emptied onto the avenue to parade behind them.

"How did they get here and where did they start?"

"They left Oregon three weeks ago. They rode trains as far as Missouri, then trucks from there. It was a real show in Missouri."

"And the railroads let them ride free?"

"They didn't like it, but who's gonna arrest war heroes? Missouri was the only state that tried to keep them from passing through."

The trucks angled across a grass lot. Walt Waters, tall and dark-haired with a long pointed nose, climbed a fender to talk to his troops. The last I'd seen him was with Eric Sevareid in St. Louis. On that day Waters was standing on top of a railroad car.

"He looks like pictures I've seen of Rudy Vallee," said Nora.

"His name is Waters. He's the one who brought them here."

Waters raised both hands to quiet the crowd. "We started this march in Oregon with 150 men, no money and no grand plan. Here we are, three weeks later, disturbing the President's lunch." A cheer sent a flight of pigeons down the avenue. "I've been told there are 3,000 veterans in the capital as of today. By tomorrow there'll be 1,000 more and by next week ten times that many. Veterans from Texas, Pennsylvania, Ohio and California are on their way. Tomorrow we'll be on the steps of the Capitol, asking Congress for what's owed us. And I promise you this, we won't be leaving until we get it."

I spotted police superintendent Pelham Glassford on his blue motorcycle. I'd met him a couple weeks earlier after a Party meeting. For reasons I couldn't figure, Cord had told him about me. Glassford wanted to talk about Negroes and the revolutionary dialectic. That's exactly how he put it too.

Nora was talking to me. "How do you know about what happened in Mizzer...?"

"Missouri. I was there." Before she could ask any more questions, Waters ordered the men to start marching back toward the White House and beyond, to the Anacostia River where they planned to set up camp.

I was going to ask Nora if she wanted to walk with them, but she was already on the move, marching down the sidewalk after her army.

NORA

IN THE WEST COAST village where they were born, Nora and her brother Brendan were known as "fairie kin" both for their green eyes and uncommon ability to find lost things. When she was seven, Nora showed up one morning at Dan Mayhew's gate with her finger in the nose ring of a prize bull the farmer had yet to miss. When the best man misplaced the ring at the wedding of the mayor's only daughter, six-year-old Brendan O'Sullivan marched up the aisle, knelt at his feet and lifted the ring from the man's pant cuff.

People came from miles around to ask where they should look for things gone queer, and more than a few seeking fairie gold. The truth of the matter was that neither of the children had any supernatural abilities. What they had was an uncommon curiosity, which carried them over as much of County Kerry their legs could cover.

Farm work and school cut deeply into Nora's explorations as she grew older, but the curiosity never died. So it was not surprising that the first chance she got to explore Washington, D.C. she exhausted herself in the effort.

She began as soon as the Bonus Army disappeared beyond the Capitol. Walker had already said goodbye (too late she thought to ask if that was his first or last name), saying he had business that needed his full attention. Fair enough, she wouldn't beg, though she did argue a bit. Following his suggestion she went northwest from the Capitol through Chinatown and the F Street shopping district, peeking into nearly every closed shop and restaurant along the way, then headed north toward U Street, which Walker had described as Washington's Negro Broadway.

In Ireland she'd seen exactly one Negro and only for as long as it took him to pass in a carriage, but he made a powerful impression. He was for Nora all the world she'd yet to see. Her uncle Dan had told her stories of his sailing days in West Africa, on a ship carrying mirrors, axes and old muskets to trade for copra and palmoil. Stories of beautiful, dark women with high cheekbones and ivory-white teeth. Walker was beautiful in his own way, his smooth skin the color of tanned leather and hair wild with curls. In a starched white shirt with the sleeves rolled above his elbows, the muscles of his forearms reminded her of cabled wool. And wasn't he a mystery, so solemn one minute and funny the next, like two people taking turns inside the same body. He would require further study.

Nora got as far as 12th and P Streets before dropping to the stoop of the Manhattan Laundry. The fatigue of her three-week journey by horseback, ship and train suddenly fell on her like a…. Nora was too tired to come up with a simile, so tired and hungry her hands shook. Fortunately she had the rest of Walker's green apple in a twist of cloth at her waist. She chewed and swallowed, taking deep breaths until her weariness smoothed into something nearly pleasant. She had to struggle to keep from falling asleep right there on the step.

She began counting the hours since leaving Ireland but was distracted by the thought of Rosario, the sailor who put his hand between her legs on the boat coming over. And that boy Metzler who tried to sweet-talk her on the train from New York. For maybe five minutes, or as long as it took her to register Metzler's intent, wonder at his American accent and study the black curl of his wet-combed hair, she was flattered by his attention. By the time she fixed him as the missing link between two boys she disliked back in Kenmare, it was too late. She'd already smiled, listened with a respectful tilt of her head and told him, in answer to one of his questions, that she was wanton. Though she didn't put it exactly that way.

"Not everyone in Ireland is Catholic," said Nora, who at the age of 10 knew the life story of every saint and could recite her Latin as well as any altar boy. But on that train to Washington, just weeks before her 18th birthday she'd said, "Myself, I'm a pagan."

Metzler fairly drooled on hearing that, the change in him like heat coming off a hearth stone. He rubbed his hands together and licked his rubbery lips and might have tried licking hers if Nora hadn't changed seats.

At Union Station he followed her off the train. "Nora girl, you listen to me," his voice buzzing like one of the American mosquitoes she'd newly met. "There's lots of people here don't like you Irish, say you're unrespectable and only like to drink and carry on. But I'm not one of them. I expect people can't be no other way than what they are."

Nora turned on him. At five foot nine, she stood two inches

above Metzler and must have looked even taller with her hair piled under her cap. In Ireland her hair had been a curious shade of red, but in this new world people stared like she had snakes growing from her head. More surprising to Nora was that she didn't like the attention. After all the years she'd spent honing her eccentricity, wearing men's clothes and professing bold and sacrilegious beliefs, here she was hiding her hair under a farmer's cap and hurrying away from a pipsqueak of a boy who'd insulted generations of O'Sullivans.

"I don't particularly care what people here think of the Irish," she said. "Neither do I care whether you share those thoughts. Now if you don't mind, I'll say good day to you and goodbye." Even as she wheeled away Nora thought—a good enough speech back home but a bit wordy here. Since the *Jerseley* docked off Ellis Island, Nora had been studying conversations around her, listening to the immigration officer interrogate an old farmer from Cork ("Why the hell are you bringing potato vines to America?") to the train conductor pulling tickets and the peanut man selling nickel bags in Philadelphia's Penn Station. Short and to the point. Blunt and final. It was a language she needed to learn.

She walked back to where Metzler was rolling a cigarette, a brown tobacco pouch held between his teeth. In a low voice and as tough as she could muster, she said "Get lost!"

Metzler's eyebrows danced like caterpillars on a hot stone, but Nora wasn't satisfied she'd been any better than plain rude. It was a start at least.

It was hard to believe that in the twenty-four hours since her arrival at Union Station, she'd been robbed by the bicycle boys, slept in the back of Briley's General Store, met Walker and marched with the Bonus Army. She allowed her eyes to close but only for an instant.

"Are you a boy or a girl?"

Nora opened her eyes to find a little girl with a dirty face, standing so close Nora could smell the lollipop in her hand.

"How old are you?" asked Nora.

"You answer first." The girl couldn't have been more than five.

Nora took off her cap and shook out her hair, which prompted the girl to make an O of her mouth and clap her sticky hands together.

Now is the time to stop hiding, she decided. "Tell your parents you got this from a fairie," she said, putting her cap on the girl's small head. When the girl looked up at the brim, Nora remembered Jamie's eyes rolling in his skull as the crowd beat him.

She rose from the stoop, suddenly eager to see Will and his gang once more. "I've got to go," she told the little girl, who'd lost interest in everything but her new, absurdly oversized cap. "I need to read some boys a story."

~

THERE WERE TWO BOOKS in the bottom of her satchel, under some hand-knit woolen clothes, menstrual pads, a bone-handled hair brush, a leather sling, a map of Washington (drawn lovingly with trees and monuments and little church towers by an old man from Breem who'd worked on the C&O Canal) and a personal journal written in a style her teacher Jack Allman once described as James Joyce with a sweet tooth. The books—*Tobacco Road* by Erskine Caldwell and *The Crock of Gold* by James Stephens—were both gifts. The first was from Allman, the headmaster of the hedgerow school where Nora learned her Latin and Greek. He offered it as a guide to the rough natives she'd meet. He gave it to her one week before she left Ireland, on the same day he asked her to marry him.

"I'll marry no one until I've seen the world," laughed Nora, pushing her fingers through his thinning hair. Sure it was cruel to take his proposal so lightly, but hadn't he disappointed her as well, refusing to have relations until they were married?

"You're a coward," she'd said, more humiliated than angry. To be nearly 18 and still a virgin was embarrassing. Most of her friends had a child or two by then and, more to the point, none of her heroines, particularly the Irish pirate queen Grace O'Malley, was a virgin at her age. O'Malley had bedded men with a frank and guiltless appetite that Nora greatly admired, though not enough to imitate, at least not with any of the town and country boys she grew up with.

She was in love with the idea of love—a letter written in blood by a dying warrior or a rose carried to her across snow capped peaks—but the physical act of sex, which she'd witnessed countless times while working the farm, had never aroused in her any of the flushed and breathless symptoms she'd read so many times in novels.

Jack Allman, being somewhat frail and decidedly sober, didn't exactly light a fire in her loins either, but he was wonderfully intelligent and the first worthy candidate to come her way. So she was deeply insulted when he refused to play his part.

"If we're found out I'll lose this position and be on the road without a penny in my pocket," he'd said. Nora knew the truth of that, but was frustrated none the less.

The other book, *The Crock of Gold*, was a gift from her father, John. Nora hadn't read it and wasn't eager to, figuring it to be too much of what she already knew—elves and fairies, giants capable of carrying mountains on their backs, talking fish, haunted hills...in short all the fables, superstitions and rank nonsense that any girl living in the west of Ireland was sure to know. But for the job at hand the *Crock* was sure to be better than *Tobacco Road*. She pulled it from her satchel under the cot and made a quick exit through the back of Briley's General Store, stopping to grab a rusty, flat-tired bicycle that was leaning against the storeroom wall.

She looked both ways before leaving, hoping to avoid the store's owner Frank Briley. The night before, when first she looked into his pink, overfed face, Nora was reminded of Cavan the baker who'd once played hide the sweets in her First Communion dress. Briley's mother and Nora's had tended sheep together in the hills above Kenmare. With that as reference she'd entered his store on 17th Street and presented herself, the only thing in sight without a price tag affixed. He offered her a cot in back and twenty cents a day for ten hours work. Nora said she didn't care about the terms, as long as she had a place to sleep and a mid-day break to search for the silver cup that had been stolen from her.

The bicycle gang's hideout was a twenty-minute walk from the store. She hoped they weren't out on a…what did American gangsters call it, a heist? The day before, when she'd first entered the alley in pursuit of her satchel, she nearly crashed into Will Cutler.

"WHOA THERE," he'd shouted, waving his hands in the air as though she was a runaway horse. With his scarf pulled down he appeared older than she'd guessed, very near her own age and handsome in a sharp way. His brown eyes looked…hungry, as though they'd spent too much time staring through restaurant windows.

"Well, look what we have here," he said with a smile so big Nora wondered that it didn't hurt his face. None of the dozen boys who came up the alley to form a circle around her was smiling, but then none looked ready to do her harm. "Either Jamie has turned himself into a girl wearing a funny hat, or a girl in a funny hat has stolen Jamie's bicycle. Now I don't claim to be Einstein, but I'm guessing the former is less likely than the latter. How is Jamie by the way?"

Nora, still a full sentence behind said, "It's not stealing if it's taking something from someone who took something from you."

"And Jamie?"

"I'm afraid there wasn't anything I could do to stop them."

"What's done is done. Pinky, Teddy, go back and get him." To Nora he said, "Thanks for bringing back the bicycle."

"I'm happy to give it back just as soon as you return my satchel."

Will laughed. "Why should we trade when we can just take it?"

"Because if you do, I'll come at you every day until I've got what's mine and as much of yours as I can carry." A few of the boys laughed. They were dirty-faced and years younger than Will. Were they orphans like she'd seen in Limerick, or just boys with parents who let them run wild?

"Aren't you the one, coming into my den of thieves, armed only with your magic hat and funny accent," said Will with such good humor Nora let the insult pass. "I'll give you your satchel and I won't even look inside to see what treasure we're giving up."

Because she'd never met anyone like this Will Cutler, Nora wasn't sure if he was a likable scoundrel or a scoundrel pretending to be likable. He was certainly interesting and at the moment that was good enough. He gave her a tour of the alley, providing a running commentary on his ambitions ("I'll be famous someday. For exactly what doesn't matter"), his hometown of Eola, West Virginia ("Where I come from the hills are so steep farmers have to tie their cows to rocks to keep them from tumbling down"), and his gang of boys.

"I've got Italians, Irish…and there, that one with the crooked haircut. He's a Polack Jew. What does that tell you?"

Nora hadn't a clue.

"We're the Outcasts."

"Oh."

"No. That's a good thing," he said to the concerned look on her face. "Since everybody already looks down on us, we don't have to care what they think."

Nora looked more closely at the boys. They were ragged but not entirely, each wearing one new or bright piece of clothing, as though they'd chipped in for a couple of fancy outfits to share. Polack Jew, for example, had an expensive leather belt slung well below his pant loops. Another boy wore a felt, tri-cornered hat that made him look like an English coach boy. All of them walked with a swagger that reminded Nora of her brother Brendan. Cocky. But then they'd have to be to steal from her.

The half-dozen shacks built against the brick wall were put together with planks, cardboard, chicken wire, blankets, even bed sheets. Like the boys, each shack had one bright spot, a wall painted a primary color. Being her first American bandits' alley, Nora was impressed with every part of it, though she did wonder at its strategic layout.

"With only one way in and out, wouldn't you be easily trapped?"

Will put a finger against the side of his nose and whispered, "We've got that taken care of. But good thinking."

A boy brought Nora her satchel. As she handed over the bicycle, Cutler made a show of studying her.

"We might be able to use a smart girl like you," he said in a slow, musical voice.

"Is that what you do all day, steal people's bags?"

"That's only a part of it," he said proudly. "We deliver things and take messages. Sometimes we work for ourselves and sometimes for other people."

"And you don't feel bad about the stealing?"

"Why should we? After what was stolen from us?" When Nora asked what had been stolen from them, Will looked amazed at her ignorance.

"How about everything? There's no money left in the world. We've got a right to whatever scraps we can find."

～

NORA HAD NO DOUBT that the Outcasts would be happy to see her again, so she was surprised when two boys jumped up from their card game to block her entrance to the alley. One whistled a warning, the other asked Nora her business.

She recognized a boy approaching from the alley. "Hello, Pinky."

It took Pinky a few seconds to get past the wonder of her hair, which hadn't been on display the day before.

"This is Nora!" he announced. "She's the one who come in here to get her bag back." The guard boys looked at Nora with sudden respect. Pinky took hold of the bicycle and steered her to Will Cutler who sat on an overturned peach basket oiling a bike chain.

"Don't tell me you stole another one?"

"I haven't. I've only borrowed it from where I work. I was hoping you might lend me a patch or two. And I wanted to see how Jamie was doing." Jamie wasn't among the boys gathered around her.

"He's doing okay," said Will. "He thinks his left arm is a dog, but he'll get over that."

Nora was sure she hadn't heard him right. "He thinks his arm is a what?"

"A dog. Come on, I'll show you."

Will led her to a shed, where Jamie sat on a mattress. One of the walls had been pulled away to let the sun in. The light did not flatter his bruised face.

"Hello," he said in a voice that sounded as beaten as he looked. He held a piece of bread in his right hand that he kept trying to press into his left palm. "My dog won't eat."

Though the boys behind her laughed, Nora was certain Jamie wasn't joking.

"You can't get better if you don't eat," he said to his arm in a low, cajoling voice.

Nora placed her hand gently on Jamie's head, the way her mother used to touch her when she was sick. Suddenly, she saw herself as if from above, looking down on Jamie with the half circle of boys behind her. That sense of being outside herself was something she'd read about but never experienced. She guessed it came from hunger.

She felt bad for Jamie's condition, but couldn't accept much blame. He'd had plenty of time to get away but wouldn't without his bicycle, yanking on the frame with both hands while Nora yanked back until they were close as lovers, his forehead against her cheek. When he finally turned to run, it was too late.

The first man caught him by the shoulders and threw him to the ground. The next, old enough to be the boy's grandfather, took careful aim and kicked him squarely in the face. Nearly everyone wanted one good lick, including a handsome woman on broken heels who reminded Nora of her favorite Aunt Sheila. Their ferocity seemed more than punishment but Nora hadn't been in America long enough to guess what.

She'd thought to help him but didn't. It was as though everything was meant to happen exactly as it did. She'd never felt that way before and wondered if America had already changed her. As she pedaled after the bicycle gang she heard a deep groaning behind her and knew it came not from Jamie but from his attackers.

Now, after saying goodbye to Jamie in his shed, she followed Will to where Pinky was pumping air into her tires. "What does the doctor say about him?"

"What doctor?"

"Don't you think he should see one?"

"He'll be good as new in no time. The same thing happened to a cousin of mine in West Virginia after he got hit on the head. Thought his arm belonged to his brother."

"And he's okay now?"

Will laughed. "Hard to tell with cousin Lester."

Nora shivered at the thought of such human oddity. In a quiet voice she said, "I've come to read the boys a story."

For the first time since meeting him, Will looked off balance. "A story? Out of a book? They're not much on books and stories."

Before she could argue her case, the boy closest to Will cupped his hands to his mouth and called to the others in a high, sweet voice. "Nora's going to read us a story." She recognized the voice— the singer in the church tower.

"Maybe if we all sit," suggested Nora and they immediately dropped to the dirt. Will gave her the peach basket to sit upon. Nora pulled the **Crock of Gold** from between the small of her back and the waist of her pants and cleared her throat.

Chapter 1

In the center of the pine wood called Coilla Doraca there lived not long ago two Philosophers. They were wiser than anything else in the world except the Salmon who lies in the pool of Glyn Cagny into which the nuts of knowledge fall from the hazel bush on its bank. He, of course, is the most profound of living creatures, but the two Philosophers are next to him in wisdom.

Their faces looked as though they were made of

parchment, there was ink under their nails, and every difficulty that was submitted to them, even by women, they were able to instantly resolve. The Grey Woman of Dun Gortin and the Thin Woman of Inis Magrath asked them the three questions which nobody had ever been able to answer, and they were able to answer them. That was how they obtained the enmity of these two women which is more valuable than the friendship of angels.

Nora looked at the boys spread below her, all pink lips and dirty faces. "Do any of you know what enmity means? It's hatred or ill will."

A boy near the front blew his nose into his hands, wiped them on his pants and said, "Keep reading!"

The Grey Woman and the Thin Woman were so incensed at being answered that they married the two Philosophers in order to be able to pinch them in bed. But the skins of the Philosophers were so thick that they did not know they were being pinched. They repaid the fury of the women with such tender affection that these vicious creatures almost expired of chagrin, and once, in a very ecstasy of exasperation, after having been kissed by their husbands, they uttered the fourteen hundred maledictions which comprised their wisdom, and these were learned by the Philosophers who thus became even wiser than before.

In due process of time two children were born of these marriages. They were born on the same day and in the same hour, and they were only different in this, that one of them was a boy and the other one was a girl. Nobody was able to tell how this had happened, and, for the first time in their lives the Philosophers were forced to admire an event which they had been unable to prognosticate; but having proved by many different methods that the children were really children, that what must be must be, that a fact cannot be controverted, and that what has happened once may happen twice, they described the occurrence as extraordinary but not unnatural, and submitted peacefully to a Providence even wiser than they were.

Nora imagined herself living in that pine wood with her brother Brendan. He'd be 16 now and surely, still her best friend. She tried to picture what he'd look like six years older but saw only the hurt look on his face the day she slapped him.

They'd been practicing kissing with their eyes closed, Nora's idea, when without any warning she gave his cheek the kind of slap women delivered in books. Nora was 11 and a little old, now that she thought of it, for wet kisses with a brother. She was glad for it though, not the slapping part but the sweet memory of those innocent kisses.

She wondered if the boy and girl in this book would get around to that. "Stop me when you've had enough," she said, settling herself on the basket for a long read.

WALKER

IT WAS NEVER EASY refusing Nora, especially that first day after walking beside the Bonus Army to the Capitol. No, she couldn't come to my Party meeting or wait outside the office until I was done. And no, I wouldn't meet her later for more sightseeing. I told her to follow the Bonus Army to the Anacostia and watch them set up camp, or take a walk through the city, but Nora didn't know why she should when it was more fun being with me.

So naturally I had to say no.

I must have known even then I wouldn't be resisting much longer, but after nearly six years of living quick and careful I couldn't jump out of my skin all at once. The way I'd come to figure it, anything I wanted too much was best avoided.

Tommy Baker used to wonder how I could be so fearless on the river yet cautious with people, but that shouldn't have been a mystery. The river might be dangerous, but it held no grudge.

Tommy was my first and best friend in Washington, though before we got there we had to beat each other bloody. It happened the morning after my grandfather, Mr. Luke, brought me home from Union Station. He was gone fishing by the time I woke but he'd left some crackers and herring on the table. I'd never had salted herring or anything like it, but I ate every bit that morning. Outside it smelled nice, like wet leaves. I could see three other sheds poking out from the evergreen, each one as homemade and unfinished as Mr. Luke's. I walked to the top of a nearby ravine and caught my breath. Thirty yards below, the Potomac jumped past in a great hurry and with a sound like a slightly drunk church choir. I went down the ravine for a closer look at an oak tree snagged in the river like a giant stalk of broccoli. I was nearly to the water when Tommy and his eight-year-old brother Penny came at me from along the shore.

"Who are you?"

It was Tommy who asked. He was 13, the same age as me. We both wore denim pants but his were patched while mine were stiff and new.

"I'm Walker. Who are you?"

"I'm Penny," said his little brother and got punched in the arm for volunteering it.

"We ask the questions 'round here," said Tommy in a quick burst, like he was still out of breath from beating up the last guy who didn't answer fast enough. He circled around, checking me up and down like I was something he'd never seen before. Finally he said, "What are you, white or colored?"

No one had actually told me, but by then no one needed to. "I'm colored," I said. "What about you?"

Penny laughed, his brother being so black. Tommy squeezed his hands into fists and held them out for me to see. "You take that back or I'm gonna whip your ass."

I asked which part he wanted me to take back.

"The whole thing."

"I can't remember the whole thing," I said, "so you better start whipping."

We went at each other full speed, our heads banging together like stones. For the first time in weeks I felt good about something, and it didn't matter if I was hitting or being hit. We rolled bloody into the river and came out swinging and might never have quit if Tommy's mom hadn't called the two of them up the ravine.

Tommy got into fights as readily as other people got into conversations, maybe because he wasn't much for talking. He was smart enough but couldn't disagree with someone without wanting to punch him. He had a sense of humor, but it came out about as often as the full moon. Once we were fighting our way out of an ambush by some white Swampoodle boys, when he turned to me in mid-punch and said, "Is it too late to tell them you're white?"

During those first weeks in D.C., Tommy took it on himself to introduce me to Negro Washington and "work the white out" of me. But I wasn't ready for it. Whenever I crossed the bridge with him to Georgetown or over to U Street I felt exactly like who I still was, a white boy staring at Negroes and being stared at in return. Everything about them was foreign to me, the way they dressed and laughed and talked. One day, watching men roll dice on a vacant lot near Howard University, I tried to imitate their talk. I dropped a consonant and burred a vowel. One of them, a nasty scar running down his cheek, shook his head like I was some idiot boy let out of the institute for the day.

After a while I just gave up and stayed by the Potomac which, believe me, was no punishment. Every day from sunup to dark I'd explore the woods on both sides of the river, following animal trails and drawing maps on butcher's wrap. The hills I shaded brown, the streams and creeks a light yellow. Every few weeks I'd stitch the maps together like a quilt. Days went by that I didn't speak a word, and there was comfort in that. The only person I had an ache to see or hear was my mother, but it was my mother who put me on the train. The last thing she said was, "You're going to live with your grandfather. I don't know when I'll see you again." That stole a bit of the thrill from my first solo train ride.

Those early months the woods were like a sick bed, my place to recover from the fall I'd taken from rich white boy to a colored kid living in a shack no bigger than the closet in my old room. I'd sit in a clearing and concentrate on smells, bird song, the wind in the trees. I wasn't searching for peace or happiness, only numbness. Empty headed, dry-eyed numbness.

Of course that was impossible. How could I recover as easy as that? Not only had I lost my family, I'd lost myself. The boy I'd been—center fielder, class cut up, next in line to go into the closet with Janie St. Clair—had disappeared. Or was he kidnapped? Some nights I dreamed about him, still somewhere in Westchester, living my stolen life.

Mr. Luke was fishing most of the time and when he was around, he looked at me like I was a bomb that might go off any second. He never asked what I did with my days and rarely talked about his own. At night, we'd sit on the outside step of the shack and eat fish, cornbread and wild greens. I liked sneaking looks at Mr. Luke's face, at his thick lips and broad forehead. I could see parts of myself there and other parts that made me wonder what my real father must have looked like. But those first months I didn't have the courage to ask Mr. Luke about his son, not even to learn his name.

It would be years before I heard any stories about Lucas Davis Jr., and only then because Mr. Luke got hit by lightning. But that's a story for another time.

~

WHEN I GOT TO THE PARTY OFFICES on 7th Street, the meeting had already started. Ken Cord was standing behind a desk with his back to the blackboard, like a school teacher before a bunch of grown-up students. A stranger walking in would have noticed what I did the first time I attended a meeting, what stopped me at the door—eight or nine Negroes sitting all mixed in with whites. If there was anywhere else in America where that could happen, I'd never heard of it.

"Do we have any more ideas on how to approach this?" asked Cord.

"I say we get in front of this thing right from the start!" said Ned Tobin, turning to face the room. "Red Ned" had been in the front lines of the Ford Motor strike in Detroit where three demonstrators were killed, and he never passed up an opportunity to remind us of it. He had a head shaped like a turnip and eyes that looked recently punched, but his voice was strong and confident. "During the Ford strike, we raised our flag right at the barricades. People damn well knew we were there."

Another man I knew as Comrade Barker got to his feet. "I like your attitude Ned, but there's a difference here. The Bonus Army doesn't want us at the front. In fact, their leaders say they'll fight us if we try. I say wait until the time is right. Stay strategic."

Ken Cord let the debate go on for another twenty minutes, until everybody said everything there was to say at least twice. That was his style and it worked. By the time he took the floor, his decisions seemed based not on what he'd decided before the meeting began, but on what other people said during it.

"I have to say I'm more in agreement with Comrade Barker on this," said Cord. "It's a dead certainty this Bonus bill will be killed by the Senate. When that happens, the veterans will be feeling a lot less patriotic than they are right now. Let's be patient. That doesn't mean we sit on our hands. I want all of you, especially the veterans, to spend time with the Bonus Army. Talk to them about the hard times. Paint a picture of how we can get past them. You know what to say and if you don't, come talk to me."

In some ways Cord reminded me of the hustlers and con artists I'd met on the streets of D.C., except that his talent wasn't so much talking as listening. I saw that the first time he invited me into his back office. He'd caught me rolling my eyes during an endless debate about putting people on street corners to testify to the benefits of socialism. He asked me about it.

"The more speeches we make, the more we sound like politicians," I told him. "And politicians aren't winning any popularity contests right now."

Cord didn't agree or disagree, just sat behind his desk, nodding his head. He asked me what books I liked, not where I was from or even why I was there. I told him I was working my way through *The Odyssey*. Most white people would have looked at me like I was a liar or a freak, but he didn't flinch. I guessed it was something he practiced, making people feel they were fascinating, but it had been a long time since anyone listened to me that way and I couldn't help liking it.

After Cord adjourned the meeting on this day, he motioned for me. "Can you come in the back office for a minute? There's something I want to ask you."

There was a Negro girl in the office behind a typewriter. She looked to be about 19, with light skin and a pretty face. When I said hello, she took a quick look at Cord before answering, as if she needed his permission to talk. It made me wonder.

"I've been thinking of what you said about making speeches," said Cord, sitting on the edge of his desk. "You may have hit on our biggest problem. How do we spread our message without lecturing. Do you think you could help with that?"

"Help how?"

"Listen to my speeches. Tell me what doesn't ring true."

"I'm not sure I know enough about Marxist theory yet."

"I'm not looking to you for theory. What I want is help in talking straight, so it doesn't sound so…."

"Preachy?"

He laughed. "Exactly. Unnecessarily didactic. What do you say?"

I didn't need time to make up my mind. All the bickering at party meetings had about scraped away my enthusiasm, but I didn't want to quit the only thing offering any hope of getting back what I'd lost. Maybe Cord's offer would let me jump past all the bullshit. I told him I'd give it a try.

"Great. I'll have some material for you to look at soon. What happened to your Irish girl?"

"I went with her as far as the Capitol and then sent her on her own."

Cord nodded. "A wise decision. She's about as inconspicuous as a unicorn."

"I doubt I'll see her again," I said, lying to the both of us.

NORA

THE WEATHER was oppressively hot for the first of May, one of the breezeless, sweat-dripping days Washington is notorious for. To Nora, who'd grown up in Ireland's cool, moist climate, it was like being inside a cook stove with no way out. She spent the morning mopping the storeroom floor, avoiding Frank Briley and thinking of Walker.

She still didn't know his full name, where he lived or worked, yet none of that mattered. He was exotically handsome and her only friend in Washington.

At noon, Nora put the dress she planned to wear to the Smithsonian into a hip pack and walked to the front of the store.

"Where are you going?" asked Briley.

"I told you this morning I'd be taking my break at noon," said Nora and went quickly out the door to 17th Street, before Briley had a chance to call her back. When she found herself following a route she and Walker had taken, she changed it. Until she'd explored every street, there was no reason to play favorites.

She remembered the grand plan she'd devised at the age of nine to walk every street and lane in all the cities of the world. Not knowing how big that world was, she spent hours after school with an atlas, copying the names of countries, their capitals and major cities into a notebook. By her rough calculation she'd have to leave home no later than her 15th birthday and travel non-stop until her 60th in order to complete the task.

There weren't many chore-free hours on a farm, but Nora took advantage of every one to walk or ride her bicycle about the countryside, sometimes with her brother but mostly alone. When her father asked where she'd been, Nora would recite a list of streets and lanes in alphabetical order.

She was out exploring country to the south and east on the day her brother Brendan drowned in a farm pond. To punish herself for not being there to save him, she abandoned her around-the-world plan. To punish God she decided not to become a nun.

"But you never intended to be a nun," said her best friend, Bridget.

There was no disputing that, but Nora was only momentarily stumped. "Well then, I'll refuse to believe in God altogether."

As she set off for the Smithsonian she felt the beginnings of a sore throat, a thin, familiar slice of pain. At a food market on P Street she talked the clerk into selling her two cents worth of apple cider vinegar and swallowed the remedy straight down.

She went south to K Street, a few blocks above the White House, then east past the S.S. Kresge's store and the Ambassador Hotel. The streets were mostly cobblestone and shared by automobiles, horse-drawn carts, pedestrians and trolleys. Every so often, a trolley line sparked with a high crackle. She loved the congestion and noise, the novelty of each new building. She was already sweating in her tweed pants and regretted not changing into her dress at the store.

Nora turned right on 7th Street and saw that the Coronet Theatre was showing *Tarzan, the Ape Man* with Johnny Weismuller and Maureen O'Sullivan. Already one stranger had asked if the red-headed actress was a relative. Nora liked pretending that she was. Playing across the street at the Reade was *Rain*, starring Joan Crawford and Walter Huston. Both theatres advertised **Air Conditioning** in letters only slightly smaller than the movie titles.

At the bottom of 7th Street, Negro laborers were digging the foundation for the new Justice Department and just beyond lay the Smithsonian Institution. Her goal today was to speak to the man in charge of acquisitions for the Smithsonian, or at least make an appointment to see him. She trusted he wouldn't be as cavalier about her search as Walker had been the day before.

"Tell me about this thing that was stolen from you," he'd asked as they approached the Capitol.

"It's a silver cup. Used in sacrifices from the pagan days before St. Patrick. I found it cutting turf." She didn't tell him about the images hammered into the silver, the cook god dipping a boy into a cauldron or the fertility goddess holding wide her vagina with both hands.

"How much is it worth?"

"I can't say. The man who took it to be appraised never brought it back."

"You must have an idea though. Five hundred dollars?"

"I wouldn't think it to be so dear. One or two cups like mine are found every few years buried in the bog."

Walker slowed to look at her. "You came all this way for a cup that may not be worth more than a hundred dollars?"

Her mother and Jack Allman had put the same question to her, but only Walker was amused by it. "Number one, I'm not sure how much it's worth," answered Nora trying to sound like the Galway barrister she'd once heard, arguing that there was no relevant difference between up and down. "But it's certainly worth more than my passage. And number two," here she let herself gush, "when I pulled the cup out of the earth there was magic to it. Bright as a torch under the earth, like it had been waiting all the years to be found by me."

"And?"

"And what?"

"And you were looking for an excuse to leave home."

On another day Nora might have argued the point but today she laughed out loud. "I was *desperate* to go and had been desperate for ages. But there are rules in Ireland for being an only child on a farm. Getting married was a way out, but I'd have none of that."

The Smithsonian wasn't one building but a few, on both sides of a wide, grassy field. The administrative offices were in a red building that reminded Nora of a storybook castle. On her way there, she stuck her head into the Natural History museum and saw Eskimo mukluks, an enormous stuffed elephant and an upright Polar bear. She forced herself to leave for fear of being enthralled there for the day, and missed the opportunity to use the toilet to change into her dress.

Directly in front of the administration building was an odd machine that looked like a chair attached to an oversized airplane propeller. A sign identified it as a Heliotrope. There was such a crowd around it, Nora had difficulty finding a secluded spot to change. She finally edged between a bush and one of the red stone walls of the administration building. When she'd stripped to her underwear, she got a feeling someone was watching and looked up to see a white head staring from a window. The man looked like a seabird, his hair straight up and his eyes bulging.

Nora pulled on her dress and jumped from the bush, snagging a bit of wool on a branch. Looking down at the yanked wool she noticed the mud on her calf-skin pampooties and regretted not having more appropriate footwear for doing business in Washington. Ideally, her hair should have been tied back or wrapped in a bun like the secretaries she'd seen downtown. Then again she was going to see a museum man, one unlikely to give her appearance a second look.

At the front desk she asked for Richard Drury, the official in charge of acquisitions. While the secretary (her hair in a bun) went to see if he had time for her, Nora studied a shrunken head in a glass case. The skin was brown and leathery, the eyes squeezed tight as if the head was still shrinking. The secretary appeared in the hall and motioned for Nora to follow.

After opening a heavy brown door the secretary announced, "Miss Nora O'Sullivan."

One step inside and Nora's well rehearsed smile cracked like pond ice. It was him! The white-haired seabird at the window, rising now from his ink black desk, wearing a look that said, yes, I recognize you with clothes on as well.

"Good morning Miss O'Sullivan. What can I do for you?"

Nora felt her scalp flush. No good, she decided, to apologize or mention her underwear at all. She waited until the secretary had closed the door. "Mr. Drury, I've traveled all the way from Ireland to speak with you."

He gestured toward a chair and sat back in his own. With only his head and chest visible above the dark desktop, he looked even more like a bird floating on a black pool. "And what is so important to bring you this far?"

As she told him about the cup, how she found it and how it was stolen, he sat with his head forward, straightening only when Nora described the images hammered on either side.

"What expression does the fertility goddess wear?"

Nora imitated the demonic smile as best she could. Drury made a sharp, sucking sound. "Wonderful," he told her. "You've captured it just so." They sat for a few seconds in silence, seabird and fertility goddess, before Drury asked why she'd come to him.

"I've been told by the curator of the Dublin Trust that James Kemper often brings antiquities to you."

Drury got up from his desk and went to the window. In the sunlight Nora could see a vein pulsing at his temple. "James Kemper has not brought me any such cup."

Nora felt a dull ache behind her right eye. "He'd be in no hurry since he doesn't know I've followed him." She put her hands on the edge of his desk. "If he brings it to you, would you let me know?"

Drury returned to his chair and folded his hands on the desk. Nora admired the dark bloodstone on his right ring finger. "We don't buy items from Mr. Kemper. He lends pieces periodically, small things that might be useful to a collection or a show. In return, we sometimes research and authenticate his more marketable items. A quid pro quo arrangement, if you will. A cup such as you describe would be marketable. So you see, Mr. Kemper would not offer it to us."

"But mightn't he bring it to you for authentication?"

"And if he did, what legal proof do you have that the cup is yours?"

Nora pulled a folded sheet of paper from a pocket of her dress and smoothed it on the desk. The receipt was for a "devotional cup" dated and signed by James Kemper.

Drury studied it briefly. "Miss O'Sullivan, I'm afraid this receipt is so vague as to be practically valueless." The ache behind her eye was no longer dull. "At the very least, a detailed description of the cup and its ornamentation would need to be on this receipt, as well as any distinguishing marks or imperfections."

"There are no imperfections," she told him. "As for distinguishing marks, an *S* like the body of a snake has been cut into the underside of the base. I can draw you a diagram exactly where."

Richard Drury returned her receipt. "Miss O'Sullivan, I wish I could help in some way. But this is a difficult area, confusing and legalistic in the best of circumstances. I'm not sure there is anything to be done."

Nora didn't answer until she'd finished drawing her sketch on a borrowed sheet of paper. At the bottom of the page she wrote her name and the address of Briley's General Store.

"Mr. Drury, I'm duty bound to find my cup. And doing business with a thief brings no glory to this institution."

As she left the building Nora wondered if seeing her in her underwear would make Richard Drury more or less motivated to help.

SEVAREID

ACROSS THE DRAWBRIDGE, past two sentries ("What's your business here?") and a line of trees, Eric Sevareid walked his long-legged walk, humming to himself: *Hinkey, dinkey, parlez vous.* The Bonus camp appeared all at once under clouds of smoke and mosquitoes—tents, shacks, packing crates, flags, people. About as ugly a thing as he'd ever seen and equally rich, he was sure, with stories. They called this one River Camp, the biggest by far of the dozen Bonus camps in abandoned buildings, parks and D.C. trash dumps. He looked at the smoke rising from so many campfires and wondered where to start.

For the first time since leaving Minnesota, he came to a full stop. Should he work from the outside in—maybe start with this guy reading a book in the back seat of the junked Model T? Or that woman on her knees, poking holes in the ground with a stick to plant seed. He passed both, as well as the two kids lounging in a cardboard box and a girl about 16, tacking a fringe of what looked like real lace to a chicken coop.

The building material seemed to be coming from a dump at the south end of the mud plain. Sevareid saw a man there, carrying an automobile fender over his head like an umbrella. The deeper he went, the more orderly the camp appeared. Near the center, the tents and shacks were arranged in military rows. Banners identified one group with Cleveland and the next with Niagara Falls. He stopped to copy a hand drawn sign into his notebook—**Army of No Occupation**. At a raised, wooden platform, a boy about eight years old tap danced with his eyes closed. Sevareid counted four pennies at his feet and wrote it down.

He turned a slow circle. Two men, one white and the other Negro, tended a smoking cook fire. Inside a half-finished Indian teepee, a man played cards with a bare-chested boy. Not far from Sevareid, a well-dressed woman stepped cautiously through the dust carrying a neatly-folded wool blanket and a white dinner jacket. Just beyond her, in a 12-by-20 foot open-ended canvas tent, sat Walt Waters talking to reporters.

That's the place to start, Sevareid decided, and took a deep breath. How would he describe the smell and taste of this air? He'd been doing that a lot lately, trying to describe smells and tastes and people in clever ways. Was there such a thing as being too clever? Sevareid didn't have enough experience to know. Except for his canoeing journal and his few Bonus Army stories, the grandest thing he'd ever written for a newspaper was an interview with Jack Dempsey. He and Arnie, a high school buddy, rode the elevator of the Niccollet Hotel for half a day, notebooks in hand until the visiting Dempsey stepped inside.

"You want an interview? Okay," said Dempsey. "Work hard. Live clean. Get lots of exercise." Tame advice from a man known as the Manassas Mauler, but it was all Sevareid would get. When the elevator door opened, Dempsey disappeared.

The editor of the *Minneapolis Star* hadn't hired him exactly, but he did give Sevareid a press card and a promise to buy any good stories he found. All he had to do was get to D.C., and that proved easy enough. With Bonus veterans coming from all directions, the railroads stopped policing the yards. Nearly every freight was packed with miners, farmers, loggers and tramps, most of them eager to trade stories. By the time Sevareid jumped off his coal car at Washington's Union Station, he knew to go directly to the camp beside the Anacostia River.

Under the green tent top, Walt Waters sat on a packing crate before a half circle of standing reporters. He wore canvas dungarees and a white short-sleeved shirt.

"The rules?" said Waters. "The rules are simple. No drinking, no panhandling and no talk of sedition."

"I thought it was the right of every enlisted man to complain," said a reporter.

"Oh, they complain all right," answered Waters. "The first week out of Oregon we had as many generals as we did soldiers and every one of them with his own plan. But now that we're here, we've got to be more disciplined. The government would like nothing more than to brand us as communists."

"And are you?"

Sevareid was surprised to hear Waters laugh at the question. "It's a funny thing. If you ask the communists what conditions they'd need to get recruits, these might be the exact right ones. But my men hate a communist. You know why? They still hope that one day they'll get their grub stake and strike it rich."

"What if they don't get their grub stake? What if this Bonus bill doesn't pass?"

"That's not for me to answer," said Waters.

A reporter with a German accent and bright blonde hair asked about outside help.

"We've got help of all kinds. Good and not so good," said Waters, bending to lift a leather mail bag at his feet. He grabbed a handful of letters and spread them on his lap. "These are from what you'd call outside help. Here's one from a flag pole sitter, wants us to set up a pole for him in camp." Waters gave the reporters time to laugh. "Another guy owns a bankrupt circus, would like us to bring his 'Riding Monkeys and Bewildering Trained Dogs' to Washington. I've got offers from human flies, evangelists, parachute jumpers—all wanting us to sponsor them for a cut of the take."

"Why don't you?"

"We don't want to make this a circus," said Waters. He looked tired but comfortable on his crate. "We already got taken in New Jersey by some chiselers who put on a wrestling match for their 'Bonus buddies.' We never saw a penny. There's more chiselers out there than you can shake a stick at."

Waters put the letters back into the bag and stood. "I've got to get this parade on. You have any more questions, come see me."

The reporters closed their notepads and stepped outside. Sevareid approached the one with the blonde hair, introduced himself and asked about the parade.

"Today at 4, from the White House to the Capitol," said Max Berga. "Are you the Sevareid who wrote that first story from St. Louis?"

Sevareid nodded.

"How'd you happen to be there?"

"Pure luck. I was just passing through."

"That's a bad way to start in this business."

"Why's that?"

"You trust in luck, you usually end up with no story."

Sevareid asked if it was okay to follow Waters around the camp.

Berga cocked his head, as though he needed a longer look. "Are you really that green?"

Sevareid blushed.

"Do whatever you can until you're stopped," said Berga. "Then try and find a way around that."

"What did you write for today's paper?" asked Sevareid.

Berga handed him a rolled up copy of that morning's *Herald*. Sevareid found his byline on a story headline "Whoopee Girl."

"Not that one," said Berga, pointing a nicotine stained finger to a smaller headline.

POLICE WARN OF COMMUNIST PLOT

Brig. Gen. P.D. Glassford, Superintendent of Police, announced tonight the discovery of a plot by Communists to physically interfere with tomorrow's veterans' parade.

The Communists, said the General, having failed to establish themselves among the veterans seeking a cash bonus, were forming "an organization of 100 men into a compact fighting unit to combat the police."

His statement read:

"Reliable information concerning Communist plans discussed at various meetings indicates that Communists may attempt to interfere with the veterans' parade tomorrow. Pennsylvania Avenue will be roped off in order that the situation may be handled by the police."

"You think this could actually happen?" asked Sevareid.

Berga rolled up the newspaper and tapped it against the side of his head.

"Kid, we can only hope."

WALKER

THE BIG PROBLEM with meeting new people during my first year in D.C. was that they all wanted to hear my story. They knew there had to be one, a high-yellow talking like I did and living half-buried in evergreen.

I used to get mad when they asked, thinking they wanted me to get all weepy about being disowned by my family, looking to see what it did to my little boy heart. Of course they didn't know any of that, only that I had a story to tell and they wanted to hear it.

So I made up stories, big whopper tales of car wrecks in the snows of Vermont, and Florida alligators attacking my family's yacht. I liked guessing what kind of story somebody would like by looking in their eyes and was only wrong about half the time.

I told my earliest lies when I started school, which was Mr. Luke's idea. He came home from fishing one day near the end of summer and said, "Boy, you belong in school. See to it." Where I belonged was beside the river, learning to fish and hunt and build my own bark canoe. But Mr. Luke had never asked anything of me before and I was glad he finally had.

The next day, Tommy and Penny took me to their school, a two-room brick building that sat behind the Hofmeister tannery. Banneker school had only two teachers, a Negro man named Eustace Curtis who believed equally in the power of prayer and his leather belt, and Mrs. Bradley, a white woman who was as scared of Mr. Curtis as the rest of us.

I got put in Mrs. Bradley's class, maybe because I was closest to her in color. She was 30 years old, wore her brown hair in a tight bun and her clothes so loose she could have hidden another person in there. That first morning after welcoming me to school and assigning me a desk that looked like it had survived the Civil War, she asked would I mind telling the class where I was from.

I stood in front of that class of forty-five Negro students I'd never seen before (Tommy was with Mr. Curtis), and lied my ass off. "My mother and father were killed by Mexican bandits in Arizona. I'm living now with my grandfather in Virginia."

I'd never told a whopper like that and had no good reason to do it then. Being in that little brick school house that smelled like skinned cattle must have popped something loose in me because not only did I lie about where I came from, I lied about where I lived, my favorite color, the pro baseball players I liked...anything that was in any way personal I reshaped, repainted or just plain invented.

One of the older girls in class, Jessie, took an interest in me straight away. She followed me to the sheltered side of the school's woodshed where I'd been sent to fetch the cart and told me my eyes were like a cat's. Then she wanted to know was I a good kisser?

Jessie was a big girl with a right eye that rolled a little left when she looked at you. I had no interest in kissing her except to show I wasn't afraid to. We stuck our faces together for about five seconds then came apart with a sound like suction cups off glass.

"You pretty good," said Jessie as if I was a cake she'd judged at a county fair. She immediately left the woodshed to share her review with anybody who'd listen, including Jimmy Earl who was sweet on her in his own sour way.

I didn't know Jimmy Earl was the school's resident tough guy because Tommy hadn't told me. So all I saw coming fast around that woodshed was a boy twenty pounds heavier than me, with long arms and a look on his face like he'd swallowed castor oil.

"You stay away from Jessie or I'll pull your ears off," he said. I noticed one of his front teeth was missing and the rest of them crooked. A scary face on a big body, so why did I feel like laughing?

"How am I supposed to stay away from Jessie when she's in the same room as me?" I could see he was thrown by the question, in the same way I'd later see him thrown by math problems at the blackboard. What struck me as funny was that here it was my first day of school and in the space of about two hours, I'd already been kissed and was about to get clobbered. But just then Mr. Curtis appeared, belt in hand, wanting to know what we were doing in the shed.

Compared to my last school, which had tiled hallways and varnished desks, Banneker was a rough and crumbling place. I guessed it had once been a church because there was an iron plate inscribed with the Ten Commandments on an outside wall. I later learned the iron had come from one of the Potomac River canons used against the British in the War of 1812.

The best thing about the school was Mrs. Bradley. When she found out I liked to read (the one thing I didn't lie about) she started bringing me books from the library. I'd always read books, but now I took to them the same way I'd taken to the river, looking between the pages for a place to hide. The poetry of Langston Hughes, novels by Hart Crane and Mark Twain, a biography of Abraham Lincoln...the faster I read, the more books she brought until I was getting six or seven at a time. Mrs. Bradley (her husband had died of pneumonia a few years earlier) got a real kick out of feeding my mind, which was fine by me. The only price I had to pay was to stay after school one day a week to talk about what I'd read and, though I complained about that to Tommy, I looked forward to it all week.

I had to be careful to limit my conversation with Mrs. Bradley to books after she nearly caught me in a lie. We were sitting outside the school under a late October sun when she asked had I ever been to the Painted Desert. I'd have been fine if I'd just said no, but I had to ask where it was.

"Why it's in Arizona, very near where you're from," she said, surprised that a boy so well read and curious would be ignorant of something so celebrated in his home state.

"My parents were afraid of snakes," I told her. "So they wouldn't have taken me anywhere near a desert." Mrs. Bradley believed me because she wanted to, but I knew she wouldn't be so gullible the next time.

Tommy skipped school as often as he went and tried to get me to skip with him. But I liked school, especially that first winter sitting by the wood stove reading my books while Mrs. Bradley taught lessons I already knew. Sometimes she'd ask me to tutor some of the slower kids in math and grammar and that was fun too, until the day she put me with Jessie.

"I told Mrs. Bradley I needed help with fractions, but I just wanted to sit with you," she said, her right eye rolling to a stop. She wasn't pretty or smart but there was something pleasant about sitting that close to a girl with breasts.

That same afternoon Jessie again followed me to the woodshed. This time she came up from behind and put her arms around my chest. As her hands moved down my stomach to my legs, I felt myself getting hard and didn't do a thing to stop her. When she turned me around for a kiss, I saw Jimmy Earl coming at us, looking even bigger in his winter coat than he had that first day. This time I knew enough to be afraid, not about getting hurt, but getting expelled. Mr. Curtis had his own commandments, the first one being that no one was allowed to mete out punishment except him.

I put my hands up and started talking fast. "Why don't we do this after school? Meet beside the tannery?"

Asking Jimmy a question, any question, was enough to slow him down and I think he might have agreed if the whole school hadn't suddenly shown up whispering, "fight, fight." Mr. Curtis and Mrs. Bradley were inside the school eating lunch, so the only one to step between us was Jessie, and she wasn't trying to stop anything.

"Let's see which one of you boys is best," she said, which must have sounded like a bell to Jimmy because he immediately charged with a wild punch that missed me but hit Jessie square in the temple. She dropped to the floor like a sack of beans.

Jimmy, supposedly fighting for Jessie's hand, stepped across her without a look, snorting like a bull. He came at me holding his right arm and fist straight in front of him, a thing I'd never seen in a fight before. When he got close he surprised me again by hitting his fist with his left hand, sending his arm down and around like a Ferris wheel. The move was so unexpected I just stood there as his fist came down on top of my head. It hurt like hell, but more than that it confused me, which was its real purpose.

As he came in for the kill, I saw him draw his right fist behind his ear for a more conventional punch, and stepped into him. Instead of catching me square in the face, the blow glanced off the side of my head. I threw a right hook to his chin and was so sure he'd go down, I stepped back to watch. But Jimmy just rubbed his jaw with the back of his hand and came at me again. By now I was less worried about getting expelled than getting hurt. I kept moving in and out so that when he did hit me, his punches were clumsy and off-balance. I gave up on his hard head and started aiming for his belly.

The first good punch I landed there made him grunt, and the sound of it stopped me cold. It took me a second to figure what was so frightening about that sound, the memory it aroused of my mother being hit. I stepped away and thought of running, but there were too many kids pressed around us. When Jimmy saw my hesitation he charged with his arms flailing. I got hit by one punch under my eye and a second against my left ear that stung so bad my eyes watered.

I don't remember knocking him down but there I was, sitting on his chest and punching his face. By all the unwritten rules, the fight should have been over but the more I hit Jimmy, the more I needed to. When somebody grabbed my arm, I turned ready to punch him, but it was Tommy. He said, "You want to kill him?"

I swear it really was like waking from a dream. Jimmy was bleeding under me, and all the kids standing in a dead quiet circle. I got up and left Banneker, passing Mrs. Bradley on the way, and never went back.

It was dark when I finally got home. Mr. Luke was finished dinner but he'd saved me some fish. He saw my bruised face and gave me one of those bomb-ready-to-explode looks, and for the first time I understood exactly what he saw.

NORA

AT 10:59 A.M., Frank Briley's niece Catherine entered his general store.

"There you are," said Frank in a voice sharp as a halfpenny nail.

Catherine dropped her head. "You said 11."

"Get the apron on," he ordered, while taking off his own. "I'll be back at three."

As soon as Frank left the store, Nora put down her metal scoop and approached Catherine at the register. "How are you, Catherine? Good to see you again."

Catherine blushed deeply. The only other time they'd met, Nora watched as Catherine shrunk at the touch of Briley's hand on her waist. Now, with her uncle gone, she managed a shy smile.

"Is it school you're in?" asked Nora.

"I've just finished."

"And what will you do now?"

"I'm not sure." Catherine's expression said as much. "I'll work here when I'm needed and keep looking for something else."

Nora sat on a pickle barrel. "If you could do anything in the world, what would it be?"

Catherine appeared embarrassed by the question but, at the same time, thrilled someone was interested enough to ask. "I'd be an actress."

"Do you take lessons or act in plays?"

"I go to movies, twice a week," said Catherine. "Then I come home and...pretend." Catherine's hair was mossy orange, the color of highly diluted juice. Her skin was pale as well, as though it didn't have the energy to be any brighter.

With Catherine framed in the large front window, Nora tried to imagine a role she might play. She asked what movie Catherine had seen most recently.

"*Rain.* Do you know it?" Catherine's eyes brightened. "It's about this woman and a minister who end up on the same island in the South Pacific, and the woman, Joan Crawford, is kind of a loose type and the minister, who's played by Walter Huston, is going to have her sent back to America where the police are looking for her, so Joan Crawford pretends to repent and gets this minister to have relations with her and then, afterwards, he cuts his throat and is found the next morning by fishermen." Catherine delivered the synopsis in one exhaustive breath.

"That's quite a tale," marveled Nora. "Maybe we could go to the pictures together some night?"

"I'd like that. Thursday is best. Bank night. You put your ticket stub into a raffle box and the winner gets money. *Virtue* is coming next week. And *They Call It Sin.*"

Somehow the news spread that Frank Briley had left the store. People Nora had only seen through the front window, flowed in until it was as busy and loud as an Irish market day. From the red brick townhouses on Q and Corcoran streets, women who hadn't bought a yard of fabric in months, hurried in to hold bolts of colored lace and cotton against the light. Unemployed carpenters bounced hammers in their hands and bowed their heads to the sharpness of new saws. Spice sniffers, bean counters, babies reaching from carriages toward every bright color—Nora had never seen the store so smart.

"Do you know where these potatoes come from?" asked a man pointing to the spud bin.

"I can tell you they didn't come on the boat with me," she said gaily. Nora let a mother with three small children have an extra scoop of beans. When an old man buying burlap was a nickel short, she scribbled a new price on the wrapper. At the register, Catherine pretended not to notice.

For the first time, Nora was happy to be in the store. Customers came to her with questions, as though she was a useful part of this new world. She was happy for another reason as well—later that day she would take her lunch break to watch the Bonus Army march down Pennsylvania Avenue, and search for Walker en route.

She'd read about the parade in one of the newspapers she cadged from Henry the paperboy. In Ireland she rarely read a paper, persuaded as she was by Jack Allman that every minute spent on gossip, politics and sporting news was time stolen from Homer or Shakespeare. But weren't the newspaper stories she read each morning Homeric? Amelia Earhardt crossing the Atlantic. Japan's Premier killed by military extremists. The funeral of slain French President Paul Doumer. ("This is only the beginning," shouted his Russian assassin.) Hundreds dead in fighting between Moslems and Hindus in India. Nora was amazed how much was happening in the world, and more than a little dismayed at all she'd missed by not paying attention.

She was sorting screws and thinking about the Lindbergh baby when Frank Briley came through the door at 3 pm.

"And what did we do today? How much stolen and how much lost?" Even across the room, Nora could see the alcohol on him. His cheeks were blood red and his eyes peculiar bright. She went to the rear of the store to sweep, determined not to let him spoil such a fine day. She looked back once to see him slide behind Catherine at the register, his head nearly beside hers. His hands moved up her stomach toward her breasts. Catherine stood still, her eyes squeezed as tight as the shrunken head Nora had seen at the Smithsonian. Nora turned away in disgust. Catherine was old enough to say no.

Nora bent over a square wooden tray, pretending to sort various sized nuts and bolts and found herself thinking again of Rosario, the sailor who put his hands between her legs on the ship coming over. Actually it was only his right hand, from directly behind and one step below as Nora climbed to the upper deck. She was wearing pants, so Rosario's hand never actually touched her flesh, which doesn't explain why she didn't immediately twist away, slap his hand or call for help. Maybe it was because she'd just emerged from three days in steerage with all those seasick passengers. Or because one of them, a four-year-old boy with skin as dry as paper, had died in the bunk above her head.

More likely it was because Nora was just shy of 18 and determined, now that she was finally on an adventure of her own, to live it boldly. What that meant exactly, Nora wasn't sure. It was easy enough to recognize in books—a pirate queen boarding an enemy ship or Finn McCool carrying Limerick on his back. But what was the bold thing to do when a sailor had his hand between your legs in the middle of an ocean?

She waited for an answer, and not finding one, waited for whatever might come next.

What came next was Rosario's left hand, yanking hard at the waist of her pants.

"No!" said Nora turning on the stair. Rosario removed his hand, but only to replace it once she'd faced him. She straightened both arms against his shoulders, shook her head and again said "No!"

Was he Italian? Maltese? It didn't matter. There was no misunderstanding her in any language. But here came that left hand, clawing at her buttons. Nora looked into his eyes. They were brown and handsome and surprisingly dull. She expected to see a fire there, like in the novels she read. Instead, there was no light at all, as if every spark had run to his hands. His breath came in short, moist huffs.

Panic rose in Nora's chest. Not a major panic like falling down a well at night or breaching her currach on a seal far out at sea, but serious enough for being so unexpected. Her breath caught below her throat, as if Rosario had his hands there instead of at her crotch. What if her boldness was all invented? The courage only cobbled together during those years tending the sheep and dreaming of great challenges to come. If she wasn't fearless, a bold girl on a grand adventure, then who was she?

Nora planted her heel against the metal stair and made a fist. On the day she turned 12, her father taught her to throw a punch that he said was equally effective against rabid dogs or men. She'd never had occasion to use it and wouldn't have then, except for her terrible need of breath. With the weight of her 110 pounds behind it, Nora hit Rosario on the bridge of his nose. He dropped to his knees like a sinner, blood dripping into his cupped hands.

Her panic gone, Nora was embarrassed to have hit him so hard when a slap might have done just as well. She put a hand on Rosario's thick dark hair and whispered, "You'd have done better just to ask."

She was still bent over the nuts and bolts when Frank Briley approached, his boozy breath preceding him like ocean spray.

"Don't fall in," he said, reaching his arms around her, one hand cupping each breast. Nora straightened and turned, lowered her head into his chest and pushed him back a step.

"Did you butt me, little lamb?" Again he moved toward her. Nora planted her foot against the bolt bin, made a fist and hit him, careful to use only half as much force as she had with Rosario. The result, however, was the same. As Frank dropped to the floor Catherine's face came into view behind him—horrified, then vengeful and finally relieved. If Catherine could do that on a stage, thought Nora, she'd have a grand career.

It took Nora less than a minute to pack her things. At the last second she decided to take the bicycle. Wasn't it useless before she fixed it? Besides, there was money due her for nearly a week's work. Frank was still on the floor, moaning softly when she went to leave. Catherine stood at the register, humming a movie score.

"Do you have somewhere to go?"

"I've an idea," said Nora.

They hugged. "Remember," said Nora, "if he touches you again, his nose will be tender for weeks to come."

WALKER

WHEN I CAME UP behind Nora, she had her toes against the base of the Washington Monument and her eyes straight up, watching the tip slice through the clouds. I'd done the same thing myself.

"You think that's impressive? You should see the Martha Washington monument. There never was a hole so deep."

That came from a Bonus vet, a skinny little guy with a moustache thick enough to hide mice. When Nora turned to him she saw me and smiled, like I was her best friend in the world.

"Thank you but I've no time for any other monuments today," she said to the veteran. To me she said, "I was wondering when I'd see you again."

"I went past the store and looked in."

"As of one hour ago, I no longer work there. But thank you for going to the trouble for someone as un-ironic as myself."

The last time we were together Nora told a story about the priest in her village getting drunk and taking a swing at a bartender. She didn't think it was as funny as I did.

"You have to see the irony in it," I'd told her.

"Irony?"

"You know, irony. Like finding maggots in an angel food cake."

"I know full well what irony is," she said giving me one of her steamed looks. "In Kenmare I'm considered one of the most ironic people around."

"Out of how many people?"

"Gobs."

I didn't know that word, but liked the way it came out of her mouth.

The morning newspapers predicted there'd be 7,000 veterans in the parade, but it looked nearly double that number lined up in regiments in the meadow below the Monument. A polished marching band from a local American Legion led the way, followed by the Bonus vets, four abreast and dressed in odd pieces of uniform. A jacket here, a pair of pants there and all of it more spit than polished.

"What's interesting to me," said Nora, "is that most of the uniforms are so loose. After 20 years wouldn't you expect them to be too tight?"

The men were oddly quiet. A few snare drums, the occasional bugle but no singing or chanting. I told Nora they'd been ordered to avoid any word or deed that might cause offense.

We watched the beginning of the parade from the edge of the Monument grounds, with a clear view to the back of the White House. Nora had tied her satchel to the handlebars of her bicycle. I figured she'd tell me why when she was ready. Standing with us were some of the men Nora had met that first day in Lafayette Park, including Party chief Ken Cord, who pointed at the White House.

"The President has time to meet with professional wrestlers and every banker in America, but won't even come to the window to watch this."

"I hear he hasn't been below the second floor in a week, afraid we'll come in and get him," said Comrade Barker.

"Don't believe that," said Cord. "Whatever else Herbert Hoover is, he's no coward. He crossed enemy lines a dozen times during the war to feed Belgians and French. And spent his own money doing it. I don't agree with him on much, but give the man his due."

We left them to follow the parade down Pennsylvania Avenue. I gave Nora the 10-cent tour.

"Right here is the start of Newspaper Row," I said at the intersection of 14th Street. "You've got the *New York Herald*, the *New York Times*, *New York World*, the *Philadelphia Public Ledger*, *Boston Transcript* and *Cincinnati Gazette*. This same stretch used to be called Rum Row for all the bars and saloons and bawdy houses."

"Are they all closed down? The bawdy houses I mean."

"Officially."

Nora burst out laughing.

"What?"

"It's nothing you said. A man back at the Washington Monument told me a joke. I just now understood it."

"About Martha Washington?"

Nora cheeks turned pink. "He must have thought I was such a child."

The crowd was four deep in places along the avenue and near-ly as quiet as the marchers. I told her Pennsylvania Avenue was where all the big parades were held and that the biggest was after the Civil War, when 200,000 men marched through Washington and took two days to do it.

"How do you know so much about all this?"

"I like history. Not the history itself, not slavery and lynchings, but knowing about it."

The parade went past Fletcher's outdoor market, the Metropolitan Hotel, Harvey's Restaurant, the Post Office building and a row of Chinese shops and restaurants. Every ten steps Nora saw something she wanted to investigate, but I wouldn't let her stop for more than a minute. I felt safer walking with the parade than taking her into any of the neighborhoods we passed. By the time things broke up at the Capitol, she'd seen a hundred places she wanted to visit. By then she'd also told me about her fight with Frank Briley.

"So where will you go?" We were at the eastern end of the Capitol grounds, under a big oak tree. Nora stroked its bark with her right hand. "To the Bonus camp, the one beside the Anacostia River."

I told her they only let in veterans and their families.

"Aren't I the right age to be someone's daughter?"

"Even so, the camp is not all brotherhood and good cheer."

Nora asked what I meant by that.

"They have strict rules and punishments. A few days ago a veteran was kicked from the camp for handing out literature. They whipped him with a belt."

"Was he a communist?"

"He was a veteran."

"Well, I'm not a communist and I'm not afraid."

"Maybe you should be."

"What are you afraid of?"

I looked into her green eyes and let myself stay there. "Besides you?"

Nora punched my arm and smiled. "Aren't you the devil?"

We joined veterans moving from the Capitol towards 11th Street but walked slowly, so no one could hear more than a little of our conversation.

Nora asked what I did for work. I told her I piloted boats and fished. She told me her grandfather had been a sailor.

"He went all over the world. He used to take us out in his currach."

"What's a currach?"

"It's like one of your canoes, only covered in animal hide or pitch."

"Where would he take you?"

"The Atlantic. To where the grey seals nest on rocks."

I said I'd only seen seals in books.

"In Ireland there are some who think the grey seal is more human than animal. They tell wild stories about magic spells and such."

"Do you believe them?"

"I do not. If you believe in one superstition then you'd have to believe them all—leprechauns, widows' curses and every other foolish thing."

"What's a widow's curse?"

"Let's say a widow is put to the road by a landlord." Nora stopped and knelt on the sidewalk to show him. "She'll kneel on stones and say a curse. Here's one I remember:

May his pig never grunt! May his cat never hunt!

May a ghost ever haunt him at dead of the night!
May his hen never lay! May his ass never bray!
May his goat fly away like an old paper kite!
May he swell with the gout! May his teeth all fall out!
May he roar, yell and shout with the painful toothache!
May his temples wear horns and his toes many corns…"

Nora put a hand to her forehead as if trying to remember something. People walked right by, as though a girl kneeling on Pennsylvania Avenue was a common sight. "Wait," she said. "That's not a widow's curse! It's Nell Flaherty's curse on whoever it was that stole her duck."

"That's a harsh curse for one small duck," I answered.

"Not for a magical duck to be sure," she said, jumping to her feet.

The afternoon light stretched our shadows ahead of us. We'd been walking so slowly that we were nearly alone when we turned down 11th, a quiet street of small, brown-brick houses. Nora put a hand on my arm. "Have you no ghost stories for me?"

I looked at the fine hairs lying across her wrist and the moon-white fingernails. Whatever thought I had about her hand was lost in the muttered curse of a man walking toward us. He was white, an older guy, wearing a freshly pressed shirt. I pulled my arm from under Nora's hand and made a fist. I'd never hit a grown white man, but I was ready to hit this one. The guy must have seen that because he went past without a word.

The Bonus camp was on the far side of a drawbridge that crossed a narrow finger of the Anacostia. We stood on a bump of land above the bridge, watching a pair of guards check visitors.

"They might be suspicious of your bag," I told her. "Let's sit and think of a good reason you're carrying it."

Nora, never one for planning said, "I'll be spontaneous. Say the first thing that comes to me."

"Better not to take chances the first time you go across. It's like casting into a pool of fish. You might only get one chance."

Nora couldn't agree. "Surely it's more like walking past a dog who's apt to bite. You don't want to hesitate, nor show any fear."

I folded my arms across my chest, ready for a long argument but Nora surprised me by giving in. She lay her bicycle down and curtsied, pulling at the seams of her pants. "My name is Nora O'Sullivan, of the cinema O'Sullivans. And I've come all the way from the wilderness of Kerry in search of me poor da."

"Who left Ireland to come here?"

"Indeed he did," said Nora. "He came here because, you see...." She closed her eyes and squeezed her palms together. "My father is American.... he went to Ireland after the war. Now he's come back and...."

She was saved from further invention by the sound of someone or something, coming through the trees behind us. Thinking it might be the man who'd cursed me, I turned to face him. Instead, out came Eric Sevareid, the hair on his head lying back like a wheat field blown flat.

"Isn't that reckless company for a young woman to keep?" he said to Nora.

"There's always some fool ready to mess in other people's business," I answered back.

Nora didn't say anything but went directly to her satchel. Later she'd tell us she was going for her sling, sure that a fight was coming. But by the time she got there, Sevareid and I were shaking hands and grinning.

"So you took my advice."

"Remember what you said about the Potomac River, that it was rough enough you'd put me in a canoe and money on the far shore? I'm here to get that money." He turned to Nora. "My name is Eric. I was only half serious about the reckless company."

"My name is Nora and he's not nearly reckless enough for my liking."

Sevareid looked from Nora to me with naked curiosity. I felt suddenly shy and annoyed with myself for it.

"Where did 'Eric' come from? I never heard you called anything but Slim."

Sevareid directed his answer to Nora. "After the age of 18, no respected man is known as Slim or Shorty."

I said I'd have to take his word for it since I didn't know any respectable men.

"I didn't say respectable. There's a big difference between respected and respectable." He looked to Nora for support, but she just smiled like the world was a funny place.

"You can give me a vocabulary lesson later," I told Sevareid. "Right now we need to get Nora into that camp."

Sevareid pulled his press card from a pocket. "Miss Nora, I believe I may be of some assistance."

~

NO WAY WOULD I APOLOGIZE for my shack. One room, no electricity, no running water—that was fine by me. So why should I care what Sevareid thought, walking around the room, studying nets and trotlines and every other damn thing hanging on the walls. Sevareid put his face up against Mr. Luke's big hickory rod, like he was trying to smell blood on the line.

"Can I hold it?" Said it like a little kid.

There'd never been a white person in this shack. Martin Hiatt got as far as the front step on the day he told Mr. Luke about my scholarship to Carver Academy. But not inside, not until Sevareid came in acting like it was the most regular thing in the world to pass through a dark woods and sleep in a colored person's home. I knew too much about white people and coloreds, having lived nearly half my life as each, to trust that. But I wanted to. I wanted Sevareid as a friend, and didn't trust that either.

I'd been resisting that impulse since we left Nora at the Bonus camp. Right off I told Sevareid about working for the Party, running numbers and almost killing a man. Instead of scaring him off, it only aroused his interest. How many communists were there in Washington? (Not many.) What were the odds of winning at numbers? (Not good.) And who was the man I almost killed? (He'd have to wait to hear that story.) By the time we got to the Virginia side of the Potomac, my throat was parched from talking.

While Sevareid studied the fishing rod, I got two bottles of beer from the cold-storage I'd dug under the floor.

"My grandfather drank two bottles every night at dinner," I told him. "The only time I ever saw him drink more than that was after he got hit by lightning."

"You said he was a fisherman."

"He was the best. He used seine nets, fishing rods, Indian stone traps, anything he could find or invent—and caught every kind of fish that swims the Potomac."

"Name some."

We sat at the table and opened our beers. "First come the herring, up from the Atlantic through Chesapeake Bay. Then white and yellow perch, and behind them rockfish and sturgeon."

"Sturgeon are big, right?"

"I've seen them two hundred pounds. Then there's the fish that stay all year—bass, chub, carp, catfish, crappie."

"When did your grandfather die?"

"Three years ago. He drowned." I took a long drink and waited for Sevareid to ask about it, but he was waiting on me. I'd never told anyone other than Tommy the story of Mr. Luke's drowning and didn't intend to now. But here I was, talking like I was getting paid for it.

"It was this time of year, during the herring run when all kinds of people come to the Potomac with nets and snag hooks. Mr. Luke didn't normally like seeing a bunch of strangers on the river, but for some reason he liked the herring run, all those fish coming up with every dip of a net. It was about as close to religion as he ever got. He called them 'mana' days and loved them more than money."

Sevareid was listening close, his elbows on the table, chin resting on his hands.

"One day he was up at Chain Bridge talking to some fishermen when a boy fell in. I was coming across the bridge and saw it happen. The boy had picked up his father's net, a big thing made from a bicycle wheel, and it pulled him right in. The water there runs fast and deep, especially in spring. Mr. Luke reached out for the boy, stepped into a hole and disappeared. No bubbles, no mud swirl, nothing. They got the boy easy enough but not Mr. Luke. We must have thrown a hundred snag hooks, but he was gone."

"That's rough."

"I got him the next morning behind Coffin Rock."

The fog that morning rose from the river like steam off hot soup. I pulled him into the boat, the surprising weight of him, and sat there for half an hour waiting to cry. I never did.

"I've got another story about Mr. Luke, a better story. From the flood in 1889."

"The Johnstown flood that killed all those people in Pennsylvania?"

"Right. By the time it got down here, the river went twenty-five feet above the canal, straight through Georgetown and up the White House stairs. People were catching fish on Pennsylvania Avenue. The water swept away 170 canal boats and their mules. One of those boats belonged to a white canaller named Jenkins. He sent his family to high ground and was riding out the flood on his 93-footer, inside one of the 100-foot long canal locks. Just before the water rose above the lock, he reattached the boat to a tree. It seemed like a good plan until the river pulled the tree straight out of the ground. It came rolling toward Jenkins, wrapping line as it came. To keep from being crushed, he had to quick cut the barge free and rudder it down river, which was quite a thing considering those boats were designed for a top speed of maybe two miles an hour. Jenkins got all the way to Long Bridge, where the 14th Street Bridge is now, before he slammed against one of the center posts. That's where Mr. Luke saw him, hanging from the only part of his canal boat still above water. Mr. Luke backferried his skiff about 100 yards above the bridge and pulled in the oars. He braced both legs against the gunwhales, reached out his arms and snatched Jenkins as he went past. A newspaper reporter for the *Washington Post* was watching from shore. The next day the story was on the front page. I've still got a copy. The reporter called Mr. Luke 'heroic' and said the rescue was a 'masterful combination of skill and luck.'"

"I'd like to read that some time," said Sevareid, his chin dropping closer to the table. I knew he was exhausted after his trip from Minnesota but I didn't want to turn down the light. It had been so long since I talked like this, the words felt alive.

"Maybe we can go fishing tomorrow," said Sevareid.

"Sure. If you ever wake up."

"Don't worry about me," he said, spreading his coat on the floor. "A couple hours sleep and I'll be ready to ride one of your sturgeon like Ahab riding his whale."

I got him a pillow, a mat and blanket, then turned down the lamp. I was glad he hadn't felt the need to explain the reference to Moby Dick.

$\sim$

SEVAREID SAID he'd never seen a boat like the one I'd built, square-sterned and curving to a sharp bow. Said it looked like a cross between a rowboat and a canoe and bet I could sell a thousand if we could only come up with a catchy name. Rownoe? Scanoat? Then we hit the rapids below Great Falls and all the talking stopped.

"You're right. This is some tough water," he said after we made it through. "This is the first I've been on a river since going to Hudson Bay. I've missed the sound of it."

Sevareid had told me about that trip. He and a high school buddy went 2,300 miles by canoe from Minnesota to Hudson Bay. If that was true, and I believed it was, he was as reckless as he was tough. But then I saw all that the first time we met.

It was in California. I was late getting back to the night freight and had to run across three closed railcars, jumping from roof to roof as the train picked up speed. At Sevareid's car I banged both feet on the tin roof until I heard the door slide open. I knelt at the edge, looking down at the dark blur of gravel running beside the track.

I said, "Somebody grab my legs," which wasn't a question but should have been, with six white men in the boxcar and me on the roof.

One of the men inside said to Sevareid, "How about you, Slim? You got long arms." Sevareid stepped to the open doorway. A second man got behind him and wrapped both arms around his waist. A third took hold of the second and then another until the chain was six strong.

I lowered myself, then let go when I felt Sevareid's arms close around my knees. He yelled "Gotcha!" and I was sure he had until my head and upper body fell back, pulling Sevareid half out of the boxcar. But he held on and the others did too, yanking us back into the car where we fell in a heap.

"Why the hell didn't you grab onto me?" he asked, pushing me off his lap. But even as he asked he saw why, a bottle of plum brandy hugged to my chest.

"It started to come out of my shirt," I said, holding the bottle toward him. "I knew you wouldn't let me go."

My catch came the next morning.

We were sitting by the tracks of the Oregon Short Line, just outside Ogden, Utah when a big man with cracked yellow teeth came out of the woods to sit beside us.

He said, "You catching the hot shot?"

The hot shot was a sealed, express freight. One jump and no trouble from police or yard goons before the end of the line. The stranger said he rode it once. "It's long and cold and you get mighty hungry." Then he said, "Tell you what, one of you boys want to walk over to my house, have my wife fix up a few sandwiches for you?"

Sevareid said he would, and followed the man down a narrow path between tall weeds and a drainage ditch. The man had strips of torn leather tied around his feet and his pant cuffs were shredded and caked with mud. There was no way somebody as dirt poor as him was offering sandwiches to strangers. I got up and followed.

When I came around the second bend, the big man was holding a knife to Sevareid. I heard him say, "Come on—got something to show you," while his left hand worked the buttons on his pants. "You do this right I'll give you a quarter."

I pulled out my own knife and went straight at that big bastard. As soon as he saw me coming, he jumped into the ditch and ran. Neither of us paid him any attention, just stood there squinting at each other, like studying something we might need to know later.

"I had that under control," said Sevareid, as cool as chipped ice.

"What I want to know is why you followed him in the first place. Didn't you know he was slimmin' you?"

"Slimmin? That's a good word," said Sevareid and wrote it down.

～

JUST PAST the last whitewater, I turned our eighteen-footer into the current and held her with short rudder sweeps while Sevareid tossed the anchor. I pulled two rods and handed one to Sevareid who, true to his word and after only a few hours sleep, seemed rarin' to go.

"Okay. Just to make it interesting, we're gonna do this without any bait." I gave him a rod with two gold hooks tied above a one ounce lead weight and pointed to the fast water near the bow. For all Sevareid knew, this was a practical joke, but he didn't hesitate. He cast out the line and let it run back with the current. When he reeled it in, he'd hooked two four-inch herring.

"Do it again," I told him. "We need about twenty."

Fifteen minutes and two dozen herring later, we paddled downriver toward a coal-fired power plant just off the Alexandria shore.

"Why did they go for those bare hooks?"

"This time of year the herring aren't feeding but they're ornery. The gold hooks look like other herring getting too close. They snap at them."

A green headed mallard flew overhead. I followed its flight to where the tip of the Washington Monument jutted above a grassy plain.

"See that scum line," I said, pointing to what looked like dirty soapsuds near the Virginia shore. "Put a piece of cut herring on this big hook and drop it just there at the edge. Change the weight to three ounces."

"What are we fishing for?"

"Something bigger than herring."

He baited the hook and dropped the line, all serious concentration. When it hit bottom, I had him raise it two turns of the reel. As I baited my own hook, I recalled the way Sevareid had studied the inside of my shack that morning, complimenting me on the trim and the radiating tin flues I'd built to carry heat across the room from the wood stove. When he started in on the hidden bookcase behind my false south wall, I changed the subject. It was embarrassing how much I liked the attention.

"I've got something on," he said, staring at the bent rod. "But I'm not sure it's a fish."

"If it's a fish, it'll get almost to the surface, then dive hard so be ready to let out line."

He played it just right. When the big cat got to the surface a second time, I saw it was ten-pounds easy and slid the net toward it. "That line is only four-pound test so let me lift it."

It thrashed for a few seconds in the boat before going quiet, its mouth opening and closing. "The first catfish I ever caught was still alive an hour later," I told him. "I didn't know about them being able to breathe out of water. It scared me so much I tried to suffocate it in a bag."

"Why do they come to this scum line?"

"That's where the warm water from the power plant meets the cold water from the river." I pointed to the dark smoke rising from the plant's round stack. "They come here to mate." I took a small wooden club from beneath my seat and whacked the catfish across his head. We caught three more before pulling anchor.

"You ready for one more stop?"

"Do I ride my sturgeon now?"

"We're too early in the year for sturgeon. Let's see if we can catch a few largemouth bass."

"Let me guess. We use catfish guts as bait?"

"You're catching on."

A light rain began to fall as we paddled downriver. Sevareid asked how far it was to the Chesapeake Bay.

"You wanna go all the way to the Chesapeake?"

"Not today," he said. "But sometime."

NORA

THE CAMPFIRE was popping sparks off the painted leg of what used to support somebody's kitchen table when the conversation turned to machine-gun music.

"Tom Halloran here was famous for it," said Dennis Diamond, pointing to a broad-shouldered guy pouring himself a tin of coffee. "Even with bullets flying past your ear, you'd be listening to whatever song he was playing on his gun."

Nora was sharing this Bonus Army campfire with six men, including Diamond, an Iowa farmer with an impressive white beard and a laugh that sounded like pebbles rolling down a pipe. She first heard the laugh when she asked him to adopt her.

"I've got a daughter just about your age," said Diamond. "I guess I can handle another. You take that space next to my tent."

It was Sevareid who picked out Diamond, on the theory that any man who looked that much like Santa Claus was bound to have a jolly heart. Walker found her a wood pallet and stuffed an old blanket with dirt and last fall's leaves for a mattress. They both promised to come back soon.

She could see half a dozen other fires from where she sat, and knew there were a hundred more. The camp was enormous, as big as an Irish village. And because everyone lived mostly outdoors, she had instant access to their near infinite supply of stories.

At the moment, Tom Halloran was explaining machine-gun music.

"What you'd do is take bullets out of your cartridge belts. The gaps in the shooting are like tempo changes in a song. Now this,"

Tom rapped his cup against the coffee pot seven times, "everybody knows is 'Shave and a Haircut, Two Bits.' But you could do tricky stuff, too. The hardest part was living long enough to get good at it."

As Halloran spoke, other men joined them from nearby fires, attracted by the conversation and the presence of a young woman. Each of the men brought with him a cup of some kind. When Diamond saw Nora studying them, he made one for her out of an old sardine can, crimping the edges with a pair of needle nose pliers that he pulled from a vest beneath his army jacket.

"Your very own Hoover mug," said Diamond. His hands were large and calloused and reminded Nora of her father's. She filled the tin with her very first cup of coffee. It was black and looked oily, though that may have been from the sardines. She gulped down a mouthful and managed not to gag.

"It's ages stronger than tea."

Diamond laughed again. "It's got to be strong. This might be the only meal of the day." As he talked, Diamond pulled a coil of light wire from his vest and twisted it into a little dog. A loaf of stale bread was passed around the fire. Nora broke off a piece the size of her thumb. She asked the men if they'd known one another during the war.

Diamond used his pliers to point to a red, yellow and blue patch on the shoulder of his jacket. "You see this patch? Anybody who wears it was in the 42nd Division, the Rainbow Division. That means you're family, even if I've never seen you before. The Rainbow had men from every state. Coonasses from Louisiana, wops from New York City and big, dumb, farm boys like me."

Nora looked at the men in the firelight. For all her studying, she knew little about the war. What she did know was that maybe half the people in Ireland wanted Germany to beat the British.

"Do you mind if I ask dumb questions? What kind of battles did you fight? And did soldiers die most from bullets or bombs?"

A man with deep-set eyes and hair grey as gunmetal, spoke into his cup. "When we got to Europe there were these two trenches about 400-miles long, from the English Channel to Switzerland.

The German army was in one trench, the Allied army in the other. They'd been killing each other between those two pits since 1914. When we got there, it was our turn. First we'd run at them through the barbed wire. Then they'd run at us. It was nothing to lose 2,000 men in a single charge."

"And for nothing," said Diamond. "Muley here and some others once made it to an enemy trench. A goddamn miracle. An hour later they get a signal to come back. Nobody expected them to make it, so there was no support to keep them there."

"Don't forget the mustard gas."

"Or the big guns that pounded us for days at a time."

"There were lots of ways to die over there. You could catch trench fever from the mosquitoes."

"Or have a gun blow up in your face."

"Our friggin' officers didn't care how many of us died. They were all in chateaus behind the trenches, sleeping in beds and drinking French wine."

"Not all of them," said Diamond. "I hear Captain Glassford was a good one. And there's another." The men looked at Diamond expectantly, waiting to hear a favorite story.

"Douglas A. MacArthur. I guess he was the best there ever was."

"The Fighting Dude," said Tom Halloran.

Diamond returned the pliers and wire to his vest. "The first battle we're in, he goes up and over. That was at Salient du Feys. Afterwards he comes out of the smoke with a German officer as prisoner."

"And him without a gun."

"He's got a riding crop," said Diamond. "Poking the butt end of a riding crop into that German's back."

The men laughed, their eyes shining in the firelight.

"He was either the bravest man I ever saw or the craziest," said Halloran. "Used to stand on top of the trench getting shot at, looking through his field glasses like a damn bird watcher. And never would wear a helmet."

"Where is he now?" asked Nora.

"MacArthur? He's here. Across the street from the White

House," said Diamond. "He's General MacArthur now, the Chief of Staff. And if I'm any judge of men, he's our ace in the hole."

Nora finished her coffee. She felt twitchy and strong, like she could jump over the fire. And wonderfully content as well, to be sitting there with musical machine gunners and fighting dudes.

The talk turned to hometowns and jobs. A pigeon-chested man with a bad cough told about coal mining in West Virginia. "The pay cuts started and the layoffs, then more pay cuts and another round of layoffs. I got so desperate I volunteered to shot-fire."

"What's that?"

"That's where a guy blows out rock with explosives. You put gunpowder in a copper tube, jam it in a drill hole, light the quick and run like hell. You get a couple more dollars a day than the other miners, and your funeral expenses guaranteed."

"It's that dangerous?"

"Let's put it this way, you won't meet any white-headed shot-firers. If you last six months and still got all your fingers and toes, it's considered a freak of nature."

"So how did you manage?"

"I got lucky. They brought some scabs in from Georgia and we went out on strike."

"People in Georgia are eating clay they're so hungry," said a colored man with reddish hair. "Whole families with their bellies popped out. Fall one payment behind and they take your farm away from you."

"We found a way to stop that in Iowa," said Diamond, pulling on his beard. "Any judge who signed an eviction order would get a late night visit. And if a farm did come up for sale, we'd go to the auction and make sure no bid was higher than a dollar."

"We should be doing that all over," said one of the new arrivals at the fire. "Workers uniting against the bosses." His comment was met with silence. Diamond dropped two wooden arms from a couch onto the fire, throwing more sparks into a cloud of mosquitoes. For some reason the mosquitoes didn't bother Nora, but the gnats sure did. Like everyone in camp, she'd developed her own gnat wave, a left handed swish like the windshield wiper on a Model T.

Dennis Diamond asked Nora what her life was like in Ireland.

"A civil war's just over, so it's not like everyone's dancing jigs. For me it's been deadly quiet, with just my schooling and the farm. But we always had food to eat, even if it was only turnips and potatoes and maybe a scallion with a few leaves of lettuce. My mother baked bread and there was always a pot of tea boiling. And sometimes we'd get lucky and catch a trout on a pin."

"That's enough about food," said a voice in the smoke.

"Forget him. What did the bread look like, was it round or loaf?"

"Round," said Nora. "I'd be up the hill with the sheep and that smell would float up like a church bell."

"I never much liked sheep," said Georgia Red. "Too jumpy. Give me a good beef cow any day."

"As far as that goes, we had a sheep dog," said Nora. "And we needed the wool as much as the meat. We'd card and spin it to make clothes. For color we'd boil a moss called crottles. It wasn't what you'd call high fashion."

"We've got sheep dogs in Iowa," said Halloran. "They can make a whole flock stand up and dance."

The conversation turned to dogs. One of the men told a story about a German Shepherd that found its way home across three states. Nora looked across the fire and saw two familiar shapes wandering near a log cabin. Catherine from the store and...Will Cutler, the leader of the bicycle gang. But what were they doing here? And why together?

"Thank God I found you," said Catherine, holding the hem of her blue and white rayon dress above the mud. "This came for you yesterday." She had a hard time pulling the envelope from her purse while still holding onto her dress. "I'm sorry I didn't come sooner, but I wasn't sure where to go."

The envelope was sealed and carried a return address: The Smithsonian Institution. Nora made no move to open it.

"I came to the store looking for you," explained Will. "Miss Catherine told me about the trouble."

"How are things at the store?"

"My uncle was awful mad after you left. He went around threatening to call the police. And he was terrible to work with."

"I'm sorry. Not that I hit him, but sorry for you."

"Don't be sorry for me." Catherine smiled. "He's always terrible to work with."

Nora invited them to join her at the fire.

"I really have to be back," said Catherine, looking past Nora to the veterans. "Isn't it dangerous or something, with all these men?"

"If I was to yell for help, a hundred soldiers would rush to my rescue."

Nora walked them to the bridge, the unopened letter still in her hand. Was she more afraid the news would be bad or good? If she got her silver cup back, what excuse would she have for being in America, for sleeping on a leaf mattress with the Bonus Army? But why should she need an excuse?

At the bridge, Will asked Nora if she'd meet him at Griffith Stadium in two days for a boxing match. There was someone he wanted her to meet.

Nora waited until they were gone to open the envelope. The letter was two typewritten sentences.

"Have seen a cup that fits your description. Meeting arranged for Friday next week, 10 a.m."

It was signed Richard Drury.

Friday was nine days away. It didn't seem too long to wait.

～

NORA WOKE the next morning to the sound of bugles. Though it seemed like she'd only just shut her eyes, she wasn't the least bit tired. The camp in daylight was thick with tents and pennants and odd constructions. A stone bird bath just beyond her pallet, was being used as a shaving stand. Further down was what the soldiers called an "outhouse" made from parts of a child's playpen and bits of plywood.

Nora planned to walk the shores of the Potomac River that morning to look for Walker and Eric, and maybe catch a fish along the way. But that changed before her second cup of coffee, when Dennis Diamond asked if she'd consider doing the men a favor.

"We're sending out a neighborhood patrol to look for food and clothes. It helps to have a woman along. Makes us look less fearsome."

The patrol was seven men, two of them colored. On their way to the bridge, they stopped to look at a crowd gathered around an open ditch.

"That's Joe Angelo," Diamond told her. "He's going to bury himself alive and charge people money to talk to him through a pipe." Nora made a face and Diamond laughed. "You're right," he said. "Myself, I'd rather sit on a flagpole."

At Pennsylvania Avenue they turned right and after a while right again. The houses were all brick and attached to one another in rows. The sky was dark and thundering, but it never did rain.

Nora asked Diamond about the rules against panhandling.

"We're not asking for handouts," he said. "We offer to do chores. The other day we painted a woman's hallway. One time we carried an old stove up a basement stairs for three pairs of socks. If people just want to make a contribution, that's fine too."

Nora had noticed something that morning about Diamond. His dark brown eyes had odd specks of color in them. They reminded her of an out-of-control peat fire she'd once seen on a trip to Cork.

They split into two groups. Nora stayed with Diamond, Tom Halloran and one of the colored men named Anthony. She told them she could sew and mend, if they wanted to offer her services.

At the first house, an elderly woman answered the door. Diamond asked would she have any work that needed doing? "Large jobs or small. Sewing or cleaning?"

The woman appeared both friendly and frightened, a combination Nora had ever seen before. She needed no work done, but gave them a loaf of homemade bread and a deck of playing cards.

"This will be most appreciated by the veterans," said Tom Halloran opening his sack. Diamond gave her one of his metal twistings, a dog with its paw in the air, then marked the curb in front of her house with a small x. He told Nora the chalk mark would let others know not to knock on her door again, at least until the rain washed it away.

Nora asked Diamond and Tom about her frightened look.

"She isn't afraid of us," said Diamond. "She's afraid of being destitute. We're bringing that to her door."

They walked the streets for five hours. Only three doors were slammed in their faces, though a good many never opened. One man invited them inside, but only to argue politics.

"What you're doing is inviting revolution," he said. "Look at all the governments around the world that have fallen in the last two years. We can't let that happen here."

A German woman gave them some old suits and a pair of rubber boots. "My husband died in the war," she said. "In the Argonne. Were you there?"

"We were there," said Tom Halloran. "God rest his soul."

On the sidewalk outside her home Diamond said, "It's a sad thing when the wife of an enemy does more for you than your own government."

Most people seemed sympathetic, even if they had nothing to give. Diamond was encouraged by that. "Hard times have done one good thing. It makes people realize we're all in it together. Maybe when things get better, some of that will last."

Nora found the day interesting and uncomfortable. She'd never asked for anything in her life, and it took some getting used to. She'd have felt better if someone needed sewing. They filled two large sacks with clothes, bread and tins of food. Besides the deck of cards, they also got a checkers set and a game of Monopoly, which looked like it would be fun to play.

"This gives me ideas," said Anthony, holding up a miniature $100 bill. "One good counterfeiter could print up our bonus in about a day." Anthony was from New Orleans. He told Nora about the French Quarter and a food called shrimp creole.

Halfway through the day it occurred to Nora that she'd never asked how much money the veterans were due.

"It's different for every man, depending on the years served. But it comes out to about $500 each," said Diamond. Five hundred dollars! That would be a fortune for these men, sure enough.

At a lunch restaurant on Pennsylvania Avenue, Diamond called a halt and said, "Let's show Nora how to get a free cup of soup." Nora didn't think Negroes were allowed to sit in restaurants with white people, but no one said anything to Anthony when he took a stool between Diamond and Halloran. They all drank nickel cups of tea, then asked for free refills of hot water.

"Toss away the teabag and pour in a good whallop of ketchup," said Diamond. "See what you got now? Tomato soup."

"That's a handy trick," said Nora.

Diamond let out a long breath. "I never expected to need it at my age."

Anthony showed Nora a picture of a house, with a picket fence and flowers. "You see that? Three years ago that was mine. Nearly paid for."

"Here, I've got something," said Halloran, passing Nora a picture of a barn. "We had forty-six milking cows and a creamery too." Diamond told her they played a game in camp like cards, throwing down bankbooks. The winner was the one with the most money in a bank gone bust.

On their way back to camp, Nora saw an elderly woman pull a rotten tomato from a garbage can. The woman brushed away what maggots she could, removed her spectacles, then bit into the tomato. Nora turned to the curb and threw up her tea and tomato soup.

"They say maggots are full of protein," said Diamond, handing her a handkerchief.

"With all the stories I've heard about our own famine, I shouldn't be shocked," Nora told him. "It just took me by surprise."

At camp they deposited their takings in a central bin. "Just like Robin Hood," joked Halloran. "All for one and one for all."

Diamond stuck his head into the bin and said, "Not a tin of beef. God, what I wouldn't do for some meat."

Nora asked if wild bird would do as well.

"That would do," he said.

From her back pocket, she pulled her leather sling then searched the ground for a flat stone. Within a minute a pigeon flew past, head high and maybe fifteen yards away. Nora sent the stone flying and knocked the bird to the ground.

As Halloran ran to retrieve it, Diamond put his arm around Nora's shoulder and asked could she pot a few more. She said there didn't seem to be any shortage.

"We've got something here," said Dennis pulling on his beard. "I'm just not sure what."

WHOOPEE

THE INFORMANT arranged to meet Max Berga at the front door of the Sky High Whoopee Club, a blunt speakeasy in a rough, low-built neighborhood far from the monuments downtown. Berga invited Eric Sevareid to tag along.

"You think this is some honest citizen?" said Berga, his German accent rising with his irritation. "These characters always want something. Reward. Revenge. Some God damned thing that's not worth getting up this fucking early in the morning."

It was 9 a.m., which to Sevareid's way of thinking wasn't exactly the break of dawn, but why argue the point. He asked Berga for some background on the girl.

Berga grunted. "You don't read my stories?"

"I've read everything since I got here but I missed the first few."

"Well then." Berga ran a hand through his mane of blonde hair. "Beulah Limerick. How's that for a name. A white girl, 18, found in her own bed with a bullet hole in the back of her skull. And no blood, which meant she'd been shot, cleaned up, then put under the covers. That would have been good enough for a couple front pagers even without the love letters from three different men in her drawer."

"Who were the letters from?"

"A golf instructor, a professor with three children, a college kid…none of them important. The story is all about Beulah, bathtub gin and five nights a week at this Whoopee Club." Berga absently kicked at the door frame of the club, which had been closed since his initial story about the murder. "Three years after everybody else put away their party hats, she's still dancing the Charleston. What does that tell you?"

"The last of the flappers."

"With a twist. This is no 30-year-old trying to hang on. Beulah was 15 when the bottom fell out, but she wanted her bite of the apple."

"Or maybe a genuine romantic, refusing to see the decay all around her?"

Berga laughed. "That would be the way to play it. Innocent flower in a weed-infested garden. Except for one thing."

Sevareid waited.

"The tattoo. Below her belly and above her bush."

"What tattoo?"

"Four words. *Pay As You Enter.*"

Sevareid felt his ears flush. Berga was talking, but not to him.

"Let me guess. You're dressed that way because you don't want to draw attention to yourself?"

The informant had come around the corner of the building wearing a trenchcoat and rain hat in the morning heat.

"Are you German?" asked the informant.

"No, I'm an Irish leprechaun," said Berga. "Now what have you got that's so important you couldn't tell me on the phone?"

The man looked at Sevareid, then up and down the road before finally leaning close. "I'm Jim Malkin."

Sevareid recognized the name. Jim Malkin was a D.C. Trolley conductor, and the last man, according to Berga's stories, to dance with Beulah.

"So you took her home that night," said Berga.

"Who says?"

"Her best friend, the cops...look, if you can't come clean on shit that's already known, how can I believe anything new you've got to tell me?"

Malkin took off his hat and used it to wipe the sweat from his forehead. He rocked forward, then back, like a man standing on wheels thought Sevareid.

"Okay, I took her home."

Without looking at Sevareid, Berga said, "Write it down."

"Who's he?"

"My butler. Go on."

"Okay, so I took her home. And that's it."

"You didn't spend the night at her apartment?"

"I'm a married man."

Berga's laugh was gleeful.

"No really. This whole thing...I mean, people think I killed her! I've never killed anyone in my life."

"I can believe that. Tell me something that will make other people believe it."

"I can give you a suspect. But not one you'll like."

"First tell me about Beulah."

Sevareid was surprised Berga had ignored his offer of a suspect. He waited to learn why.

"I knew her from the Club. Beulah and her girlfriend Theresa. The two of them always together. Both good dancers, but Beulah was the best. People would stand around just to watch her." Malkin's face softened momentarily. "So anyway, I drove her home. As a favor."

"Just her and not her friend?"

"Somebody else drove her friend," said Malkin. "And I never even got inside with her."

"Why not?"

"Because she wasn't having it. Not as wild as she pretended. And then there was the cop."

"What cop?"

"My suspect. I don't know his name. But Beulah showed him to me. He was standing across the street from her place. She said he'd been bothering her for weeks. Banging on her window at night."

"Did he talk to you?"

"No. He stepped back into the shadows when Beulah pointed him out, but I got a good enough look."

"Did you tell the police?"

"Tell the police that one of their guys is a better suspect than me? I told them there was a copper standing across the street who saw me leave without, you know, going in."

"He must have backed your story."

"Why do you think?"

"You're out here talking to me."

Malkin considered that. "You're right. He must have backed me. So maybe you shouldn't write about him, huh? I mean, just put in the story that I never went inside, so I can show it to my wife."

"You have a telephone? I'll tell her myself."

Malkin's eyes narrowed. "That's okay. You put it in the story and I'll show it to her. Then we can forget this whole thing ever happened."

"I'll put it in the story," said Berga. "And you be sure and let me know when your wife forgets it ever happened."

On the way downtown, Berga read Sevareid's notes. "Malkin. Brown shoes. Laces frayed." He closed the notebook. "Kid, when I said write it down I didn't mean what color socks he was wearing."

"Those are things I notice."

Berga smiled. "Okay, you did good. Here's your reward. There's a guy in the Bonus camp who's gonna bury himself alive and breathe through a tube for money. The story's even better if you can figure out why he's important. That's all I'll tell you, let's see what you can dig up."

"If it's such a good story, why aren't you writing it?"

"I am. It'll be in tonight's edition. But I'm giving you a head start on everybody who'll play catch up."

"Why did you stop Malkin from telling you about the cop? Wasn't that his best information?"

"Sure. But that was all he planned to tell me. I needed the other stuff too. I wanted to keep him eager."

"About Beulah's tattoo? Was she a prostitute?"

"That's the funny thing," said Berga. "By all accounts she wasn't. The tattoo was some kind of joke. How do you like that for a sense of humor."

Sevareid wasn't sure why, but he was relieved to hear it.

FIGHT

I GOT TO GRIFFITH STADIUM at the same time as Police Commissioner Glassford, but didn't recognize him right away without his uniform and cap. He recognized me, stuck out his hand and said, "Hello Walker, are you a boxing fan?"

There must have been two hundred people close enough to see Glassford's hand hanging there a full second before I took it, and none of them more surprised than I was. But Glassford acted like that was the way you were supposed to shake somebody's hand, only after you'd checked it for concealed weapons.

"I am a fan," I told him. "I'm looking forward to seeing the Pep O'Brien fight."

"Good middleweight," said Glassford. "I saw him nearly beat Junior Wilson ten years ago in New York."

At six foot three, with shoulders like a lumberjack, Glassford has the size for a policeman but not the face. I don't know any other way to put it, but he is actually pretty, with a straight nose and eyelashes a woman might envy. The first time I met him, after the Tuesday party meeting, I thought somebody with a sense of humor might have stitched an artist's head onto a prizefighter's body. Even his hands were an odd match—long delicate fingers growing out of wide, callused palms. I found out later that he actually is an artist, a painter, and not completely talentless.

"Superintendent."

"Major."

A man with piercing blue eyes and a head as round as a bowling ball joined us. Glassford made the introductions.

"Walker, this is Major Dwight Eisenhower." And damn if he doesn't stick his hand out, too. I grab his so fast the Major looks down to make sure he's still got his watch.

We were at the stadium with about ten thousand other people, for a night of boxing matches between war vets, all the money going to the Bonus Army. I was there to work the Negro crowd, invite them to a Party picnic. And I was keeping an eye out for Nora. The last I saw her was three days earlier in the Bonus camp. She made me promise to come back soon, a promise I was happy to keep.

I let myself drop a few yards behind Glassford and Eisenhower as we walked through the gate. I knew Glassford was a Brigadier General in the army before he retired to Arizona to raise horses and paint. Something must have gone wrong to give that up for the police job. What I didn't know was how popular he and this Eisenhower were. Every ten feet someone stopped them to talk about the war. One guy left, then came back with his wife and teenage son, pointing at Glassford and Eisenhower as if they were proof of some tall tale he'd been accused of telling for years.

Of the two, Glassford looked more comfortable with the attention, maybe because he was used to it from his visits to the camps. Eisenhower reminded me of a kid at an amusement park, flashing this big smile whenever he remembered a name or face. After we passed through the portal to the open stadium, I could hear their names being repeated in every direction, like ripples on a pond— Glassford and Eisenhower.

∼

NORA WAITED at the north entrance to Griffith Stadium as the crowd flowed past. Her only concern on this warm evening was how to find Will in such a throng. That worry proved laughably misplaced. From two blocks away, she saw him coming up 7th Street leading a one-man parade.

"Miss Nora, this is Virni Tabak," said Will, introducing a dark-skinned boy in purple pantaloons and blouse, topped by a bright yellow scarf. It was not, Nora guessed, what the average American wore to a boxing match. In fact, Nora had never seen a person dressed like this for any occasion and, judging by the reaction of the stadium crowd, neither had anyone else.

"I am very pleased," said Virni with a slight bow. Will had told Nora that Virni was 16 and some kind of minister who made things appear out of thin air. He looked younger than that, his skin butter smooth and his lips shaped like a heart.

"Virni is an Elevated Master type," said Will, putting his hand on Virni's shoulder. "He works at the Mighty My Temple over on 13th Street."

"I've never met an Elevated Master," said Nora cheerfully. "I'm very pleased."

When Virni insisted on paying for everyone, Will gave Nora a wink. Was it money Will wanted from this Virni? If so, how would he expect her to help?

They moved beyond the stadium's outer walls, up a sloping ramp and through a twenty-foot portal flanked by District of Columbia policemen. The field and wooden bleachers opened below them like a box lined with green felt. On a field marked for baseball, a boxing ring sat at second base, surrounded by squared rows of wooden benches and folding chairs. The sound of singing came at Nora from the opposite bleachers.

> *Another little drink*
> *Another little drink*
> *Another little drink wouldn't do us any harm*

Their ten-cent admission allowed them to sit anywhere but the field seats. Nora led them toward first base, waving as she went to men who called out "Nora" or "Red." Will was impressed that so many knew her.

"You got something special there, Nora, something too good not to use."

"It's only my hair."

Dressed as he was, Virni garnered his own share of attention. "Someday I would like to do a show here," he told Nora.

She heard someone below calling Will Cutler's name, and traced the voice to a hatless man at the edge of the infield. "That's Mr. Gold. He runs the best speakeasy in town," said Will in a reverential whisper.

They met Gold at a gate separating the stands from the field. He was wearing a tan linen suit and blue necktie with white boxers stitched in the wool.

"Mr. Gold, this is Nora O'Sullivan. She's come here from Ireland. And this is Virni Tabak."

Neil Gold welcomed them while at the same time pressing money into the palm of a gatekeeper. "I have some seats you might like, close enough to catch any boxers flying from the ring."

Gold had a high forehead and wavy brown hair. Like a boxer, thought Nora, but only because he resembled a photograph she'd seen of Gene Tunney. Except Tunney was handsome and this man was not. He was as close to handsome as a person could get without actually getting there, but instead of being nearly handsome, he was somehow ugly. No feature on his face was unpleasant by itself, but all of them together were at war with one another, the pointed nose threatening the full lips, the square chin like a hammer between the rounded cheekbones. His face looked as if it had been put together with spare parts and too much haste.

The seats were four rows from the ring. Gold sat Nora, Virni and Will to his right. On his left was a newspaper reporter.

"Max Berga of the *Washington Herald*, this is Nora O'Sullivan and Virni Tabak of the Mighty My Temple."

Berga nodded to Nora, then leaned forward to speak to Virni. "I saw you last week at the Temple. With the flower and sword."

Virni smiled serenely. It was the first serene smile Nora had ever seen. It made Virni look more than a sixteen-year-old boy dressed like a grape.

"I read your story today about the Whoopee Girl," Nora told Berga. "It was brilliant."

Berga straightened up and studied her for a moment. "Where in Ireland are you from?"

"The west. Have you been there?"

"My grandmother was born near the Burren. She said there are enough rocks there to cover half the world."

"We are a country rich in rocks," said Nora.

After the heat of the day, the relatively cool night air was a pleasure. Nora turned to study the bleachers filling with spectators. Coming from a small village, large crowds excited her and this crowd particularly, since nearly everyone she'd met since landing in America was likely here. She hoped to find Walker and Eric before the night was over.

The first pair of boxers climbed into the ring, one holding an American flag, the other a military service pennant. The roar of the crowd was like a wind across her face. Nora remembered the afternoon she saw the Irish lightweight Jim Nance fight in Dublin, dancing and slipping punches, then risking everything in attack. It was the only time she'd ever wanted to be a man. The sound of the bell brought her back to the present. She opened her mouth, as if to swallow the first punch.

～

Buried Alive
by Eric Sevareid

It's often said that Washington D.C. is a city of contrasts—Democrat and Republican, white and Negro, rich and poor. Yesterday two veteran soldiers proved the truth of that cliché.

Sevareid paused to re-read his first paragraph. A confident tone if he did say so himself. Not to mention a large helping of bullshit, given that he'd been in Washington barely long enough to find the main streets, much less report on the indelible character of the city. He looked up at the huge statue of Lincoln in his Memorial and wondered if he'd really said, "I cannot tell a lie." A year ago he'd never have questioned it.

On one side of the city, in East Potomac Park, Major George O. Patton unholstered his pearl-handled revolvers and climbed atop a thousand dollar polo pony, one of the three he would ride during his afternoon match.

At the same time, three miles to the east, a retired infantryman named Joe Angelo was taking his place on another field. But Angelo's place was six feet underground.

"You tell your readers, this is a swell country where you got to be buried alive if you want to eat," said Angelo, a small, thin man with dark eyes and hollow cheeks. "You tell them to come see me."

George Patton came to Washington from West Point and old money.

Joe Angelo came at the head of an unemployed march of World War veterans from Camden, New Jersey.

Now Angelo is buried in a pit, ready and willing to tell his story to anyone who'll fork over a dime. Just put your ear to a tube that snakes through six feet of mud, ladies and gentlemen.

When it comes to story telling, Major Patton is a master. Many a night he entertains friends and reporters with tales of war and heroism. And all for free.

Joe Angelo is not quite so mesmerizing. And yet he wants to charge his listeners 10 whole cents for the privilege of listening. Ask about his trip to the Nation's Capital, for example, and you hear, "I just said, 'Fall in,' and we started. I walked most of the way here."

Not exactly gripping.

But Joe Angelo does have one great story to share. And Major Patton, as it happens, figures prominently in the telling. It goes like this:

Fourteen years ago, Joe Angelo went on a night patrol in a dangerous part of France with five armed men. The leader of that patrol was Major George O. Patton. An artillery shell landed among the men, killing everyone but Patton and Angelo.

Patton was badly wounded. He lay on open ground, exposed to enemy fire. Angelo braved that fire, crawling across the ground to pull the Major into a shell hole where he nursed him through the night until help arrived.

Joe Angelo was cited for exceptional bravery outside the line of duty and awarded the Distinguished Service Cross.

Yesterday, in this city of contrasts, Major Patton was asked about that bravery, and the man now buried in a living grave.

"Undoubtedly the man saved my life. But his several accounts of the incident vary from the true facts," said the Major.

Does Patton mean it was raining rather than dry that night? The enemy fired bullets instead of shells? Details are important. Pay a dime to Mr. Angelo and hear for yourself.

Sevareid laid down his pencil. He'd planned on writing more about Angelo and Patton, where they came from to end up here, but this was the obvious place to stop. Besides, there was the fight to see and he still had to take this story to the Associated Press office. He gave it one last read and allowed himself a small swallow of pride. Too bad nobody in Washington would get to read this. His parents would, and friends in Minnesota, but they weren't on his new list of people to impress. All of those lived here.

WALKER

EACH OF THE FOUR bouts was scheduled for three rounds. Before the first, an announcer in a cream white suit told Depression jokes.

"What do you call a family pet in 1932? *Dinner.*"

In the Negro section where I sat, we waited until each fight began to pick favorites and make our penny bets. The boxers were past their prime, but suitably eager. It was good fun sitting up there, a part of the big show.

The last fight was between the former middleweight contender, Pep O'Brien and Negro veteran Jimmie Williams. There was no question where our loyalties were in this one. Both men still looked like fighters, with flat stomachs and muscular backs. We all roared when Williams charged O'Brien at the bell, staggering him with an uppercut. But when he stepped closer to press his advantage, O'Brien banged him with a quick right. When the round ended, we stood and cheered with everyone else in the stadium.

The second round started slowly, O'Brien stalking Williams in a clockwise circle. The punches were more measured, like stone masons tapping a wall for weak spots. Halfway through the round, O'Brien found his opening and blasted through, putting Williams against the ropes. When I was sure he couldn't take another punch, Williams slipped to the side and hooked a blow to O'Brien's head. Now it was O'Brien's turn to cover until the bell.

Between rounds the crowd began a rhythmic clapping, like the beat of a giant heart.

~

THE FINAL ROUND began and ended with both men in the middle of the ring, bucking and grunting like exhausted rams. Nora saw arcs of sweat and saliva spray across the spotlights. She worried for both men's safety and was pleased when the fight was judged a draw.

"Fantastic," said Virni, shaking his head as if emerging from a trance. "Wonderful."

Neil Gold, smelling of mint and shaving soap, leaned across Nora. "You're a surprise, Mr. Tabak. I might have to join this religion of yours."

"It's not a religion," said Virni. "But you're welcome all the same."

"If it's not a religion, why do all those people come to your Temple?"

"For the same reason they come here. To feel something which is bigger than themselves."

"That's a little slippery for a Jew to grab hold of," said Gold.

Gold didn't look anything like Nora's idea of a Jew, but then she wasn't sure what her idea of a Jew looked like. She studied his profile and wondered if Jews prayed on their knees.

Gold turned to her. "Will you come to my club tonight? With your friends."

Nora said she would.

~

IN THE FIRST YEARS of Prohibition, Washington D.C. saw every kind of illegal drinking establishment that home-grown and imported entrepreneurs could conceive. But until Neil Gold opened his Criers Club in the summer of 1930, the city had never seen a drink joint where an Italian diva sang arias above the craps table, an artist painted portraits beside the bar, and a Mexican juggler spun dishes while being led through the room by a monkey on a leash.

Sevareid learned all this from Max Berga. "Meet me there after the fight," he said. "I'll buy you a whiskey and introduce you to the monkey."

He left the stadium and immediately spotted Nora O'Sullivan. It had only been three days since he and Walker dropped her at the Bonus camp but she looked changed, brighter somehow, and happy. He felt a tickle in his throat, like he'd swallowed a feather. He'd meet the monkey some other night.

"I'm not sure I should be talking to you," said Nora with an unconvincing pout. "You and Walker promised to come back. How did you know those veterans wouldn't sell me into white slavery?"

She wore a blue shirt that made her hair look lighter and her green eyes brighter, a dazzling combination that kept him staring until Nora snapped her fingers in front of his face.

"Eric, this is Virni Tabak. He's an Elevated Master. And Will Cutler here has himself a small business."

"I'm impressed," said Sevareid, "and glad to meet you both."

"We're going to a speakeasy," said Virni. "Perhaps you'd like to join us?"

"I'm not sure Mr. Gold would want us inviting strangers to his club," said Will to Nora.

"That's okay," said Sevareid. "I've already been invited."

"Mr. Gold offered to drive us in his Pierce Arrow car, but a certain person wouldn't allow it," said Virni, glaring at Will.

"I still say we should take Virni back to the Temple," pressed Will. "A speakeasy isn't the place for a master type."

"Don't be such a stick. Didn't your Jesus withstand temptation? I'm very much ready to be tempted."

Will reconsidered. "You wouldn't feel the need to smite anything, would you?"

Virni grinned. "I don't do smiting."

As they walked, Will gave Sevareid the scoop on Gold. "He was down to his last dollars when his luck changed. And guess what day it was? October 19, 1929—the day Wall Street crashed. The first thing Mr. Gold did was buy that car—a green 1929 Pierce Arrow, bright as a waxed apple and nearly as long as a trolley. The seats are leather, I've touched them, and the dashboard is mahogany. Brand new, the car cost $1,750. The morning after the stock market crash, Gold bought it from a man on Third Avenue for $100."

"How did that change his luck?" asked Sevareid.

"That's the mystery," said Will, putting a finger against his nose. "Good things happen when you take risks."

～

ON A DARK STREET, Neil Gold's building was the darkest, as though everything that reflected light had been covered or chipped off. The building shared a half-acre lot with a weathered carriage barn.

"This place?" asked Virni, clearly disappointed by its black, abandoned look.

"Hold your horses until we get inside," said Will, leading them through a basement door and up a dimly-lit stairway. At the landing, Will pushed through a thick, velvet curtain into a closet-sized hallway. The hall was occupied almost entirely by a double-breasted suit. The head atop the suit was bald as an egg. Nora recognized him immediately—a gangster guarding a door.

"We're here to see Mr. Gold," said Will. The suit opened the door to smoke, lights and laughter. There were at least two-hundred people in the main room, some playing roulette, others blackjack and dice. A woman in an evening dress and elbow length white gloves rattled dice above her head. Nora tucked a loose corner of her shirt into her pants.

More than the smoke or the crowd, it was the light that struck Nora—bouncing off glass and metal, rings, necklaces and chips of ice. Where she came from, nights were mostly lit by lanterns or hearth fires. This light dazzled.

Virni was immediately impressed by the music—swing piano, drums and saxophone. "Boogie woogie!" he shouted and plunged through the crowd in the direction of a Negro quartet. Will was left behind, staring at a monkey in a round hat and vest dangling from the chandelier.

"I bet a monkey would make good company," he said wistfully, then realized he'd lost Virni. "I better go follow that boy."

Sevareid and Nora snaked their way through men and women who danced without touching, to a serving bowl big as a horse trough with iced seafood and bottles of champagne.

"Tell me about the camp," said Sevareid. "Are the soldiers behaving themselves?"

"They are perfect gentlemen. Really, they've been so kind to me, as though I actually was someone's daughter. And the stories they tell about the war and what happened afterward. I had no idea. It's all so sad. Did you go to Walker's cabin after you left me at camp?"

"I did. The next morning we fished the Potomac. Walker was right about that river, it's big and fast!"

"Fishing? Without me?" Nora was genuinely mad.

"Have you tried an oyster?" Neil Gold, now in a tuxedo, had come up behind them. He reached into the ice for a half-shelled oyster, squirted it with lemon juice, and held it just at Nora's forehead.

Nora opened her mouth and stuck out her tongue.

"That's it," smiled Gold. "Like taking communion back home."

Nora chewed, her eyes squinting in concentration.

Gold laughed at the look on her face. "You ever hear of John Smith? A long time ago he said, *'He be a brave man who first ate an oyster.'*"

"This is my friend Eric Sevareid," said Nora.

"Max Berga told me you might come," said Gold. "He's playing poker in the back room."

"Thanks," said Sevareid. "I'll find him later."

"Your club is so extravagant," said Nora, accepting another oyster. "I wouldn't be surprised to see an elephant here."

"We tried Shetland ponies once. But the smell never came out of the curtains."

Nora was dressed for the fight, in tweed trousers and a blue cotton shirt. It was an outfit that made a statement, though tonight she'd have liked to say something finer, like the beautiful ladies who sailed through the club.

"They're so pretty. And clean," she said, as much to herself as Gold.

"Some of them have less than you think. Some have only their dresses."

Nora looked again at the women. "So this is all pretend?"

"That's the business I'm in."

A woman's smoky voice drew Nora's attention. The singer was Negro and beautiful in a sheer peach gown. Nora had never heard the song but guessed where it was heading and hummed along.

"So you're a singer," said Gold.

"Only to the sheep back home."

"Some night we'll have to get you up there."

"I might drive away your customers."

He leaned close, "Then I'd have you to myself."

Nora smiled. Eric didn't.

A blonde woman in a silk dress with bright blue eyes and skin too white to have ever seen the sun, joined them just as Will and Virni approached from the other direction.

"Look," gushed Virni, holding a yellow poker chip between his fingers. "A woman gave it to me. She called me Lucky Swami. I believe it's worth a dollar."

"Cash it in while you're ahead," advised Gold. The woman in silk spoke into his ear. As she walked away, Nora saw Will staring at her hips. He blushed at being caught, which surprised Nora. Since when did tough gang leaders blush?

"We should be heading back to the Temple," Will told Virni. "If Madame Blisky finds out you're gone, they'll send people with swords to bring you back."

"You can't leave without one glass of champagne," said Gold and reached into the oyster ice for a bottle.

"Champagne!" Virni looked as though he might levitate.

"Here's to a bright future," said Gold, raising his glass to Nora.

"And health to the company," she answered.

They'd barely drained their glasses when Will began nudging Virni toward the exit. "Nora, we have to go."

"Go ahead, I'll be just out."

"I'm sure Will can get the swami home without you," said Gold, holding the champagne bottle before her eyes.

"No. I promised Will."

"I'll go with you," said Sevareid, putting a hand on her elbow.

"Eric, stay and see your reporter friend. But get Walker and come find me tomorrow at the camp."

~

ON THE SIDEWALK, Will was teaching Virni the words to a song:

> *Well I'm ragged, I'm hungry, I'm dirty too;*
> *I'm ragged, well I'm broke and I'm dirty too.*
> *If I clean up, sweet mama, can I stay all, all night with you?*

"Teach me too," said Nora, "I need to learn American songs."

"That's a Negro song," said Will. "Not the kind a white girl sings."

"I'm not a white girl. I'm Irish."

They went west to 13th Street, then north under a canopy of oak trees. Nora walked between them.

"So, who'll go first?" she asked.

"Go where?"

"Tell a story. About your mother or father. About where you come from. Will, how about you."

Will pushed out his chest as if he was about to recite something heroic, then apparently had second thoughts. "You're the guest, Virni. Why don't you go first?"

Virni told his story in a soft, hypnotic voice. "I was six when my mother died and the visions began. They weren't dreams exactly or clear like photographs either. It's hard to describe a thing that is both sharp and blurred at the same time. Anyway my father would ask, 'Will it rain tomorrow?' Or 'If I flip this coin will it land one side or the other?' I had no answers to those questions. I didn't choose my visions and they revealed nothing that could be used to advantage. But still people came to sit beside me and touch my face, first from my own village and then from far beyond."

Will asked if he liked the attention.

"I didn't. My mother and I had the same fever. She died, I lived, and then the visions came to me. I didn't know if they were a punishment or some message from my mother, but either way I didn't want to share them with strangers. Then one morning, playing on the dirt road that led through our village, I saw a shiny black automobile approach. In the back seat was a woman with golden yellow hair, like a Christian angel.

"She was dressed in a purple robe that matched exactly the purple of my visions. She reached her long white hands toward me and said, 'Hello, Virni. I've come for you.' Twenty minutes later, I was in the automobile on my way to London. My father told me only that I was going on a trip with this woman and that she would show me special things. I didn't see my family again for nine years."

Nora waited for Virni to continue, but he was done.

"Here we are," he said with a laugh, and spun on the sidewalk like a dancer. "This is where I do all my tricks."

The Mighty My Temple, a former Masonic Lodge, rose from the crest of Cardozo Hill. As they climbed its wide, outside steps Nora wondered at a pair of Egyptian sphinx and the all-seeing eye above them. The temple's massive iron doors were closed.

"How will you get in?" she asked.

"The same way I got out." He went behind one of the four Greek columns and was gone.

Will had seen this disappearing act before. "There's a hidden door in the pillar. But pretty good, huh?" A distant thunder rumbled behind them. As if on cue, Virni reappeared.

"I forgot to thank you," he said to Nora. "Will must bring you here some night for my show. I'll do my sword and flower trick."

WALKER

MARTIN HIATT tried for months to convert me to fly fishing. Showed me the pretty imitators he tied, the elegant, looping casts of his ten-foot cane rod, the tiny scissors, clips and other gadgets tucked inside his vest pockets. I'd have none of it. Why spend time on all that when I could catch any fish I pleased with worms, spinners or spoons?

What finally sold me was a big brown trout in a deep pool of Seneca Creek.

"Okay, Randolph. Let's see you catch him," said Hiatt, after driving us an hour west of Washington to confront the beast. "You can use anything short of explosives."

I'd never fished for brown trout before, but how hard could it be? I started with worms, switched to crawfish and crickets, then methodically went through everything in my tackle box. That fish might as well have been a log for all the interest he showed me. If Hiatt hadn't been there, I might have gone after him bare handed.

"Let's fish upstream," said Hiatt. "We'll come back in an hour when things have settled and I'll have a go."

Sure enough, an hour later Hiatt casts a black and brown puff of feathers above the pool and lets it drift down. I was crouched low to keep the trout from seeing me through the clear water, so when he smashed that fly not three feet from my face, I nearly fell on my butt.

Hiatt kept his line taut and let the trout take him. Up the creek then back down, though shallows and hip deep water. The only time Hiatt insisted on controlling the direction was when the trout tried to run the line against sharp edged rocks. He must have walked a quarter mile before that fish was spent enough to be reeled in.

He put the fish in my hands. "What do you think, Randolph, shall we let him go? Give you a chance to catch him yourself some day?"

I didn't answer. I had no room in my brain for anything but that trout. So muscular in my hands, eight pounds at least, with smooth skin in deep colors of brown, olive green and yellow. The black and red spots on its back were circled by light, like a halo. The mouth looked prehistoric. This was a fish to fall in love with.

I lowered him into the water, his head into the current and opened my hands. He stayed on my palms, calm as sleep for about ten seconds, then shot forward with one swish of his tail. I went back to Seneca many times after that, but never even thought to bother that fish.

Tying flies became a pleasure, figuring the right weight for something nearly weightless and which colors might appeal to a fish's eye. I looked for bugs under submerged rocks and watched what the trout slurped from the surface, then tried to imitate that menu—mayflies, caddis, the ugly black beetles and other bugs that fell into the water from stream-side rocks. It was fun creating a little zoo of artificial creatures. Like being a kid again.

The morning after fight night, I decided it was time to replenish my artificial fly box. The sky was clear and windless, but my mood didn't match the day. As flat as I felt, the bright piles of feathers, wool and fur on my outdoor work table might as well have been heaps of dead leaves.

I was still beating myself up for what happened the night before with Nora. More accurately, for what hadn't happen. I'd spotted her climbing toward the exit with Will and the kid in purple, laughing and waving to her fan club of Bonus vets. She was the brightest thing in that stadium and I knew she was searching the crowd for me. Okay, for Sevareid and me.

I pushed toward her, but every step took me deeper into a sea of white people pushing the opposite way. By the time I exited the stadium, Nora was gone. I knew she was probably on her way to Gold's speakeasy and knew I could find a way inside, but instead I turned and started for home. I couldn't have told you just then why I gave up so quickly. What I did learn is it's a hell of a hike from Griffith Stadium to Virginia when you're kicking your own butt all the way there.

I put the fly material away and went across the river to the Boat House, which sits on a slope of land between the Potomac and the C&O Canal. There's no actual boat house, just a few sheds, one with a covered porch for selling bait and renting rowboats. Nobody seems to know exactly how old the place is. One old timer likes to point out reeds near shore as the spot Moses was found floating in his basket.

The Boat House is one of the few places in town that's not

totally segregated. Negroes can rent rowboats and fish anywhere they like. The only place they're not welcome is at one outside table where white fishermen tell stories and, even there, they can sit around the perimeter on tree stumps.

I began going to the Boat House the month I moved to Washington. At first I stayed away from the story table, just roamed the shoreline, studying the way people fished. Gradually I moved close enough to listen to the dozen or so regulars who gathered there, each with his own spot around the table like reserved stools at a bar. Except for a house painter named Zachary who hated coloreds only a little more than he hates everybody else, the regulars were friendly enough. They respected Mr. Luke for being an old time fisherman and came to respect me for being a good young one.

The river was muddy this day from overnight rains and running fast. Higher up the bank, driftwood from the spring floods lay in oddly neat stacks. There were five regulars at the story table, including the one I was hoping to see, my fly fishing mentor Martin Hiatt.

"You hear about that man in Brandywine the other day?" asked Fred Stinson, a milkman who rides his horse-drawn wagon to the Boat House each morning directly after his last delivery. Stinson tells stories in great, outlandish detail and never seems to care if anybody believes them.

"What man was that?"

"Nearly got himself killed catching a bass. When he cut her open, this little snake jumps out, some kind of poisonous thing, and bites him right on the hand. The largemouth must have swallowed it just before he got caught. How do you like that?"

"I got something to top that. Happened to me this morning," said John Hardy. John and his brother Larry own a plumbing business. Except for a shared reputation for knowing fish, the two couldn't be less alike. John is heavy, talkative and quick to laugh. His brother is thin, deliberate and quiet. The reason Larry so rarely talks, it's said, comes from childhood when he opened his mouth and swallowed a bee. The Hardy family has worked on the

Potomac for dog's years—as fishermen, bootleggers and fur traders. Their cousin Oliver T. Hardy owns the *Lighthouse*, one of the river's largest gambling and prostitution barges, and a place I once worked.

"I'm taking the hook out of this catfish and I hear a croak that sounds like 'Let me go.'" Hardy daubed his head with a handkerchief. "I don't think a thing about it, knowing the air bladder a catfish has. But then I hear it again, and this time there's no mistaking what it says—'Let me go.' I know nobody in the world will believe a fish talked to me. But I also know I can't eat one that might have. Just as I let it loose, what do you think that fish says to me?"

"Thank you?"

"Hah! Turns in mid-air, gives its whiskers a shake and says, 'Sucker!' just as clear as ringing a bell."

Martin Hiatt left the table to greet me. "How's everything, Randolph? I haven't seen you for months."

"I went to California."

"What did you think?"

"The sky is bigger. I went fishing with some Indians and caught steelhead trout."

Hiatt is a retired government printer who always wears a bow tie and, except on the hottest days, a tweed jacket. It was Hiatt who first hired me as a fishing guide, for a quarter a day, and got me the scholarship to Carver Academy. Over the years we'd come as close to being friends as I'd allow. What held me back was not being able to figure why he had such an interest in me. That and the way he smiled when I talked, like he could see me more clearly than I saw myself. The fact that he probably could only made me more uncomfortable.

I did enjoy fishing with him. We could spend a whole afternoon hunting fish and speak no more than a dozen words. When we did talk, it was almost always about fish or local history, and Mr. Hiatt knew a lot about both.

Our fishing partnership ended after I was expelled from Carver Academy during my junior year. But later, when I was arrested for murder, it was Mr. Hiatt who helped set me free. Though it had only been six months since I'd seen him, he looked considerably older.

"I thought about you during my travels," I said, dropping my usual reserve. "About what a good friend you've been and how badly I repaid you."

He turned his face to the river. "That's not necessary."

"Maybe, but I need to say it."

He straightened his always straight bow tie before facing me. His eyes were pale blue and wet, but then they always looked wet. "I am curious about one thing."

"Anything."

"Why did you hit the boy at the Academy?"

"I didn't hit him. I pushed his face into a bowl of custard. It was my first day back after Mr. Luke's funeral and he said to me, 'I hear you've got a whole new source for worms.'"

"He meant....?"

"He did."

"Well, you had every right."

I laughed. "I'd been wanting to hit him for months, ever since he told a girl I liked that I lived in a shack."

"You hadn't told her?"

"Worse, I'd let her think I was rich. One of the 500 families."

"What a tangled web, eh Randolph?"

I thought to put a hand on his shoulder, but wouldn't with so many people around. Instead I said, "Let's go fishing next week. I'll show you my favorite rockfish hole, one I've never showed to anyone else." He seemed pleased.

THE PARTY

THE OFFICE of the New Masses magazine was on 7th Street N.W. near the corner of G. The word Communist was nowhere visible and neither was there any sign of a hammer or sickle. From the chipped look of the storefront, Nora guessed contributions weren't pouring in.

There were three people inside the office, including the Party chief she'd twice met with Walker. He looked up from a table where he was writing.

"You're Walker's friend."

"I am. Nora O'Sullivan. I was hoping to find him here."

"I'm Ken Cord." He shook her hand. "He'll probably be here soon. You're welcome to wait." He offered her tea.

"Are you a writer then?" she asked while waiting for the water to boil.

"I'm a candidate," he told her. "For the Vice-presidency."

"Of...?"

"Of the United States."

Nora could think of nothing to say but "Oh."

Cord smiled. "I'm not expected to win in a landslide."

"I'm afraid I haven't a vote to give. I'm just visiting."

"They say the Irish are lucky. You can wish me luck."

"If the Irish were lucky, there wouldn't be so many of us here," said Nora. "But I'll wish you luck all the same."

Cord went back to his papers and Nora picked up the January issue of *New Masses* magazine. Inside was a story headlined "Women on the Breadlines," by Meridel LeSueur:

> I am sitting in the city free employment bureau. It's the woman's section. We have been sitting here now for four hours. We sit here every day, waiting for a job. There are no jobs. Most of us have had no breakfast. Some have had scant rations for over a year. Hunger makes a human being lapse into a state of lethargy, especially city hunger. Is there any place else in the world where a human being is supposed to go hungry amidst plenty without an out-cry, without protests, where only the boldest steal or kill for bread, and the timid crawl the streets, hunger like the beak of a terrible bird at the vitals.

Nora turned to the title page to see what city the woman was writing about—Minneapolis.

It's no wonder these young girls refuse to marry, refuse to rear children. They are like certain savage tribes, who, when they have been conquered refuse to breed. Not one of them but looks forward to starvation, for the coming winter. We are in a jungle and know it. We are beaten, entrapped. There is no way out. Even if there were a job…for a few days, a few hours, at thirty cents an hour, this would all be repeated tomorrow, the next day and the next.

Nora had seen fear and hunger in Ireland, but never experienced it herself. Her parents, with only one surviving child, adequate acreage, three cows, some chickens and a flock of sheep, were well-off by Irish standards. That wasn't something she advertised, particularly not in the Bonus camp.

At the end of the article, Nora read an Editorial Note:

This presentation of the plight of the unemployed woman, able as it is, and informative, is defeatist in attitude, lacking in revolutionary spirit and direction which characterize the usual contribution to New Masses.

Her respect for the magazine tumbled.

Walker and Sevareid came through the door in a rush. Walker was wearing denim pants and a small, green backpack. Sevareid had the sleeves of his white shirt rolled to the elbows. Both were breathing hard, like they'd just finished a race.

Walker saw her first and stopped just inside the door. Sevaried had eyes only for the magazine covers and labor posters mounted on the walls. He walked the room, nodding his head and humming softly. He didn't see Nora until he was directly above her chair, then jumped in surprise.

"For a reporter, you're not very observant," she joked, giving him a quick hug. He felt nicely muscular inside her arms. She went to Walker, curious to compare hugs.

They went outside to talk. The rain Walker smelled that morning had passed to the west, and the clouds there were thinning.

"Were you ever coming back for me," Nora demanded of Walker, "or did you think once you found me a father you were done?"

"We planned to come back but...."

"No need to tell me why you didn't. Eric already has." She took hold of Walker's right thumb. "You promised to take me fishing as well, or is that just a thing you tell Irish girls?"

Walker shrugged his shoulders. "I promised Mr. Cord I'd help him with a speech today."

"You're a speech writer?" asked Sevareid.

"I don't write his speeches. I listen to them. Suggest things."

"Then you're an editor," said Sevareid.

"Or like a piano tuner," added Nora.

Walker laughed. "A piano tuner? I like that."

"Mr. Cord can do without you for one afternoon," said Nora. "I've talked to him. He's not yet working on his acceptance speech."

"It *is* a good day to show me Great Falls," said Sevareid, studying the slash of blue on the horizon.

Walker had them wait while he went inside to talk with Comrade Cord.

～

NORA LEFT her bicycle in the office, under a poster celebrating an Akron, Ohio tire workers' strike. "My country was like that once," she said pointing to the photograph of six muscular men around an oil slick machine. "Full of heroes."

They chased down a trolley on F Street, the three running stride for stride. Sevareid was surprised at how fast Nora ran, but then nearly everything about her surprised him.

When she sat between them on the trolley, he saw the others on board stare daggers. Wouldn't his friends at the University be jealous? All their talk of equality and human rights, and hardly a Negro in the state to practice on.

"I could do this all day," he said as they rode past Woodward and Lothrop's huge display windows and the National Theatre's flapping blue pennants. "Just ride around and look at people."

Walker said that was the reporter in him talking. "You'd probably like to follow all of them home."

"Not all of them," said Sevareid. "And maybe not the ones you'd guess."

Nora turned her head from one to the other. She said she was happy and told them why. "We look good together. Like Dumas' *Three Musketeers*."

"I don't recall there being a woman Musketeer," deadpanned Sevareid. "We'll have to come up with something else to be."

WALKER

THE TROLLEY turned up Connecticut Avenue, rounded the massive fountain at Dupont Circle where a gang of kids waged a water battle, then crossed over Rock Creek on P Street just downstream from the Buffalo Bridge. When the trolley hit Wisconsin Avenue in Georgetown, I pointed up Virney Place to my old school.

"It used to be a foundry. Cannons from the War of 1812 were forged there."

"Was that secondary school?"

"Elementary. I went to secondary school at a private academy."

"Were you rich?" asked Nora.

"No," I said and stopped short of adding that I used to be. "One of the men I guided on fishing trips got me a scholarship."

Nora looked down the cobblestone streets lined with small, elegant houses and ivy-covered churches and said it was the nicest neighborhood she'd seen in Washington.

I told her Georgetown wasn't always colored. "Congressmen

and bankers and high society types lived here. When the rest of Washington was swampland, ships sailed out of Georgetown to Africa and the Indies. Then the canal died and everybody moved closer to the Capitol."

Nora said, "I'm trying to picture you as a boy on these streets, but the image won't come." I'd tell her later she was right.

The trolley stopped at the car barn on 36th Street where we transferred to the electric railway to Great Falls. When a couple of 16-year-olds stared at us on this trolley, Sevareid took a deep breath and growled. The boys looked away so fast I had to laugh. It made me feel good, not Sevareid staring them down so much as the idea that we were in it together.

The rail ran north along the Potomac, under Georgetown University. Nora said it looked like a castle. She stood and bent across me for a better look, her hair touching my cheek and her hip my shoulder. I was confused enough that I nearly let her get decapitated. It was Sevareid who pulled her inside by the shoulders to avoid a low limb.

Where the trees thinned, Nora got her first good look at this part of the Potomac—wide and fast, with a steep bank on the Virginia side and sharp rocks in the middle that she said looked like fins cutting the water. The Shannon River in Ireland, she told us, was wider but not as swift. She recognized the C&O canal from a hand-drawn map she carried and asked how far it went.

I told her 184 miles to Cumberland, Maryland and plunged right into a history lesson. "At one time they say you could barely see the water for all the barges."

"What happened?"

"They built a railroad that was faster and cheaper." I leaned back and wondered was I talking too much and could I stop even if I tried? "Sometimes the kids who lived in the lockhouses along the canal would unhitch the mules and we'd have races."

Nora asked if the families still lived there. Sevareid wanted to know about the mules. I promised to take them along the canal and show them the old, mostly empty lockhouses and two old mules that still pull a little barge for kids' birthday parties.

The tram left the river at Little Falls and went inland, through woods, farms and little clumps of stores and houses. When Nora asked about the water reservoir, the sound of her voice merged with the bump and rattle of the trolley vibrating through my seat. The sun was shining directly on her face. I saw again the tiny freckles near the bridge of her nose that I'd noticed the first day in the Stead.

Just before we left Washington to cross into Maryland, Nora jumped from her seat like she'd been stung and grabbed each of us by a wrist.

"Get up. Pull the cord. We're getting off." The car hadn't even stopped before she was off and racing down the footpath, pointing as she ran to an orange Ferris wheel and one visible hump of a roller coaster. She looked back to find me standing pretty much where she'd left me and Sevareid not much further along. It was Sevareid who pointed to the sign she'd missed, just above the entrance to Glen Echo Amusement Park.

NoColoreds

It wasn't a warning but an advertisement, like Clean Rest Rooms or Quick Service. Nora looked at all the white faces beyond the gate, eating caramel apples and throwing darts, then stormed up the avenue, mad as hell.

When we caught up to her she was mostly mad at me. "You should have stopped me from making a fool of myself."

"You're a hard one to stop," I said. Sevareid added an "Amen."

We followed the road for a mile, passing little houses cut into the woods and the occasional shop. I knew nearly everyone we saw, white and colored, well enough anyway to nod my head or say hello. But their response wasn't so casual. I'd never come through with a tall, redheaded girl and someone as big and white as Sevareid. You'd have thought I was leading a pair of Martians and I liked it, the ripple that trailed our wake.

When we'd passed the last tin-roofed house, Nora said to me, "How do you stand it?"

I knew what she meant. "A teacher told me once, 'Nobody can

make you feel inferior without your cooperation.' That's the way I deal with it."

"It can't be as easy as that," said Nora. "It has to change the way you look at things. Or the way you grow, like trees you see on a windy coast."

"Maybe that's a good shape to be. Besides, what should I do? Climb that fence at Glen Echo? Fight everybody who calls me nigger?"

"You could leave," said Sevareid.

"And go where, back to Africa?"

Nora asked why not.

"Hunting lions with a spear isn't something you just pick up after a couple hundred years. Besides, I've got as much right to stay as anybody."

Nora stopped. "But to stay and do nothing?"

"Who says I'm doing nothing? I'm working to bring down the machine."

"The machine. I like the sound of that," she said and smiled. "But are you doing it with 'correct revolutionary spirit'?"

I didn't know where she'd read that, but I refused to be baited. "That's just words some people need to hear."

We left the road to follow a narrow path to the canal. For maybe a second, Nora wobbled. It wasn't all the trees that made her dizzy, she said, but the giant pileated woodpecker, his flame red head hammering at a nearby trunk. Sevareid thought it might be an O'Sullivan woodpecker.

We crossed the canal on a foot bridge above lily pads. Near the bank, a white swan ducked its head under the dark green water. The swan had been there for a month. I was surprised nobody had eaten it.

"Fifty years ago, the sharpers would get around Great Falls by taking the canal to here."

"What's a sharper?" asked Nora.

"River boats, pointed at both ends. They stretch canvas over hoops to protect the cargo, like old covered wagons in the west." I promised to show them one of the half-dozen still around.

"With all the things you're promising to show us, we'll have to get you one of those caps that tour guides wear," said Sevareid.

It wasn't all that funny, but it made Nora smile and that made me happy as well.

We turned from the tow path, onto a steep animal trail. Nora and Sevareid handled the rocks and downed trees like they'd been walking it all their lives. More patches of water showed through the woods as the trail climbed and fell. We stopped at a frog-backed rock on top of sheer cliffs a hundred feet above the Potomac. Below us the river was half as wide as in Georgetown and twice as fast, cutting through boulders the size of small houses.

"On my canoe trip to Canada, I saw a bear chase a deer off a cliff about this high," said Sevareid. "We had a nice couple of meals thanks to that bear."

I asked if he carried a rifle on the trip.

"A .22. But you wouldn't want to face a brown or polar bear with a .22."

"I can't believe this is here, so close to the city," said Nora. "It's like pictures I've seen of your wild west."

"This is the start of Mather Gorge. We'll follow it to the bottom of Great Falls. But let's eat first." As I unpacked our lunch I pointed to some cliffs on the Virginia side. "The Indians call it Lovers' Leap."

"Tell us the story," said Sevareid, leaning against the trunk of a shrub oak.

"You already know the story. An Indian maiden, daughter of the chief, falls in love with a white fur trader. Her father forbids her to see him again, which she does anyway. After they're caught, they hold hands and jump from that pointy rock."

"Romeo and Hiawatha," said Sevareid. "I bet people tell that same story everywhere in the world."

I handed each of them some smoked fish. "This is rockfish. Some people call them striped bass. You might find a few bones."

Sevareid said the fish looked like charred leather, but after one bite he was humming along with Nora.

"I've been living on bread and bean soup so long, I'm drooling like a rabid dog," said Nora.

I quartered two apples and a chunk of cheese.

"So Mr. Tour Guide, can we see where you were born from here?" asked Sevareid.

"That's the first probing question you've ever asked me. Kind of shocking for a reporter, don't you think Nora?"

Nora smiled but kept her mouth closed around the cheese.

"Actually I was born in New York. Not the city but a little north, in Westchester County."

"How did you get here?"

"I'm too thirsty to tell a story that long," I said. "Come on, I'll take you to a fresh spring where my grandfather used to fetch water for his Christmas beer."

"Maybe that's why I never asked you a probing question," teased Sevareid as we moved down the trail. "You don't exactly talk a guy's ear off."

The spring fell like a twist of silver from a high crevice. Nora put her head underneath and let the water splash her cheek.

"You know what that is?" I asked Nora, pointing at a leafy green plant.

"Something bad?"

"Poison ivy. It blisters your skin and itches like hell for days, so take a good look. Three uneven leaves on a smooth stem. This plant beside it is jewel weed. The juice is a natural antidote to poison ivy. And the two of them grow by side. What does that tell you?"

Nora didn't answer. She was listening instead to the sound of Great Falls, which was still more than a quarter mile away, but rumbling like wagons on a wooden bridge. We finished drinking and followed the trail until we came to some boulders below the last fall. Nora climbed a wet rock, turned into the falling water and immediately lost her balance. This time I was there to catch her as she tipped backwards.

"It's a strange feeling, isn't it?" I said, one hand on her lower back the other just below her shoulder. "Your brain knows you're standing still, but your body won't believe it."

Nora tried again, and this time righted herself. "It's splendid, like being drunk but with a clear head. Better than any of those amusement park rides."

Great Falls is not one drop but a staircase of plunges over a quarter mile. The sound of it is a physical thing, as real as the spray. I studied Nora's face, remembering the first time I stood before these falls. Did she feel the same way about them? And if she did, could I ever really know? The difference between us wasn't just male and female, color and country. It was frames of reference, patterns of speech. Even if Nora found words to exactly describe her feelings, could I trust the translation? The same was probably true of Sevareid, but somehow that didn't seem as important just then.

I touched his shoulder and pointed downriver to a narrow spine of rocks that divided the Potomac. We followed the shoreline until we were directly opposite the spine's lower tip, beside a cove fed by the eddy current.

"I almost drowned here once," I told them. "But not because the water's dangerous. I was with a friend who couldn't swim and he pulled me under."

"That's a good idea," said Sevareid, unbuttoning his shirt. "Let's go for a swim."

I'd have gone behind a rock to undress but since Sevareid already had his shirt off, I took mine off too. Nora watched as we stripped to our shorts. I'd had a girl or two watch me undress before, but never with such a cool, straight look.

We dove in and came up yelling from the cold. Sevareid's hair lay plastered forward. I told him he looked like a Roman Centurion, but he might not have heard me, staring as hard as he was at the shore. I turned and saw why—Nora taking off her clothes. She got down to undershorts and a cotton shirt before diving in.

"This is warm compared to Ballybunion," called Nora as she

swam toward us. "Nearly like bathwater." When she was close enough to see the looks on our faces she laughed. "You think I'm brazen!"

"I think you're bold," said Sevareid.

"Why shouldn't I swim, and me wearing more clothes than the two of you together?"

"Take it easy," said Sevareid. "Bold isn't bad. I like bold."

I wouldn't have believed it possible in that frigid water, but I swear Nora blushed. I said, "Maybe we should start calling you Nora the Bold."

"Let's wait until I do something bold instead of merely sensible," she said and disappeared beneath the surface. It was too murky to see where she'd gone but I could feel the waves from her hands and feet move across my legs.

～

THE PROBLEM was where to sleep. With only a single bed in the cabin, I laid blankets for myself and Sevareid on the floor. But Nora wouldn't have it. All for one and none above the other she said, handing out coins to flip.

"If it's really one for all, then shouldn't we all sleep in the bed?" said Sevareid, who'd gotten funnier with each beer. "I can certainly be trusted not to take liberties. But can we trust Nora?"

"I'd as soon sleep standing than get between the pair of you," said Nora, who was only one beer behind Sevareid.

"Let's have another drink and study this," I suggested.

We'd come to the cabin after our swim, the sun cutting through the trees like bright splinters. It was a flattering light for Sevareid to show off my woodwork.

"See this piece here, that's oak. Look at the way it blends with the pine. And the windows are all cut from the same maple." I laughed to hear him talking about my little bits of carpentry like they belonged in a museum.

Nora was more impressed by my collection of books than the cases that held them.

"Have you read all these? History. Poetry. Detective novels."

"I've read them. That doesn't mean I learned anything. What do you like to read?"

Nora rattled off a list of writers including Shakespeare, Homer, Cicero and William Butler Yeats.

"That's an impressive list for a farm girl," said Sevareid.

"I've learned just enough to rattle off a few quotes. I only study a thing for as long as it keeps my interest."

Sevareid suggested a game "We take turns reading the first paragraph of a book and see who can guess where it's from."

Nora already had a book in hand, a textbook with a dollar bill showing between two pages. "What have we here?"

"Nothing. A bookmark," I said reaching for it.

Nora held it above her head. "I think we've discovered something, a key to our friend's radical politics."

The book was *American History,* by a Professor Thomas Marshall. Nora opened it to the marked page and an underlined passage.

"Read it," ordered Sevareid.

Nora read silently, then closed the book. "It's not what I thought."

"Give it to me. I used to read at Sunday services," said Sevareid, clearing his throat. "How many souls I saved can only be imagined." Laying the book open on the table, he raised his arms, looked down at the passage and...faltered.

"Go ahead, read it," I said. "It's in a school history text. How bad can it be?"

Sevareid read the passage in a flat voice:

> **The slaves.** Although he was in a state of slavery, the Negro of plantation days was usually happy. He was fond of the company of others and liked to sing, dance, crack jokes, and laugh; he admired bright colors and was proud to wear a red or yellow bandana. He wanted to be praised, and he was loyal to a kind master or overseer. He was never in a hurry, and was always ready to let things go until the tomorrow.

I asked if they wanted me to sing some spirituals.

"Don't throw that at us," said Sevareid. "I wasn't born when that was written."

"Don't be so damn sensitive," I said. "I hate it when people are too damn sensitive."

Dinner started in an awkward silence but by the time we finished our potatoes and white perch, the history book was just that—history. We joked about the swimming and Nora's redheaded woodpecker. Sevareid asked if my grandfather taught me to brew beer.

"He did."

"Then pass me another one, so I can drink to him."

I felt a flush of pleasure. Such an ordinary thing, to have a spirited conversation with friends, yet so damn rare for me. Some of it, I knew, was my fault. I'd grown so disgusted with people— whites who couldn't spell C-A-T thinking they were superior to me, and Negroes who accepted the lie of inferiority as truth. How could I be comfortable in either camp?

But here, in my tiny shack, was a nation I could pledge allegiance to. Friends who didn't give a shit about color. Wasn't this what the Party promised society could be in the future? And I had it right here, at least for one night.

"So tell me," said Nora, looking at us through her beer bottle. "How exactly did you two meet?"

"We hopped the same train," said Sevareid. "And then he wouldn't leave me alone."

"Were you together in Missouri?"

"The battle of East St. Louis. Oh yes," I said. "But only accidentally. Our train stopped because of the Bonus Army, so we walked down the track and joined them. You should have seen your boy Slim here, interviewing people, writing down everything, white bits of paper sticking out of every pocket."

Sevareid laughed. "I didn't know what the hell I was doing."

"He wrote the very first story about the standoff and a good one too. I've got it right here." I went to the bookcase and returned with a folder of Sevareid's stories. "I got these from newspapers at the Library of Congress. Here you go, read aloud the last one."

"I will not."

"Give it to me. I'll read it," said Nora jumping to her feet.

Battle of East St. Louis Ends In Draw
by Eric Sevareid
Special to the *Washington Evening Star*

May 25, Mo.—The Battle of East St. Louis, a three-day standoff between 300 war veterans from Oregon and about that many Baltimore & Ohio Railroad guards, climaxed today with a wild, six-mile race between a lone locomotive and a few dozen automobiles packed with veterans trying to reach an east-bound train.

"All we wanted was a ride in a few of their empty box cars," said Walt Waters, a former Army sergeant and the current commander of the veterans who call themselves the Bonus Expeditionary Force. "But somebody doesn't want us to get to Washington."

"There's a good start," said Nora. "Like one of the Zane Grey westerns the men in camp have given me to read. Okay, sorry, I'll continue."

The veterans, who marched out of Portland two weeks ago under a hand painted banner and to the beat of a borrowed drum, are on their way to D.C. to lobby Congress for immediate payment of bonus money already promised but not payable until 1945. A bill authorizing the immediate distribution of that compensation was introduced last November but has been shelved "indefinitely" by the House Ways and Means Committee.

Veteran Bill Amber, for one, thinks 1945 is too long to wait.

"My family will have starved to death by then," said the out-of-work plumber wearing a frayed Army jacket. "If the government can bail out banks and steel companies, I don't see why they can't give us money that's rightfully ours."

Nora used a rough male voice for Bill Amber, raising her fist in the air.

The delay in St. Louis was the first serious obstacle the group encountered since leaving Oregon but there have been smaller hurdles to overcome. After waiting 24 hours in a Portland rail yard, the first train they managed to hop was a cattle freight that hadn't been cleared of dung. Then there was the train that nearly ran them over in Pocatello, Idaho when the conductor panicked at seeing so many men lining both sides of his track.

"This isn't exactly first class travel," laughed Commander Waters, a former cannery worker. "We've got less than $30 in our treasury."

Help has come from veterans groups and others along the way. In Cheyenne, Wyoming a veteran working for the railroad arranged to have a field kitchen meet the men and provide them their first hot meal. And wherever they changed trains, the veterans would parade through the nearest town to collect contributions.

Reception in St. Louis Not So warm

"It looked like the entire police force was waiting for us in St. Louis," said Waters. "They had side arms, night sticks and riot guns like they were expecting to see a howling mob of roughnecks pile out of the boxcars and swarm the streets. What they got was a well- organized, disciplined group of men who only wanted to ride a train out of there."

For three days veterans and rail yard workers played a game of feint and parry, with a near-constant series of maneuvers and track switching that resulted in the complete stoppage of east-bound rail traffic.

"I told them there's no way we're going to let them ride our trains without paying the fare," said Dick Young, a B&O superintendent who conceded that his terminal sheds were filling with perishable freight. "I've got orders and there's nothing I can do about it."

The final showdown occurred this afternoon. Veterans had noticed large shifting engines moving single rail cars out of the yards during the night. The rumor was that the cars were being taken six miles east to be reassembled at a town called Caseyville. So when a locomotive started out of the yard in that direction, a dozen veterans climbed its tender, guessing correctly where it was headed.

The rest of the veterans grabbed their packs and began running down the tracks in what appeared to be a futile effort until a number of local civilians, who'd been watching this drama unfold, came to their rescue. Driving private automobiles on the road that paralleled the tracks, they called for the veterans to get in, then joined the chase. Traveling at 60 miles an hour, they arrived in Caseyville at the same time as the locomotive. The veterans ran and stumbled to close the 100 yards between the road and the rail yard but were apparently too late, as the engineer hooked his locomotive to the waiting train, blew his whistle and pulled away.

Or tried to anyway. The few veterans who'd hitched a ride on the locomotive found a way to tighten the brake wheels enough to keep the train from moving. Once again things were at stalemate.

Finally a local sheriff, Don Munie, called a draw to the battle by rounding up 50 cars, trucks and even trash dumpers to carry the veterans to the Indiana line. But if the battle of East St. Louis was officially a draw, the mood of the two sides didn't reflect it. While Mr. Young and the other railroad officials appeared frustrated with the turn of events, the veterans climbed happily into the waiting vehicles, singing a song composed for the occasion:

We didn't ride the B&O,
The good Lord Hoover told us no,
Hinkey dinkey, parlez vous.

"A chase at full speed and a song in French to boot!"

"A one-armed baboon could have written a good story with that material," said Sevareid.

"But it's the rare baboon who knows bastardized French," I said.

Nora got up from the table to look at a framed photograph on the window sill of Mr. Luke and his wife Tessie, my grandmother. She'd died a year before I arrived. The small, white-haired woman and tall white-haired man, both eyed the camera with suspicion. Nora said it reminded her of the day she was 11 and her mother took her to Limerick, to sit for a photographer in a studio with fake flowers and painted hills.

"I cried the whole time and wouldn't tell anyone why."

"What was the reason?"

"I was missing my brother Brendan. He'd drowned a few months earlier. I don't know what it was about that studio, but I couldn't stop crying." She replaced the photograph on the sill and looked at me. "Do you have a picture of your mother?"

"My mother…" I stopped to think. Was I that drunk? How else to explain my eagerness to tell the story I'd refused to tell just a few hours earlier. It wasn't just the beer, I decided. It was the easy way we were together. And probably, mostly, it was the beer.

"Forget I asked," said Nora gently.

"No. I mean, yes, I do have a photograph of my mother." From the closet I fished out a sepia-toned photo of a young woman in a high-collared dress. Nora studied it, and passed it along to Sevareid who said, "She's beautiful."

"And?"

"And what?"

"I thought you were a reporter. You didn't notice that she's white."

"It's not the first thing I noticed."

"That my mother is as white as Mary Pickford?"

Nora took the photograph and tilted it to the light. "How old was she when she married your father?"

"She didn't marry my father. She married a banker, four years before she ever met my father. A rich, white banker with a fifteen-room house and a backyard big as a city park."

"I'm confused," said Sevareid.

"So was the banker. Until someone whispered a secret in his ear."

"How old were you?"

"Thirteen."

"So until you were thirteen, you thought you were white?"

"Until I was thirteen, I *was* white. My teachers, classmates… everybody thought I was white. With maybe some Italian blood in me."

"But your hair."

"My mother kept it summer close year round. And I always wore my baseball cap outdoors. I think my mother invented some story about my skin blistering. People knew me as Hat Boy."

"It's so…biblical," said Nora pleased to find the word. "Like being expelled from the Garden of Eden."

"I wouldn't go that far. Even when he thought I was his son, my father was a cold fish. And I had an older brother who was pure evil. Used to dress like a minister and sacrifice birds and mice and anything else he could catch. When he couldn't find anything else, he'd torture me."

"When did they tell you?"

"They didn't. One day I was in the living room doing homework when they started yelling and breaking dishes in the kitchen. I jumped to the door and put both hands against it, not to push it open but to keep it shut. Then I heard my mother crying for help and I opened it just enough to see him holding her by the hair and slapping, one side of her face and then the other. Hard."

Nora leaned closer. "What did you do?"

"I went to the living room and grabbed a poker from the fireplace."

"To hit him?"

"I don't know what I was going to do. But it felt good in my hands, like I was meant to pick it up."

"And then?"

"Then nothing. When I got back to the kitchen he was gone."

We sat in silence, nobody wanting to say anything. Nora changed the mood with a song.

"On a high green hill, my lover called to me…"

As familiar as I was with her musical way of speaking, this singing voice came from a girl I didn't know. The high notes were sweeter than I expected and the low ones wet and growly, like a fast moving creek.

When she finished, Sevareid reached across the table and touched Nora's hand. "I was picturing you way out at sea on your uncle's boat."

"Have you ever been far out to sea?"

"No. But I'd like to go."

"We'll all go together," commanded Nora. "But first sing us a song."

Sevareid considered for a moment. "I won't. That would be punishment after yours. But I'll recite a poem I learned from some gold miners in California. It's called 'The Joy of Being Poor':

Let others sing of gold and gear, the joy of being rich;
But oh, the days when I was poor, a vagrant in a ditch!
When every dawn was like a gem, so radiant and rare,
And I had but a single coat, and not a single care;
When I would feast right royally on bacon, bread and beer,

And dig into a stack of hay and doze like any peer;
When I would wash beside a brook my solitary shirt,
And though it dried upon my back I never took a hurt;
When I went romping down the road contemptuous of care,
And slapped Adventure on the back — by Gad! we were a pair;
When, though my pockets lacked a coin, and though my coat was old,
The largess of the stars was mine, and all the sunset gold;
When time was only made for fools, and free as air was I,
And hard I hit and hard I lived beneath the open sky;
When all the roads were one to me, and each had its allure . . .
Ye Gods! These were the happy days, the days when I was poor.

Nora applauded. "That's so handsome. Who wrote it?"

"Robert Service. He wrote a lot of handsome poems."

Nora turned to me. "A song or a poem?"

I went back to the closet and returned with Mr. Luke's old guitar. I sat at the table and strummed jazz chords.

Nora walked to the bed with her arms stretched high. From behind, I couldn't tell if she was yawning or trying to fly. Either way she was doing a nice job of it.

"I need to listen to this laying down," she said and flopped on the bed. "One should be totally relaxed for this kind of music."

When I stopped playing five minutes later, Nora was asleep. Sevareid helped me unfold a blanket and together we covered her.

"She's a different kind of girl, isn't she?" I said, looking down at her hair which in the dim light was a flat brown color, as though the red had gone to sleep as well.

"She is that," agreed Sevareid. We looked at each other above the sleeping girl. The floor under my feet seemed to shift.

CAMPAIGNS

ERIC SEVAREID found Police Superintendent Glassford sitting on his motorcyle in front of the Capitol building, reading a newspaper story about yesterday's action:

Police Guard Congress and Supreme Court,
On Rumors of Red and Bonus Demonstrations
By The Associated Press

WASHINGTON—Congress and the Supreme Court convened today under police guard to prevent demonstrations by bonus advocates and by Communists.

A score of metropolitan police were marshaled about the Capitol to guard against any disturbances by a group of "pay the bonus now" advocates and Communists. Threats of a demonstration sent another police detail to the Supreme Court chamber as a precautionary measure.

The rumors linked the predicted demonstration with the Scottsboro (Ala.) conviction of seven Negroes for assaulting two white girls. The rumors of the two demonstrations were not borne out.

War veterans from widely scattered States toured the city in a half-dozen automobiles, with a detail of police on their trail, and one group of about twenty-five from Bethlehem, Pa., stood in front of the Capitol until a burly police inspector convinced them that they were wasting their time.

Sevareid asked if he believed the Communists were planning violence.

"I don't want to," said Glassford. "Because if John Pace and his Communists take over the Supreme Court chamber, even for a few minutes, the Bonus Army will suffer for it."

Sevareid started to reach for his notebook, then thought better of it. "I heard what Pace said to you the other day in camp. He didn't sound like a man worried about holding anything back."

"You snuck up on me," said Glassford, with something between a grin and a grimace. "But are his men feeling as reckless? I'm hoping they aren't."

That meeting between Glassford and Pace came the day after

Sevareid and Nora spent the night at Walker's cottage. Nora woke in a dreamy mood, yawning and playful as a cat. Sevareid spoiled that mood by announcing he had a story to cover at the camp that morning.

"But we haven't come up with a name for ourselves yet," she argued.

"I'll be thinking of one today at the Party headquarters," said Walker.

"No, you won't abandon me as well," pleaded Nora.

"This is the price I had to pay for skipping out on Cord. Let's call it the Great Falls reparation."

Sevareid was relieved to hear that Walker wouldn't have Nora to himself, but had he known of Walker's obligation, he'd have found a way to stay. His mood improved when he saw Glassford and Walt Waters walking together toward the west end of the Anacostia river camp, where Pace and his men had separated themselves. Waters looked a different man from the one he'd met in St. Louis. He'd traded his threadbare sergeant's jacket for one nearly new, and he walked about camp with his arms behind his back, nodding regally to the men he passed. Waters looked as confident as two colonels, right up to the moment he and Glassford found John Pace.

"Good morning Mr. Treasurer," he said, addressing Glassford who managed the Bonus Army's money. "Nice of you to visit your assets." Pace was sitting in a junked dentist's chair, at the center of a circle of shacks and tents. Pace's encampment was as uncomfortably spartan as every other part of the camp but unlike other veterans, his men displayed no photos or family mementos. This group looked ready to pick up and go at a moment's notice.

"Mr. Pace. You were with the 143rd at Avignon if I'm not mistaken," said Glassford.

"That was a long time ago. Another war ago," said Pace, a short man with receding hair and one dark eyebrow that ran above his eyes like a hedge. Even sitting, he seemed jumpy.

"I hope this campaign is as successful," said Glassford.

Pace gave him a long, sneering look. "This campaign, as you call it, will only succeed if we're willing to fight."

Sevareid took note of the iron in his voice. Such a hard, uncompromising approach could be attractive to angry or desperate men and there was no shortage of them in this camp. But as far as Sevareid could tell, Pace's call to radicalism hadn't recruited more than a handful. Sevareid would have to ask Glassford if there was a worry in that as well, if losing an apparently winning hand might push someone like Pace to extremes.

"I'm going to expel Pace and his men from the camp," said Waters when he and Glassford resumed their walk. "And I wouldn't raise any objection at all if you ran him out of town."

"Let's not make a martyr out of him. Better to let things take their course," said Glassford. Only then did he turn to find that Sevareid was close enough to hear.

Now the Superintendent rolled the newspaper into his bag and started his motorcycle. "Did I see you with Walker the other day?"

"Probably," said Sevareid. "We met on the way to St. Louis."

"He appears to be a very bright young man."

Sevareid nodded his head. "He is. But his politics are probably closer to Pace's than yours."

"Oh, that's okay," said Glassford. "It's not politics that worries me, only personality. Off the record, I'd be worried about John Pace if he was a bishop."

After watching Glassford motor away, Sevareid continued toward the Capitol. The House was debating the Bonus bill this morning and he wanted to hear some of the oratory. He passed the regular crowd of veterans on the Capitol steps, went across the empty chamber of the U.S. Supreme Court and climbed a stairway to the House gallery. An usher led him to a bench reserved for local officials, press and visiting celebrities.

On the floor below, a Congressman from Texas was proposing that the U.S. government repeal Prohibition and get into the business of brewing and selling beer. The money made by the government (the Congessman used a figure of 500 million dollars a year) could be used to pay the bonus. The argument seemed popular with the veterans sitting behind Sevareid until another Texas Congressman, Wright Patman stood and attacked it.

"Linking Prohibition with the bonus is a sure fire way to kill it!" said Patman, who as sponsor of the Bonus bill sat only half a step below God. "Let's not drown the bonus in political barley."

Another Congressman from Tennessee stood to speak in favor of the bill.

"When the war was over, the government paid the contractors not in promises but in cash, $3,000,000,000. It aided the railroads with $2,000,000,000. More than $125,000,000 was given to feed the hungry hordes in Europe, but when it came to the soldier, you gave him a promise to pay in 1945, twenty-seven years after the original Armistice Day."

Sevareid listened to his words without trying to make sense of them. He thought of Nora, the bed cover tucked under her chin. And without intending to, thought of his own mother. He hadn't written in a week, but as long as his stories kept coming, she at least knew he was alive. How would she and Nora get along? He had the pair comfortably settled in his mind when he heard a cry of surprise from the gallery.

He looked down to see a man lying on the floor of the House.

"Who is that?" he asked the usher.

"That's Edward Eslick of Tennessee."

A woman, presumably Congressman Eslick's wife, ran down the center aisle of the chamber and knelt beside him. By her reaction Sevareid knew the man was dead. Quickly turning to the man sitting to his right he asked, "What did he say?"

"Something about alcohol and...."

"No, only his last words," urged Sevareid. "Come on, remember for me."

DEATH MARCH

THE WAY I heard it, the Death March began under a quarter
moon and the spray of lawn sprinklers.

One of the Capitol cops was making his rounds at 3 a.m. when
he bumped into a bunch of veterans just in from California, led by
a guy in a scary-looking neck brace that kept his chin pointed at
the moon. The cop wasn't supposed to let anybody sleep on the
Capitol grounds, but he was so spooked by the metal spokes growing from Royal Robertson's head, he backed off and let them sleep.
By the time the next shift arrived, the vets were in no mood to
move. So the cops turned on the sprinklers. Robertson delivered a
liberty or death speech to his men and started them circling the
Capitol. There was no law, he said, to prevent them from sleeping
on their feet.

I came into this march with sandwiches and coffee, donated by
the Party. I didn't think Robertson and his men cared one way or
the other about politics, but they liked the food and didn't mind
answering my questions about California.

I'd been thinking of what Nora said, about finding a place to
live where I wouldn't have to keep an eye out for lynch mobs and
flying elbows. Josephine Baker found her perfect place in Paris, but
I didn't have her legs or voice, and didn't speak any French.

Harlem was a possibility. The one time I visited there, I listened
to some writers claim a Negro Renaissance was underway, that all
we had to do was learn good manners and shuck all our low down
jive talk. In other words, we needed to act more like white people.
As much of a head start as that would give me, it didn't sound like
much of a plan. What was so great about white people? I enjoyed
the people I met in New York but couldn't get comfortable with all
the noise and concrete, everyone living one on top of the other, all
the way to the sky.

Now California, there was a place for taking big gulps of air. I
only spent a day and a half in San Francisco, but felt nearly at
home in some of the neighborhoods. I'd never seen a city with so
many hills, so many opportunities to admire itself. Of course it was

filled with white people, who weren't likely to welcome me with open arms. But I guessed Nora would like it, and that was a pleasant thought to hold while I passed out coffee and sandwiches.

DIAMOND

IN NORA'S DREAM her mother was a bird, hopping around the hearth fire, her feathers coated with a fine sprinkling of flour. Her father was still her father, but his pipe was enormous, shooting sparks that ricocheted around the kitchen like lightning. It all meant something, she was sure, but before any meaning came clear, she was pulled from sleep.

"Nora. Wake up."

Dennis Diamond was gently shaking her shoulder. It was past midnight but the camp fire was bright enough to light the policeman and lady stepping into the circle of bonus veterans. Max Berga and another man in a chauffeur's uniform followed behind them.

"I'm Evalyn McLean," announced the woman. She was wearing a chiffon dress beneath an open, black opera coat and looked as though she'd come directly from a fancy dinner party. "I'm hoping you might tell me what you could use here in camp."

"A hot cornbeef sandwich," said the man closest to her.

"A cigarette that hasn't already been half smoked," said another. It was obvious this wasn't the first time the subject had come up.

A veteran wearing a leather billed cap raised his hand like a schoolboy. "Are you the Mrs. McLean who owns the Hope Diamond?"

"I am."

"Can I ask what shape it's cut in and how heavy it feels in your hand?"

"Would you like to see it?" she asked.

"I didn't bring my museum-going clothes with me on this trip," he joked.

"Not in a museum," said McLean. "Here. Now."

Nora sat bolt upright. Was she still dreaming? No. People didn't have headaches in dreams and that policeman, Superintendent Glassford, looked like he just got one. She'd read that the Hope Diamond was worth $2 million and here was this woman about to show it to an army of desperately poor men.

"It will look best close to the fire," she said removing the diamond from its black, velvet box. "It's a very old stone. You can hold it if you like."

Glassford positioned himself at one of McLean's elbows, while her chauffeur moved to the other. Nora wiggled close to touch the gem. But just before her fingers reached it she pulled back, mindful of the stories she'd heard about its power to bring misfortune.

"The stories are not all true," said McLean with a smile.

"I'm not superstitious," said Nora. "But others are."

"You are such a beauty," said McLean, reaching out to touch her cheek.

After a few more minutes talking to the men, she asked Supt. Glassford if there was an open restaurant nearby.

"There's Childs on Pennsylvania Avenue, not far from here."

"Can we go there to get some food for these men? You're welcome to come, Mr. Berga. As are you. What is your name dear?"

"Nora O'Sullivan. I'd be delighted. Thank you."

Her limousine smelled of leather and jasmine perfume. Nora sat in the back seat between Mrs. McLean and Max Berga.

"May I offer my condolences to you on the loss of the *Washington Post*," said Berga.

"It's my fault," she said. "My husband let the paper run down and I didn't pay attention until it was too late. Ned McLean wouldn't recognize a piece of news if the man who bit the dog likewise bit him."

Nora knew nothing of the newspaper or its history, but she loved the whiff of gossip.

Childs was two dozen tables and a bright counter that ran to the back wall of the restaurant. Glassford started toward a table, but Mrs. McLean went directly to the counter and the cook.

McLean: "Do you serve sandwiches?"

The cook: "We do."

McLean: "Well I'd like 1,000. And wrap them if you please."

Nora watched the cook. Of all possible reactions, this short, bristle-chinned man in a white apron gave only a slight nod and said, "That's gonna be awhile. Why don't you take a seat and have a cup of coffee."

"Lovely," said McLean. "That will give us time to talk."

∽

SEVAREID FOUND Eisenhower coming out of the State, War and Navy Building.

"Major Eisenhower. We met at the fight night. I'm a newspaper reporter working for the *Minneapolis Star*."

"I'm on my way to lunch," said Eisenhower, a paper bag in hand. "Normally reporters are referred to the press officer on the first floor."

Sevareid nodded but didn't move. "I only have one or two questions."

"Okay, I'll give you a minute. Let's cross to the park."

"What is it you want to talk about," asked Eisenhower when they'd settled on a bench beneath the trees.

"The Bonus Army."

Eisenhower took a bite of his sandwich and waited.

For a long moment, Sevareid forgot what he wanted to ask. "I heard a rumor that the military schools have had their rifles confiscated?"

"Not true," said Eisenhower. "None of the rifles at any of the military schools in this area have firing pins."

"So you've checked?"

"It's something I know."

"What about the Navy Yard munitions? I hear they've doubled the guard there."

"The only guns they manufacture at the Navy Yard are for warships. It would take half the men at the Anacostia camp just to lift one."

Sevareid slumped against the wood backed bench and closed his notebook.

Eisenhower took another bite of his ham sandwich. Two secretaries walked by, arm in arm.

"That doesn't look like Lafayette," said Sevareid, staring at the central statue of a soldier on horseback.

"That's Andrew Jackson."

"Then why call it Lafayette Square?"

"When Lafayette visited the White House in 1824, people packed this square to see him. There's an interesting statue of him over there." Eisenhower pointed to the southeast corner where Marquis de Lafayette stood holding clothes in his arms. Nearby was a statue of a bare-breasted Columbia holding forth a sword. "The joke is that Columbia is saying, 'Give me my clothes and I'll give you back your sword.'"

Sevareid stared at Columbia's breasts. Any questions he had for Eisenhower disappeared behind his memory of Nora, rising from her bed in the middle of the night to squat and pee in the clearing just beyond Walker's cabin. Watching her in the moonlight roused something in Sevaried nearly as powerful as lust. As he lay on that hard wood floor Sevareid thought, I could share a life with a girl like that.

He stood abruptly and offered his hand. "I should go. Thank you for talking to me."

"Eric."

"Yes sir?"

"It's only natural to be confused about a girl."

"How did you know?"

"I spent a lot of years training 19-year-olds. It wasn't that tough a guess."

~

ONE BLOCK from the Smithsonian, on the morning she hoped to retrieve her silver cup, Nora O'Sullivan stopped at a traffic light and had a thought:

Preparations could have been better.

It wasn't a whopper as thoughts went, but for Nora it qualified as both radical and new. She'd always regarded planning as something for the old, the slow or the timid. Straight ahead, directly as it comes was infinitely more fun. And how easy it had always been, she realized, never before wanting anything enough to fear its loss.

The cup. Walker and Sevareid. This new life in America. She couldn't imagine losing any of it. Her last years in Ireland now seemed as quiet as a painting. Jack Allman. The sheep on the hill. All as unreal as one of her father's bedtime stories. Here in America she was living at a faster speed and reveling in the insecurity.

But as she waited on her bike at the stop light, her lack of foresight loomed like a brick wall. What else could she have done? To ask one of her new friends for help would be the same as inviting them to commit a crime, since it would take a mugging to get her cup back. Without proof of ownership there was no way to do it legally. What she needed was a plan, a brilliant, criminal plan. She wondered why it had taken her this long to realize it.

∽

"COME IN Miss O'Sullivan. You're right on time." Richard Drury greeted her without ever taking his eyes off James Kemper, so he saw in profile what Nora saw head-on—a major flinch of Kemper's shoulders and neck, as if a bee had stung him between the shoulder blades. The flinch was followed by an effort to pull himself together.

From Drury. "Have you two met?" Kemper coughed on the question, gave himself more time by clearing his throat into a red-checked handkerchief, then lied.

"No. I don't believe we have."

Nora laughed triumphantly. "Do you need more proof than that?" She kept her eyes on Kemper, measuring the space between his chair and the door. "The man acts like he's seen a ghost, then denies having seen anything at all! And how would I know the secret markings if he'd gotten that cup from anyone but me?" Nora couldn't see the cup but guessed it was in the black case at his feet.

James Kemper picked up the case and stood, making a show of being offended. "I won't stay here and be called a thief by a 17-year-old girl." Chunks of cockney sounded through his high church accent.

"How would he know I was 17?" asked Nora, moving toward the suitcase.

Drury scooted around his desk to block her. "You will not fight in this office."

Nora was sure she could win a fight with Kemper, even if he did outweigh her by a hundred pounds. But it would be a spirited brawl, maybe wipe out a wall of the Smithsonian. At the moment there was nothing to do but bite her hand and let him pass.

As Kemper reached the door, Drury called to him. "Mr. Kemper, based on what I've seen and heard today, the Smithsonian is no longer interested in maintaining a relationship."

Kemper turned as if to speak, but only moved into the hall.

"I suggest you make a complaint to the police," said Drury.

"Without proof of ownership, what chance would I have?"

"I'll tell them what I saw."

"That wouldn't be enough. Thank you Mr. Drury, but I'll have to do this my own way."

"That will undoubtedly lead to trouble."

"If this isn't worth a little trouble," asked Nora, "what is?"

∼

KEMPER JUMPED OFF the trolley at the New Capitol, a run-down hotel on the northeast corner of Third Street and Pennsylvania Avenue. As it happened, the New Capitol was one of the few hotels Nora knew something about. Walker had pointed it out to her on one of their walks—not for the marble pillars at the entrance, which were salvaged from the U.S. Capitol building after the British burned it in 1814, but for the slave pens still visible

under the sidewalk. In its glory days the New Capitol was fre-
quented by Daniel Webster, Martin Van Buren and Andrew
Jackson, who made speeches from the little balcony above the
street. It was also the favorite hotel of visiting Indian chiefs. Now
it was shabby and soon to be demolished, a suitable place for a visiting thief, thought Nora.

Across the street from the hotel squatted a row of buildings
also scheduled to be torn down. They were currently occupied by
Bonus Army veterans with families. Nora backed into one of those
doorways and smelled beans cooking inside.

Did Kemper know he was being followed? Nora had kept her
bicycle well behind the trolley and her hair tied back. She remembered him complaining about his eyesight the first they met, but
then he might have been lying about that as well.

That first meeting occurred on a Saturday morning, in the back
of Murphy's Pub where Michael Murphy, who doubled as village
undertaker, stored his bodies and beer. At a plank table below the
room's only window sat Kemper, his yellow hair and salmon-pink
skin like a fried egg in the bright morning light. Nora sat opposite,
dressed in her best vest and cap. Murphy, Father Connelly and
Nora's father John stood above them, resting their jars on a closed
casket.

Kemper had traveled all the way from London to see this pre-
Christian silver cup which Nora uncovered while cutting turf. He
was coming to Kenmare anyway, he insisted, on his way to study a
pair of prehistoric beehive huts and other treasures beyond imagining. With a cough to clear his throat, he pulled a pair of gold-
rimmed spectacles from his vest pocket and peered at the cup.

"I've seen better," he said.

"If it's so poor a thing as that, you've no need to bother," said
Nora reaching for the cup. Kemper eased it away, holding the cup
to the window. Outside, farmers with lucky pennies in their pockets, pushed sheep and pigs to another disappointing market day.
Inside, all eyes were on the images hammered into the silver—a
round-bellied cook god dangling a boy above a cauldron by his

ankle and a fertility goddess wearing a demonic smile while holding wide her vulva with both hands. Kemper took a deep breath of pipe smoke, stale beer and embalming fluid and brought the cup back to the table. "As I said, it's not the best of these I've seen, but I'm thinking I can find a buyer. And if I'm not entirely mistaken…we might get something close to 50 pounds."

Murphy gave the sharp whistle of a man who purchased cups by the case. "Fifty pounds did you say? Now wouldn't that be a fair profit for an afternoon's dig."

"A high price for a graven image," clucked Father Connelly, rubbing his bristle black hair. Rumor was that Father Connelly had betrayed confessional secrets in the civil war just ended, but no one dared make the accusation to his face.

Nora's father said nothing, just looked at his only remaining child and repacked his pipe. Nora knew her father was of two minds about the cup and neither of them indifferent. A few nights earlier, she'd found him asleep at the fire cradling the cup in both hands. When he opened his eyes, he looked at her as though at a stranger. The cup had taken him that far away. But as long as it remained in the house, Nora's mother would give him no peace. Like the priest, her mother judged the cup an over-bright sacrilege.

"I'm not interested just now in selling the cup for fifty pounds or a thousand," said Nora, pulling it from Kemper's hands. "This is a thing more than money. And anyway, it isn't likely to get less valuable with age."

"Now that's foolishness," said Murphy, who'd suggested sending for the "collectibles man" and now risked losing his finder's fee. "To hold onto something that could be of great help to your da here."

"I, too, must advise against keeping it," announced Father Connelly with an authority built for a different room. "The sooner we're rid of this the better." He placed a hand on Nora's shoulder. "Do you remember the First Commandment?"

"I do," said Nora, sounding for a moment like the pious school girl she'd once been. "But the commandments haven't a thing to do with this. It's my cup to sell or keep. And for now, I'm keeping it."

James Kemper startled them with a loud slap of his palms against the table. "The girl is entirely right. There's no rush to sell this. But at the same time, there's no reason I cannot take it to Dublin for an expert appraisal." He snapped shut his mouth with a click of teeth. "That is something we can surely agree upon."

Nora didn't want to agree to anything with James Kemper. Everything about him reminded her of the scoundrels she'd met in Dickens—wide-browed and low reaching, with darting eyes and lips that curled like nesting snakes. She'd met so few people in her life, each new one had a distinct taste and Nora had no desire for any further bites of Kemper. On the other hand, she was curious to learn everything about this cup, including its value in coin.

In the end, she allowed herself to be persuaded.

Kemper wrote out a receipt with great sweeping strokes of his black ivory pen and promised to return her cup within eighteen days.

Four and a half weeks later, Nora O'Sullivan was on a blunt-nosed freighter, chasing him across the Atlantic.

I've come too far to let the cup get away now, thought Nora, suddenly hungry for some baked beans. The trick was to retrieve it in a way that fooled Kemper into thinking it had been lost or destroyed, otherwise he'd set the authorities on her. Was Kemper likely to run? If the answer was yes, she'd need to watch the hotel day and night. But if he was as arrogant as Nora guessed, she had time to seek help. And the closest place to look for that was only a few blocks away.

∽

IT WAS 11 A.M. when Nora knocked on the door of the Criers Club, a time when Neil Gold was likely fast asleep in the arms of the woman in the white dress. The thought made Nora envious, not so much of Gold or the woman, but of her dress.

Gold pulled open the door wearing a denim jacket, riding pants and boots. In a merry voice he said, "You look like you need a drink!" and led Nora inside.

"I'm trying to find Will," she said. "He isn't in his alley and I need him to help me make a plan."

"A plan? This is no place for making plans," said Gold handing her a glass of brandy. Nora took a small sip. "For plans you need wild beasts and open spaces. I know just the place."

⁓

AFTER A CHILDHOOD riding ponies and the occasional plough horse, mounting Ruby was like climbing a different species. She was glistening black, fourteen hands and eager to run.

"Keep a tight rein or she'll go out from under you," said Gold, astride a white stallion named Rum.

"I'd be thrilled to have a horse run out from under me," said Nora. "Does she like to jump?"

"Oh yeah. She likes to jump."

The barn was in Arlington, Virginia, in hills above the Potomac. Nora guessed they weren't more than a mile or two from Walker's house. She entertained a fantasy of riding there as Gold and his stallion led the way up a narrow, wooded trail. Nora's horse Ruby pulled at the bit, anxious to lead. Nora thought of Anthony, the Criers Club bodyguard back at the New Capitol Hotel watching for Kemper. When Gold suggested Anthony stand guard, at least until they concocted a plan, Nora didn't even fake an objection. He was the right man for the job. But when Anthony asked, "You want I should get the cup and bring it back?" she said no. Kemper could have both Anthony and Nora arrested. Besides, what self-respecting heroine would hire a stand-in?

They followed the trail out of the woods and into a pasture of grazing cattle. The rain had stopped but the clouds looked capable of more. For a long moment the horses stood side by side. Gold adjusted his black polo helmet, Nora studied the patchwork of fields and woods spread before her. Without any coaxing, the horses set off at a gallop. Nora bounced forward, grabbing Ruby's mane to keep from falling. By the time she got her feet back in the stirrups, Gold was twenty yards ahead. She loosened her grip and whispered, "Go!" Ruby went, nearly pitching Nora again. The horses were even as they approached the stone wall at the edge of the field. The open gate was only wide enough for one, but neither horse was heading for the gate.

Nora put her face against the mare's neck, breathing in the warm, beasty smell. Up and over the stone fence they flew, landing so softly Nora couldn't tell when Ruby's hind hooves touched.

"Well done," said Gold, rapping his helmet with his fist.

"It was all Ruby," said Nora, short of breath. "I just hung on."

Another trail took them a long, looping way through a pine wood. As they descended toward the river, the trees rotated from willow to cedar and oak.

"Where I grew up, the woods were short and marshy," said Gold.

"And where was that?"

"New Jersey. The pine barrens. The rivers are red there, like strong tea. A horse this big would sink straight in."

"I thought you were from somewhere else."

"I was born in Russia, but I left when I was seven."

"Do you remember it?"

"Only as pictures in my head. A snow-covered hill. A favorite climbing tree."

"And your parents?"

"My father died the same year we arrived and my mother when I was 10."

Through the trees Nora saw the flat water of the Potomac.

"What is it you want here?" asked Gold.

"Here in America? What does anybody want?"

"Three years ago I could have told you. To get rich. But that dream's gone. Haven't you noticed? Everyone walks around like they've been hit over the head?"

"I've noticed," said Nora. "But I've nothing to compare it to. Aren't you rich, with your club and horses?"

"I'm only rich by comparison. And I'm not so far from being a failure that I've forgotten it."

Nora slowed Ruby's gait. "You're being modest."

Neil Gold laughed. "I failed at touting phony stocks, a patent medicine business, bait-and-switch con games with counterfeit ten-dollar bills. One of my first scams was selling cheap neckties and dress shirts out the back of a fancy cart I'd boosted from a Fifth Avenue clothing store. Nobody was fooled. I was the worst hustler in America. While everybody else was getting rich, I was scraping bottom. I only started making money when everybody else lost theirs."

They led the horses to water at the lower end of a cove. A line of twigs and foam rode the edge of an upriver eddy. A beaver had piled sticks and driftwood in a way that reminded Nora of the western forts she'd read about in one of Tom Halloran's cowboy novels. Wouldn't that be an adventure, to ride on horseback through the American West. Maybe after she retrieved her cup she'd go there with Walker and Eric, Will and Virni, Dennis Diamond and Tom Halloran. She turned to ask Gold if he'd like to join her wagon train of men, but he was too close to ask. He leaned in to kiss her and she let him, opening her mouth and closing her eyes. His lips tasted...red. His hands were warm against her back. During her first kiss in America, Nora thought: In five days I'll be 18.

Nora broke off the kiss. "We should get back. In case something is happening with the cup."

Gold laid a hand on her arm and smiled. "We'll have to do this again."

Nora wasn't sure. She loved riding Ruby and liked kissing him too, mostly for the reckless feeling of it. But it was probably a mistake given that she had no desire to kiss him again.

PISTOLA

"I'M DEAD ASLEEP, dreaming of a blonde I used to know in Dusseldorf, when somebody starts pounding on my door with what sounds like a hammer."

"What did you do?"

"I did what any fool would do, yanked it open, ready for a fight."

"And was it a hammer?"

"It was not. It was a pistol with a barrel as wide as a sewer hole. At least that's how it looked from where I stood. The man on the trigger end was dressed in the uniform of a D.C. cop. Younger than I'd pictured, with fair skin and, except for his skittery eyes, handsome in a completely ordinary way."

"John Tobin woke you up in the middle of the night with a pistol?"

"He did. Said, 'You're telling people I shot that Whoopee girl.'"

"And you said?"

"Officer Tobin, I'm not saying any such thing. Come inside, I'll make some coffee."

"I'm not sure I'd have done that."

"I'm not sure I should have. But it did get him to lower his gun somewhat, which unfortunately left it pointing at my crotch. I concentrated on his index finger, afraid that something would go horribly wrong if I thought of anything other than that for the smallest moment."

"Obviously you succeeded."

"I didn't. Within twenty seconds I found my mind wandering back to the large-breasted woman of my dreams. Maybe that's the thought that saved me. Can I buy you another beer, Eric?"

"No thanks. I have to go find a story. But take my advice, don't open your door before you see who's on the other side."

"It wouldn't have mattered. I'd been hoping to interview him all week. In that situation, what reporter wouldn't open his door?"

NUMBERS

I DIDN'T EXPECT to win any Party converts on the day Congress voted for the Bonus Bill. Comrade Cord had told me the fix was in —the House would vote it up and let the Senate vote it down later. That meant, for one day anyway, a whole city full of happy veterans, and happy people don't sign up for revolutions. All I expected from the day was some conversation, maybe a chance to plant some seeds and to find Nora in the crowd.

But I'd hardly made it over the bridge into Georgetown when Tommy Baker caught me from behind.

"Where the hell you been?" said Tommy, as unhappy as his words. "I went all the way to your place and got shit all over my Sterlings."

In his yellow-brimmed hat and mud-spattered buckle shoes, Tommy looked like he'd come directly from his favorite U Street spot, the Poodle Dog Cafe. We'd barely touched hands before he started in on me again.

"How come I ain't seen you? Back in town for weeks and you don't even stop by to say hello?"

"Where am I supposed to stop by?" I laughed. "You're never in the same bed two nights in a row."

"That is the honest truth," said Tommy, turning his profile to me like he always did, lifting his chin for dramatic effect. "But shit, boy, you could find me in half a minute any time you tried. And you should have too, because I've got news for you that isn't good. Fat Carlos been asking about that liquor you dumped. He's thinking maybe you didn't dump it at all."

I had to laugh at Tommy, looking so dead serious. His skin was even darker than when we first met, with another color like bruised plum mixed in. When we ran together, people called us salt and pepper. It wasn't a name either of us liked.

"That liquor is history," I told him. "And what if I did steal it? After the way I was set up?"

"Shit. How long were you in jail? Two weeks? I could do that holdin' my breath."

I believed him. In the two years since we'd stopped running numbers, he and I had pretty much gone our separate ways. Tommy started hanging with a late-night crowd, while I stayed by the river either fishing or working the gambling ferry. The times we did go out always seemed to end up with somebody drunk and fighting. But Tommy was still my best friend, the one I'd always trust to cover my back.

We walked through Georgetown to P Street and followed it across Rock Creek, Tommy talking non-stop in his quick, excited way while I stole things. An apple here, a knit scarf there, batteries, pencils, matching tea cups. I replaced each new thing with one I'd taken just before. Tommy never could figure what that was about and I couldn't explain it to him, except to say I was keeping in practice so I'd be ready when something worth stealing finally came along.

When I asked how his brother Penny was doing, Tommy's voice changed. "Cops caught him three times delivering whiskey. Once more and he'll go to jail, maybe for a year. My moms is after me to put him right but...."

"But you're not one to talk."

"I already talked too much to the boy, braggin' about all the serious shit I was into. How am I gonna tell him anything now?"

When Penny was 12, he liked fishing with me, especially when I paid him to help with the seine nets. He was good company, even if he did talk too much. But as soon as he turned 15, all the boy in him seemed to disappear. He was determined to make himself into a gangster. Started styling himself the Negro Al Capone. No way he'd want to work at fishing now. I told Tommy he could offer it to him anyway. Tommy laughed at the thought, the first good laugh I'd heard from him in a long time, and it made me realize how much boy had disappeared in both of us.

"I got to leave you here," he said when we reached Dupont Circle. After all my stealing, the only thing I still had was a rubber ball. I threw it into the fountain for a dog to fetch. Tommy leaned close, the brim of his hat brushing against my face. "Right or wrong, having Fat Carlos after you is what counts. So keep your eyes big and stay out of alleys."

The first time I met Fat Carlos was at Jimmie's card room on 14th Street near U, a place with big nudie paintings on velvety walls and armed men blowing cigar smoke. A person could disappear forever inside that card room and I knew a few who had.

I was 15 at the time, one week after Mr. Luke died, and the same day I was expelled from Carver Academy. I came to Jimmie's directly from pushing Rupert Gordon's face into a bowl of lemon meringue custard.

"Who's this?" asked Carlos when Tommy Baker brought me in. I was still wearing my green-and-white Carver uniform.

Tommy put his hand on my back. "He's a friend of mine, Mr. Carlos. I been meaning to talk to you about him. About maybe finding him some work. He's smart and tough, too."

Fat Carlos ran half the colored numbers racket in Washington. His territory covered most of the Northwest, from Georgetown to 7th Street by Howard University. The rest of the city belonged to Juan Wilson, a Jamaican Negro with a reputation for hurting people in creative ways. Tommy had been running numbers for Carlos for nearly two years.

"A private school boy?" Carlos looked at me, then turned to the three other men playing cards. He was not so much a fat man as a big one, with long straightened hair and diamond rings on both hands. "Anybody goes to private school has got the kind of parents I don't need," he said. "Come back when you're an orphan."

I told him I was already an orphan. "I buried my grandfather this week."

That got his attention. "A private school orphan boy. I don't believe we've ever had us one of them." He looked hard at me. "You come back on Monday, hear? I got me a route on 7th Street that needs a smart, tough, private school orphan boy. We'll see what you can do."

Tommy didn't look as happy as I expected when we got to the street, especially since he'd been bugging me for two years to come work for Fat Carlos.

"That route he's talking about is worse than shit. The last boy got himself stabbed."

"Who did it?"

"Most likely Juan Wilson's boys, looking to steal turf. That's nothing to get between."

"If it comes to that, I'll quit."

"No you won't, stubborn as you are."

"Stubborn as you?"

"Stubborn enough to get yourself cut." He shook his head, the same way his mom used to shake her head talking about him. "Come with me today and I'll show you what the job is about."

Tommy's route went from 15th to 17th Street NW and from K to Florida Avenue. Most of that neighborhood was white, but there were colored shops that did a big business, and maybe a thousand Negroes living in the alleys. The alley homes had started with maids and servants of white people, building little places in back of the houses where they worked. When the boll weevil hit the south and all those people flooded north, speculators realized there was money to be made renting whatever shacks the newcomers could build for themselves. I read in a newspaper that one third of all Negroes in Washington, 20,000 people, were living in about three hundred alleys. At 15, the only one I knew well was Poplar Alley in Georgetown, behind the Hopfenmaier animal rendering plant.

"This place here, Steadtown is all right." Tommy told me that first day as we entered the square of alleys behind Briley's General Store. "Some of the others you need permission to walk through, or else you carry your knife where everybody can see."

I said I didn't plan on carrying a knife.

"You may not plan on it, but you damn sure will carry a knife if you want to keep at this job."

That first day I didn't see anything that looked even a little rough. Tommy stopped at stores to pick up envelopes filled with names, numbers and money. In the alleys he found himself a corner and let people come to him. A few asked for credit, but Tommy looked right past them. "Man, if they don't have a nickel today, how they gonna have a nickel tomorrow." A nickel was the price of a three digit number that might win as much as $500. I asked Tommy about the odds of winning.

"It's long odds, I can tell you that."

"Then why do people do it?"

"There's always a chance, right? If they don't play they got no chance at all."

Only one thing shook me that day. After we'd finished collecting, Tommy took me to Murder Bay, a bunch of shacks built over the nasty-smelling canal that bordered a lot near the Smithsonian. I'd walked past it, but never through it. The people living there were thick as maggots in a trash bin.

"I used to stop here," said Tommy. "But these people are so poor they'd steal your breath."

Tommy had never been very good in school, but at the end of the day he knew exactly how much money he'd taken in and how much of it—three dollars and seventy six cents—belonged to him. It looked like easy money.

My territory bordered Griffith Stadium and Howard University, two of my favorite places in the city. The bad aspect of the route was being right on the edge of Juan Wilson's territory. Tommy compared it to frontier days with cowboys and Indians. He wanted me to take along a bodyguard, at least that first day but I wouldn't have it. If I did take a bodyguard (and where would I get one?) it would show I was scared. Sooner or later I'd have to go alone.

I had a map that the last runner drew, but some of the stops were hard to find. Goat Alley was so well hidden behind fence posts and trees, I had to ask one of the neighborhood kids to take me there. Two men playing craps with guns stuck through their belts, watched me go past without ever losing sight of each other.

The boy who showed me the alley also showed me where to stand. People came and dropped nickels in my box, some wearing clothes that didn't look like they cost much more than that. By the end of the day, I had $27, which meant $2.70 for me. Three boys about my age followed me, but only for a block.

I bought myself a steak dinner at Lonnie's on U Street to celebrate the start of my new career.

The second day I took a walk through the university. I'd been to the library lots of times, but had never seen the campus in this light. The pretty Negro girls looked untouchable, now that I'd closed the door on ever being their equal. And if I had any doubts about my status, it was made clear by a group of Howard students who stopped me to buy numbers. One suggested they pool their nickels to play three numbers every possible way. When they stumbled over how many ways that was, I told them six.

"Well, thank you Professor," said one in a mocking voice and dropped his nickel into a puddle at my feet to see if I'd pick it up.

"You want this number? You pick it up," I told him. His friends hooted, egging him on but nothing came of it.

When trouble did come, it was from the ass-end of Goat Alley where two guys with scarves over their faces appeared from behind a wall. Another came at me from the street, holding his hand out for the box. I didn't see any weapons and decided to fight. The problem was how to do that while holding onto the box. Before I could come up with an answer, all three were on me.

I dropped to the ground and curled myself around the box. A kick caught me in the back and another in the ribs. What really got my attention was a brown boot that missed my face by about an inch. I rolled quickly, one way and then the other, sticking money into my shirt at the bottom of each roll. When I had it all tucked away I yelled "Here!" and tossed the closed box down the alley. When all three of them went chasing it, I ran the other way. I didn't stop till I got to Jimmie's card room, every breath a knife in my ribs. Carlos sat me down and leaned close.

"Did you lose any number slips?"

"I've got all of them here," I said touching my front pocket. "The wind blew some out of the box in the morning, so I figured…." Carlos put up his hand.

"Did you lose any money?"

"Maybe half a dollar in change."

Carlos sat back in his chair, pleased. The whites of his eyes were as yellow as old wax on a linoleum floor and the hair in his nostrils moved with each breath. Carlos leaned close again and put his hand on my knee.

"You gonna quit on me like the last boy?"

"I don't quit."

"Good." Fat Carlos stood, slapped me on the back and returned to his card game.

The next day after spending a few nickels for information, we found all three of those boys outside a candy store. They were smoking Chesterfields and talking up some girls. Tommy walked straight at the two brothers while I grabbed the big one in the heavy brown boots. They barely raised a fight.

I'd never hurt anybody more than was needed to win a fight. But this was no fight. We had to hit them where it would show most, a warning to anybody else who might make a run. I hit the big boy until he was down and then hit him again above the cheek bone, just enough to purple.

When I remembered to look for Tommy, I found him holding a barber's razor at one kid's ear.

"No!"

Tommy turned to me, slow as December.

"What exactly do you mean by 'No?'"

"It was me that got hurt. I decide."

"This is Fat Carlos' business too," said Tommy. "It's got to be done right."

I told Tommy to put away the knife and he did. We came home by way of Aspen Street, where the canopy of trees was thick as a blanket.

"You got a lot to learn about the street," he said.

"I learned a lot already, just from watching you."

~

NOW, AS I WALKED onto the Capitol grounds, I patted my front left pocket to feel the outline of the knife I still carried. Folded, it wasn't much longer than my middle finger, but I always felt more comfortable on the street knowing it was there.

There were maybe six hundred people below the Capitol steps. It didn't take long to see that Nora wasn't among them. While I was debating whether to go looking for her at the Anacostia camp, I felt a hand on my shoulder. It belonged to Neil Gold, the owner of the Criers' Club.

"Don't look so disappointed," said Gold. "I've got a job I want to hire you for."

I'd met Gold a few times and he seemed okay, but I told him I wasn't interested in any jobs.

"You might be interested in this one," he said. "It has to do with a girl you know and a cup she's trying to get back. Come to my club tonight and I'll tell you all about it."

VOTE

ERIC SEVAREID stood on the top of the Capitol steps, mildly disappointed with the peaceful scene below.

Twenty five thousand men had marched on Washington with an eye to this day and yet here it was, just hours before the first of two crucial votes on their bill and fewer than five hundred were gathered. A deal had been struck and the veterans appeared to be living up to their end of it. For Sevareid's purposes, a more raucous crowd was preferable. Of course, he wouldn't share that hope with Superintendent Glassford.

"I'm feeling optimistic," said Glassford. "The House will approve the bill today and whatever the Senate does won't happen until later. All I'm concerned about today, is today."

He'd barely finished when the Death Marchers came into view in a slow, ragged line. In the seventy-two hours since they started marching, their numbers had increased to three hundred. They trudged through the 100-degree heat, many trailing loose leg wrappings.

"It's like watching a bunch of mummies come undone," said Police Captain Dexter Largent, pushing past Sevareid to stand beside Glassford. Largent was as opposite Glassford as a man could get. Short, with a short man's complex, he hated women, Negroes and the bonus vets. He wasn't exactly fond of Glassord either, believing he'd taken the job that should have been his. Sevareid had heard him say as much to a Capitol policeman one night while watching the Death Marchers.

"He's a soldier. He knows as much about policing as a woman knows about telling the truth."

Walt Waters came across the plaza wearing shiny new boots that looked as though they pinched from the way he was walking.

"We shouldn't be playing footsie with these people," said Largent, pointing a finger at Waters as he climbed the stairs. "I'd believe the devil before I'd believe anything that he had to say."

"He hasn't lied to me yet," said Glassford.

Waters reached the top step and offered a salute. Glassford returned it and shook his hand. Largent refused to do either. Waters responded to the snub with a half smile.

"So what's the mood of the troops today?"

"Hopeful," said Waters.

"And John Pace?"

"You can never tell which way a snake will slither."

Glassford invited Waters to take a turn with him through the crowd of veterans below. Sevareid followed. He could always tell how things were going by the way the vets reacted to Glassford. Today they greeted him like a long-lost brother.

"Hey General, thanks for them sandwiches the other night."

"Don't thank me," said Glassford. "That was from Mrs. McLean."

"I hear she went up to Childs to get all that food. How much was it?"

"I don't know," said Glassford, raising his voice as the circle of vets grew. "She never paid."

"How's that?"

"When the sandwiches were ready she told the cashier she left her money at home. Then she said, 'You can trust me. I am Mrs. Evalyn McLean.'"

"I guess I'd get some credit too if I owned the Hope diamond," laughed one of the men.

"Who knows," said Glassford. "Someday you might."

Captain Largent broke into Glassford's circle with news that Pace and his men were on their way to the White House, and offered to take men to stop him.

"I need you here," said Glassford. "Find Captain Wyrick and tell him to follow me with reinforcements."

～

EVERYONE CAME HOME from the war changed in some way. Wounded, shell-shocked, exhilarated at having survived and guilty that so many comrades hadn't. John Pace came home furious. He'd been nearly killed a dozen times and for what? To protect property owned by other people, rich people.

"When I got back to Detroit and Henry Ford's assembly line, the unfairness of things only came clearer," he told Sevareid. "My father was nearly dead from twenty-five years in a steel mill, coughing up his lungs in an attic room. My mom up and left him. It hit me hard that I'd been conned by life, played for a fool. Nobody let me in on the scam."

Sevareid was happy to get the interview, even if no newspaper wanted to run it. He figured that might change in time and now, hurrying to catch up to Pace's men, he was sure that time had come.

WALKER

IT ALWAYS surprises me how white people spill secrets in front of Negroes, as if we don't have ears to hear. But maybe it's because they know we have nowhere to take those secrets. Last week I overheard a police captain whisper that Glassford had infiltrated Pace's outfit with a few of his cops. That should have been major news to Pace, but when I warned him he brushed me off. Said he trusted his men more than he trusted the word of a...he never said nigger, but I know that's the word he swallowed.

I kept even with them as they marched down the middle of New York Avenue toward the White House, under a red flag painted with half a dozen white stars. Every block the crowd grew thicker with tourists and office workers taking lunch. One called out, "Who are you guys?"

As they got to the Treasury Department, a few blocks before the White House, I saw Glassford waiting in the middle of the Avenue with a line of twenty uniformed men. Pace had at least sixty.

Pace stopped about twenty-five yards from Glassford. I noticed again how jumpy he looked, even standing perfectly still. Glassford, with his hair curling under his cap, was the picture of calm. Both seemed to be waiting for a sign. It finally came from behind Pace—a fist-fight between a bearded vet and another one trying to talk the men into turning back. You can guess which one was undercover.

Somebody yelled, "He's a cop," and a bunch of Pace's men jumped him. When four of Glassford's cops came running to his rescue, Pace charged the gap they left. Glassford immediately closed on Pace, but that weakened the left side of his line. For the first time since the Bonus Army arrived in D.C., police and veterans were fighting hand-to-hand.

Above the fight, I could hear the honking of stalled automobiles and people cheering like spectators at a boxing match. Pace's men were slipping through the line a few at a time, then returning to attack the police from the rear. The situation was moving from bad to desperate when I heard a metallic clank. I looked past Glassford and saw more of his officers coming, tear gas bombs attached to their belts.

Pace's men gave up the fight and ran into the crowd. The bearded vet who'd fought the undercover cop lunged at Captain Wyrick's holstered pistol, knocking him over. I couldn't see if he had the gun, but a woman nearby was screaming that he did. He was about to disappear into the crowd when he tripped, or someone tripped him, and he fell face down on the sidewalk. By the time Glassford got to him, Wyrick's gun was back in its holster.

Pace and one of his lieutenants stood in the middle of the avenue waiting to be arrested. Glassford left that to Captain

Wyrick and hurried after George Eicker, another of Pace's lieutenants who served as his public relations guy and court jester. I followed Glassford and three patrolmen. They caught up to Eicker at a baseball field on the edge of the Monument grounds. He was wearing a buckskin coat with leather fringe dangling from the shoulders. When one of the officers put a hand on his arm, he yelped like a coyote and sprinted to a tree behind home plate.

A crowd of tourists and veterans ran after him, cheering as Eicker went up the tree and out on a limb. The cop who'd let him go was blocked by a Negro, comically shadow boxing. With one man in a tree and another punching the air below it, the crowd couldn't have been happier.

The cop tried to push past the boxer but was blocked again. This time he punched the Negro on the side of his head and sent him sprawling. The crowd started to get ugly. Glassford sent a second cop to replace the first.

Eicker, who'd been sitting quietly above the show, perked up as the new cop reached his limb.

He yelled, "Hi, comrades!" The crowd below shouted hello. "This is just the beginning, men. The rank and file will organize..." The rest of the sentence was choked off by the policeman's hands around his throat. Though clearly on Eicker's side, the crowd laughed. I guess the whole scene was too much like Keystone Kops to take seriously. After a few breathless seconds, both Eicker and the cop climbed down.

When the police wagon opened for Eicker, John Pace stuck his head out the door and pointed at the White House. "Hoover's lucky if we don't decide to move into some of those spare bedrooms in that chateau of his. He'd better not crowd us."

I thought about following Pace to jail, but went instead to the Capitol. One fire was out, but others could still be burning and that's what the Party was waiting for.

BUMP

THE STING was hard enough to plan—a moving boat, a big river, and an unpredictable target. Then James Kemper threw a bomb into the works by showing up at the dock with two uninvited guests.

Nora's first thought was that the two men in the black limousine with Kemper were police. But there hadn't been a crime committed, not yet anyway, and they weren't dressed like policemen. Though just dark, Nora could see each man clearly as he stepped beneath the gas light near the dock. The first was blonde and muscular, with a perfectly round head. The other was taller and dark-haired. Nora was distracted from looking more closely at his face by the long, white cigarette holder clenched between his teeth.

This was definitely not part of the plan, but far from being alarmed, Nora was made more jealous. Here she was hiding behind a building that smelled of dead fish while Neil Gold, Will Cutler and Walker were about to sail into a grand adventure. Her adventure.

"I can dress like a cabin boy," she'd argued. "Pin my hair up under a cap." Gold didn't bother to answer. Walker looked at her like she was coming down with something.

"After all this work, crossing an ocean, you're ready to risk losing your cup for some excitement?"

"I might be useful. You never can tell."

"That's a chance we'll take," said Gold.

Gold was to play the part of the buyer while Will, in a bright white yachting cap, had the role of first mate. Walker would spring the trap from the boat's wheel.

Virni begged for his own part to play, but Gold didn't want to crowd the 50-foot Bayliner and certainly not with someone semi-famous for making objects appear and disappear. He didn't invite Sevareid because he was a reporter, and no matter how much Nora and Walker vouched for him, Gold said you couldn't trust a reporter to not report.

With the Bayliner gone, Nora walked to the dock, careful to

stay out of the light. She sat on the creosoted planks and tried again to figure the two men with Kemper. This circle was growing larger. Maybe Jack Allman had been right when he said the cup was meant to pass from hand to hand. If that was true, her time might already have come and gone. Though she refused to believe that, she had to admit she was more interested in regaining the cup than keeping it.

Walker had guessed as much.

"Are you going to sell it, take it back to Ireland or what?"

"I'm not at all sure."

"If it's as valuable as all that, you wouldn't want to leave it sitting around," he said. "And it would be a little awkward hanging from your belt."

That was two days ago. Now Walker was chugging across the Potomac, taking all the risks while she sat on a pier. The night was dark and moonless. A few gnats hovered before her eyes. She had a sense of events coming to a close. Congress had passed the Bonus bill as promised. What if the Senate followed suit? If she retrieved her cup and the Bonus Army went home, what was she to do?

Thoughts of home were sweet, but not the thought of actually going home, not with America barely a taste in her mouth. She'd long put off thinking about her future and probably should have for a little longer, because while she sat there picturing her father smoking his pipe and her mother cooking soda bread, she missed the sound of the limousine door closing.

"Waiting for the boat?" The driver was in the uniform of a soldier, not a chauffeur. Nora jumped to her feet.

"No," she lied as sweetly as possible, her blood pounding. "Just looking at the river. I come here every night. I should be going."

She walked toward the darkest part of the night as casually as she could, but inside she was shaking. What a fool she'd been. Had she done any harm? There was no reason to connect her to Neil Gold and his borrowed boat. She was just a girl sitting on a pier of a summer's eve. So why did she feel as if she'd loosened a thread and left it dangling for anyone to pull? She may not have done any harm, but she certainly had done no good.

~

I'VE PILOTED boats nearly as big, but none so sweet as the *Patriot* —fifty feet of mahogany and teakwood with brass railings and a plush, carpeted cabin. Not to mention the best view in the house for our floating drama.

After the handshakes and introductions, Neil Gold led James Kemper, Dwight Eisenhower and General Douglas MacArthur to a table on the foredeck, flush against the starboard gunwhale. The table had been built at a slant so an orange placed there would roll into the Potomac. What I didn't like was the obvious smell of sawdust, a giveaway that this odd table had only recently been planted there. What I didn't like even more was having MacArthur and Eisenhower on this boat. Were they going to bid on Nora's silver cup? If not, what the hell were they doing here?

Kemper sat with his back to me, a thick black case at his feet and his right arm over the starboard side. Neil Gold sat beside him. Across from them and facing me were Eisenhower and Douglas MacArthur, who just happened to be the one man in all of Washington I was eager to see up close. During the early chit-chat he sat smoking a cigarette in his holder and staring at the dark water. Gold drew him into the conversation.

"A cousin of mine served under you General, during the War."

"Which Division?"

"The 42nd."

"The Rainbow!" MacArthur's face lit up. The Rainbow was a division made up of troops from every state. It was as commanding officer of the Rainbow that MacArthur earned his reputation for bravery, and a chest-full of medals. The men in the camps who served under him spoke of MacArthur with great affection and not a little bit of awe.

"And where is your cousin now?" he asked.

"He died taking the village of Sergy in France."

"Sergy." MacArthur stood. The weather was calm and the river flat. He began to pace. "That was as brutal a battle as I've ever seen." He stopped to put a new cigarette in his holder. In the light of the match his eyes looked black as oil. "The village was on a cliff, two hundred feet above the Ourcq River. We crawled forward in twos and threes against each stubborn nest of enemy guns, closing in with the bayonet and the hand grenade. It was savage and there was no quarter asked or given. It seemed to be endless. Bitterly, brutally, the action seesawed back and forth." MacArthur's voice was hypnotic. I forced myself to concentrate on my navigating.

"A point would be taken, and then would come a sudden fire from some unsuspected direction, and the deadly counterattack. There was neither rest nor mercy."

"And was it worth it?" asked Gold.

MacArthur didn't hesitate. "Of course it was worth it. France was cut in half. England was starving. Another month or two and the Germans would have been drinking beer in Buckingham Palace." He turned to Kemper. "Our boys arrived just in time, didn't they?"

"Oh indeed," said Kemper cheerily. "A grateful nation and all that. Shall we talk art?"

"Not before we have a drink," said Gold, excusing himself to get a bottle and glasses. MacArthur was still standing, transfixed by something beyond the rail. Kemper set his black case on the empty chair. Eisenhower looked into the cabin, where Neil Gold was opening and closing cabinet doors in search of two extra whiskey glasses. I hoped Eisenhower wasn't a sailor because if he was, he'd know that every task on a boat was made intentionally repeatable, from coiling rope to stowing dishes. He'd know that Gold had either just bought this boat or didn't own it at all.

The General took his seat as Gold emerged from the cabin with a bottle of brandy and four glasses.

"So how long have you owned the *Patriot,* Mr. Gold," asked Eisenhower.

"Not long at all," said Gold. "I haven't even had time to figure out where to find the extra whiskey glasses."

My opinion of Gold jumped two rungs.

"It must be hard," said Gold as he poured MacArthur's drink, "to see these good fighting men in the camps brought so low."

"I doubt many of these men fought bravely or, for that matter, fought at all." He took one sip of the brandy and returned the glass to the table.

"You think the Bonus Army is made up of imposters?"

"Not every one, no. But the great majority. Opportunists. Radicals. Communists." He spoke with measured calm, turning his head first to Gold and then to the Englishman. In profile his nose reminded me of a hawk's. "I will say this for them. They are remarkably brazen. At a meeting in the offices of the White House, this Waters fellow offered to help protect the President from 'radical elements.' Incredible!"

Comrade Cord had told me that during that meeting, Waters asked MacArthur for his pledge that the Bonus vets be given the opportunity to salvage their belongings, form columns and retreat in orderly fashion if the military was called out. In return, Waters promised to stop resisting the Treasury Department's order to vacate three buildings on Pennsylvania Avenue at Third Street.

"I have every expectation that your men will leave the field peacefully," said MacArthur, which wasn't a guarantee but at least it wasn't a spit in the eye.

When we hit our first mark I gave Will Cutler the signal. In a white coat and yachting cap, he bent to whisper the message in Gold's ear. Turning to the others Gold said, "Shall we take a look at this unholy cup?"

"I've also brought some dueling pistols for the General. I'm sure he wouldn't mind if we had a look at them as well," said Kemper, opening his black case. I held my breath, afraid he was going to bring out the pistols first. I let the air out when I saw him pull a cup from the case. Nora had only described it to me as silver. But this was to silver cups what the Washington Monument is to tall buildings. Kemper held it by its base and turned it with ceremonial slowness.

"The figures are pre-Christian. Here we have a cook-god about to drop a boy into the sacrificial pot. On this other side is a fertility goddess. Wicked thing she is. Look at that face. The dark side of pleasure, eh." The goddess had both hands between her legs, pulling herself as wide open as a gate. "The Irish were still performing human sacrifice at the beginning of the Fourth Century. 'A savage race in a savage land.'"

The men stared at the cup. MacArthur turned his head as though fixing his trigger eye on it. I know nothing about pre-Christian artifacts, but I knew for sure that this cup of Nora's was the real thing and wondered if human blood had ever filled it.

Neil Gold was playing his part as a bargain-minded buyer. "Where did it come from?" he asked. "And who found it?"

"A girl, cutting sod in the wilds of Ireland. For all she knew or could appreciate, it came from the local pub. Her father made arrangements with me. I have the documents right here. Did I tell you the curator of the Smithsonian Institution examined this cup just last week? A most distinctive pedigree."

At the same moment that Gold reached for the cup, Kemper bent to his case and pulled it out of reach. For a moment Gold's hand twitched forward, as though he might snatch it. The only one who seemed to notice was Eisenhower.

"Still to come, just here the Kaiser's dueling pistols," said Kemper placing both cup and the pistol case on the table. "They have a history all their own."

Gold picked up the cup and set it back down six inches closer to the edge of the table. I needed a few more seconds to reach my target but Kemper was moving his right hand toward the cup.

His fingers were nearly touching the cup when the *Patriot* lurched violently. Two remarkable things happened then—MacArthur was thrown backwards, yet somehow managed to land on his feet while Neil Gold lunged forward, following the clump of objects hurtling toward the river—the brandy bottle, the four glasses, the silver cup and pistol case. He was half over the rail before his legs caught. Eisenhower would have stayed standing too if Kemper hadn't slammed into him. When Eisenhower rolled to his feet, I could tell he was suspicious, alert to whatever was coming next. But nothing came next. The boat drifted free; MacArthur stood where he'd landed, his eyes on me; Kemper groaned from the deck and Neil Gold remained folded over the rail like a string of wet spaghetti.

"Where is my cup?" cried Kemper.

Gold came off the rail holding the dueling pistol case in his right hand. He presented it to General MacArthur.

"But where is the cup?" asked Kemper, now on his knees, a bruise glowing below his left eye.

"I could only grab the one thing," said Gold. "Too bad you had to bring them both."

～

AS SOON AS the *Patriot* spilled Kemper and the two strangers onto the dock, Nora knew. She knew by the look on Kemper's face and the angle of Will's yachting cap. She knew by the way Walker stood at the bow, coiling rope. It was all she could do to wait until the limousine disappeared before running to the dock, fast as a thief.

"Tell me everything. From the start." She had Will's sleeve and Walker's hand and would have hooked Neil Gold by the leg if he'd come closer.

"Not here," said Gold. "Some place safe."

～

AT A TABLE by the bar of the Criers Club, Neil opened a bottle of champagne, then nodded to Will who'd been as impatient to talk as Nora was to listen.

"Man oh man, when I saw that Kemper fella pull the cup away just as we were heading for the bump, I said to myself 'Goner!'"

"That's always the problem with split-second timing," said Gold filling glasses. "Sometimes it just splits."

The "bump" Nora knew—a V of moss-covered logs held in place by a web of underwater rope. The bump was not meant to stop the boat, only to give Walker an excuse to throw the engine into reverse.

They told Nora the story in no particular order, trusting her to arrange it.

Gold pointed at Walker. "Didn't our friend here hit his target right on the nose?"

Walker raised his glass to Gold. "The thing I'll remember is you following that pistol case over the side."

"You should have seen it, Nora!" Will was out of his seat. "Mr. Gold stretched out like a left fielder."

"If you'd missed," said Walker, "it wouldn't have troubled my conscience any."

"And deprive General MacArthur of the chance to pay good money for fake dueling pistols? Where's your patriotism?"

Nora asked Walker if the cup was safe in his net.

"If the current didn't take it."

"And if it did? Wouldn't the cup just lie on the bottom?"

"The bottom might be two foot deep with silt. Or the current could carry it under rocks. It's not like looking on dry land." Walker knew the bottom was firm and the current predictably steady. But the river held other surprises.

"How safe is it for all of us to be here with Kemper staying in a hotel just down the avenue?" asked Walker.

"My bouncer knows him well enough," answered Gold.

While the monkey swung from the chandelier and the sketch artist drew caricatures near the bar, the club filled with a crowd that looked very nearly elegant. It may be the third year of a depression but not everyone is deadly poor, thought Nora. When the piano player flubbed a bar of Scott Joplin, Will mentioned that he hated piano lessons as a boy. Nora took the opportunity to examine Walker's right hand. "You've got good hands for piano. Long fingers."

Walker turned his palm up. "Do you read fortunes, too?"

"Absolutely. But not forever things. I can only see what will happen just next."

"And what do you see?"

"I knew, for example, that you'd ask me that question."

Nora kept his hand, making no pretense of reading it. The loudest thing in the room was the feel of it across the table. She saw a look pass between Walker and Gold but couldn't read it and didn't care to.

Will broke the spell, holding out his palm to Nora. "What about my future?"

Gold's laugh turned heads at the dice table. "Enough with the future. I've got something to show Nora now." He led her through a curtain to a door disguised to look like wood paneling. Inside a small room was a deep tub of steaming water, surrounded by lit white candles. The smell of wax reminded Nora of the afternoon she snuck into the sacristy with her friend Kitty, determined to touch every sacred and forbidden thing.

"There's soap and a brush beside the tub," said Gold, backing out the door as his blonde assistant entered carrying two towels, a hair brush and a shimmering green dress on a wood hanger.

She introduced herself as Ineke. "I can get you cold water if that's too hot."

"I don't think that will be a problem."

When it became obvious Ineke wasn't leaving, Nora turned her back and undressed, letting her clothes fall to the floor.

"You have lovely long legs," said Ineke. "Are you 18?"

"I'm nearly 18." She turned to Ineke, resisting the impulse to cover herself with her hands. She hadn't stood completely naked in front of anyone since she was 11. "How old are you?"

"Twenty-eight."

Against her white skin and blonde hair, Ineke's eyes were a shocking blue. It should be a pleasure to be looked at through such eyes, thought Nora as she lowered herself slowly into the steaming water.

Ineke sat on the edge of the caskwood tub. "When I was a little girl in Sweden, my father built a sauna by the edge of a cold pond. We'd go from the sauna to the cold water and back again."

"In Ireland we had our baths on Saturday night in a metal tub. My brother and I would sit and wash each other's back while my mother poured hot water from the kettle."

Nora lay back in the tub. Her body didn't seem her own, more like a painting or a table.

"Are you and Mr. Gold lovers?"

Ineke didn't seem surprised by the question. "Not in the way you think."

Nora was satisfied with the answer, though she didn't understand it. She closed her eyes, let her head sink beneath the water and blew slow bubbles. When she resurfaced, Ineke was gone. The dress hung on a hook by the door and beneath it stood a pair of high-heeled shoes. The tub was a pleasure and no reason to leave it except for the dress, which seemed to be moving on the hanger, glimmering with its own light. Nora climbed from the tub and tossed her clothes into it—pants and shirt, socks and underwear. Dripping wet she knelt on one of the towels, scrubbed the clothes and hung them on the side of the tub nearest the fire. Gently, she rubbed herself dry.

That done she took the dress from the hanger and pulled it over her head, breathing in the fabric as it shimmied down. She stopped wearing dresses at the age of 13, after she and Kitty decided that they were unnatural things, invented by men for their own purposes. But that was an idea and this was silky green against her naked body, like the touch of a strange hand. She ran both her fingers down her sides and purred. If Kitty could see her now.

The high-heeled shoes were a fascination, but so wide and wobbly they were impossible for Nora to manage. She brushed her hair in front of the fire and for a moment forgot there was any other place in the world. Was this the bliss Virni spoke of, a natural, unthinking state? It was impossible to know without thinking about it, which disqualified it as unthinking bliss.

Gold knocked at the door. "All set?"

Nora invited him in.

He looked at her with satisfaction, as though he'd guessed how the dress would fit. "The band wants to talk to you about some songs."

"You want me to sing?"

"Isn't that what you're here for?"

Hearing Gold say it, Nora knew it to be true.

"What if I don't know their songs?"

"They know your songs."

Nora saw heads turning as Neil Gold led her barefoot to the stage. She looked for Walker at the table but couldn't find him. The club had gone strangely quiet. As she consulted with the three musicians—piano, bass and clarinet—Nora was amazed at her own self-confidence. "Rose of Sharon" in the key of C. This was easy, something she was meant to do. She stepped to the microphone, waited for the musical cue and began to sing.

It took about one-and-a-half bars for the panic to set in. It wasn't her voice, which was strong, but what to do with her hands. She tried keeping them at her sides and felt like a school girl. When she let them go, they flew to her chest and fluttered there like captive birds. Her eyes were another problem. Should she look at faces in the audience or at a fixed spot on the back wall? While worrying of that, Nora forgot the words to the song she'd sung a hundred times. They came back to her, but not before her throat went suddenly dry.

She was almost through the first song, and dreading the next, when a loud bell rang in the club. The musicians stopped abruptly. Without any coaching the audience moved toward rear exits. Neil Gold appeared beside her.

"They're two hours early," he said looking at his watch like a man noting the arrival of a train. "Stay close to me."

They went back through the curtain to the hidden door. As it opened, Nora felt someone at her hip and turned to see Walker. Gold led them to a dark corner of the room where he pulled a latch disguised to look like a radiator valve. A piece of the floor lowered away, leaving an opening big enough for a good sized man. Gold put his feet onto the top rung of an iron ladder and invited Nora and Walker to follow him down. Nora grabbed her wet clothes.

"It's solid down here," he promised and it was, the ground hard as stone. When all three were at the bottom, Gold tugged on a counterweight and the floor clicked shut above, leaving them in blackness thick as sleep.

"What about Will?" whispered Nora.

"Northing to worry about," Gold assured her as he put a match to a kerosene lantern. "A regular part of doing business. At worst, he'll spend a couple hours in jail."

They were in a stone cellar surrounded by barrels and kegs.

"How long do we stay?" asked Walker.

"We don't. This will take us to the street." Through a plaster archway into a brick-walled tunnel, the light flickered over puddles and a scurry of rats. Nora shivered as a drip of cold water hit the back of her neck. "This goes all the way to the Capitol," said Gold. "Congress built it to escape the British and anybody else who wanted to wring their necks.

"Is it still used?"

"Only by outlaws like us."

Nora loved being in the secret belly of the city with the lantern throwing shadows and was disappointed when, after what seemed only minutes, Gold stopped at a second iron-rung ladder.

"Stay low going out," he said.

Nora climbed between the two, one hand on the ladder and the other holding her clothes. She emerged through a metal grate, between a five-foot hedge and the statue of a mounted soldier.

"One block that way is Pennsylvania Avenue," said Gold, who looked comically overdressed beside the wild hedge. "To get back to Massachusetts Avenue you go there."

"Wait and I'll change from the dress," said Nora.

"It's yours. Wear it the next time you come to the Club. You still have songs to sing."

~

THINGS CHANGED the second we turned down U Street, and this time it was all my doing. I walked closer and let my hand brush against hers. Given my history on Washington sidewalks, that was rank boldness.

"They call this the Great Black Way," I told her. "This is where the Negro half of Washington carries on."

Ahead were bright lights and crowded sidewalks. A man in a startling yellow suit hurried past, turned to look back at Nora, touched the brim of his hat and winked at me.

"The night I got to Washington, my grandfather met me at Union Station and walked me through this neighborhood. It was about a mile out of our way, but the safest route for two Negroes at night."

Nora looked to see if I was telling a story or making a point. I wasn't sure myself. We passed the Jungle Inn, Club Bengasi, the Capital Pleasure Club and the Parrot Room, each club loud and crowded on a Tuesday night. Nora walked as slowly as I let her, not wanting to miss anything. I finally stopped at the corner of 11th Street, above basement stairs leading down to the Club Crystal Caverns.

"Let's go in here and have a drink," I said and led her down.

The white stucco roof and walls of the Caverns club are shaped with stalactites, turbaned genies, minarets and other oddities. I could see that Nora was fascinated. She was the only white person in the club.

"It's a prickly feeling, isn't it? Having everybody look you up and down."

"At least I'm dressed right for once," she said, smoothing her green dress, which was more than a match for any in the club. We sat at a small table near the empty bandstand. I ordered two grape fizzes.

I told Nora about seeing Duke Ellington at the Caverns before he went to the Cotton Club in New York.

"I've heard him on a Victrola," she said. "*The Savoy Stomp.*"

"He grew up in this neighborhood. So did Cab Calloway. The first time I smoked reefer was at the Howard Theatre just down the street, watching Cab Calloway. When I closed my eyes, I could see the music. All different colors dancing around."

"What's reefer?"

"Reefer? It's like tobacco but gets you…it changes the way everything looks. Makes it all funny."

"You mean, ha ha funny?"

"That too."

"I'd like to see you act funny. Ha ha and otherwise."

The drinks were spiked with the same liquor I used to smuggle, lightly- flavored stuff that didn't hit you right away. Nora swallowed hers in one gulp and ordered another. When she turned to me, her face was bright and dreamy, like she'd swallowed a light bulb. It made her look more like a kid than a woman in a sexy green dress and that was fine by me. Somewhere in the middle was where I wanted her to stay.

The lights flashed to let us know the show was about to begin. A man in a white tuxedo walked to the front of the stage and played a clarinet, soft and low. Nora closed her eyes and let her head move to it. When she opened them again, she took my hand across the table and this time I let her keep it.

～

ON THE WAY to the cabin, I tried to explain to Nora where I fit into Washington's Negro society. She was just drunk enough to be interested.

"The good people were too good for me. They wore clean, new clothes and went to church."

"But you were smart."

"How would they know? I was a rough little high yellow with patches on my knees. Besides I wasn't ready to fit in. I didn't know how to act around Negroes."

Nora said she felt the same way the first time she visited Dublin.

"All those city people looked at me like I was a savage from the hills." A few steps later she stopped and apologized. "I know that's not the same thing. It's the grape fizz making me talk such rubbish. Let's talk about something else."

"Okay. What kind of man is your father?"

"He's a big, melancholy man. Loves to read poetry. He should have been a professor at a university instead of a farmer. Oh, and he can do magic tricks."

"What kind?"

"With cards. Sleight of hand, that kind of thing. Remind me to show you a few when I'm wearing a shirt with sleeves. And what of your father? Did you ever meet him?"

"I did, but that's not a story that would interest you."

"Let me be the judge of that."

I felt irritated with her for asking. Then again, I'd asked about her father. The only person I had a right to be annoyed with, I decided, was myself.

"Okay, miss inquisitor. I did meet him once. It was the day of my grandfather's funeral. I came back to the cabin from the cemetery to find a man sitting at the table, drinking one of Mr. Luke's beers."

"You always called your grandfather Mr. Luke?"

"I did. Anyway, the man at the table was light skinned with pomaded hair…"

"Pomaded?"

"Straightened, to make it look more like white peoples' hair. He wore peach-colored shoes and a red vest. I knew immediately who he was.

"'So how was the old man's sendoff?' he asks in a voice so much like Mr. Luke's it throws me. I told him he should have been at the funeral. He says that would have been dangerous, with all the people around D.C. still looking for him.

"Mr. Luke told me a story about him stealing a horse carriage from a white man in Georgetown. Said he escaped the police by racing it across the frozen Potomac. The carriage and horse sank just before he reached the far shore. I asked if the police were still looking for him on account of that.

"'I only stole it after the man who owned it hit me with his whip,' he said, 'I don't let nobody lay hands on me, white or colored.' Then he put his head back and said, 'So the old man was telling stories about me?'

"I could see he was dying to know but I wasn't looking to please him. Instead I said, 'The story I never heard was how you met my mother.'

"He dropped his head and looked at the floor, exactly the way Mr. Luke used to when he wanted to avoid a subject. Then he says, 'Damn boy, that was a long time ago.'

"I kind of blew up at him. Like I didn't know how long ago it was! He puffed his chest, like he was ready to fight back, then sat back in the chair and started talking.

"'I was working for your mother as a gardener, up there in New York. She used to come out in the afternoon and talk to me, about flowers and trees and that kind of thing. A good-looking woman, too.'

"I said, 'Tell me something I don't already know.'

"'You wanna hear this? So you know what she looks like. And here she is coming every day to talk to her Negro gardener, except now she's not talking about flowers. Now she's asking what it's like to be colored. And how disgraceful the white man has been.'

"I felt the tiniest bubble of hope grow in my chest and asked, 'So you got to be friends?'

"He finished his beer, then popped my bubble. 'No, we never got to be friends. I waited until one day we were out the back, where nobody could see. I kissed her and waited to see what she'd do. She just stood there, like she had it coming. When I saw that, I kissed her again and pulled her down on the ground. That's just the way it was. I left and never went back. Hell, I didn't even know about you until two years later. By then you'd passed as white. Wouldn't do no good for me to be showing up.'

"When I said that was awful considerate of him, he says, 'Shit boy, you got more in your first years than most niggers get in a lifetime. Good food, a big house, rich boy school. What you got to complain about?'

"He knew damn well what I had to complain about. I could see it in his eyes, that same bewildered look Mr. Luke used to get. I'm not sure why, but as soon as I recognized it, I felt relieved, like a weight had rolled off my back.

"I opened two more beers for us and said, 'Mr. Luke told me there never was a person could grow things as good as you.'

"He narrowed his eyes, wondering had I let him off so soon. Convinced I had, he leaned back and started telling stories, about the gardens he'd designed and rich folk he'd worked for. But having forgiven him, I wasn't much interested in what he had to say. I did like looking at him though, and listening to his voice. After about half an hour he said, 'Well, I guess I better be going, huh?' It sounded like he was hoping for an invitation to stay.

"And did you offer one?"

"No. I said, 'Guess you better go, what with people around here still looking for you.'"

Nora stopped on the sidewalk and looked me in the eye. "Did you, you know, feel like a son to him?"

"Not in the way you're asking. But I was glad I'd met him. I could finally throw away all the other versions of him I'd invented over the years. One thing that struck me was watching him walk to the door. It was as familiar as anything in the world. It wasn't Mr. Luke's walk, but mine. The last thing he said to me was, 'You take care of yourself, hear? I can't be coming back here for no more funerals.'"

We crossed the river and walked the trail to my cabin. Clouds smothered the night sky. I could hear Nora better than see her, humming a song and crunching twigs. I'd have been happy walking for hours, especially since I was suddenly nervous about what we were going to do at the cabin. I wanted to kiss her and was pretty sure she'd let me. But where would that lead? Dogs and cats and Nora not one to pretend it never happened. That said, I still wanted to kiss her and knew I'd try.

We made the last turn and saw a lamp burning in my window.

"It must be Eric," cried Nora. She ran up the step and through the door. I got there in time to see the look on Sevareid's face. He was sitting at the table above an open volume of Langston Hughes' poetry.

"Don't be so shocked. It's only a dress," said Nora dancing across the floor. But Sevareid and I both knew it was more than a dress.

"You look…great," said Sevareid, and might as well have said she looked tired or wet for all the enthusiasm in his voice.

Nora looked from Sevareid to me, standing stone-faced at the door. "Why are you both so grumpy?" Getting no answer she tried to make things right by pulling me to the table and sitting between us. She told Sevareid the story of the bump and General MacArthur, of the limousine driver and Neil Gold diving over the rail of the *Patriot,* and clapped her hands together when she was done.

"We need to celebrate the return of my cup with an adventure," she said, leaning playfully close to each of us in turn. "A canoe trip somewhere. What do you say?"

"The Bonus bill," said Sevareid. "I need to write stories about it."

"The Senate won't vote on it for another week," countered Nora. "What's to write about until then?" To me she said, "You've nothing to say to people now either, not until their dreams are dashed."

"You make me sound like a vulture waiting for a corpse."

"We'll talk about it tomorrow on our voyage," insisted Nora. "One day is all I ask. Maybe two."

I told her I'd sleep on it. Sevareid just nodded. We took the floor and left Nora to the bed. With the lamp extinguished, she talked about her drowned brother and how her mother started counting things afterwards, everything from the number of steps to town, to the times each day that a certain bird would sing. It was her way of keeping track, so she wouldn't lose her daughter like she'd lost her son.

When she finished we let the silence be. Quiet as it was, I could almost hear Sevareid's brain working the opposite end of our common problem.

RIVER TRIP

THE SMALL BOAT reminded Nora of early days on the Atlantic with her father and uncle, her first measure of great men. Because her father was oldest, he inherited the farm. That was fine by Uncle Dan who liked farming even less than Ireland's climate. Her uncle had been eager to take to sea and all the sun-drenched lands beyond and, at least as far as Nora could judge, was the happier for it. One afternoon with the ocean slapping against their currach, she tried to imagine what each would be like with their personalities switched. She decided her father would get the better part of that deal, but then a girl her age would.

Eric and Walker reminded her of them in certain small gestures. Eric had the same way as her father of cocking his head to one side when spoken to. And a look would sometimes play across Walker's face, as though he was both present and far away, that was uncannily like her uncle's. It was a look Nora envied.

Getting Eric and Walker to agree to this trip had been surprisingly easy. Though the night before they'd been as eager as prisoners facing a firing squad, come morning Eric announced he was game and Walker said he'd better go as well, if only to keep them from sinking his boat. That settled, they busied themselves with gear and packing. If Nora hadn't known better she'd have guessed Eric and Walker had been partners for years.

"We'll visit the Kemunkey," said Walker, and Nora was only temporarily disappointed to learn the Kemunkey were not exotic American tree monkeys. Much better, she discovered, they were Indians who wrestled two-hundred-pound drumfish.

"It's a sight you'd never forget," said Walker, while attaching fishing poles to fixed straps inside the boat.

Walker's boat was big enough for the three to sit as long as Nora didn't mind squeezing onto the stern bench, first with Eric and then Walker. She didn't mind one bit. Paddling was a pleasure, though steering was tricky with two in the stern. But after she and Eric got 'the hang of it' (another bit of American slang she'd come to like) her back muscles were grateful for the work. She'd had nothing to pull or push since landing in America, certainly nothing as weighty as the new lambs she carried over the Kenmare hills, and this paddling reminded her of them.

Though the morning was hot, a comfortable river breeze blew from the south. Other than a few puffy white clouds, the sky was as blue as a robin's egg. As they moved past the Georgetown docks, below church steeples and homes made from Seneca granite quarried a dozen miles upstream, Nora marveled at how different the world looked from the middle of a river.

"Isn't it grand to be leaving?" she said and pointed to shore where miniature people moved through their undersized day.

"A puny race those landsmen," said Eric in a voice like god's own.

Walker pointed his paddle at half a dozen turtles sunning on a log and said, "We'll live on fish and turtle soup and never again set foot on land."

"I might like a cup of coffee every day or so," said Eric.

"And the occasional sweet," added Nora. "How about once a week we visit land to buy books and go to the cinema."

"You pilgrims!" teased Walker. Nora was gladdened to see him smile and Eric smile back. The ill wind from the night before had blown through. They were the three musketeers once again, or whatever alternative Eric might come up with. All for one and on their way to an Indian reservation. The trip was less than an hour old and already Nora judged it the finest she'd ever made.

〜

ERIC SEVAREID was no less aware than Nora of the tight seating and rhythmic rub of their thighs. As fantasies went this was certainly the top of his list, paddling a canoe with a girl who actually liked it, and not just any girl but maybe his perfect girl. Of course in a true fantasy, Walker wouldn't be there. But then Sevareid knew he was likely intruding on Walker's ideal fantasy as well.

That morning over a breakfast of biscuits and honey, he saw a look on his friend's face that surprised him. It was the same look

Sevareid would have seen in a mirror, but he wasn't a Negro letting his affection for a white girl show. Not that Sevareid saw anything wrong with that, but most other white people would. In fact nearly every other white person would.

He'd already congratulated himself for being open-minded, so why did he keep coming back to it, like a tongue that couldn't let a chipped tooth alone? Maybe it did bother him, but not because he believed it should. He decided to blame Carl Jung's "collective unconscious," inherited by each generation from all those past. Sevareid wasn't sure he understood the concept, much less believed it, but he was happy to lay blame for his prejudice at the feet of the dead.

Walker stopped paddling and pointed to the water ahead of the boat. "Right about here."

"What is right about here?" asked Sevareid.

"Nora will tell you."

Nora looked as confused as Sevareid.

"The cup? The one you crossed an ocean to find?"

"Oh! Here? I wasn't on board," she explained to Sevareid. "Do you want to see it? Shall we get it now?"

"Why not wait a bit," urged Walker. "It's safer there than in our boat."

"The Captain has spoken," said Sevareid.

~

I SHOULD HAVE put Sevareid in the bow from the start. I knew the fast water far better than him and besides, the Captain's place was in the stern. Of course the main reason to put Sevareid up front was to put myself beside Nora. Wasn't I an idiot to play things cool and slow. This was the time to be reckless and direct. It hit me at breakfast that morning—I'd finally found something worth stealing.

I was jealous of Sevareid, but one part of me was glad to have him along. It was fun working with somebody who didn't need to be told every little thing. For the first time since my last baseball game at the age of 13, I was part of a team again.

"I've got a friend on the reservation named Henry," I told Nora and Sevareid. "I hope he's still there. The last time I saw him was when we traveled together to the Grand Canyon."

"How grand is the Grand Canyon?" asked Nora.

"A mile deep, 23 miles long and ten thousand shades of brown, yellow, red and purple. It's just as spectacular looking up from the bottom as down from the top."

"Did you paddle the river?" asked Sevareid.

"We swam in it and camped on shore. Henry gave me some Indian mushrooms that made my head open like a suitcase."

"What happens when your head opens like a suitcase?" asked Sevareid.

"All the thoughts and feelings in the world, stuff you didn't even know you knew, fall in and out again without any effort."

"I'd like to try some of that," said Nora.

I warned her it took my body two days to recover.

"Isn't that a small price for all the thoughts and feelings in the world?"

I looked at Nora over my shoulder. The sun was shining on her face and hair and she'd pulled her cotton dress just above her knees. I took one deep breath and needed another.

Sevareid asked how Henry and I became friends. When I said it was kind of a long story, he laughed. "We've got ten hours of paddling ahead of us and you don't have time for a long story?"

The river here was flat and, except for the occasional barge, fairly harmless, so I turned on my seat to face them. "My grandfather always talked about the Indians that lived in our woods, said there were only a few left and were hard to see. They'd learned to be invisible to escape being killed by the white man. Every day, no matter what else I was doing, I kept a lookout for them. But I never found one until a day I wasn't even looking."

Nora had stopped paddling and Sevareid was using his only to keep the canoe pointed downstream. A hawk screed overhead.

"I was hiking the shore a little south of here when I came across a cove, hidden from the river's main flow. I decided to call it Snapping Turtle Cove because of the air bubbles popping on the surface and sat down to add it to my map. All of a sudden something big flew out of the water, a square-headed thing with whiskers thick as clothesline. It was a flying catfish, the size of a dog...with a human hand in its mouth!"

"It didn't!" cried Nora happily.

"It did. And a great, scary pleasure that was, thinking the catfish had the hand rather than the other way around. But soon enough an arm appeared, then a head of long black hair. The hair made me think it was a girl, just like Nora's cap had me fooled into thinking she was a boy at first. But it was definitely an Indian boy, holding a catfish in his fist.

"He said, 'Hey keep an eye on this' and heaved the google-eyed monster at my feet. When I looked back to the water the boy was gone."

"An invisible Indian?"

"Yeah, but only because he'd gone under to get another fish. Next time up he was talking before his head came out of the water, finishing an argument I hadn't started. 'I'm not saying they're the prettiest things, but how can you say they're not tasty?' With his long hair and high cheekbones he looked exotic. It was the first time I'd ever thought of using that word to describe a person.

"When I asked how he caught fish without a net or hook, he shifted the cat to his left hand and showed me his right. The pinkie finger was missing its tip. He said, 'The big ones like to work into bottom mud or find a hole along the bank. You just wiggle your hand in there slow like, get behind the gills and whoosh...out it comes. You want to make sure you don't try it with a fish that's got teeth.'

"I asked was it a fish that bit off part of his finger?"

"'No, a girl did that,' he said all serious, then burst out laughing and danced a little circle.

"He told me he was fifteen and his name was Henry. I said it out loud, trying to make the name fit. He said, 'You were expecting Sitting Bull?'"

"That's funny," said Sevareid.

"Now, sure."

Nora hopped on her seat like she'd sat on a bee. "I keep forgetting to ask," she said. "What's *your* name?"

"You know my name."

"All I know is Walker. Is that your first or last name?"

"Last. My first name is Randolph."

Sevareid laughed. "And here you're wondering about an Indian named Henry? Randolph isn't exactly a Negro name."

"I wasn't a Negro when I got the name. I mean I was but they didn't know it, my father anyway…."

Sevareid waved his hand. "It's a good name. A great name. I'm just saying."

"So what happened to Henry?" asked Nora. "Was he one of the invisible tribe of Indians your grandfather told you about?"

"No, he was a Kemunkey traveling through. Said he was on his way to find the source of the Potomac. This will sound stupid, but I'd never thought about the Potomac having a beginning. Like the Hudson in New York, it seemed too big and powerful to ever be that small. I asked Henry if I could tag along. He said no, but he let me help him cook and eat the fish. Before he left he invited me to come visit him on the reservation, said he'd show me what makes the red man red."

"What does?" asked Nora.

"He was only kidding. Anyway, I went to see him the next year and I've been going every year since."

I turned back to the river, thinking about Henry. It had taken me awhile to figure why I was so comfortable with him. He wasn't white and he wasn't Negro, so I didn't have to pretend to be either. Being with Henry was a nice break from trying to be what I was not.

I'd planned to stop for lunch at a bend in the river where I knew we'd find small rockfish. I pulled over instead to a spot with good tree cover and a fresh water inlet I'd never fished. The main appeal of that place was it came an hour earlier than the other one, and I was past ready to change seats with Sevareid.

We set up a cookfire, then started fishing with worms, spoons and artificial flies. It turned out Nora was pretty good with a fly rod, so I was cheated out of giving her a hands-on lesson. Sevareid took my casting rod and tied on a small spoon. He tossed it twenty yards down river, bouncing the lure off a big rock so it dropped like a frog or salamander into the deep pool below. A few seconds later he was reeling in a pretty decent largemouth bass. Nora caught some sunfish and I was lucky to find two rockfish. That gave us enough to eat.

We roasted the fish on sticks and cut up some apples. When we were done, Sevareid surprised us with a small bag of sucking candy.

"I'm enjoying this," said Nora, sitting between us with her back against a rock. "I could do this forever."

I was pretty sure Sevareid and I had the same reaction to that —forever was a long time to sit on a triangle. We'd hooked the same fish and only one of us could reel it in.

～

SEVAREID was lying on his back in that half state between sleep and waking, the sound of the woods and river merging into a thin dream about a cocker spaniel walking on hind legs beneath a girl sitting in a tree. Only it wasn't a dream (except for the dog walking on hind legs) because when he fully opened his eyes, he saw a girl sitting on a tree limb ten feet above his head.

"Are you awake?"

Sevareid nodded.

"Good." The girl slid off her perch, caught the limb with her right hand, and let herself drop to the ground a few feet from Sevareid's face. In that short descent, Sevareid saw she was about 16, wore black hobnailed boots, held a hand-rolled cigarette between her teeth, had hair the color of cedar bark and skin as white and fleshy as a mushroom. Oh, and she wasn't wearing any underwear beneath her brown cotton dress.

"Who're them?" asked the girl, jerking her head toward Nora and Walker, now sitting up from their own naps.

"They're with me. Who are you?"

"I'm Sophie. And we better get up and goin' before the fella that owns this land gets here with his shotgun."

"How do you know there's somebody coming here with a shotgun?" asked Nora.

"I know because he's chasing me." The girl smiled, not like it was a joke but a truth she didn't fear. "Joe Holman ain't a nice man which you'll see if he finds us here."

"There's no room in our boat," said Sevareid.

"That's okay, I got a canoe. Maybe you could help me paddle just til we get downriver some."

"Sounds good to me," said Walker. "We're done here."

Sophie looked from Walker to Sevareid. "Is he like a servant or something?"

"No, he owns the boat. And he's our friend."

"Well, any friend of yours is a friend of mine," she said. "We can make our introductions when we're free of here."

～

IF YOU ASKED Nora what her reaction would be to a high-spirited girl dropping from the sky into the middle of a river adventure, she'd have said great. Anything to add more spin to the earth's rotation.

But her reaction to Sophie Landry dropping into *her* adventure was considerably less enthusiastic. Nora didn't like this girl and not just because she had designs on Eric. Though really, what kind of girl would make such an obvious play less than half a second after meeting a man? And not wearing any underwear? She'd seen that all right and knew Eric had too. Low class, from pillar to post.

Then there was the way Sophie treated her and Walker, as though one of them wasn't there and the other shouldn't be. And that story, about a crazed farmer with a shotgun. It didn't just stretch credulity, it shredded it.

With those dark thoughts she climbed into the bow of Walker's boat and began paddling downriver to where Eric and the girl waited.

"Do you think we'll be invited to the wedding?" asked Walker.

"She's about as suited to Eric as a mouse is to a cat."

"You know what they say about love making strange bedfellows."

"No, I do not. And I'd just as soon not talk such nonsense," said Nora, unable to hide her irritation.

Sophie's canoe was painted bright green and yellow and patched in a dozen places with tar and tape. Eric looked uncomfortable sitting in the stern of such a slovenly duck, while Sophie appeared well pleased.

"What good luck that I found y'all on the same day I planned to run away. We're free and clear now." No sooner had she said it than she was contradicted by a voice from shore.

"Get back here with my boat and wife or I'll blow you out of the water!"

Everyone turned toward the voice except Sophie who began paddling furiously. The others soon followed suit.

"Keep low!" ordered Walker as if Nora could get any lower and still work her paddle. Behind them came a crashing sound of someone moving through woods, but no gunfire. After another half minute Nora relaxed enough to look back. The bald-headed man standing on shore was pointing a shotgun in their direction. As Nora watched, a puff of smoke rose from the end of the barrel. The sound of the shot arrived just ahead of the buckshot, ten yards to their left. Either Joe Holman was a terrible shot or he was aiming at the wrong boat, her boat, which was one more reason to dislike this Sophie.

Holman reloaded and fired again, but this shot fell short. Walker and Eric brought the boats abreast.

"You didn't tell us it was his canoe. Or that you were his wife," said Nora.

"We never went before a preacher," said Sophie. "And I needed the canoe. There ain't much a girl can do against a two-hundred pound man except to run."

"Well, you're safe now," said Eric.

"I truly hope so. If he doesn't come after me by tomorrow morning I'll be sure."

"You can stay with us until then," said Walker. Nora saw a look pass between him and Eric.

"Thanks," said Sophie. "That's white of you."

∿

THE QUESTION was whether Walker could jump higher and run faster than Sevareid.

"It's a fact," said Sophie. "The nigras where I grew up were all good that way."

" Maybe they had to be," said Walker. "To get away from all the white people chasing them."

"Now that makes a lot of sense, don't it?" asked Sophie of Sevareid.

His only answer was "Mmmm."

Eric Sevareid had never been shot at before. Thanks to Sophie he now had that experience under his belt. And he had to admit, a girl jumping from a tree showing all her parts was, if nothing else, a good story to tell. There was also something about the girl's looks—her excessively white complexion and potato-plump cheeks, the way her eyes shifted from side to side when she talked and the exceptional tint and stiffness of her hair—that combined to create a certain fascination. But against all those positives was Sophie's inability to keep her mouth shut for more than five seconds.

Not only was she a non-stop talker, but the things she said made either no sense or bad sense.

" *You see that bird? Don't he look like a pigeon that got upwind of a rooster?*"

"If we used to be monkeys, then why didn't all the other monkeys come along and become us?"

"You ever wonder what it would be like to be buried? Not dead, just buried?"

"Most colored people are more interested in carrying on than taking care of themselves."

That last bit was said while they were setting up camp for the night. Sevareid expected Walker to jump on Sophie with both feet, but Walker just smiled. It was Nora who bristled.

"And isn't that the same pack of lies the British always said about the Irish? Colored people had civilizations in Africa when white people in Europe were still living in caves. How do you explain that?"

Sophie shook her head. "Who said anything about Irish or Africans? You got to pay a little closer attention."

It was dark by the time they finished eating and nobody was working very hard to keep the fire going. The mood was so settled that not even Sophie could keep conversation alive.

"I think I'm going to turn in," said Walker. "We've got about three hours more paddling tomorrow morning before we reach the Kemunkey reservation."

"Kemunkey? I've heard stories about them I don't want to believe," said Sophie.

"Then don't," said Nora. "I guess you'll be leaving us tomorrow morning, now that you're safe. If I don't see you, good luck." With that Nora left the fire and followed Walker.

Sevareid wasn't particularly tired, but he didn't want to get stuck with Sophie. He also didn't like the idea of Nora and Walker getting too cozy in the dark. "I'll see you in the morning," he said to Sophie. But as he started to rise, she reached out a hand and stopped him.

"I don't have a blanket. Maybe you could sleep close to keep me warm."

"I'll do better than that," said Sevareid, escaping her grip. "I'll pile this wood on the fire. It'll burn pretty much all night."

Sophie laughed like she knew he was kidding. When she saw he wasn't, she laughed again. "Well, I'll be. You sure now? You might be sorry in the morning."

A fascination to be sure, thought Sevareid. "Sophie, you're probably right. But that's a chance I'll have to take."

~

I WAS 14 YEARS OLD when I first visited Henry at the reservation. I told Mr. Luke I'd be gone a few days, but didn't tell him where. He wouldn't have cared one way or the other but I wanted the trip to be all mine, with no ideas about it coming from anyone else.

After surviving my first year in D.C., I was determined to change, to remake myself into somebody unafraid of anything that walked or swam. But as I paddled up to the Kemunkey reservation, I couldn't help imagining Indians staring at me from the brush. In every book I'd read about Indians, they always ambushed the unsuspecting trappers or settlers from exactly the kind of narrow, covered shore I was passing.

I froze at the sound of whooping, until I saw it was only a gang of Indian kids wanting to race me along the shore. They were dressed like any eight-and nine-year olds, in denim pants, shorts and summer undershirts, but these kids had thick black hair and copper-colored skin. I was excited, knowing I was about to meet a whole tribe of them.

When we paddled up the Mattowack this time, another group of kids swooped down on us at nearly the same spot. But they didn't whoop or holler. This time it was them that froze. Nora had her hair down, Sevareid his shirt off and Sophie, who'd managed to keep herself attached to our little group, was wearing a hat of vines and leaves that made her look like a floating bush.

"They act like they've seen a four-headed sea monster," said Sevareid.

"We are a little strange, but I bet they'll be racing us any minute." And I was right.

The Kemunkey used to be known mostly for fishing, but a lot of them farm now or work in mills, so it wasn't a complete surprise that we made it nearly to the dock before we saw any adults. When we were close enough to tie up, I heard Henry coming down the hill, bellowing like a carnival barker.

"Well look what we have here! Randolph Walker himself, and brought with him a princess wearing a garland of laurel."

I doubted Sophie had ever heard the word garland, but she knew he was talking about her and stood to make his acquaintance. It wasn't the best time for that gesture, not because Henry or anyone else would think it odd, but because Sevareid was leaning out of the canoe holding a tie line. Sophie's first step to that same side flipped the canoe clean over.

As icebreakers go, that one would have split a glacier. Every one of the thirty men, women and children on shore laughed like Sevareid and Sophie were the funniest act since the Lone Ranger and Tonto. Even old Chief Alli came off his cushioned seat inside his ceremonial teepee to see what the commotion was all about.

Sevareid was mad as a hornet, capsizing in front of a whole tribe of fishermen. What Sophie felt was hard to gauge since she only surfaced for a second before sinking again. Sevareid waited to make sure she wasn't just fooling, then took a stroke toward her, but Henry was already knifing into the water.

He resurfaced with Sophie under his left arm. With his right he reached across the water for her leaf hat, floating like a funeral wreath, and replaced it on her head. The Kemunkey laughed again, like they'd been waiting a month to see it. Even Sevareid looked pleased. Someone was taking Sophie off his hands.

"I apologize for our river. It's usually more polite to visitors," said Henry after pulling Sophie to shore. I remembered how he looked coming out of the water the first day with the big catfish in his grip. He'd gotten a lot bigger across the shoulders in the last four years and more scuffed up, but he still owned an ear to ear smile.

Henry said there wasn't time for Sophie to change out of her wet clothes, not if we wanted to hunt ducks, explore One Mile Cave and wrestle giant drumfish.

"We'll let the afternoon sun dry you off," he said and gave her hair a quick rub with his shirt. Sophie looked warmer already.

We hunted the ducks on a narrow tributary of the Mattowack, with canoes and shotguns. It's called jump shooting because the stern man, after paddling as close as he dares, signals to the gunner lying on the canoe bottom with the gun across his chest. In this case her chest.

Sophie missed her duck by the width of a football field. Nora would have missed hers too if she'd taken a shot. Just as we were getting into range, Sophie sneezed. Nora came off her back in perfect firing position but the wood ducks were a second too far gone. That she knew enough not to waste the shot impressed the hell out of me. But then I was in a pretty impressible mood.

After the ducks we explored the cave, which wasn't half as deep as advertised but did have great stalactites and stalagmites, and nice echoes of water dripping into pools.

"Don't let that torch go out," said Sophie, putting both hands on Henry's bicep. "This place gives me the creeps."

Nora wanted us to sit in a circle in the cave's deepest part and tell stories, but Henry said it was exactly the right time of day to wrestle drumfish. He took us back to the Mattowack and pulled off his shirt.

"If you get a big one, anything over a hundred pounds, hold tight with both hands and talk to it. That seems to calm them down."

I knew it was months early for big drumfish this far north and so did Henry. He was looking to wrestle something a little softer than a fish, and Sophie looked ready for the match. Every time I looked, they were poking or pinching each other. He held up his tipless pinkie finger and whispered something into Sophie's ear that made her squeal.

"What is it Americans say, 'they're getting along famously?'" Nora was down to her underwear and shirt. Though I was taller than her by an inch, her legs were longer than mine and much nicer to look at. I loved the way the river mud squished between her toes.

"He's conning us, isn't he?" asked Sevareid. "About the drumfish?"

"We're about six weeks early," I told him, "but it's a good excuse for a swim."

It was just past sunset when we visited Chief Alli in his teepee (he also had a nice log cabin for winter) and presented him some small gifts, including a fishing rod I'd made since my last visit.

"Okay, you're all honorary Kemunkey now," said the Chief who'd honorarized about half of surrounding county in the last thirty years. "Let's have a smoke on it."

Chief Alli brought out his peace pipe and special tobacco and passed it around our little circle. When I saw Nora and Sevareid weren't inhaling, I told them they should. But the pipe never came back. The dinner bell rang and everyone in the tent hurried toward the sound.

We ate under a thatched roof wide enough to cover fifty or so people in case of rain. On the menu were the ducks we'd shot and a variety of fish, some greens, corn bread and a Kemunkey corn whiskey that Henry called "keek." When I asked what the word meant, he took a big sip, squinted his face and screeched "keek!"

The stuff tasted better and better as the meal wore on.

After dinner we walked down the hill to a five-foot-high wood pile stacked like a teepee. I went around the circle, visiting the Kemunkey I hadn't already seen at dinner. A couple of old people had died since my last visit, about the same number as babies born. Hard times weren't as bad on the reservation because they fished and grew a lot of their food. But as Three Finger Billy told me, "It ain't been a year to brag about."

The fire was roaring when I came back to sit with Henry, Nora and Sevareid. I asked about Sophie.

"She said she wanted to put on some paint," said Henry, passing the jug. "I hope she isn't getting ready to go to war."

"I don't think she means that kind of paint," explained Nora.

"I wouldn't have thought so either if I hadn't spent the last six hours with her," said Henry, who held his deadpan expression as long as he could before breaking into laughter.

I asked where he'd gone after we left the Grand Canyon.

"I went south to see Mexican people and some of their cities. I ended up at a place called Isla Mujeres in the Yucatan. It means Island of Women."

"And was it?" asked Nora.

"It was an island of beautiful women. Unfortunately it was also an island of jealous men. But I saw great things in the Yucatan. Huge pyramids made by Indians like me."

"I don't think there are too many Indians like you," I said and was glad to get a laugh out of him.

Nora wanted to know about the night we ate mushrooms at the bottom of the Grand Canyon.

"I remember looking at Henry across the fire and his face changed into something else."

"Like what?" asked Sevareid.

"It was still his face, but very old and wrinkled like a dried prune. After that I didn't look at him again."

Henry wasn't the only thing that scared me that night. The taste of the mushrooms almost made me throw up, then I started sweating and had a hard time breathing. I closed my eyes for a second, which was a mistake—strange shapes came flying at me under my eyelids. But when I opened them again and looked into the fire, I saw something even scarier—myself leaning against the kitchen door while my father beat my mother on the other side. My mind knew it wasn't real, but I couldn't convince my body. It wanted to get up and run but there was nowhere to go except the darkness and we both agreed, mind and body, that darkness was the wrong place to be.

"I had my revelation the next morning. You remember Henry?"

"Sure. Maybe. Where was I?"

"Asleep in the sand. As the sun climbed higher, the canyon walls started changing color from dark grey, to red and then pink. That was my revelation."

"I don't get it," said Sevareid.

"Color is only illusion, right chief?" asked Henry.

"That and you get very hungry after sitting up all night having hallucinations."

~

WHEN NORA saw the pipe making its way around the campfire she took a few practice breaths. This was the ha ha tobacco Walker had told her about, smoke that made the world seem funny. As big as the circle was, maybe forty people, she wasn't sure the pipe would make it around again so she took a lung full of smoke and added a touch more. She'd smoked her father's pipe a few times as a girl but never tried to hold it in. This smoke wasn't as harsh, at least not immediately, but the longer she held it in her chest, the more it expanded until suddenly, with a great gacking sound, it exploded from her mouth and nose.

"That…" cough, cough, hack, gag, cough, deep breath, cough, short breath, cough, cough "…really hurt."

Eric took a short puff, blew it out then inhaled again. His coughing fit was only half as bad as Nora's. Walker handled the pipe like a Kemunkey and didn't cough at all.

"So when does it happen?" asked Nora.

"What?"

"Everything get funny."

Henry looked at Walker and shrugged his shoulders.

" I'm not feeling a thing," she complained. "Except for the hair in my nose."

"What about the hair in your nose?"

"It's tickling me."

Walker was the first to laugh, followed by Henry and then Eric. Once they started, they didn't stop until all three were bent nearly to the ground. What were those African animals…hyenas, thought

Nora, annoyed at being the only one sober. She looked away, looked back. Looked away, looked back. That was a funny thing, not ha ha but peculiar, the way her head kept turning left and then right as if controlled by an invisible motor.

"I may have no irony," she announced to her friends. "But my head has a life of its own."

That sent Eric, Walker and Henry back into a laughing fit and this time Nora joined them.

~

THE FIRST TIME Sevareid woke it was still dark and the fire only a bed of glowing embers. It took him a second to remember where he was and a little longer to recall what happened after they smoked the reefer. Had he really stood up and sung the Minnesota fight song? It was the first one that came to mind when it was his turn. Nora's song was the crowd pleaser, a Negro blues thing. The Kemunkey loved that, thumping on their drums and cracking wooden poles together. Walker...he couldn't remember what Walker sang but he acquitted himself well.

Henry and Sophie disappeared after the singing started. When it was time for sleep, he, Nora and Walker curled together like spoons, with Nora in the middle. They were all a little drunk from the corn whiskey and giddy, whispering back and forth. The Three...something or others. Too bad it had to change. But there's no getting around that, he thought, and slid back into sleep.

The second time he woke, the sky was showing a ribbon of pink and someone was talking in his ear.

"You want to get up now."

It was Henry.

"Why would I want to get up?" asked Sevareid.

"To get a ride home in a truck."

Sevareid understood every word but couldn't tie them together in any way that made sense. And why was Henry talking to him and not Walker. He looked over his shoulder and saw Walker coming up the hill from the river.

"I have a friend who's driving a truck to Washington," said Henry, loud enough for Walker to hear. "It will save you about sixteen hours of paddling upstream. But you'll have to leave now."

"Sounds good to me," said Sevareid.

"Do we need to check with Nora?" asked Walker.

"Naw. You pick up her feet, I'll take her head. She won't wake until we're back home."

"Great," said Walker. "But I better take her head. You can be a little clumsy."

"I'll help you load your boat," said Henry. "And don't worry about Sophie. She'll be staying here with me."

JENNY

THE FIRST THING Nora wanted to do when we got back from the Kemunkey reservation was dive for her cup. Sevareid, who still hadn't seen it, was all in favor. That left me to play the bad cop.

"Where are you going to keep it? What if that Englishman found out something while we were gone? Wouldn't it be smarter to keep it safe for at least another two days?"

Nora bit her lip and rubbed her hands together but couldn't come up with any better argument than a big fish might eat it. Sevareid wondered how many fish in the Potomac were partial to silver cups and before we could run away with that idea, Nora backed down.

"I'm going back to the Bonus Camp," she said. "I need at least a day to recover from the pair of you."

Sevareid and I paddled across the Potomac and unpacked the boat, all the while joking about Henry and Sophie, the reefer we'd smoked and farmer Joe's buckshot. Later we took a swim in one of the feeder canals, riding the rapids belly down. By the time we went to bed we were as tired as twins.

But when we got up the next morning, I looked at him and he looked at me and damn if we weren't back to working the same piece of rope.

"I guess I'll head over to the Bonus Camp and see if I can rustle up a story," said Sevareid.

"I'm going there myself," I told him. "On my way to the Party office." He didn't want to go with me any more than I wanted to go with him, but neither of us could risk letting the other find Nora first.

Nora was with Dennis Diamond, the white-bearded vet pretending to be her father. They were drinking coffee and tossing bits of wood onto the fire. She was glad to see us until we got close enough for her to see our faces. Cloudy and threatening rain. Nora was wearing a linen skirt and her hair tied back with a piece of string. She'd lost about five pounds of butter fat since the first time I saw her. With all the sun she'd gotten in the last few weeks, her skin was nearly as brown as my own. She'd never looked more beautiful.

"Let's take a walk," she said, and led us like a couple of kids trailing a schoolmarm. She stopped beside the log cabin where someone had tacked up a drawing of President Hoover's head that looked like a squashed pumpkin. "I need a few days to think about things," she said, and didn't have to explain which things. "Why don't we meet up Tuesday when the Senate votes on the Bonus bill."

There was nothing to like about that idea but nothing to do about it either. She gave us each a hug and went back to Santa Claus. Sevareid and I walked toward the bridge.

"Max Berga, that reporter at the *Herald*, said I could stay at his place in Adams Morgan a few nights. I might do that," said Sevareid.

"You'd be a lot closer to downtown that way."

"That's what I was thinking."

We stood looking at the bridge, at our own feet and then each other's. I'd never noticed how big his were. I wished him luck and he knew I meant it in a limited way—luck in finding stories, keeping out of the way of trolleys and the D.C. jail. Luck in love he'd have to wish for himself.

I'd have gone to the Party office but didn't want to call anyone comrade just then, so I walked toward the Maine Avenue docks to take a look at my old ferry boat, the *Edie*, which I hadn't seen since getting out of jail. The closer I got to the water, the more I thought about Jenny Broom.

How I became a communist started with wanting to sleep with Jenny Broom. Not directly, but then Jenny liked to say that everything a man did eventually got back to the stiffness of his cock. The word she used for cock was "thingy."

"Climbing mountains, writing poetry, robbing banks, it's all the same—a man trying to get his soft thingy hard or his hard thingy soft."

Two and sometimes three days a week she came aboard the ferry boat while I was napping. She was so quiet I sometimes didn't wake until she was sitting in her spot near the wheel, reading one of her detective novels or a pamphlet on tea readings and astrology.

I told her I could understand the first part, wanting to get the soft thing hard, but the hard thing soft?

"To save it from being broke off," she told me, like it was the most obvious thing in the world. "That's why some men don't trust women. They're afraid we'll break it off."

My job was to pilot customers and workers from Washington docks to the *Lighthouse*, a double-decker gambling and prostitution barge anchored in the Potomac just off the Alexandria shore. I got the job two-and-a-half years after I started running numbers. The new job didn't pay as much as numbers, but I was glad to be back on the water and happy to see Jenny Broom twice a day, especially days she came early. On those days she sometimes talked to me about her job and the different levels of pleasure.

"Some of the girls don't enjoy it one bit, not in any way whatsoever. One of them said to me the other night, 'Jenny, it's the same as if somebody was poking me with a stick.'"

"But you don't think that?"

"It's all what you make it. Now me, I try to study a man and understand what he wants. The secret things he wouldn't even tell a whore. Once I figure them out, the rest is easy."

"So you get pleasure giving them exactly what they want?"

"I didn't say that. It's not what I give them, it's what I hold back. That's why so many come here just for me. I get pleasure knowing that."

I was 17 when I started piloting the *Edie*. Jenny was just 21 but carried herself like a grown woman. She had olive skin, high cheek bones, curvy lips and eyes the color of wet sand. Once I nearly ran the boat into a river buoy because I had my head turned to look at them. She didn't sit and gossip with the other prostitutes on the ride back each night, but I noticed they sometimes went to her with their problems.

"I'd like to run my own whorehouse. That's a thing I'd be good at," she told me one day as I ferried a small chest of drawers for her to the *Lighthouse*. Doing favors for people who worked there was an unofficial part of the job. The prostitutes and musicians, the kitchen help and waiters would ask if I minded showing up early or working late, to take something across the water for them. Hutch, the cook, had me ferry over a little pig one morning. He said he was going to keep it for a week or two, then butcher it. But weeks and months went by and the pig kept getting bigger and bigger, eating all of Hutch's leftovers, until one day it was too big to get out of the anteroom where Hutch kept her. I named her Petunia and teased Hutch about being sweet on a pig.

Running liquor wasn't an official part of my job either, until the night Pete McGovern told me it was.

"The cargo comes in Tuesdays and Fridays, at different places and different times. Your job is to get it to the *Lighthouse*. All of it." McGovern was right-hand man to Kelly Coleman, the head of Washington's Irish mafia. Oliver T. Hardy owned the *Lighthouse* but it was Coleman who controlled the liquor and gambling. Later I learned that Coleman used both Fat Carlos and Juan Wilson to manage distribution. That arrangement would eventually bring me grief.

I'd never met Kelly Coleman and only saw McGovern twice, the second time when he handed me a pistol in a paper bag. "Let people see you've got it. That way you'll never have to use it."

I was surprised how much I liked that gun. The black shine of it and the weight it put in my jacket pocket. I practiced drawing and shooting in the Virginia woods, slow and steady and then fast and wild.

My first liquor run was on a perfectly dark night, with clouds low enough to nearly touch my head. At about 10:30, I dropped a load of passengers at the *Lighthouse* and motored to a spot just above Slattery Point. McGovern had told me to look for a square-ended barge. The first one I saw belonged to the Skeffington brothers.

"Tie up downriver," said John Skeffington. "You'll get away easier if you have to shove off quick."

I tied up fore and aft and began loading the cases of bottled whiskey and beer. John helped while his brother George kept the wheel. Though Mr. Luke worked with the Skeffingtons for years, no one listening would have guessed we'd ever met. We loaded forty five cases in less than fifteen minutes.

"If you get caught, don't bother trying to throw anything overboard," said John. "You won't have time."

"Don't the police get paid off?"

"They do. But there's other people out here besides the police, this much whiskey is a temptation. And the police might get you too. Whenever they want a raise, they make a few arrests. A week in jail is the worst you'll get."

I thought about that on the way to the *Lighthouse*. A week in jail was seven days too many. There had to be a quick way to ditch the liquor. Maybe I could tow it behind on a raft. But the police or thieves would just retrieve it. What about a raised deck, with all the boxes stacked on a slope? One tug of a rope and the cargo could slide into the sea. But the platform couldn't be obvious or in the way. I remembered a raft Tommy and I built when we were kids and thought it could be done.

~

ONE MORNING Jenny showed up at the ferry on a horse cart carrying a clothes bureau that weighed about eighty pounds. I told her it was too bulky and heavy for me to carry to the second deck, that we'd have to get some help.

"Too heavy? Not for the two of us. Feel this," she said making a muscle of her bicep. When I squeezed her arm, a jolt went through me and I yanked my hand away. Jenny laughed, wrongly thinking I was trying to be funny.

After a beautiful sunrise it was clouding up in the west. Jenny looked gorgeous in her long black dress, which was too tight for her to sit comfortably. When she pulled it above her knees, she caught me staring.

"So what's your idea of heaven?" she asked. We'd been talking lately about religion.

"Besides this? Taking a beautiful woman on a boat ride."

"You are easily pleased."

"I don't believe in heaven or hell. And even if I did, who's smart enough to tell me what they're like?"

"If there's no heaven or hell, then why should we even try to be good?"

"Because it feels better to be good than bad?"

"You should be a preacher," said Jenny with her rough and honey laugh.

We'd had this conversation a few days earlier after Jenny took me to see Sweet Daddy Grace at his United House of Prayer for All People, a repainted pool room. People spoke in tongues while others sold "Daddy Grace" coffee, tea and healing creams. Jenny wasn't a member of the congregation but she was curious, in the same way she was curious about astrology, psychic healing and time travel. To Jenny it was all worth a shot. I didn't have to ask which one was Sweet Daddy. He came into the room from the rear, dressed in a purple cutaway with gold cufflinks and epaulets. He was a Negro from Cape Verde Islands. His fingernails were about four inches long and painted white. People fell in a faint when he touched them. He said a bunch of stuff about equality and donating to his church, but what really got my attention was something he said at the end of the service.

"Grace has given God a vacation, and since God is on His vacation don't worry Him…. If you sin against God, Grace can save you. But if you sin against Grace, God cannot save you."

"I had a dream about God," I told Jenny as we motored toward the *Lighthouse*. "He was on a beach drinking rum while Daddy Grace punched his time card."

Jenny laughed. "Don't they say God works in mysterious ways?"

True to her word, when we tied up at the *Lighthouse* Jenny grabbed one end of the bureau and helped me hump it up the stairs. I'd only been in her room once before, on the day I delivered the chest of drawers. Today there was a fresh flower on it. A painting hung near the door, a bright water color of a stream running through a meadow.

"Sometimes I look at that when I'm working and imagine myself on a mountain somewhere. With this job you want a good imagination." We were pushing and pulling the bureau, trying to get it around a corner of the bed.

"Is it hard to be with different people every night?"

In a grunting breath she answered, "Didn't your daddy tell you never to ask a whore if it's hard?"

We'd just about made the turn when she said it. I started laughing and leaned into the bureau. She gave it a shove that sent me backward onto the bed.

Jenny sat next to me. "You don't get out much, do you?" I reached out my hand and touched her face. She looked surprised but didn't push me away, so I slid my fingers down her face to her throat. All the clichés I'd read in books about being on fire and weak with desire didn't seem so ridiculous anymore. Jenny just sat there, like she was making up her mind. Finally, she stood and went to the door. Instead of booting me out, she wedged a chair under the door knob (none of the rooms on the *Lighthouse* had locks) and came back unbuttoning her dress.

"We've got to be fast about this," she said. "Don't just lay there, come on." She was naked before I had my pants off. Her body was even more beautiful than I'd imagined it, and I'd imagined it plenty of times. Every line of her body led to the dark hair between her legs. My desire was painful, but still I held back. The look on her face was cool and steady, like she knew exactly what I was thinking.

I said, "Maybe we shouldn't do this."

Jenny's eyebrows went up high and she covered her breasts with her hands. "Is this your first time?"

That one thing, covering herself, made me want her even more. "It's not my first time," I lied.

"Then what?"

"It's just, you know, me being a Negro."

Jenny put her hands to her mouth to keep from laughing out loud. "Lord, boy, don't you know I'm part Negro myself?"

I didn't ask any more questions.

~

THE PICKUP was scheduled for midnight on the dark side of Key Bridge. I was wary because of rumors I'd been hearing, and because the police boat had stopped me two nights earlier. I had nothing to hide that night except my gun, which I always kept stashed in one of the life buoys.

The Skeffington brothers were just as nervous. George suspected that Juan Wilson, the Jamaican, was looking to steal a load of whiskey. In the last three months, Wilson had been openly grabbing turf from Fat Carlos as if he wanted to pick a fight. My little boat was open game.

Before we started loading the whiskey, the brothers took some time to look at the tilted platform I'd finished the week before. I showed them the latch springs and the weighted net, designed to keep all the cases together underwater. John was most impressed with how the platform folded down to look like a hatch cover. He said Mr. Luke would have been proud.

I drifted downriver, letting the current take me. A half moon drifted in and out of clouds. I thought of the catfish Jenny caught that afternoon. She'd never looked happier than holding that fish. Meanwhile, I'd never been more tormented than the two weeks since we had sex on the *Lighthouse*. Jenny told me it was sweet and good, but she also said it wouldn't happen again.

I demanded to know why I was the only one she wouldn't do it with, and offered her a handful of money. She looked like she might cry.

"I have friends and I have customers. I thought we were friends."

To patch things up, I took her for a boat ride to where the big catfish were mating by the power plant. While I showed her how to bait a hook with chicken livers, I studied her hands. Which part of her was Negro? She'd told me her grandfather was a freed slave and her great-grandmother was one-eighth Indian. So that made her....a human fraction. And like me, nothing in particular. On the ride back to the dock she said, "What you need is a girlfriend. A nice little 17-year-old virgin. The problem is I don't run into too many of those in my line of work."

I was thinking about that when I heard a motor downriver. The police boat was cruising again. I took my best chance and drifted close to the Virginia shore. I'd have easily snuck by if the moon hadn't peeked out. I started my engine, and at the same time yanked the rope, hoping to cover the sound of the cases going overboard. By the time the police caught up to me, I was two hundred yards from where I'd dropped the whiskey.

Officer Farquar, a big, square-shouldered cop who was called "boxhead" behind his back, knew something had happened but couldn't figure what. He searched the *Edie* up and down, then dragged a long-handled hook from bow to stern. Disappointed wasn't the word for the state he was in. He looked at me like I'd kidnapped his favorite hunting dog, and said my luck had about run out.

With no chance of getting the whiskey that night, I steered toward the *Lighthouse*. A wet gust of wind carried a muffled sound of music. At maybe thirty yards I heard a scream quite clearly, and not the kind that comes from gamblers or drunks. It was the scream of a scared woman, a long, piercing sound I didn't recognize until it stopped. I throttled up the engine and went broadside to the *Lighthouse*, grabbed my gun and jumped into the crowd bunched on the lower deck. The cook's pig Petunia squealed as I ran past the galley and up the steps. Pete McGovern stood just inside Jenny's open door. I looked past him and saw everything at once—Jenny naked on the floor below the bureau I'd helped her move, her chest and stomach covered in blood. Beyond her stood a man wearing only black sox. He was big and hairy-chested and held a bloody knife at his side. The man was shivering, looking from Jenny to Pete McGovern and back again. I pulled the gun from my belt and aimed it at his head. Did I intend to kill him? I don't know. I felt completely calm, like this was something I was meant to do. The man dropped the knife and threw his arms across his face. I thought to myself—pull the trigger, slow and steady just like in the woods. If I hesitated, it was only for a second.

~

I WOKE in a police holding cell with two white men standing above my canvas cot. They were arguing over which one would get my leather boat shoes. My head hurt when I opened my eyes and exploded when I tried to lift it. But I wasn't giving up my shoes. I'd never been in jail before, but I knew the first day there was no different than the first day on a new playground—you couldn't get it back.

"Take off those shoes, nigger."

The bigger of the two was bent over me. He was maybe 30, a scar through his right eyebrow and acting confident as you please. But no man shopping for shoes in a jail cell could be that confident. I sucked up all my strength and whip-kicked him between the legs, jumped up and elbowed the side of his head. Now it was my turn to fake confidence. My energy was draining from me like water down a hole and a hard breath might have knocked me over. But the man I kicked was on the floor and the other had retreated to a corner.

There was a second colored man in the cell, sitting as close as he could to the dim corridor light, squinting over a book. As far as I could tell, he hadn't taken his eyes off the page. It occurred to me that this would be a good place to have a book.

Before I learned anything about the charges brought against me, I discovered what it was that always scared me about jail. Not being locked up, or even attacked by other prisoners, but the act of landing there. Every time that cell door opened and closed, the sound hit me like a hammer. I'd always believed I was special, that when the time came I could find a way to rise above anything. Tommy called me on it once when we were running numbers. He said, "Your problem is you think you're better than a nigger."

It wasn't that so much as thinking I was different. Not white, not colored but some special mix that kept me separate from both. Finding myself in jail put me below everybody. Hard as I'd been pumping my arms and legs, I'd finally hit bottom.

My cell was in the basement of D.C. lockup, one of six cells that served as a temporary holding area for prisoners awaiting trial. I was there for two full days without any word about what to expect. Did I kill that hairy man? I must have, otherwise why would I be there. The only thing I remembered was the room going black. I tried not to think about that or anything else. For most of a day I sat unmoving on the edge of my cot, pretending I was in a tree somewhere hunting deer. When Rufus McPherson came over with his book, I was ready to be distracted.

"You know how to read?"

"Why?"

"There's a few words here I don't understand. I thought maybe you could help."

"Because I've got light skin, you think I can read big words?"

"Am I wrong?"

I took the book from him and opened it to the marked page. Rufus squatted beside me with a half smile on his face, like he'd played a trick and wanted me to know it. I looked at the cover, *Manifesto of the Communist Party* by Karl Marx and Friedrich Engels.

"Which part don't you know?"

"That first paragraph. Read the whole thing."

I didn't want to do what he told me, but it was hard to resist a printed page.

1. BOURGEOIS AND PROLETARIANS

The history of all hitherto existing society is the history of class struggles. Free man and slave, patrician and plebeian, lord and serf, guild master and journeyman, in a word, oppressor and oppressed, stood in constant opposition to one another, carried on an uninterrupted, now hidden, now open fight, a fight that each time ended either in a revolutionary reconstitution of society at large or in the common ruin of the contending classes.

I knew of Karl Marx and Friedrich Engels, Lenin and Trotsky. But I'd never read them. Why study the rules to a game I wasn't allowed to play?

I asked Rufus what this had to do with him or me.

"Only everything!" He was almost spitting with excitement. "The difference between Communism and what we got now is the difference between the bicycle and the automobile. And with Communism, Negroes will get to ride up front."

I asked why he thought Communists would be any different.

"Didn't I just read that the history of society is class struggle? As soon as Communists get to the head of the class, we'll go back to struggling."

"You read this," said Rufus, pressing the book into my hands. "Then you tell me if you still believe that."

I read the book. Fifty pages so dry I felt like I had cotton in my mouth. How could stuff like "conditions of appropriation" and "superincumbent strata" have lit such a fire under Rufus?

The first direct attempts of the proletariat to attain its own ends, made in times of universal excitement, when feudal society was being overthrown, these attempts necessarily failed, owing to the then undeveloped state of the proletariat, as well as to the absence of the economic conditions for its emancipation, conditions that had yet to be produced, and could be produced by the impending bourgeois epoch alone.

Dry and thick at the same time. Maybe it was better in Russian, over a glass of vodka. It sure didn't do anything for me except take my mind off the stink and damp of the cell and the fact that I'd probably killed a man. And that was reason enough to read it again.

My two white cellmates left for a court hearing. When they came back they gave me a queer look. Rufus found out why.

"They don't know about any man being shot. You've been charged with the murder of some *Lighthouse* whore."

I was eventually found not guilty, thanks to the efforts of my fishing patron Martin Hiatt and a detective he hired. But for the two weeks I waited in that cell for the trial to begin, Rufus' book was the only thing that gave me any hope.

BURIED MAN

HIS FATHER called it a "heebie jeebie" and said everybody had one. Eric Sevareid was eight years old when he found his. On a cold night in December little Sevie (the first of half a dozen nicknames he'd take on and then shuck) snuck from his bed, lit a kerosene lamp and opened the book he was reading to page 236. A north wind swept across the North Dakota wheat fields rattling the outside shutters. A quarter moon threw the skeletal shadow of a leafless oak tree against his bedroom wall. The book that did him in was *Blackbeard*, specifically the scene where the pirate is buried to his neck in sand as the incoming tide laps against his face.

Sevareid closed his eyes and imagined it, his arms trapped at his sides, the fish and crabs and whatever else lived in oceans, ripping chunks from his face. He never felt scared by the thought exactly, just sick to his stomach, like he'd swallowed too much saltwater. From that night on, Sevareid suffered from claustrophobia, but of a type so narrow he only had to steer clear of open ditches and tall sand dunes (which was easy enough in the midwest) to be free of it.

"Everybody's afraid of something," said his father. "You're lucky to have found a thing as rare as being buried alive."

Every time Sevareid imagined he'd outgrown his childhood fear, something would happen to disabuse him, like the day he used too much dynamite while gold mining in California. He was stuck in the creek bed for less than a minute, the dirt and rubble burying him only to his arm pits, but it took all his concentration not to throw up as his partner dug him free.

So Sevareid was less than eager to do a follow-up story on Joe Angelo, the veteran who'd buried himself. Every time his Minnesota editor suggested it, Sevareid telegraphed that the time wasn't yet ripe. But after saying goodbye to Nora and Walker at the camp, he heard someone mention Angelo's name and a minute later heard it again. Something was up with the buried man and he couldn't afford to ignore it.

He was moving toward the southwest corner of camp when he saw Joe Angelo, resurrected. He was standing beside an open pit, his face and hair streaked with dirt and his eyes blurred red, look-ing exactly like a man who'd been buried alive.

"The Health Department dug me up. Said I was endangering myself." Angelo's lips were caked with a fine mud that cracked and flaked as he spoke. "Ain't that a laugh. Now I'm safe to starve."

The bottom of the pit was about two inches deep with scum-my water. Every few seconds, dirt from the walls slid down with a splash. Sevareid felt his stomach jump and turned his back to the hole.

"How much money did you make?"

Angelo looked at the two veterans standing with him and

laughed bitterly. "You'd have to ask my good buddy Tim Kelty. He's the one who held the money. Once the Health boys started digging, buddy Tim disappeared."

"He stole it?" The shock in Sevareid's voice gave all three veterans a laugh.

"Yeah, he stole it. At least he didn't take my fillings like that cocksucking dentist."

"What dentist?"

"Where you been? This dentist comes down from some damn place and volunteers to fix all the veterans' teeth for free. First he takes out all the gold fillings. Next thing he does is disappear. Just like my friend Tim."

They were interrupted by the sound of Police Superintendent Glassford's big blue motorcycle, coming across the 11th Street Bridge. Sevareid was relieved when Joe Angelo and his friends walked away from the pit to meet him. He asked Angelo what he planned to do next.

"I think I'll take a swim in that river, then go look for my buddy Tim."

Two hundred men gathered where Glassford stopped.

"Captain Marks is coming by in a minute to make you an offer," said Glassford to a good-natured chorus of boos. "He's been asked by the city commissioners to come and make that offer. What you do with it is entirely up to you. No hard feelings. Those of you who know Captain Marks know he's a good man, a veteran like yourselves."

Captain Marks arrived on the running board of a closed police car, followed by eight empty trucks.

"If you are tired or distressed. If you want to get back to your homes, we have trucks...." When a wave of laughter drowned him out, Marks laughed along with the men. "Well, I suspected that, and so far as I'm concerned I don't want to see you leave. I hope you stay here and get your bonus."

The ovation for that was loud and long. Someone suggested naming the encampment "Camp Marks." Walt Waters called for a voice vote which passed without dissent.

MOVIES

NOW THAT Nora had time to think, she didn't want to. Walker or Eric. It wasn't fair to ask her to choose, and impossible even if she tried. Eric and Walker were mixed together like sugar in milk. The feeling she had hugging Walker? Exactly the same as hugging Eric. Maybe not exactly, quite different now that she thought about it, but only different in the way of musical notes in the same scale. Shouldn't she be pleased with such a dilemma? In Ireland her choices would have been herding sheep or helping Jack Allman prepare lessons for his class. But Nora didn't trust herself to make any choices just now, even good ones. For the first time in her life, she worried that things were happening too fast.

So Nora did what she'd become practiced at since coming to America—she put it out of mind. Eric and Walker? Into the same bin as thoughts of her parents in Ireland awaiting her return.

She needed to stay busy, find something to keep herself from revisiting her buried thoughts. Will Cutler's hideout sprang to mind. She'd been thinking of him and his gang of boys since her dream last night. A boy with a red scarf over his face bicycled circles around her on a Limerick street. He never came close enough to grab and the scarf stayed high across his cheeks, but she knew, in the way you know things in dreams, that it was her brother Brendan.

Nora had been having unusually vivid dreams of late, including one that featured her best friend Brigid, lying naked in a field of flowers beneath a statue of Jack Allman. But the dream of her brother was the first to shake her awake. She'd opened her eyes in the dark of the Bonus Camp to a chorus of snores. One in particular sounded very much like her father's. Into the bin with that as well.

She left the camp for Will Cutler's alley, dressed in one of her cotton shirts with the sleeves pulled above her elbows, and a wraparound skirt she'd taken from a clothes bin at the camp. It was too hot for wool and though she'd never admit it, Nora had taken to heart what Neil Gold told her at the Criers Club. "You can wear men's pants when you're 60. But now is your time to wear dresses and pretty blouses." Friends back home had said the same thing, but it sounded different coming from the nearly handsome owner of a classy speakeasy who'd taken her horseback riding and kissed her full on the mouth.

She was a block from the alley when Will emerged from it. Behind him came Pinky and Jamie pulling a newspaper wagon that held a large, metal box.

"Nora. You look so…different," marveled Will. He was wearing oversized brown-and-white spats, red suspenders and a derby hat. He reminded Nora of a character she'd seen in one of the newspaper funny pages.

"I'd perish in my wool pants," she said, shaking his hand. "Hello Pinky, hello Jamie. What have you in the cart?"

"It's a cinema," said Jamie.

Nora heard him clearly enough to know he wasn't making any sense. To Will she whispered, "Is he not getting any better?"

"Of course he is," said Will. "And he does have a cinema in the box. A cinema camera."

"How did you come upon such a thing?"

"Walk with me and I'll tell you. Better yet, I'll show you," said Will. "We're going to the Mighty My Temple right now to make a cinema of Virni Tabak."

They walked north on 13th Street through a tunnel of overarching elms whose leaves were a fresh wet green. Will explained how the camera had passed from Brian Donaldson, a maker of training films for the United States Army, to Neil Gold and finally to Will himself.

"This Donaldson owed Mr. Gold some money. Probably a lot of money, because these cameras are not exactly cheap."

"Why did Mr. Gold give it to you?"

"He didn't exactly give it to me. He wants me to get good at it and then…. I don't know. Except that he wants something out of this."

"Is it one of the talkie kind of cinema makers?"

"Silent, but we've got a way around that," said Will. "Jamie, show her the recorder."

Pinky stopped the wagon. Jamie opened a second, smaller metal box. Inside were tubes and wires and something octagonal-shaped that Nora guessed was a microphone.

"What you do," explained Jamie, "is use this recording thing and play it back with the movie and then it's just like a talkie, see?"

"Jamie is our recorder guy," said Will. "Pinky works the camera. I'm the director."

"And how many of these cinemas have you made?"

"This will be our first."

At the top of Cardozo Hill they paused to rest and look at the city below.

"There's the Capitol, the Washington Monument, the Lincoln Memorial," said Nora, less the awed tourist than an explorer studying landmarks. "All spread out like a stage, don't you think? Somebody should make a movie down there."

"About what?"

"I don't know. Maybe the Bonus Army."

"That's kind of a ragged thing," said Will.

"Aren't Charlie Chaplin's movies about ragged things?"

"I guess…." Nora could see Will trying to work something out, his lips twisting down as his eyebrows scrunched up. She'd seen that face once before, when Will was figuring how to make money by inventing a machine to automatically scoop up horse manure.

The Mighty My Temple was past the crest of the hill in a former Masonic Lodge. It was the first time Nora had seen it in daylight. The temple's iron doors were closed tight, but Will knew where to find the bell.

Madame Olga Blisky opened a door, nicely disguised within one of the large ones. She was wearing a loose-fitting white robe and a necklace cut from something black and hard. Instead of stepping back to let them enter, she reached out and pulled them inside, taking one of Will's hands between her own and kissing Nora on both cheeks. Jamie and Pinky waited just outside.

"Such an aura you have. Blue like a sapphire. Are you a believer?"

"I am. But of what I'm not exactly sure," said Nora, suddenly shy before this tall, blonde woman who was quite beautiful in a thin, severe way. Nora was fascinated by her thick, strawberry lips and her accent which she guessed was Russian, only because every accent beyond the few she recognized sounded Russian.

"I am Madame Blisky. Welcome to the Mighty My Temple." She nodded to Jamie and Pinky, before turning her attention to Will. "How much light will you need?"

"As much as you can give me."

"It will have to be a spotlight. Nothing on the ceiling."

"That's fine. We'll figure it out."

She led them down a marbled hall unlike any Nora had ever seen, squared and quarry white like a headquarters building in heaven. They passed through a large door into an auditorium where fifty women sat facing an elevated stage, empty except for a wooden table and chair.

Pinky set up the camera in the middle aisle while Jamie unpacked the recorder. Will went to study a pair of spotlights leaning against a wall. Nora was eager to study the camera, but Madame Blisky led her to the rear of the auditorium.

"This is a private audience," she whispered. "Transcendentalists."

"What do they hope to gain from this?"

"That's an interesting way to put it," said the Madame, not unkindly. "They're hoping to see the unseeable."

Nora liked that. To see the unseeable. The lights dimmed.

Virni Tabak entered through a curtain at the back of the stage, wearing a bright purple blouse, silk pants and dark slippers. He stopped and bowed to the audience with his hands joined as if in prayer, then sat behind the table. He looked beautiful to Nora, his hair thick and black above the blouse. Will switched on one of spotlights. Madame Blisky put her arm around Nora's waist.

"Welcome," said Virni. "I am here to tell you that there is no present, no future, no past. There is only time. And time is an illusion." His onstage voice was so much more full and deep than his regular one. "Time and space are like windows in a room. We can open those windows together. But I will need your help. Please chant with me. *Hoooo, hoooo….*"

As the audience joined in, the chant sounded to Nora like owls singing off key. She might have laughed if not for Madame Blisky's right hand which was now pressed against her belly.

"Close your eyes," whispered the Madame. "And chant with him."

Nora did as she was told, helped along by Madame Blisky's hand, which seemed to be moving her stomach in and out. There was something interesting in this, a tingle in her fingertips and a relaxation of her stomach muscles. But it might have been Madame Blisky's touch more than the chanting.

"Six hundred years ago, on the land where this temple sits, a warrior sacrificed his life for God." Virni's voice had dropped even more and seemed to be coming from far away. "Concentrate on bringing something of that warrior through a window in time."

Nora tried to imagine a six-hundred-year-old soldier being sucked through time, but all she could picture was an Arthurian knight falling off his horse into a lake. Maybe time was like that, something that reflected back the world so you couldn't see it, until after you passed through. This chanting thing was a bit like the funny tobacco they'd smoked with Kemunkey Henry. She was wondering where she might get some more when she heard a sharp thump, followed by a gasp from the audience. She opened her eyes and saw a sword, gold and in the shape of a scimitar, stuck in the table. It was still quivering before Virni Tabak's closed eyes.

The chanting was replaced by an excited chatter. Virni called for silence, insisting there was more work to do, and led them in another round. Nora kept open her left eye, the one furthest from Madame Blisky. It was dark above Virni's head but not impenetrable. If there was somebody in the ceiling, or a trap door, she was certain she'd see it. But when the white flower floated down, landing softly on the table, Nora had no idea where it came from.

"Thank you for helping to make this happen," said Virni rising

196 c *Nora's Army*

from his chair, the sword in one hand and the flower in the other. "Did you feel it? The power we have unlocked? I ask you now to go and meditate upon it, as I will."

Just before he turned to leave the stage, Virni looked directly at Nora and made a small movement with the flower. He wanted her to wait for him outside. How she knew that from a twist of his hand, she couldn't say.

~

"THAT WAS quite a show in there," said Will when Virni met them outside the Temple.

"It is a good trick, especially today," said Virni softly. "The sword doesn't always stick."

Virni had changed into baggy silk harem pants and tied a black cape around his shoulders. He wanted to know how he looked.

"You look...fine," said Will awkwardly.

Nora was more blunt. "Like an Indian prince set loose in a costume shop. Don't you have any normal clothes?"

"I'm not supposed to look normal," he said. "Now, where are we going? Is it too early for the Criers Club?"

"It sure as heck is," said Will.

"You know where I'd like to go," said Nora. "I'd like to go to a movie."

Virni clapped his hands. "Wonderful. Which movie? We shall let Nora pick. *Tarzan*? *Grand Hotel*?"

"I want to see *The Front Page*," she said. "That's about newspaper reporters, right?"

"*The Front Page* it is," said Will. "That's showing down by Dupont Circle. Let's go find Catherine. You know how much she likes movies."

Jamie and Pinky had already started down Cardozo Hill. Now Nora followed between Will and Virni, a hand on each of their arms.

"Okay, Will, it's your turn to tell a story," said Nora. "Virni went last time."

Will didn't need persuading.

"My father was a minister man, back in West Virginia. It was a real strict kind of religion. No dancing or singing or any of that. I'd listen to the colored field workers singing their songs and it would just about kill me not to join in. Of course I have a terrible singing voice, so religion wasn't the only thing stopping me. Anyway, one day we had a flood. It come down the mountain and brought a whole lot of mud and rocks with it. It knocked the back wall off my daddy's church. He said it was a sign and I took it as such. I left the next day and came up here."

"What about your mother?"

"She was already gone. Died when I was just a baby. At least that's one story. I heard an uncle once say something that made me think she hadn't died but just lit out. But he was a drunk and said a lot of crazy things."

Nora asked how old he was when he left.

"I was 14 when I got here, about a month before the stock market went kerflooey."

"What was that like?" asked Virni.

"One day everybody was thinking they were gonna be rich. Secretaries and street sweepers, buying shares on their lunch break. The next day everybody was looking in the gutter for pennies. It kind of put everybody in the same place as me, money wise."

"You were lucky," suggested Virni. "You were the only one who didn't lose anything."

"I don't know about that," said Will. "I'd have liked to know what it feels like to be rich."

Nora asked Virni about Madame Blisky. "Does she do what you do, make things fall from the ceiling?"

"She does different things. In England, before we came here, she conducted seances to contact the spirits of soldiers killed in the war. But the war has been over for twelve years, so it's time to change."

"You mean a mother would come to Madame Blisky to contact the ghost of her son?" asked Nora.

"A mother, father, wife, child. There were millions killed in the War and many of them weren't officially buried. That's a lot of loose spirits."

Will slowed his walk. "So she actually talks to dead people?"

"Something like that," said Virni.

"But I thought you said it was all tricks," said Nora.

"No. It's not all tricks. But it's not always real either. You can't just snap your fingers and make a sword from the Crusades drop out of the sky."

"That's a little ahead of me," said Will, steering them across Dupont Circle, past a man in rags who stood in the fountain singing. "But I always say each to his own and all to all."

∼

THEY LEFT the theater talking all at once.

"It went so fast, I feel out of breath," said Will. For the second half of *The Front Page*, during the entire time convicted killer Roy Williams was hiding in the pressroom desk, Will sat with his derby hat between his knees, rocking back and forth.

"I want to play poker. Like those reporters," said Virni. "And smoke a big cigar."

Nora confessed she'd fallen in love with one of the stars of the second movie—*Possessed*. But not Clark Gable. "Wasn't Joan Crawford brilliant? Didn't you desire her?"

Will and Virni considered their desire.

"The actress or the woman she played?"

"Either. Both."

"Telling Clark Gable she was only interested if he was rich?" Will shook his head disapprovingly. "I couldn't love a girl like that."

"She was only doing what men do all the time. Only men insist on a woman being beautiful. What's the difference?"

"The difference is chemistry," said Virni. "People don't decide to fall in love."

Nora wasn't convinced, but knew there was no arguing it. "I

liked what Joan Crawford said to her first boyfriend, 'If I was a man you wouldn't think there was anything wrong with me getting everything I could out of life. And using anything I had to get it.'"

"Yes but she isn't a man. That's the difference," said Virni.

"That's not a chemistry difference. That's just rules that men make."

At the corner of Connecticut Avenue and L Street, Virni asked if they might look again for Catherine.

"Let's do," said Nora. "And then we can see another movie."

THE DUKE

"YOU'RE A REAL GO-GETTER, aren't you, Slim?"

Sevareid hadn't been called Slim since he jumped off the rail-car at Union Station. He was determined not to let the nickname resurrect itself here. But he didn't want to sound defensive in front of Max Berga, especially when the reporter was buying him lunch.

"I'm going nowhere," said Sevareid, who'd come to Bassin's Restaurant to give Berga a heads up on the Joe Angelo story. He figured he owed him for his help those first days in Washington. "I've got no place to live, no real contacts and the clerk at the Associated Press office hates my guts for some unknown reason."

"He's jealous," said Berga. "He's been applying for jobs as a reporter for three years. Now you come along and start writing stories."

"I'm writing them all freelance. Nobody's paying me a salary."

"Exactly. He could have done the same thing but didn't, and that really twists his nipple. Cheer up. Order whatever you like." Berga raised his hand to get the waiter's attention. "They've added a game hen to the menu that I hear is very good."

The game hen was a little stringy but filling. While they ate, reporters stopped to talk to Berga, others called to him from across the restaurant. Sevareid did his best not to look too impressed.

"That one makes up quotes," said Berga. "And the one over

there, eating the sausage? Don't tell him anything unless you want to see it in tomorrow's paper. Under his byline."

After lunch Berga offered to take Sevareid to his place. "It's hard to find. Besides I've only got one key."

"Don't you need to interview Joe Angelo?"

"Why? You already did. And a damn good job I'm sure. I'll just rearrange the quotes a little. As a reward I'll tell you a secret. Duke Ellington is coming back to D.C. to play at the Caverns Club Thursday night. Go hear him, It will do your spirit good."

Berga wasn't exaggerating about his place being hard to find. Up 18th Street, down a cobblestone alley and...there! It was smaller than a house but more than a shed. It reminded Sevareid of the earthquake cottages he'd seen in San Francisco. This one was about fourteen feet high with a tin roof and walls covered in wood shingles. The most unusual aspect of the place was its door, a double-hinged plank of oak that opened nearly as wide as the house.

"Robert Fulton built the scale model of his first steamboat in this cottage, sixty years ago. Come in, I've got the lithograph."

The interior walls were rough-planked oak and pine. Besides the lithograph, Berga had hung paintings and photographs of wolves, eagles and other wild animals.

"I prefer their company to humans," he said, taking a seat on a cushioned wicker chair hanging from the beam ceiling by thick rubber straps. "So don't overstay your welcome."

The cottage had a small, open kitchen and one bedroom. When Sevareid asked where he was supposed to sleep, Berga pointed to a platform built atop two ceiling beams.

"There's a mat and blanket up there and a folding ladder behind that table. You're not afraid of heights, are you?"

"No. How do I get in and out?"

"We'll get a key made. Any other questions?"

"Nope. I appreciate this."

"Maybe you'll do the same for me some day," said Berga. "Or maybe something else."

"Anything," said Sevareid, then thought better of it. "Within reason."

~

AS SOON AS he left Berga's cottage, Sevareid went looking for Pelham Glassford.

"I know you like jazz and since Ellington's from here...."

"Ellington is from everywhere," said Glassford. "He's the hottest jazz man on the planet."

A year earlier Sevareid would have been embarrassed to curry such obvious favor with someone who could help him. It seemed so...blatant. Berga had mocked him for his timidity. "I'm guessing your parents didn't haggle at the local fish market," he said. "You better get used to it if you want to succeed in this racket."

Berga was right. Cultivating sources was no different than cultivating tomatoes. Or was it cucumbers? They'd both had a few drinks during that conversation. At any rate, he liked Glassford and was pleased when he invited Sevareid to join him at the Caverns.

"We're waiting for Major Eisenhower," said Glassford as the two shook hands at the entrance to the U Street club. "I haven't told him about Ellington. Let's keep that a surprise."

Sevareid was embarrassed to recall his meeting with Eisenhower in Lafayette Park. He'd acted like a nitwit. But when the Major arrived he made no mention of it.

"Ike, don't take this the wrong way," said Glassford with a smile that nearly matched one of Eisenhower's. "But you're probably the whitest person ever to step foot in this club."

"Blame my parents."

The interior stucco walls of the club were shaped with genies, gargoyles and cherubs. Blue and amber lenses on the lights added to the surreal look.

"The closest thing I've seen to this was in Paris, just after the war," said Eisenhower. "Have you been there?"

"No. I was headed there but stopped to see a show in Cologne and couldn't tear myself away."

"Is that the show you mentioned last year, where the audience entered through a public urinal to find a girl in a first communion dress, reciting obscene poetry?"

"It was," said Glassford. "The poetry was written on toilet paper. That's where I discovered the dadaists. Do you know them? Duchamp and Arp?"

"I've only heard of Duchamp."

"You might be surprised to know that your boss, MacArthur, is well-versed in the European surrealists and dadaists. When I met with him last week he wanted to talk about them."

"It does strike me as odd that he'd like art that celebrates chaos."

"He didn't say he liked it. Just said he found it 'interesting.'"

Sevareid, with no idea what they were talking about, buried his head in the menu.

"I'll have a ginger ale," ordered Glassford from a waitress in a red sarong. "They've also got something called a grape fizz that's a little stronger."

Eisenhower and Sevareid ordered ginger ales. When the waitress left, Glassford told them about his first visit to the Caverns. "They recognized me as the Police Superintendent and weren't sure if I was here to listen to music or arrest them for serving spiked drinks. The owner came to my table like he had cats in his pants."

While the quartet—piano, drum, horns and standup bass—set up on a round stage ringed by tables, the men talked music. Eisenhower liked the mainstream swing of Dorsey and Goodman. Glassford was more interested in the new jazz personified by Ellington. Sevareid said he liked it all.

"I played the tuba in my high school marching band," said Eisenhower. "But that's pretty much what you'd expect from a guy as white as me, huh?"

"Hey, I played trombone myself," said Glassford.

Sevareid was enjoying this. Most of the military men he'd interviewed in Washington seemed stiff and cautious. But that might have been because he was trying to pry out information that could get them in trouble. These two were educated and witty. He made a mental note to learn more about the dadaists.

The Zoot Mayfair quartet started with something called "Slow Motion." The clarinet and piano traded leads, each keeping to the low octaves. In the break between songs, Ike leaned close to Glassford.

"The Bonus bill is still dead, right? And what comes next?"

Before answering Glassford turned to Sevareid. "Can we trust you not to quote us directly?"

"Sure. Of course," said Sevareid.

Glassford turned back to Eisenhower. "That might be up to your General."

"Congress adjourns next week after the Senate vote. Maybe the men will leave…?"

"I'd like to see that, but I'm not sure the Commissioners want it to end that easily. Not without breaking a few heads first," said Glassford. "Don't get me wrong, there are men in the camp who feel exactly the same. It's hard to give up without some kind of fight."

Sevareid's right hand twitched toward the notebook in his pocket. Now he understood why reporters hated off-the-record conversations. Glassford's quote was money he couldn't spend.

The horn player traded his clarinet for a saxophone. The musicians played a blues pattern that varied with each repetition. It was complicated and not altogether sweet and allowed Sevareid to guess where the music was headed without spoiling the surprise in getting there. The way it kept building on itself, made him think of ascending stairways. Sevareid was distracted by a white, upright piano being rolled from the back of the stage toward the front, where it was pushed against the first piano until the stools stood back to back. The Duke was coming. Eisenhower looked at Glassford for an explanation, but he just smiled and nodded his head like it all made wonderful sense.

There came a sound from behind them. Duke Ellington, in white tails, passed through the room like a twist of wind, touching hands and squeezing the shoulders of people who might have known him as a boy practicing scales behind his 12th Street window. He jumped the last step to the stage and sat on the piano stool, his back nearly touching Zoot Mayfair's. Back and forth they went on their pianos, asking questions, finishing each other's sentences, neither man willing to end the conversation. Sevareid didn't presume to understand all of what they were saying, but it was enough to get a sentence or two, an exclamation point here and a small joke there. The music touched on *A Train* and *Savoy Stomp*, on four or five of Ellington's most popular songs, but it didn't stay anywhere for long. They may have rehearsed it, but to Sevareid it sounded like pure improvisation. The music carried him back to his early boyhood in North Dakota, listening to Saturday afternoon banjo pickers at a farm co-op. That recollection was cut short when Ellington and Zoot, without any apparent signal to one another, hit the same C note and jumped to their feet. The audience rose to join them, none quicker than Sevareid. He hadn't felt so uplifted since he sang in the youth choir in fourth grade. Here was ecstasy in another basement room.

While they were still standing, Randolph Walker appeared. "You better come quick," he said to Superintendent Glassford. "There's trouble cooking down at Murder Bay."

∼

THE TROUBLE started when fact mixed with rumor. The fact was that Joan Caudell had sex with a man who was not her husband. The rumor was that the man was a Negro, and the sex had been forced.

"Where?" asked Glassford.

"Down near Swampoodle," I told him. "A crowd is getting worked up to head for those buildings on Pennsylvania Avenue. They're looking for a colored veteran named Poole."

Glassford's motorcycle wasn't going to carry all four of us.

"You'll have to find another way," said Glassford. "There's only room for two and I need Major Eisenhower."

"I'll be right behind you," said Sevareid, running onto U Street holding a dollar bill above his head. "Remember this is my story."

~

THE BONUS ARMY had taken over three buildings on Pennsylvania Avenue—the Showroom, Fort and Morgue—all three scheduled for demolition. Each of the buildings was shabby and abandoned but only the Morgue seemed ready to collapse in a stiff breeze. Clotheslines were strung where the west wall used to be, and smoke from a cookfire escaped through a broken front window. Glassford had taken a lot of heat for letting veterans with wives and children stay in these buildings, but then he took heat for most everything he did concerning the Bonus vets. I'd been told that whenever he needed to boost his spirits, he'd drop by the Pennsylvania Avenue buildings to play with the kids and compliment their mothers for their domestic miracles inside buildings without running water or electricity.

The Showroom was interesting to me for another reason. Two Negro families shared what had been a Ford dealership with three white families. I'd seen that same racial integration in the outdoor camps, but it was more impressive inside, even under only half a roof. Still, I wondered if the whites would stand with their Negro neighbors in the face of a mob.

I got my answer when our taxi reached the former armory. On the steps and sidewalk in front of the Fort, and atop an adjoining hillock, stood two dozen men armed with clubs and bricks. Only six or seven were Negroes. It was there we caught up to Glassford and Eisenhower, still on the motorcycle with the engine running.

"Stay calm and let the police handle this," said Glassford.

"You better have more police than just you," said a man pointing down the avenue toward the Capitol.

In the darkness I could see the vague shape of a crowd coming toward us. I heard Glassford tell Ike, "I can't let them get to the veterans. If I have to, I'll ride straight down their throats."

I knew what could happen if a fight started between whites and

Negroes. Thirteen years earlier, just a few blocks north, the same mix of fact and rumor (fanned by false newspaper reports of white women being assaulted by Negro men) led to a race riot that left a bunch of people hurt. Mr. Luke told me things would have been much worse if not for a sudden rain storm.

Sevareid and I ran down the sidewalk to keep in contact with Glassford's motorcycle. When we got close we saw something hard to believe—a half dozen policemen seemed to be leading the mob. Turns out they were only in front to slow it. Glassford jumped off the motorcycle and whistled an order for his officers to halt. It took about twenty yards of bumping and stumbling, but the six somehow stopped the fifty men behind them. Glassford must have known he didn't have much time before they pushed past.

"We've got your suspect in custody," he shouted in a voice that was half cop and half town crier. "And I guarantee you he'll get what he deserves."

The crowd was so surprised by the lie, it took some time to digest. Glassford used the lull to reposition the six officers, each of them sweating like a prize fighter.

"One more thing." Glassford lowered his voice to something more conversational and soothing. "This is Major Eisenhower. He's talked to the veterans back there and told them not to bring discredit on their uniforms by shedding the blood of American citizens."

"Have they got guns?"

"I'm saying they've agreed not to use any of their training and war time experience to cause you serious harm."

"How many are there?"

I saw Glassford's body relax. A posse hunting one man was dangerous, this one was now picturing an army. "Does it matter? A hundred, two hundred? I've already told you we have your suspect, now go home and let justice do its work."

The crowd was slumping back to Murder Bay when Max Berga arrived.

"It's over already? What did I miss?"

"Nothing," said Eisenhower. "The Superintendent just told them all to go to bed."

"Seriously, what did you say to stop them?"

"I said I had a table reserved at the Caverns Club," said Glassford, "and I was going to be very annoyed if they made me lose it."

I turned to say something to Sevareid, and found him crouched behind a parked car.

"If he sees me, I'll have to tell him everything," he said. "I need this story for my own."

VERDICT

DURING THE SUMMER Nora turned 11, a caravan of tinkers set up camp just outside Kenmare. They'd barely finished unhitching their horses when Nora came down the hill carrying a freshly baked loaf of her mother's bread. Her idea was to trade the bread for stories of the wider world. She walked up to the first person she saw, a woman tending to a pair of black horses and offered her the loaf.

"Aren't you the one," said the woman who, except for rings on every finger, looked disappointingly normal. "What is it you want with us?"

"I'd like to hear about the places you've been," said Nora.

The woman smelled the bread approvingly then wrapped it in cloth. "I can do better than that. I can let you look into my crystal and see the places you've yet to go."

"You mean the future?"

"Not all of the future, just your own. Come into the wagon."

Nora followed a few steps before stopping. "Even if I believed in fortune telling, which I do not, I wouldn't want to know."

"It's all the same to me," laughed the tinker. "But I'll be keeping the bread."

Nora hadn't thought of that day in years, which persuaded her there was no coincidence it returning now, the day Eric and Walker expected her to choose between them. Knowing how this ended might at least relieve the pounding of her heart.

She'd spent the night at Catherine's house, drinking tea and discussing their last double feature—*Platinum Blonde* and *Strictly Dishonorable*. The cinema! It was too much really, like being thrown about in a small boat. The more she saw, the more she wanted to see. The actors were so big on the screen, especially their eyes and lips. When they kissed, it was as though she was being kissed.

After the night's hard rain, the Anacostia was running high and fast. Nora passed six District policemen at the 11th Street Bridge without giving them a thought. She hid her bicycle in a thicket of bushes beside the bank and began the slow walk to her pallet, the mud sucking at her leather pampooties with a will. Under the hot sun the camp itself seemed to be cooking, wisps of steam giving the shacks and tents a strange glimmer. She was still a dozen yards from the camp's outer ring when she heard a pair of bugles. Within a minute the entire camp seemed to rise as one and start toward her. Nora stayed where she was, sunk nearly to her ankles in mud. When Diamond and Halloran reached her, they each took an arm and lifted her like pulling a cork.

"Where are we going?"

Dennis looked to see if she was joking. "Darling daughter, the Senate votes today." His Santa Claus cheeks were a good deal thinner than when first they met, or maybe it was only that his hair had grown so long. She'd teased him about it the last time they talked, said he was passing from a Santa look-alike to John the Baptist.

"I thought the vote was later this afternoon."

"We need to get there early and let Congress see our teeth."

"Like in that movie, the one where the Confederate General parades up and down the enemy line on horseback......I can't remember the name," said Nora.

Dennis laughed. "So you've given up your books for moving pictures."

"I've done no such thing. But books I can read anytime. These movies come and go so fast. If I was a man I'd be in love with Carole Lombard."

"She's a little thin for ranch work," said Dennis. "Mae West might do."

Tom Halloran handed Nora two dollar bills. "Your share," he said. "From the pigeons."

Nora didn't know what he was talking about. She'd killed a few dozen pigeons with her sling two weeks earlier, but those were for the Bonus vets.

"We've been selling them to restaurants all over town," explained Diamond.

"What restaurant would serve pigeon?"

"They're not pigeons when they leave us." said Tom. "They're Iowa game hens."

"And how do they taste?"

"I wouldn't know," laughed Diamond. "They're too expensive for my wallet."

∽

SEVAREID WAS SITTING outside Walt Waters' pup tent when the Bonus Army leader woke.

"Damn this tent," cried Waters, thrashing around inside. "It's like being swallowed by a worm."

His feet came out first, half into a pair of pants. When Waters tried to yank them higher he fell backwards and hit his head on a metal canteen. He cursed the tent once more before emerging.

"Why don't you get a bigger tent?" asked Sevareid.

"I didn't want to put on airs," said Waters. "But you're right. It's about time I moved into something that suits my rank."

Sevareid liked Waters, not only because he allowed him unlimited access but because the man was helplessly honest. Any thought that entered his mind was soon rolling off his tongue. Because Sevareid had been with him since East St. Louis, nearly from the beginning, Waters trusted that he was partial to the

Bonus Army. While that was true, Sevareid was uncomfortable with the assumption. A good reporter didn't take sides or pull punches and today he was determined to write something less than positive, to sketch Waters as a commander in defeat. But other than the frustration with his tent, Walt Waters seemed remarkably jolly.

"Oh wait, I almost forgot," he said, reaching into the tent. "Take a look at this. My Sacred Scroll." He held up a copy of the Bonus bill, tarted up to look like a Roman proclamation.

"I found a sympathetic printer who did it for me cheap. The men have been asking to see this since the first tent was raised beside the Anacostia. I tried explaining that the bill was only words typed onto cheap paper and stapled together with a hundred other bills. But they wouldn't hear it. They had a picture in mind, and pretty much the same picture—a rolled parchment, crinkly brown at the edges and written in script. So I'm giving them what they want."

"You seem to be in a pretty good mood today, given that the Senate is sure to kill the bill."

"It's worse than that," laughed Waters. "As soon as the bill is killed the communists will attack me from the left and the fascists from the right. But that's the nature of battle, right? Who'd have thought a couple years ago that I'd be negotiating with generals and the president and have newspaper reporters like you copying down my every word."

"Where were you two years ago?"

"Let's see. That was before I got the job in the cannery. I must have been working as a bakery helper or farmhand. Son, I've had more jobs than a cat has lives. But I don't have time to get into all of that now. We've got a battle to fight."

Waters brushed the dirt off his pants and approached a group of veterans playing horse-shoes. "Gather 'round men," he called, unrolling the scroll. "I've got something here to show you."

WALKER

IN THE THREE DAYS since I said goodbye to Nora at the Bonus Camp, I'd been wandering the river looking for something to take my mind off its sorry state. Nothing worked.

When I tried fishing, the only thing I caught was the back of my ear with a bad cast. That was unusual enough, but then I went swimming in water I knew like the back of my hand and banged a knee on a submerged rock. If I was the sort to believe in bad luck, I'd have started nailing up horseshoes.

I dragged out my broken-backed copy of *Ulysses* (which I did not steal, despite the library markings Nora discovered), hoping to sink myself in the confusion of dogsbodies and rolypoly poured jampuffs, but I made the mistake of starting at the beginning. Right away I pictured the mailboat clearing the harbour mouth of Kingstown with Nora on deck, holding hands with someone who wasn't me. I read the first ten pages of the *Legend of Sleepy Hollow* hoping it might at least put me to sleep but it didn't have the power to comfort or sedate.

In bad times past I could always sit in the woods and recharge, like topping up an old battery. Nothing there—rocks, earth, tree squirrels—cared whether I lived or died and there was comfort in that. On even the stillest day the trees whispered the truth: life is greater than any man—white, colored or otherwise and no amount of money or advantage could change that. If there was a God, he was deadly fair.

When I went to the woods this time though, I didn't hear a thing. The trees weren't talking and the air was so still, I could hear a dog moving over leaves seventy yards away. My dog Smoke would have been embarrassed to claim him as kin. Smoke wasn't actually mine, but then he didn't belong to anyone else as far as I knew. He snuck up on me one afternoon at the end of my first year in DC. I was sitting against a tree when I heard breathing to my left. There was this big, pure white dog with a bushy tail that curled up like a question mark. He was standing sideways to me not 10 yards away. I said hello in my best, dog friendly voice. I even offered him a strip of deer jerky. He never looked my way, didn't even blink. I got up to go, but left the jerky on the ground.

We repeated that same drill the next two days, and each day he moved closer. On the third, I called him over and he let me touch his head.

I never had a dog as a kid, maybe because my family knew my older brother would torture it. I don't remember ever wanting one, but once I started traveling with Smoke I realized what I'd missed. That gave me one more reason to hate my father. I refused to believe my mother would be that cruel.

I acted like a fool with that dog, talked to him about all kinds of crazy stuff, sang songs I made up on the spot, and he never seemed to mind. Even when he was working a fresh scent, he'd just cock his head to the other side and get on with his business.

My favorite fishing spot back then was on the west side of a small island in the Potomac. The only way to reach it, without spooking the fish, was to swim. The first time we went together, I swam across with the rod strapped to my back. When we were ready to leave, Smoke put the rod in his mouth and paddled across. I laughed so loud the fish were scared for a week.

I figured he hunted with a pack of dogs and finally saw them one day from the top of a ridge. Below me, I spotted what I thought was the white tail of a deer until the rest of Smoke appeared in the clearing, leading three smaller dogs. I didn't call out, just stood watching, proud and a little jealous. As they left the clearing Smoke lunged toward bushes on his right and came up with a black snake. He shook it hard from side to side, then flung it behind him for the other dogs to tear into. My heart was still racing long after he disappeared.

About four months after he found me, we were moving through unfamiliar woods upriver when he stopped to dig at a hole. I followed the trail into an open field and waited. When I looked back, I saw a spot of orange and thought it was the late sun peeking through the trees. But the sun was more than 20 degrees west of where I was looking.

I started running and yelling Smoke's name, hoping I was

wrong. Then I heard the rifle shot. A kid about 12 in an orange hunting cap stood with his father above Smoke's lifeless body.

"I thought it was a deer," said the kid in a cracked voice. "His tail."

I buried Smoke in those woods, didn't mark the spot and never went back.

The worst part of losing Smoke was how afraid I was to mourn him. If I let one tiny hole open in the dike, I might risk a flood. I felt a little of that same fear in the hours before the Senate vote on the Bonus bill. The odds of Nora choosing me over Sevareid were 50-50 at best. Once I factored in the race thing, my odds dropped considerably. I'd really let myself go with wanting Nora, and wouldn't have chosen to give anything less. But now, with my heart beating in my throat, I couldn't help but wonder how deadly the approaching flood might be.

On my way to the Bonus Camp I stopped to read a discarded newspaper.

SENATE VOTE ON BONUS BILL
Special to *The New York Times*

WASHINGTON, July 16. – The full Senate will vote on the Patman bill for the payment of $2,400,000,000 to World War veterans after the Finance Committee reported it adversely.

With today's developments the morale of the bonus expeditionary force, which has remained high in the face of amazing difficulties, began almost visibly to sag. The adverse report of the committee and the growing expectation of defeat began to weigh heavily on the thousands of destitute ex-service men encamped here, and the movement of the veterans homeward, only a trickle thus far, was notably increased.

Officials believed that the beginning of the long-expected breakup of the camp was at hand, and would begin in earnest after the Senate vote.

Officials Plan Evacuation

Hence they began planning for what they concede is the most dangerous period of the bonus army's existence —the period in which the men will start roving about the country as isolated bands of unemployed, without funds, without food and without the discipline to which they submitted voluntarily when they thought there was a chance of achieving their objective.

The plight of the men was the most serious tonight that it has been since the bonus army began arriving in force, notwithstanding the miracles of sheltering which have been wrought and the announcement that the expeditionary force had food supplies sufficient for a week, with $5,000 still left in its treasury. An all-night rain almost set the camp at Anacostia awash, and today the veterans, still soaked, were under another downpour of many hours.

Few in high places here will admit that they fear any serious disturbances from the men themselves in Washington. But they believe there will be real danger when the men break up into small bodies and start home.

They fear that many of these bands will be tempted to settle in the "jungles" on the outskirts of industrial centers and that, with their food supply abolished and with the population gradually losing interest in them, clashes with the authorities will be inevitable.

"It's tragic," said an army officer who had a front line command in France. "Here they are, the ghost of the greatest army America ever put in the field. They're shattered in health, many of them, these men who trod the roads so magnificently just fourteen years ago. They are being beaten now by an enemy they cannot get to grips with. What is to become of them?"

I was bound to be at the Capitol when the bill died, to talk with veterans about their hard times and the Party's way around them, but it was the last place I wanted to be. The job required missionary zeal and I didn't have a spark in me. The day was beautiful, but my body couldn't enjoy it. The sun was too bright, the sky too clear and the soft breeze, a gift any other time, was sandpaper against my skin. I walked with my head down, as oblivious as I'd been during my first walk with Nora. But instead of being completely focused on her, I was working to stay completely focused on nothing. The result was the same—I didn't see the punch coming.

"There you is," said Benny the Wolf, knocking the wind out of me. Chuckie, another of Fat Carlos' gang, stepped behind me and put a grip on my shoulders like ice tongs.

"Fat Carlos wants to see you," said Benny. "Wants to see you last week, dig? So don't be saying you got somewhere else to be."

I considered surrender. If I never got to the Capitol, Nora wouldn't get the chance to lay me low. Was I really more afraid of seeing Nora than Fat Carlos? Apparently so. Benny and Chuckie must have felt my resignation because they loosened their grip. Without really deciding to, I stepped on Benny's foot, whirled an elbow into Chuckie's ribs and sprinted away. There was no point in postponing the inevitable.

～

THE MEN, assembled in regiments a hundred yards before the 11th Street Bridge, looked a wonder in their bits and pieces of uniform. Whatever crease or sparkle the outfits had during the first parade down Pennsylvania Avenue had disappeared, yet the men snapped to attention so smartly it squeezed Nora's heart.

Walt Waters faced them with his hands clasped behind his back and his legs spread. He'd later write that he debated with himself all morning whether this speech should be brief or epic. He didn't have anything new to say but figured a general's job was to say something.

"Whatever else happens today, you men have come a long way

and I want you to know I'm proud. I remember the day we arrived at this camp…" he was interrupted by a harsh creak of metal behind him.

Standing on her toes, Nora saw two policemen on the other side of the bridge working a hand crank. The end of the bridge closest to them began to rise in the air.

Without the bridge, they'd either have to swim the river or march a 90-minute loop down Good Hope Road into Prince Georges County, Maryland and then back into the District. Three men near the front broke ranks and charged, but the mud and distance were too great. By the time Waters led the rest of them to the bank, the bridge was pointing straight up like a middle finger.

"We're American citizens!" called Waters over the water. "You have no right to keep us here."

One of the policemen shrugged his shoulders while the others stood with arms crossed, as though they had nothing to do with this bridge deciding to raise itself.

Nora moved closer to Dennis Diamond and Tom Halloran. Diamond, normally a deep pool, was blowing air out of his cheeks like a bellows while machine-gun Halloran raked his hair with his fingers. As a group, the men were eerily quiet.

A veteran at the front threw off his jacket, climbed down the bank and dove into the river. The current pulled him nearly a hundred yards downstream before he could reach the far shore. He dragged himself up the bank, twice slipping in mud. No one made a move to follow.

Waters gathered his officers to discuss strategy. Across the water Nora saw Max Berga interviewing police. A big blue motorcyle arrived carrying the Police Superintendent. Pelham Glassford. He talked with the policemen, then went to the crank and lowered the bridge himself.

Nora expected cheers, but heard only a collective sigh of relief.

"That's a good sign," said a woman near her, holding an infant in the crook of her arm. Nora wanted to think so, but she had a premonition things would go badly. Then again, she thought, maybe the premonition had only to do with herself.

Berga was waiting for Nora on the other side.

"So here we are. Approaching the sad, anti-climactic end." His words were cynical, but his voice was not entirely unsympathetic.

"Do the stories you write stay with you?"

"Forgetting is as much a skill as remembering," said Berga.

"I'll remember every bit of this." Nora had been saving another question for Max Berga and she asked it now. "Mr. Berga, do you think you'll ever move back to Germany?"

"I'm not sure I could."

"Does that happen, I mean if you stay here too long?"

"Are you worried about yourself?"

"I'm not worried, just wondering."

"There's a big difference between you and me. I lived the important parts of my life in Germany. The most important parts of your life are still to come."

Nora felt someone behind her and turned to find Eric Sevareid. He was wearing a white shirt (how did he keep them so clean?) but his normally well-behaved hair was loose and unruly with a lock hanging over his right eye. Nora gave him a hug.

"I've come to hear your verdict," he said with a weak smile. A most handsome man, smart and funny. She could easily picture herself with him. Their children would be tall and fair and the family would canoe all the world's great rivers.

"I can't announce my verdict until we find Walker," she said, reaching out to touch the back of his hand.

"What verdict?" asked Berga who'd been standing to one side watching this drama.

"It's only a game we're playing," said Sevareid. "Nora, walk with me."

As they moved toward the Capitol, Nora sensed Eric's impatience. He barely looked at her and answered questions with an uncharacteristic economy of words. She needed to give him something, even if it wasn't the thing he wanted.

"Did you know that today is my birthday?"

He stopped in his tracks. "Your birthday! Why didn't you say something?"

"It's good to have some secrets, don't you think?"

"Sure, with other people. But not with…friends."

"I need a present from you."

"Name it."

"I need you to be patient until we find Walker. I need you to not be mad at me."

"I'll never be mad at you," said Eric. "Mad about you. Mad for you. But never mad at you."

At the edge of the Capitol grounds. Nora put a hand on his arm. "If I don't see you, we'll meet here after the vote."

"I won't leave without you," said Eric. He leaned close and kissed her.

It was their first real kiss, full on the lips and as good as Nora had imagined.

~

"IN MY JUDGMENT the Senate is mistaken in its idea of the temper and mentality of these men." Senator Byron Thomas, the Bonus bill's chief defender, was speaking on the floor of the Senate. Above him Eric Sevareid listened from the edge of a crowded gallery that smelled of damp clothes, dried mud and cheap tobacco. It reminded him of summer days working in a neighbor's corn silo. Senator Thomas was reading from a prepared speech, his white head bobbing up and down like a robin working a worm. The large oil paintings and the blood red carpeting provided a vivid backdrop for his words.

"If they cannot get work and cannot collect their honest debts what are they going to do? Even the monkeys in Africa eat and find their cocoanuts in the jungle."

A senator from Indiana stood to speak against the bill. "Our country's life is more in danger today than in the days before or during the World War." As he spoke, the sound of singing floated through the windows and filled the Senate chamber: "Hail, Hail the Gang's All Here." How many are out there, wondered Sevareid.

Twenty-thousand at least. Despite his desire for a good story, he hated to think the veterans might prove this gasbag right.

WALKER

I MOVED THROUGH the plaza, searching for Nora as well as clues to the veterans' disposition. They seemed fairly cheerful in the face of defeat. At one point the Bonus Army's field kitchen was being pulled onto the plaza by a brown mare, when two Capitol cops in black brimmed hats stepped in front of it with their hands up. One called out, "We can't have that here."

"If the men don't eat, they get grouchy," said Winkie, a camp cook notorious for his temper and a fondness for putting hot sauce and pepper on everything but the custard desserts. I expected trouble when a group of men gathered round to see what the commotion was about, but just as quickly things calmed.

"We've got no problem with you feeding the men, just not here," said the policeman in a friendly voice. "Put it back behind those trees and you'll be okay." The kitchen was moved without further argument.

I did see one sign of tempers flaring. A newspaper photographer tried to get three veterans to move into the light so he could take their picture. Normally, veterans were happy to oblige but these refused. One of them barked, "You can go to hell. We came here to get our bonus, not to be photographed. What are you paying us to pose?"

That small act of dissension should have encouraged me, but I didn't have the energy for it. This whole day was unreal. The Senate debating a foregone conclusion, while the crowd outside refused to give up hope in what it knew was hopeless. I couldn't help thinking it matched my life exactly.

～

THE SUN was dipping behind the dome of the Capitol when a bugle called the men to mess. They formed a line that snaked through trees and across a stone walkway, patiently edging forward for "mystery stew."

Nora sat on the lawn below the Capitol steps. On her right sat Catherine and Virni. On her left stood Will, Pinky and Jamie packing away their movie camera.

"It's getting too dark," he said. "Besides, I've already used up a whole reel."

The black camera stood on metal legs. Two reel cases rose from its top like giant eye sockets; the lens was protected by a square hood. There was a hand crank, a cylindrical viewfinder and assorted metal discs that may or may not have had anything to do with film. Nora had never seen a machine so complicated and handsome.

"It's too bad there wasn't enough light to get that last speech," said Virni sitting cross-legged with his palms facing the sky. "When the man on the steps said of congressmen opposed to the bill, 'Nothing human ever reaches their hearts.' That was very good, yes?"

"Sure," agreed Will. "But the best was from the fella who said Al Capone got eleven years in jail because he started a bread line in Chicago. When people boo Congress and cheer Al Capone, that tells you something."

Catherine sat with her legs tucked under her rayon dress looking entirely at ease, Little Miss Muffet among the hairy veterans. She asked Will what his movie would be about.

"It's about the Bonus Army," he said with a wink to Nora. "Some might think that's a raggedy thing, but aren't Charlie Chaplin's movies about raggedy things?" He cleared his throat. "Miss Catherine, would you consider being in my movie?"

Catherine puckered her lips as though trying to keep the notion from jumping out of her mouth. Would she like to be in a movie? Ever so much.

While Catherine and Will discussed their cinematic future, Nora talked to Virni about an idea for his next show. "I was thinking you might do one at the Bonus Camp."

"But how could I? Without a ceiling?"

"Would a big tent do as well?"

"A tent? In the big camp of soldiers?" Virni's dark eyes drifted together as though studying something at the tip of his nose.

"I'm not sure they'd let you," warned Nora. "But I bet lots of the men would find it interesting."

"I will think on this," said Virni happily. "I will visualize Madame Blisky in the mud."

Dennis Diamond and Tom Halloran brought two plates of stew for the group to share. Diamond in particular had been worrying that Nora might disappear if she lost any more weight.

"You're trying to fatten me up like one of your cows," laughed Nora, holding up something from the stew that looked like meat but squished like sponge. "I'm just not hungry in this heat."

A muted cheer rose with the appearance of Senator Thomas, who'd earlier made the speech about the monkeys in the jungle. He came halfway down the steps before raising his hands for quiet.

"You've made a wonderful record so far and everybody respects you. For God's sake, don't do anything tonight to spoil it," said the Senator. "The truth is, this bill is not likely to pass."

It was not unexpected news. From the beginning the men had been told that the House would pass the bill and let the Senate reject it. But hearing it from one of their chief sponsors was sobering. Though Nora had found Walker earlier in the afternoon, she excused herself to wander the Capitol grounds and look for him again.

She passed Eric, who stood laughing with one of the Capitol policemen. On the quiet side of the Capitol, Roger Cord was talking with three men Nora didn't recognize. She could have asked him about Walker, but didn't. She finished her circle of the Capitol and returned to sit between Will and Dennis Diamond. Walker would come eventually. He had to.

"Hey Will, tell Nora about what you filmed yesterday," urged Diamond.

"Have you heard of the Amazing Regurgitator?" Nora hadn't. "He's an Egyptian fella who swallows things."

"What kind of things?"

"Buttons, coins, live goldfish…just about anything. But that's not the amazing part. The amazing part is when the audience, he was in a theater off F Street, calls out one of the things he swallowed. And then…."

"What?"

"He spits up that very thing. Not from his mouth, but from his stomach."

"Tell her about the castle."

"Oh yeah, the castle. It's made of cardboard. So the Egyptian guy swallows a gallon of water and then a pint of kerosene. The lights go down, which was bad for my camera, the drums beat and the Regurgitator lights a match and spits out the kerosene in a big flame right at the castle. He lets it burn for about five seconds and then comes the gallon of water to put the fire out. Talk about your grand finale!"

"Is that going to be in the Bonus Army movie?"

"Sure."

"But how will it fit?"

"I haven't figured that out exactly but the way I see it, everything should be able to fit, especially the interesting parts. Virni will be in it too. The sword and flower thing."

A veteran with a banjo had climbed the Capitol steps and now began to play.

"There's an interesting sound in that," said Nora. "We don't have banjoes in Ireland."

Will suggested she go up and sing.

"It's not my place," she said, though the idea was nearly as thrilling as intimidating. Since her night at the Criers Club, she'd thought about what to do with her arms and practiced holding her head three or four different ways. But here, in front of twenty-thousand people was not the place to try again. She was disappointed by her timidity and blamed it on growing old.

The banjo player gave way to a man in a tight infantry jacket. He had greasy hair and blunt features and didn't look anything like a singer to Nora. But as soon as he opened his mouth, Nora realized she'd misjudged him. He was so good, the veterans waited until nearly the end to join in on "There's a Long, Long Trail a Winding." On "Tipperary," which was as singular to these veterans as a secret handshake, they joined in loudly and with emotion. A bear of a man in front of Nora sang heroically off-key, tears rolling down his face. Nora guessed the whole place would be sniffling after the next sad song but the singer changed pace.

> *All you here—here and there—*
> *Pay the bonus, pay the bonus everywhere,*
> *For the Yanks are starving, the Yanks are starving,*
> *The Yanks are starving everywhere*

A few heads appeared in the windows of the Senate gallery as he finished with, "My bonus lies over the ocean."

A congressman from Texas named Blanton followed immediately after the singer, his hands held out as though trying to catch some of the singer's applause. Nora remembered Blanton from a day she spent in the House gallery, when she couldn't understand a word he said. He was either talking more slowly today or her ears had adjusted to his speech. "You boys have more friends in the House than you realize. They will stay here 'til hell freezes over, and you'll get your bonus before you quit." After the long, disappointing day, it was the best thing they could have heard.

Twenty minutes later they heard the worst.

A messenger walked slowly from the Capitol to the top step. He said, "They've taken the vote. Sixty-two to eighteen. They killed it dead."

For a long moment there was no response. Sixty-two to eighteen? That wasn't even a contest. A low, rumbling sound rose from the ground, growing higher and louder until it sounded to Nora like a great engine running low on fuel. Walt Waters, the Bonus Army commander, appeared on the steps above them, hunched over as though he'd been punched in the stomach. Nora could barely hear his words. She caught the phrase "time to go home" and heard it echoed again by men sitting near her.

"Go home? Is that what he said?"

"God damn if I'll go home."

"He'll have to fight me if he's ready to surrender."

It was the first time Nora had heard any of the soldiers openly challenge Waters, though Max Berga had predicted it would happen. He said the sound would be like "barrel staves giving way." Walt Waters must have heard it too because when no one responded to the bugle's assembly, he pulled himself erect and shouted out something that sounded like "HUP." They could all hear what he said next.

"We're not telling you to go home. We're telling you to go back to your camps. We're going to stay in Washington until we get the bonus, no matter how long it takes. And we are a hundred times as good Americans as those men who voted against it."

The men began moving from the Capitol slowly, their heads down, like mourners leaving a funeral. Nora wondered, was this just a battle lost or was their war truly over?

～

"THE WAY things look now…I mean looking at things the way they are…I'm kind of ready…thinking I might have to…." the ex-soldier was having trouble finishing his thought and Eric Sevareid was in too great a hurry to wait.

"Call it quits?"

"No, not exactly…."

"Make a tactical retreat?"

"Now that's a little closer…."

"Reconsider the overall plan?"

"Yeah, that's good. The way things look now I'm going to have to reconsider the…what did you call it?"

So what if it wasn't good journalism, Sevareid had his own overall plan to attend to, which included a fast-approaching deadline. But before he could write and file his story, he needed to find Nora and learn his fate. Under the trees of the Capitol, a great setting and an even better plot. Two champions vying for a fair lady's pleasure. A month ago he might have wondered at how easily he saw his situation as a story, and worry that he was not following his heart but only his best idea of where his heart should lead. His father had called him on that when he was 16, the night Uncle Ben threw his fit. Uncle Ben, not a real uncle but one of his mother's first cousins, had been staying with them for about a month, drying out from his latest gin binge. One night before dinner, Sevareid heard a loud thump in Ben's room and poked his head inside to find him on the floor, his eyes rolled up into his head and his body shaking. Sevareid went into the hall and called his father in a voice so calm it surprised him. After they got Ben onto the bed, his father looked at Sevareid's impassive face and said, "Aren't you the cool one." It wasn't a compliment.

But there was nothing calm about him now. Nora was more than some prize in a contest. She was keeping him awake nights. No girl had ever done that before. The other day, during an interview with Walt Waters, he realized only half his mind was concentrating on the job while the other half was thinking of Nora's smell. Not a perfume smell but real orange blossoms. And this afternoon when he came up behind her, the sun painting all those new shades of red in her hair.

"I've come to hear your verdict." That was a stupid thing to say straight off, especially with Max Berga standing there. He almost didn't kiss her, not because he was afraid to but because the thinking part of him got bogged down with questions of timing, and wouldn't that have been a tragedy.

The kiss lasted maybe four seconds but he'd already taken an hour to replay it and wasn't done yet. The look in her eyes as he leaned close was worth ten minutes by itself. And then there was the moment before their lips touched, when she opened her mouth, not a pucker but soft and accepting. He'd only ever kissed one Catholic girl before, Sharon LaFrange, and her lips were squeezed so tight he couldn't have hammered a needle between them. Now, as he walked toward his meeting place with Nora, he thought again of their kiss and the faint hum that came from the back of her throat.

Not calm. Not by any definition.

WALKER

LOSING THE VOTE on the Bonus bill, and by such a whopping margin, was enough to make a person depressed or angry. I was looking for the angry ones. Under tall sycamore trees and the lowering night, I handed out a pamphlet inviting veterans to the next meeting of the Washington Communist Society. A few weeks earlier I wouldn't have dared be so open in a crowd of Bonus veterans, but this night I was confident things had changed.

"Here's something to look at and think about. Decide for yourself if our system is working the way it should." My voice was soft as an undertaker's, all sympathy and eternal rest and it seemed to be working. In the last half hour only one person had cursed me and he was cursing everything in the world.

I kept an eye out for Nora and Sevareid and wondered again why she wanted to tell us at the same time. She had to know it would be harder that way, but I didn't want to start an argument so close to the finish, especially after the bright look she gave me that afternoon.

I tried to put Nora in my pocket and concentrate on how Fat Carlos found out I'd stashed the whiskey. Could the Skeffington brothers have told him about my hidden platform? I hated to think that. Maybe the bootlegger I sold it to had talked. I either had to leave town or come up with a plan to appease Carlos. Tomorrow, after I learned my fate, I'd start working on a plan. Tomorrow I might be able to think of something other than Nora.

When she found me in the afternoon, I couldn't help but wonder how the skinny girl I first thought a boy had grown so damned beautiful. Nora seemed to suck the color out of everything around her. How else could her eyes glow so green and her hair so red? She was wearing a skirt that showed off her hips and a white shirt with the top two buttons undone and I couldn't figure which half of her to stare at. She saw me looking and not only let me but pushed back her shoulders and made a slow turn to show herself off, like she'd just gotten this new body in the mail.

She said, "You, me and Eric under the trees just before the avenue. After the vote, okay?"

I'd have agreed to anything.

It was Sevareid who came through the trees first. When he saw me he stopped, like he wanted to go back the way he came. But it was too late.

"Hey. Any sign of Nora?"

"Not yet. This is where she said for us to meet, right?"

"Yeah."

He said to go ahead with my handouts but it was too dark and I was pretty much done, so we stood there waiting for Nora, looking everywhere but at each other. We'd always been comfortable not talking but this silence was filling up the space between us like a balloon. I had to say something before it popped.

"So what do you think?"

"It can't work."

"What can't work?"

"You and Nora."

"It's working okay so far."

"So far isn't what I'm talking about."

"What the hell are you talking about?"

The conversation was strange enough, but with the fireflies popping on and off it was like a scene from a book I'd just finished, *All Quiet on the Western Front*. Sevareid came a little closer, but didn't lower his voice.

"Most of the time when you've been with Nora in public, I've been there, too."

"So?"

"So the two of you alone is different."

"I'm done worrying about what white people think is 'different.'"

I waited for him to say the obvious, that if I wasn't worried for myself, I should at least be worried for Nora. Of course he didn't say it, he never said anything predictable. I liked that about him when we were just friends, right then I hated it.

228 « *Nora's Army*

"Tell me the truth," I asked him. "What do you feel about Nora and me being together?"

"I've told you what I think."

"No, not what you think. What do you feel, about a white girl being with a darkie?"

"That's a cheap shot."

He was right. It was low and cheap and I didn't care. "So you'd have no problem with me marrying your sister."

"I don't have a sister."

"That's an easy excuse."

We were heating up now, our voices growing louder. The last time somebody talked to me that way I hit him in the mouth and I admit the idea had some appeal. Then Nora showed up to scold us.

"Are you two finished?"

I didn't know how long she'd been standing there and it didn't matter. For a guy who didn't let himself get worked up, I was in high gear. Sevareid, too. When Nora said we should go somewhere and talk, he growled.

"I'm tired of carrying this thing all over town. Let's talk here."

A look came to Nora's face I hadn't seen before. She was scared. Miss-always-rock-solid was worried the floor might be dropping out from under her. It didn't make me feel good to see she was in the same spot as me, but it didn't make me feel any worse. She took a deep breath and licked her lips a couple times as if tasting what she planned to say.

"Okay. Where is it written?"

"Where is what written?"

"The rules. About how people are supposed to be with one another."

I didn't have a clue what she was talking about.

"Since when do you care about rules?" asked Sevareid.

"I don't. That's exactly my point," she said and clapped her hands together. "Why should any of us care? Somebody who's dead now made a rule about something that was none of his business."

When I said that made things clear as mud, Nora shot me a

look like I was only being stubborn. A thought did come to me then, but it was too outrageous to consider.

"None of us has family here. We're all orphans that way," she said, half pleading and half rock-solid again. "We've nothing to lose. That makes us free."

"Free to do what?" asked Sevareid.

Nora was really exasperated now, like she'd never had to deal with such simpletons. She grabbed one of Sevareid's hands and one of mine. It wasn't the first time she'd done that but it was the first time I felt a static shock, like you'd get after walking on a rug. The idea I'd swatted away came flying back. Judging by Sevareid's bug-eyed look, the thought had come to him, too.

"You can't be serious."

"I've never been more serious," she said. "Or has all our brave talk been just talk?"

It's probably a trick of memory, but I swear the lightning bugs stopped blinking. The silence was like being underwater and about as dark. I was glad to be holding someone's hand.

CUP

SEVAREID was glad to have something to think about other than the unthinkable. As he, Nora and Walker left the Capitol grounds he concentrated on the Bonus story he needed to write and telegraph to Minneapolis in the next twenty minutes. Not Nora's kiss that afternoon, or the naked statue that greeted them at the west end of the park, and especially not any undressed visions of himself and Nora and….

He'd always been a slow writer, going over sentences with the speed of a stone mason. The remarkable thing now was how easily this story came to him. He didn't even need to look in his notebook, the quotes and descriptions settling into place like geese landing on a pond. By the time he got to the Associated Press office, all he lacked was a snappy ending and this wasn't a story that wanted one.

"Where do we go now?" asked Walker, as Sevareid came out of the AP office.

"Home. Along the river," said Nora.

Her calm command. Sevareid remembered the Irish queen she'd told them about, who bedded men with a pirate's zest. He'd always liked traveling the city with Nora and Walker, the crooked looks bouncing off them like wads of paper. But now the disapproving eyes under their ridiculous hats (were he and Walker the only two men on the streets tonight not wearing hats?) and the old women shaking their heads annoyed him, and annoyed him more because he let it. A part of him was standing in judgment beside them. He was relieved when they reached the dark quiet of the river below the Fish Market.

"That reminds me, we need to go fishing soon," said Walker. "I'm nearly out of food."

"And get my cup while we're at it," said Nora. "Don't you think it's time?"

The cup was their adventure, not his, thought Sevareid and was disappointed in himself for feeling jealous. But how could he help it? There was no way he could keep cool and calm about something so upside down and backwards.

Mormons had multiple wives. Mormons and African chiefs. So there were precedents. But one man and a bunch of wives was a different beast entirely. He looked left at Nora and Walker moving along the shoreline and wondered what each was thinking.

"Did you make any converts tonight?" he asked Walker.

"I got some interesting reactions." His voice seemed to swim with the sound of the river. "People said sorry, they weren't quite ready, or let me think it over for another day."

"What's so interesting about that?"

"I'd never had three people in a full day promise to even read the pamphlet."

"I've been thinking about this communist thing," said Nora. "Thinking that it's good."

"So you're ready to join the party?" asked Sevareid.

"Not at all."

"Then why is it a good thing?"

"Did you ever debate in school?"

"Sure."

"I did as well."

"And you were good at it."

"There was one boy better. He was brilliant at the synthesis part."

"Explain," said Walker.

"I'd give my side, the thesis. He'd give his side, the antithesis. When it was time to have a final go at one another, I'd stick to my side while he'd move to the middle. Marry some of my arguments to a few of his. The synthesis. The judges thought him the picture of reason."

"And Communism?"

"Communism is at one end and Capitalism at the other. After all the debating, what's met in the middle will be the picture of reason."

Sevareid had an image of himself meeting Nora in the middle. And there was nothing abstract in that.

~

NORA LIT the candles while Walker went to the trap door. "Open these," he said, handing Sevareid three bottles of beer. "We're almost out, time to brew some more."

"Shall we?" began Nora then stopped.

"Shall we what?" asked Walker.

"Nothing."

"You want to start brewing beer now?"

Walker and Sevareid had every right to look at her that way. But what else was there to do? Now that she was in the cabin (had it gotten smaller since the last time she was there?) her confidence was dropping like…he pictured a pair of pants and cleared that image from her head.

"I do not want to brew beer. What I want is to eat a piece of fish, a carrot and two radishes."

"Did you know the Greeks thought radishes were apples that had been condemned to the underground by a vengeful goddess," said Sevareid.

"Do you have a vengeful side?" asked Walker.

"Oh I do," said Nora. "I've only been waiting for the right time to show it."

"Vengeance to all vegetables."

"Where do you get these," asked Nora. "I don't see any garden here."

"The soil is too acidic," said Walker. "I trade a woman in Alexandria fish for vegetables. And sometimes venison, though deer are harder to come by the last two years with all the poaching."

"Where's your gun?" asked Sevareid.

"Up there." Walker nodded toward an apparently solid beam in the ceiling.

"Is there anything you don't hide?" asked Sevareid.

Nora knew he was referring to the bookcase and the invisible trap door, but the question covered other territory as well. She looked at Walker and laughed. "A man of mystery."

"Our Minister of Secrets," added Sevareid.

"There's a difference between keeping things secret and keeping things safe," said Walker. "I'm not sure what the difference is exactly, but another beer might give me a clue."

"I've got a game," said Nora. "Let's each tell one secret, something embarrassing."

"Something just popped into my head," said Sevareid in a slow mid-western twang. "I was six years old, my first day at school and I wet my pants. I haven't thought about that in years."

"How did it happen?"

"I was too shy to raise my hand and ask."

"You, too shy?"

"I walked to school holding my older sister's hand every day the first week. You see before you a sensitive soul."

"Did anybody in your class see you, you know, wet?" asked Walker.

"One girl. Betty Rosedale. She blackmailed me into carrying her books home after school."

"I had a girl in third grade own me for a while after she caught me looking through a window into the girls' bathroom," confessed Walker.

"You little pervert," said Sevareid.

"I wasn't really peeping. When she came around the corner I was looking at my reflection in the glass to see if anything was stuck in my hair."

"That's even worse," said Nora, "admiring yourself when you could have been looking at naked girls."

"What's your secret?" asked Sevareid.

Nora felt herself flush.

"Ooh, this looks like a good one," said Walker. "Tell it."

"Mmmm...I don't know."

"Has Nora the Bold lost her nerve?"

"All right then. Last night I had a dream about the pair of you."

"Go on."

"I shouldn't."

Walker and Sevareid leaned closer.

"Well, we were in a bright, white room on a bed the size of this house."

"And then?"

"And then Eric wet his pants and Walker wouldn't leave his mirror."

"Come on, we told you our secrets."

"You call those secrets? I've heard naughtier bits in church," laughed Nora. "Get the cards, let's play that pinochle game you taught us."

"I better warn you, I'm feeling lucky tonight," said Sevareid.

Nora thought it best to bite her tongue.

WALKER

YOU WANT to know what happened next? So do I. Seriously, one minute we were drinking beer, playing cards and laughing at how Nora pronounced penny ("pinny"). The next thing I knew the three of us were on our mats with Nora in the middle and the candles blown out.

I was half drunk when I lay down but I sobered up fast in that howling silence. What was happening? What was I supposed to do next? Sevareid cut the quiet.

"Remember when you said you'd rather sleep out in the rain then get between the pair of us?"

"You want me to say I was wrong? I've likely contracted some American disease. Out of my head delirious."

"You were out of your head delirious before you met us," I said. She reached over and pinched my shoulder then kept her hand there to rub it out. I couldn't see what she was doing with her other hand and didn't want to. I reached to where I thought I'd find her shoulder and touched her neck instead. It was warm against my hand. My eyes had adjusted enough to see faint light coming through the window. I closed them against it. My hand required every bit of my attention as it drifted from her neck to her shoulder.

Nora put her palm against my chest and my breath grew shallow as leaf water. I reached to touch her stomach, which was a great mistake and another lesson in leaving well enough alone because what I found there was not the unimaginably smooth skin of a half-naked woman but the coarse and bony hand of Eric Sevareid.

Which one of us yanked our hand away first is impossible to say.

Nora laughed but let it die fast. "Well…." She took my right hand and I knew she had Sevareid's left. For a second I was afraid she was going to bring them together, like a referee forcing fighters to shake after a foul, but she just held on and let things settle. By the time she said, "Why don't we sleep on it?" I was as tired as if I'd climbed a mountain on my knees. I woke once with that dull surprise you get sleeping somewhere new and found Nora's hand still holding mine. I passed the rest of the night in a coma.

~

NORA WATCHED him standing bent-legged in the center of the canoe, naked except for a pair of black shorts, and knew she'd never seen a thing so perfect, not just the way his body was smooth in all the smooth places and muscled everywhere else but the easy way he stood against the grey sky with his arms hanging loose and his fingers moving like he was counting to himself.

"Keep it as close to here as you can," said Walker looking at her over his right shoulder, the same shoulder she pinched last night, then dove a loose arc into the brown water with such ease the boat barely moved.

Her cup was ten feet below the surface in a fishing net, staked to the bottom with marine rope and 12-ounce buoys. That's what he told her anyway. She'd have probably judged him right not to trust her with the cup while Kemper was still around asking questions. She didn't really want it now except to let Sevareid see it, and because she'd pestered Walker too much to back off. The truth was she had enough to take care of at the moment.

The Potomac was wide and flat here, empty except for one coal barge that looked like a black derby hat drifting downstream. A small airplane crossed the river on its way to Hoover Airport, while a green-headed mallard flew to the opposite shore. A week earlier Nora would have been reminded of shorebirds back home, but now she saw the mallard without any context but its own.

She wondered what Eric was doing at the moment and in what frame of mind. It still amazed her how things had worked out that morning. There was so much to talk about, yet not a word needed to be said. Eric had to write a follow up story back at the camp. She and Walker were free to stay. So there it was.

"I'll see you tomorrow," he said, like saying goodbye to people he'd met on a train. Glad as she was that Eric had made things easy, Nora hoped it wasn't as easy for him as all that.

Walker surfaced fifteen yards from the canoe, empty-handed. "Lost?"

He held up an index finger, took a deep breath and dove again, his legs together and feet pointed at the sky.

She'd wanted to touch his legs last night and Sevareid's as well. She had no idea why their legs had such sudden appeal, unless it was the sensation in her own. The books she'd read hadn't prepared her for that, a feeling like honeyed milk moving from her toes to the top of her thighs and higher. In books heroines never ached to wrap their legs around somebody and squeeze.

Nora felt herself blush remembering the way she'd rolled her knees open and shut in the dark. Even before Walker and Eric's hands touched she knew nothing would happen, which is why she felt so safe letting herself go like that. Otherwise she'd have been as nervous as a cat.

She heard the coal barge behind her and was startled to find it so close. She paddled hard left but the barge loomed larger. There was no gain in looking back but she couldn't help herself, not out of fear but amazement that a thing so bulky could move that fast. The waves from its black bow nearly capsized her before she could point the canoe into them. The barge's pilot, a white-haired man dozing on a wooden stool behind the wheel, lifted his chin and popped open his eyes as the barge passed, so close Nora might have splashed him with her paddle, yet never saw her.

The great lump of coal slid past to reveal Walker, swimming toward her with the silver cup in his right hand. She didn't paddle to meet him but waited and watched, his arrhythmic stroke, scoop, stroke, and the sheen of water rolling off his copper shoulders. He was coming to her. Everything was coming to her and that was a scary thought, that all her life 'til then had only been preparation for this moment and a few more soon to come.

The day she found her cup she'd been as certain as rain it had been waiting for her alone to pull it from the earth. She still believed that but only with some effort. Just because she'd stopped believing in a God with white whiskers didn't mean she had to stop believing in fate. To reject everything you couldn't taste or touch seemed as childish a notion as the other. And there was still the cup, which had came out of the ground as bright and clean as an orphaned piece of star. She concentrated on it now, looking for the hammered details. She wanted to watch Walker's face the first time he looked at the fertility goddess spreading her vulva wide enough to swallow a man, and caught her breath at how far she'd already gone, beyond modesty and all hesitation and they hadn't even had their second kiss.

Walker was at the boat now, holding out the cup. She looked at his upturned face, the flecks of water dripping from his eyebrows to his lips. Maybe she'd get nervous again when they reached home, but looking at him now, his eyes bright as schist, she had no reason to believe it.

WALKER

WE WERE putting dinner on the table when things started. Nora bent past me with the cornbread and let her hair brush the side of my face. That reminded me of the trolley ride to Great Falls and Nora swimming with us in her underwear. I put down my plate of grilled fish and touched her waist. By now the table was completely set, with knives and forks and little glasses filled with store-bought wine. We turned our backs on all of it and went to my bed.

"It's narrow," I said, as if she couldn't see for herself. My voice sounded thick, like my tongue had grown too big for my mouth. We sat holding hands as the last, flat light came through the window giving her hair a combustible look. I asked her to close her eyes so I could see what the light would do to her eyelashes. When she opened them again, I could tell she was as calm as I was. We were partners in this, co-conspirators with a whole night ahead to break the rules.

I kissed her and she kissed me back but not in any hurry. I put my hands through her hair and was surprised how soft it felt. I'd always imagined her hair as thick and tangled, like sea grass. I wanted to touch her eyebrows but that would have been awkward while we were kissing, so I followed the curve of her cheek to her ears and pinched the lobes between my thumb and forefinger. Every part of her needed touching. I was breathing like one of those Indian yogis, through my nose and all the way to the top of my chest, and Nora's breath was just as slow. She had all ten fingers touching my neck, like a blind woman reading Braille.

"Can we lie down?" Nora asked, or maybe she didn't. Maybe she just rolled onto her side and pulled me with her. I was sure she could hear my heart pounding in my chest and put her hand against my shirt pocket. She undid one of the buttons and slid two fingers against my skin.

"You're burning. Like a stove. What about me?"

I undid enough buttons on her shirt to pass my whole hand through and felt her stomach shiver, if that's the right word, and suddenly my patience was overwhelmed by a desire for everything at once.

We undid each other's shirts but got tangled pulling at the sleeves. Neither of us laughed. I'd jumped straight from the soft appreciation of her cheek bone to undoing at her skirt and Nora didn't slow me. She rolled onto her back and lifted herself so I could slide it off, all the while keeping her eyes on mine to show me what was in them.

"I feel so good it scares me," I said.

"This morning, watching you swim to the boat, I realized I'd spent my whole life getting ready for right now."

"It's the opposite that scares me. I've been getting ready my whole life to never have what I'm having now."

"You mean a white girl?"

"No, I mean the right girl."

"Aren't you the sweet talker," she teased and undid her bra. She put her hands on her breasts, not to hide them but to massage them back to life. "I hate wearing that. Like you with hats."

It seemed strange talking to each other this way, so light and easy like we were setting down to eat a snack. I'd have liked to see her body in a better light but didn't want to break the mood by getting up to light another candle. I got my pants off the same way she had, then lay as close to her as I could without touching. I'd slowed down again, and could feel the heat come off her legs. Nora reached over and gave my shorts a tug. I pulled them off then helped with hers, careful not to touch her. I wanted more time to anticipate this. I did the same thing on big rivers, taking time above a rapid to appreciate the drop.

When I finally put the flat of my palm on her chest, she slid against me. I touched her breasts and between her legs and she took me in her hand and squeezed so softly I nearly jumped.

Nora pulled me on top of her and whispered, "I haven't done this before so it might be difficult."

Neither had I, not with a virgin anyway and that worried me. Was there a way to do this the first time without hurting her? That was something I should have known and felt I'd let her down. But Nora didn't look worried, her eyes half closed and a smile on her face like a cat in mid-purr. She spread her legs and reached up to guide me in. I didn't get far before she caught her breath and bit down on her lip, but when I tried to pull out she kept me there. I rested my weight on my elbows and let her move slowly under me. It was torture not to push back, but a sweet kind. I had to stop her every once in a while so I wouldn't finish—six or seven times right to the edge and back again and each time the pleasure spread until I swear I could feel it in my elbows and knees.

I was ready to stay like that for hours, propped above her slow motion and the humming sounds that excited me nearly as much as her touch. I closed my eyes and was just floating in it when she reached out and knocked my elbows from under me. I fell on her chest and must have gone in deeper too because Nora dug her fingernails into my back and made a sound that went straight through me. I lost whatever fear I had of hurting her.

Afterwards we lay a long time without talking, like we both knew this was something too big for words. It was only when I moved my arm from under her that she said something and then so softly I had to put my ear to her mouth to hear.

"So glad," she murmured, like talking in her sleep. "Jack wouldn't...."

I waited to hear why she'd brought this Jack character into bed with us, but Nora was done talking. I'd never seen anybody fall asleep so fast and deep, and it made me proud in a stupid kind of way, like I'd loved her into a fairy tale sleep. I pulled a sheet over her, put away the food then sat by the table with my guitar, too tired to play.

As much as I wanted to, I wouldn't let myself sleep. I knew when the sun rose it would be Sevareid's day.

SEVAREID

IT WASN'T just the story that made him leave, though the story had the potential to be a bell ringer and he hadn't had one of those since the Battle of East St. Louis. And it definitely wasn't the awkward situation he found himself in. Three on a rope seemed a lot less sticky after sleeping on the idea with his stomach pressed against Nora's hip. The deciding piece that pushed Sevareid out of the cabin that morning was the look Nora gave Walker over breakfast. Not love or lust but something more dangerous—curiosity. Sevareid didn't want to spend his day with Nora while she was still wondering about Walker.

As inexperienced as he was in matters of the heart, it seemed a wise decision to let Walker have his day first. And besides, his story wouldn't wait.

He'd come across it the day before while putting together a profile of Walt Waters. A vet at the Bonus Camp showed him a one-page newsletter being circulated which slammed Waters as "Puss in Boots." Slamming Waters wasn't a rare thing in the camp these days but the new twist was an accusation that Waters had made a secret deal with Hoover in exchange for $20 a day in expense money. It was laughable to think Waters would betray his obvious ambition for that little, but the rumor did show how desperate things had gotten, and so Sevareid held his nose and followed the smell.

It led to veterans Nortie and Ben, a pair of unemployed bricklayers. They didn't look like any writers Sevareid had ever seen but they did have two things going for them—a friend who worked at a print shop downtown and a well-developed sense that everybody was out to screw them. They were not particularly happy to be tracked down.

"I need your help to get to the bottom of this," explained Sevareid with a weak attempt at sincerity. "What proof can you show me that Walt Waters sold you out?"

Ben, the bigger of the two, with a lower jaw that jutted out like a tusk, shook his head at Sevareid's thickness. He'd heard the story from another Ohio veteran, a man as upright as summer corn. And that man heard it from someone definitely in the know. How much smoke did it take to prove a fire?

"You must not be much of a reporter," said Nortie, tossing a piece of brick through the space where a wall had once been. "Everybody knows that story by now."

Sevareid knew a couple of Oregon veterans who'd been friends with Waters since the war and found one of them, Scott Pearson, in the plaza.

"Walt wouldn't double-cross his men for any amount," said Pearson with a dismissive laugh. "I've known him dog's years, since the days he called himself Bill Kincaid. He's not in this for the money."

Bill Kincaid? Sevareid made a show of closing his notebook and putting his pencil into his pocket. "Bill Kincaid, sure. That was after the war right? Back in Oregon."

Pearson started blinking fast, like trying to get his mind airborne "He told me he did it as a lark. Changed it back soon enough. Hey, if his wife didn't care why should anybody else?"

When did his wife know he wasn't Bill Kincaid, before or after they were married? Pearson said he didn't know, then scooted into an outhouse and stayed there.

That was only yesterday, on the morning of the Bonus bill vote, but Sevareid knew the clock was already ticking. By now Pearson would have told at least one other person. ("I can't believe that fucking reporter was asking about Walt changing his name to Bill Kincaid!") And that person would be telling three or four more. He had to get the story today, even if it meant leaving Nora and Walker alone in the woods.

But as soon as he crossed the river, Sevareid stopped to consider his own idiocy. Had he actually believed that abandoning the field to Walker was a good idea, or just let his own ambition play the saboteur. He'd never known anyone as un-ordinary as Walker. Black and white, cautiously fearless, a guy who'd survived what everybody else most fears—the loss of everything. With any other girl, Walker being a Negro would be a fatal negative. But Nora was intrigued by it. Hell, that aspect of Walker had intrigued him too.

By the time he got to Walt Waters' command tent, he was feeling about as sympathetic as an executioner. Waters was sitting behind a table, dressed in his military pants, a dress shirt and bow tie. Straddling both worlds.

"Commander Waters, for the profile I'm writing. Have you got a few minutes to talk?"

"Sure thing," he said. "Shall we sit here or take a walk?"

There were two men in the tent with him, separating one huge pile of letters into four smaller ones. Sevareid suggested they walk. He'd planned to bluff Waters the way he bluffed Pearson, by assuming he knew more than he did. But as they went through the camp, Waters was so open and encouraging that Sevareid changed his mind. "So which do you want, optimism or despair?" asked Waters in a cheery voice. "Should I tell you I've got everything under control or admit I'm hanging on like a cowboy on a wild bull?"

"I guess riding a bull makes for better copy," said Sevareid, "but I'm not here for that story."

As they approached the spot where Joe Angelo had buried himself alive, Sevareid saw that someone had stuck his air pipe into the pile of loose dirt and attached a cardboard sign that read —Bonus Army R.I.P.

"Yesterday somebody told me you once changed your name to Bill Kincaid and that your wife didn't know about it until later."

Waters didn't look particularly surprised. In fact he nodded his head like he'd heard that same story himself.

"I'll tell you the truth," continued Sevareid "I don't have enough for a story yet. If you decide not to talk to me it might be a day or two before I do. But it will come out."

Waters came to a stop and looked directly at Sevareid. One eye was a lighter brown than the other and smaller too, like a little brother.

"How old are you?"

"Twenty."

"I was two years younger than you when I went to war."

"It must have been terrible."

"No. Terrible is your house foreclosed. The war was a hundred times that. Your best friend lying dead just out of reach and starting to stink. And you knowing that sooner or later some asshole officer is going to order you to get up and run across that same field where 10,000 men died trying. Terrible is coming home to a hospital and feeling that the guys who didn't make it were the lucky ones."

Sevareid looked up from his notebook. "So what does that have to do with changing your name?"

"I was back about three years and been fired from as many jobs —garage mechanic, car salesman....everything was slippery and hard to keep hold of and I could feel myself getting smaller. You can't imagine that, can you? To actually feel like you're shrinking." Waters smiled as he said it and his eyes brightened, like he was remembering his first homerun. "That's when I decided to do it, make myself into somebody else."

"How do you do that?"

"Easy," said Waters. "You hitchhike to Washington State without telling anybody and start over. The first time somebody asked my name, I said Bill Kincaid and liked the sound of it. So where's the crime? And you know what? It worked. I started thinking, what would a guy named Bill Kincaid do in this or that situation and it slowed me down, enough anyway to start choosing things instead of letting every damn thing choose me."

"What about your wife?"

"When I met her in Seattle I was calling myself Bill Kincaid. By the time I told her my real name, she liked me enough not to care."

Sevareid was glad to hear that for a couple reasons. First, the woman he married would have to be at least that understanding and secondly, if that woman was going to be Nora O'Sullivan, he had to believe he could remake himself the same way Waters had. One thing was sure, the person he was now couldn't share Nora with Walker or anybody else.

He thanked Waters for the interview and waited for the inevitable request to kill or hold the story. But Waters was either a very good actor or genuinely unconcerned.

"Good luck Mr. Sevareid."

"Same to you," said Sevareid, wondering at Walt Waters's apparent peace of mind.

NORA

LIKE ALL great sleepers Nora liked waking slowly, one level of consciousness at a time. Growing up on a farm she'd had precious little practice waking at her own pace and so she coveted the rare opportunities.

On this morning, she first became dimly aware of a bird singing and folded that sound into a dream about her brother. They were floating on a green river under low hanging trees. He was happy and so was she, knowing that something good waited for her on the other side of her dream. Walker. Sharing her bed. And with that she was carried up and out of sleep like an air bubble through water.

She felt a sheet over her bare legs and a vague soreness between them. No longer a virgin. She reached back and brushed her hand against Walker's knee. Even with her back to him she knew he was awake, about to put his arm across her shoulders and say something sweet or funny. She gave him a low, encouraging hmm, but he didn't move, just like last night, keeping himself from her like Christmas Eve. That was perfect then but this morning...could he still be asleep? No. She tried to remember the last thing they said and only remembered a steep slide into sleep. And why wouldn't she, after so long a wait and all that pleasure mixed with pain. Wasn't it Walker who liked to say some things couldn't be put into words?

"As I was saying last night," she began and rolled toward Walker, a dreamy smile on her face. She was right about him being awake, but not so his romantic intentions. His eyes were cave dark. It was so unexpected that Nora found herself apologizing for what needed no apology. "I couldn't have pulled myself back from sleep with a team of bullocks."

Walker put two fingers on her lips, either to caress them or keep her quiet.

Nora nibbled at the fingers and nearly took a bite. "You look tired. Like you've been cutting sod all night."

"When does Sevareid come?"

As softly as he asked it, it still hit her like a slap. "Why are we talking about that now?"

"I should leave, in case he comes early. Besides, we're nearly out of fish."

"Fish?" Nora felt a spasm of anger. "I don't give a tinker's damn about fish." Why was he spoiling things? They were supposed to lie together this morning, talk softly and then make love again. She knew that, not because she'd read it in books, but because that's what her body told her and because she could taste it, like sugar on the tip of her tongue.

"I don't want to be here," he said, climbing out of bed.

She watched him move away, the angles of his back and hips and the long curve of his arms. She forced herself not to let disappointment dilute her anger.

"You know perfectly well Eric won't come here this early. You're only trying to punish me. Why are you punishing me?"

Walker had his shirt on and was stepping into his pants. He looked at her with false politeness, like an over-worked store clerk.

"We haven't talked. We haven't…hugged," said Nora and tasted only bitterness now, and how much more was there to come?

"We'll talk later," said Walker, sounding short of breath.

Now Nora saw the pain behind his artificial remoteness, in his quivering lower lip. She reached a hand towards him, but he wouldn't take it.

"Later," he said. "After everything's been done."

Such an odd way to put it, thought Nora, as if an outside force like wind or rain would be responsible for whatever she and Sevareid decided to do. He'd once teased her for believing she had control over her life, said it was like believing you could make a river change course or water run uphill. She loved that about him, his willing acceptance of whatever came his way. But right now she needed him to swim against the tide, to show enough reckless disregard to shove her off the path she felt duty bound to follow. She couldn't ask him. Or could she? He was dressed now and walking out the door. It had to come from him, she decided as he crossed the clearing and disappeared into the trees. She waited for him to reappear, absolutely certain that he wouldn't.

CAPITOL STEPS

The man looks as worn down as salt lick left in the rain.

No, too corny, decided Sevareid and besides, he wasn't sure how salt lick wore in the rain. Walt Waters was definitely worn though. Standing on the steps of the U.S. Capitol, about to give a speech to 30,000 who wanted him to promise that bad as things appeared—with the Bonus bill shot dead and Congress adjourning in an hour for the rest of the summer—the future still looked bright. Sevareid knew they weren't likely to believe it, most of them

shorn clean of hope, but he also knew it was something they needed to hear. Otherwise their future was only more mud and mosquitoes. There was no surprise in what kind of speech was called
for, just as there was no surprise in a hundred pound bag of sand,
but you still had to lift it.

His defeated army is spread below him like pieces
spilled from a sack. What can he possibly offer them except
surrender?

"Now men, I want to warn you," began Waters, his voice so
hoarse and worn Sevareid barely recognized it. "There will be
many factions and groups with pet hobbies and crazy ideas of government who will try to get the support of the Bonus
Expeditionary Force. I want to pledge that I will not allow myself
to be influenced by their oratory or their beautiful pictures of special heavens, as I will ask you to pledge yourselves to me, as red-
blooded Americans, not to listen to them. We are Americans in
principle and can only join that which is wholly American, and
that which represents true American ideals."

A few weeks ago that would have brought them to their
feet. Now they sat and clapped with the same energy they
used to swat gnats.

Sevareid couldn't blame them. Except for Superintendent
Glassford, everybody had let them down, especially Hoover. He
still didn't understand why a guy like Hoover, who just about sin-
gle-handedly rebuilt Europe after the war, couldn't see clear to give
his own people a little of that same help. Hoover's excuse was that
charity would make Americans weak, but how much weaker could
they get?

"I don't blame any of you for feeling angry. And I understand
why some might be disappointed in the leadership." Waters rested
both hands against the wooden microphone stand and waited as a
murmur rolled through the crowd. Waters, scanning the faces
below him, stopped for a moment on Sevareid's. He knew what

Waters was thinking—why hadn't he used the Bill Kincaid story? Sevareid wished he had an answer for that himself.

"Let me just say that we've come through a lot together and I'd like to see us finish that same way," concluded Waters. He appeared as unexcited delivering the message as the Bonus Army was in receiving it. It was just a thing that needed to be said.

A dozen steps above Waters stood Pelham Glassford, in leather boots and motorcycle britches. His uniform cap looked odd, until Sevareid realized he'd gotten a haircut. The curls were gone. He must have figured his picture would be in a lot of newspapers tomorrow.

Glassford started down the steps. The polite applause for Waters had died out, but as Glassford reached the podium it rose again, louder and more enthusiastic. Both Glassford and Waters looked confused. It occurred to Sevareid that the vets were calling for some kind of resurrection, praying that the two might join forces and win this war together.

A dozen veterans slipped under a rope and began climbing the steps. Glassford bent to Waters ear, probably asking him to order them back down. Waters appeared not to hear him. Glassford put an arm across his shoulders and asked again, but Waters only stared unblinking at the advance. Another group started up the other side.

Glassford signaled Captain Largent to come to the podium. Sevareid read Glassford's lips: "Take Commander Waters into the tunnel. And gently."

With the crowd now moving up in force, Glassford set his men in a double line, five steps above the platform. He remained where he was, a token of trust, guessed Sevareid. Glassford was rewarded by the veterans who stopped at the podium. One woman, holding a cat on a leash, hoisted herself half onto the platform before a plain-clothes policeman nudged her off. A new chant rose from below: "We want Waters." Glassford nodded and sent for him.

"I told the Vice President I would keep the plaza clear, and I mean to keep my word!" said Glassford. The crowd jeered at the mention of the vice-president. "You know I'm on your side, but you can't win a war by fighting losing battles."

A veteran answered back. "Maybe, but how can you win a war without fighting any battles?"

Glassford didn't argue the point, only waited while Waters came down to the microphone.

Waters was eager to speak now. "I want you to keep a lane open for the white-collared birds in there, so they won't have to rub into us lousy rats," he said, pointing to the windows of the Capitol. "We're going to stay here until I see Hoover."

"Ask them to sit," said Glassford. Before Waters could respond one way or the other, the Death Marchers appeared at the west side of the Capitol, led by Royal Robertson, his neck brace glinting in the sunset. Though they made no sound, every head turned toward them. Stooped and shuffling, their exhaustion added a charge of electricity to the air.

A Bonus scout appeared on the Capitol's top step to deliver the latest bulletin. Not only had Congress adjourned, but the members snuck out of the Capitol through underground tunnels. Someone shouted, "Let's go!" The crowd surged past the platform toward the police line, leaving Waters and Glassford stranded like sailors on a raft.

Sevareid looked into the faces of the men and women as they moved past, at the cat woman holding a now empty leash, and the pack of reporters running for cover. None of it seemed real, especially when Glassford dove from the platform.

"Don't shoot, don't shoot!" he yelled, swimming through the crowd with overhand strokes. He was trying to reach…Captain Largent. The idiot was waving a gun over his head. Here it is, thought Sevareid, the spark to set things burning. But in the moment it should have happened, nothing did. The veterans paused at the police line long enough for Glassford to reach Captain Largent and shove the gun back into his holster. Then a familiar voice rose above the tension, female and achingly sweet.

> *Oh beautiful for spacious skies*
> *For amber waves of grain*
> *For purple mountain's majesty*
> *Across the fruited plain*

The voice had the pull of the moon on a cresting tide. The space between the Bonus Army and police grew wider as the veterans turned to look at the red-headed girl standing on the platform, singing this most familiar song to a tune none had heard before.

When Nora was done, her head lowered and arms hanging by her side, Walt Waters leaned into the microphone and barely whispered, "Men, let's regroup at camp and see if we can come up with a plan."

And damn if his army didn't obey him one more time.

~

"YOU BROUGHT me back," said Dennis Diamond, who smelled of cut grass and a sour/sweet sweat. "I swear I was ready to break through that police line to do God knows what. You brought me back."

"I guess it's for the best," said Tom Halloran, sounding less than convinced. "Anyway, you sang real nice."

The men walked with her, down the steps to where half a dozen reporters waited. Nora knew they were waiting for her and wasn't sure how she felt about that, just as she wasn't sure why she'd climbed the platform to sing, except it occurred to her someone should.

She'd never have done it three days ago, but she had no need for it then. Today her heartache required shock treatment, and she only realized how much when she stepped to the microphone. All her rehearsing was forgotten, as well as any thoughts of what to sing or how to sound. She was halfway through the first verse of *America the Beautiful* when she realized she'd improvised the tune. Afterwards, she felt exhausted but strangely fortified, as if she'd rid herself of some paralyzing tension. She looked over the crowd for Walker and Eric and, not finding them, felt some of that tension return.

It was still a mystery how everything had fallen apart. Eric she expected to lose, especially after greeting him at the doorway on that morning, red-eyed and folded in on herself from crying. He'd put his hand on her cheek, which nearly brought her again to tears, and asked what was wrong.

"I can't do this or surely I'll die," she answered and felt, if anything, that she was understating things.

Eric said he understood, though Nora could see he didn't. She'd have told him everything if he'd asked and was grateful he never did.

As for Walker, there was no excuse for Walker. Hadn't he won the day? And then abandoned the field. At first she feared he'd been hurt fishing. But after waiting at the window of his cabin for a full day, her fear turned to anger. She waited another half day for the chance to hit him over the head with his guitar. By the time she crossed the river and returned to the Bonus Camp, that anger was an ache behind her breast-bone.

"What's your name?"

"Did somebody tell you to do that?"

"Is your father one of these veterans?"

The reporters' questions came in an unhurried way, as though their stories were already written and only need filling in some blanks. For a moment Nora was tempted to make things up, or at least create a Nora more like the one who'd stepped off the boat from Ireland a few months earlier. But she was too tired for that much creativity.

The oldest and best dressed of the men carried a cane rather than a notebook and asked no questions. He had white hair and his right eye was half shut as though gripping an invisible monocle. When the others left, he stepped forward and introduced himself as Ned Grant, the managing editor of the *Washington Evening Star*.

"That was quite a thing you did."

"It's this city."

Grant leaned on his walking stick, topped with the brass head of a bulldog. "And how is that?"

"The statues and monuments. It's like we're all on a great stage."

"A keen observation," said Grant with a laugh. His eyes were grey and intelligent, or maybe they only looked intelligent, thought Nora, because he'd flattered her. He asked if she had a few minutes to talk.

Dennis Diamond and Tom Halloran waited for Nora a short way off. She told them to go ahead and began walking with Ned Grant in the direction of the White House.

"What you said about all of this being drama. That's exactly what I'm looking for."

Nora turned to him. "You'll have to explain that."

"I'm looking for someone to write a story for my paper, but not a regular reporter." When a clump of veterans bumped past, Grant lowered his voice. "Think of it as a journal, or a diary. A first-person account of things."

"You want me to write a story about the way things really are in the camps?"

"Exactly. And particularly about these final days. We'll pay you, of course."

"But how can you be sure these are final days. Not all the veterans are leaving."

"I'll be frank with you, Nora. It's our belief that whether or not they want to, the Bonus Army will be leaving soon. Mr. Hoover will have them out long before the presidential election in November."

They came to the buildings on Pennsylvania Avenue occupied by the Bonus Army. Nora had been inside once, to watch over two children while their mother gave birth to her third. She danced that night with a six-year-old boy to Duke Ellington's *Savoy Stomp* on a beat up Victrola.

"These will be the first to go," said Grant, pointing at the buildings with his walking stick. "If you could be inside when it happens, talking to the women about their husbands and children. That kind of thing."

"But what if they don't want a story written about themselves?"

"It's best to be as anonymous as possible. We've discovered over the years that you get a more realistic picture that way."

"You mean don't tell them I'm writing a story? I couldn't spy on them, Mr. Grant."

Ned Grant nodded vigorously, as though in complete agreement. "Spying would be unethical. What I'm talking about is writing a story about yourself, with the others as just a part of that." He put a hand on her shoulder. "Nora, this could lead to bigger things for you."

Nora didn't promise anything more than to give it some thought. She'd already considered what it would be like to be a newspaper reporter, while watching Barbara Stanwyck play one in *Forbidden*. Couldn't she write a story at least as well as the ones she read in the newspapers? She wasn't sure but she was ready to try.

After she and Ned Grant parted, she walked slowly, picturing herself assigned to stories in Paris or Rome. She looked back at the building they called the Morgue and saw candles burning in a second floor window. It occurred to her that she'd never gone back to see how the newborn was faring, and that this might be as good a time as any.

ELEVATED MASTER

THE FIRST three men they saw in the Anacostia camp were running scared. Just beyond, another pair sat still as buddhas.

"Ecch!" The sound came from behind them, a woman spitting out moldy bits from a piece of bread. When the woman saw Virni Tabak watching, she quickly turned her back as if to keep him from stealing her bread.

"People are spooked, like the world's coming to an end," said

Nora to Virni. "The tent is spread out over there, next to the dump. Waters wouldn't let us set it up inside camp lines."

"I didn't expect anything more," said Virni. "Commander Waters said if he let me into the camp he'd have to let in Father Coughlin, Sweet Daddy Grace, the Theosophists, the Baptists and the Holy Rollers. I don't know who most of them are, but that would be a good show, don't you think?"

Nora tried to put the best shine on things. "The tent will be visible from parts of the camp and the smell from the dump won't be bad as long as the wind doesn't change direction."

"I don't care about any of that. If this is meant to succeed it will. Early this morning, in a storeroom inside the Temple I had a vision, my first in a year."

"What was it, the vision?"

"Something falling from a ceiling, though not a ceiling exactly. And I couldn't really see what fell. But I took it as a good sign."

"What does Madame Blisky think of this?"

"She said, 'You risk everything. All our work.' I said, 'It's time for me.' And then she let go. I was so surprised how easy it was. When I left the Temple I felt a great joy. Out on a limb, as they say here."

They found Will waiting beside the tent that Neil Gold had scrounged from a bankrupt circus. It lay flat on the ground, round and cheesy with holes. More than a few of the poles were broken and the ropes were a tangle. They had only three hours to set it up, find a table, chair and wooden benches and hang kerosene lanterns.

"Don't worry, this will work," said Will putting an arm across his shoulders. Virni turned to Will with a look of surprise.

Will grinned at him. "Hasn't anybody ever hugged you before?"

"Not like that," said Virni.

Will looked closely at Virni, gave him another squeeze, and looked again. "I can see that now," he said thoughtfully.

WALKER

I COUNTED twenty people pulling ropes, apparently happy to raise anything from that barren ground, even an old sack of canvas tent that smelled like elephant shit and stale popcorn. It reminded me of my first circus in New York. I was just five and more afraid of the clowns' deceiving smiles than any lion or bear. What I liked best was this juggler who caught burning torches and sharp-edged knives with all the confidence in the world. For years after that, when anyone asked what I wanted to be when I grew up, I'd say circus juggler.

A man pulling rope next to me said he once worked in a circus.

Another guy, holding penny nails in his mouth, asked if it was true what they said about trapeze ladies.

"It is," said the rope man, "and then some."

I was glad for the company. During the last four-and-a-half days I'd traveled alone to the Kemunkey reservation and back again, full-speed both ways like a lunatic. I left the day after Nora and I had our night together. As heavenly as that night had been, the next day was equally hellish. I knew I didn't own her, but that wasn't the same as accepting it. When I left her waiting for Sevareid at my cabin, I felt like I'd swallowed broken glass.

I crashed through the woods all that morning trying to come up with a solution short of murder. By the afternoon I'd made a decision: it didn't matter what I decided. Sooner or later we were bound to fail. Better to get it over with before the wounds went deeper.

And then there was Fat Carlos to consider. Visiting Henry seemed the logical thing to do. I snuck back and got my boat, grateful to avoid any sign of Nora and Sevareid. If there was any relief in doing what had to be done, I didn't feel it. I didn't feel anything but doomed all the way to the reservation.

Once there, I had a quick meal of wild turkey and some corn bread with Henry, said hello to a few old friends and was suddenly hit by another revelation. Even if it *was* a case of sooner or later, why the hell would I choose sooner? My wounds couldn't go any deeper.

"Stop by again when you're in the neighborhood," said Henry as I pointed the boat for home. Jesse was still with him, wearing a deer skin skirt decorated with little painted totem figures and a genuine Indian feather vest. A few of the Indian women seemed to be mocking her getup, but she and Henry looked happy and I was encouraged by that.

I didn't expect to find Nora at the cabin, but I was surprised she wasn't at the camp. No one had seen her since her performance at the Capitol steps, a performance described by half a dozen people in as many different ways. One of the wives told me she'd put some kind of magic spell on the men. I didn't doubt it.

I guessed my best chance of finding her was at Virni's show, so after we raised the tent I sat and waited, my chair turned to the entrance. When Virni and Will came in to thank everyone for helping, I asked about her.

"She was here earlier," said Virni. "Said she'd be back for the show."

"I think she was going to one of those Pennsylvania Avenue buildings," added Will, resting his arm on Virni's shoulder. The pair were chummy as wood ducks.

Sevareid came into the tent looking like the fittest man in Washington. I'd hoped to find Nora first but Sevareid needed seeing as well.

"Hey stranger, how's it going?" he said, smiling like nothing but good had ever come between us. I smiled back, glad to share the pretense. Losing him as a friend was no small sacrifice, especially since it was the only proof I had that whites and coloreds could actually get along like the Party promised. I told him I'd just got back from seeing Henry.

"He asked about you."

"You and Nora paddled down?"

Now I was definitely confused. If he was asking that...three possibilities occurred to me, all of them good. As casually as I could, I told him Nora hadn't made the trip. He pushed a strand of hair off his face to get a better look at his possibilities. "So you haven't seen her either?"

"I'm supposed to meet her here," I lied.

He didn't believe me, but then neither of us knew what to believe except that one of us would find her first.

～

THEY CALLED IT the Ladies Room and invited Nora to take a cushion on the floor. "There's no men in here after supper," explained Kristina Sworzek, holding the baby girl she'd delivered the night Nora watched her kids. Kristina was from Poland. She had bunchy brown hair, light grey eyes and a clear forehead that appeared and disappeared behind the smoke from her hand-rolled cigarette. She'd been in America long enough to pick up some swear words and fractured slang. "You can love men and still take a getaway some damn time."

Nora knew the other two women in the room from her previous visits. Jennifer Owens, a proper Bostonian, had just come back from a tour of restaurant trash bins. Dorothy Dowd, an out of work school teacher, was explaining fractions to five children in a Mississippi accent so strong her number three had two-and-a-half syllables.

Nora sat on the floor next to Kristina, who was knitting a sweater, occasionally flicking her ashes with one of the needles. Nora found her own fingers moving in sympathetic rhythm.

"You have beautiful skin," Jennifer told Nora. "When I was a girl I treasured my little box of makeup. The only thing I have to put on my face here is coal dust."

"I don't think my husband would notice one way or the other," laughed Dorothy. "But then noticing things isn't really what they're good at, is it?"

Nora laughed with the others though it seemed to her most men in America paid closer attention than she liked. Even Walker and Eric...no, she wouldn't think of them right now, she was worn out with thinking of Walker and Eric. When Kristina's four-year-old daughter bumped her knee and began to cry, Nora was glad to take on the job of comforting her.

"He pushed me," said Patty pointing at her three-year-old brother Ben.

"He needs to be punished," decided Nora. "Let's kiss him and make him laugh."

Patty was hoping for a less affectionate sentence, but didn't want to lose Nora's attention. Soon enough she, Nora and Ben were on the floor laughing.

"You have babies soon, yes?" said Kristina.

"Not soon," said Nora. "Maybe when I'm twenty-five."

"Twenty-five? That's a lifetime away," said Dorothy.

Nora looked at Patty, Ben and the other children in the room. A week ago she'd have sworn she was more akin to them than their mothers. Now she recognized that as wishful thinking and was glad to admit it. All those years on the farm, inventing herself without fear of contradiction. The world was a more interesting place knowing it had the power to change a person. She looked at the women and wondered where she'd be at their age. She'd never before thought half that far ahead. Once again she wondered if writing about these women would be a betrayal. They'd told their stories to her, a virtual stranger. Putting them in a newspaper was only repeating the stories to a larger group of strangers. Ned Grant said Depression stories were like a tribe's oral history, everyone's to share. She wanted to believe that.

"I might like to write stories about all this for a newspaper," she said.

"I'm still planning on finishing the novel I started when I was 14," said Dorothy.

Kristina patted her hand. "It's good to have dreams."

Nora hadn't exactly "come clean" as Americans liked to say, but she felt better for having brought it up. Sitting with these women was a pleasure, but if she was to keep her promise to Virni she had to hurry.

She'd parked her bicycle between the Morgue and the Armory,

behind a pile of bricks. When she bent to it, someone pressed something hard into the small of her back.

"Please don't call out or try to run, Miss O'Sullivan. I just want us to have a little talk."

James Kemper! How had he managed to sneak up on her, big as he was? And had the nerve to stick what she guessed was a pistol into her back. She spun around to grab it, but Kemper's hand was concealed inside his jacket.

"Tell me you aren't so stupid as to threaten me."

Kemper looked flustered by her boldness. He removed his empty hand from the jacket and held it palm up. "I just wanna talk," he said, his native cockney leaking through this adopted accent. "We can do it here or in my room across the avenue."

The only reason to go to his hotel room was to maintain the charade that she believed he had the cup. She couldn't think of a reason not to.

"You lead the way. But I warn you, if I find my cup in your room I'll take it straight back."

They dodged traffic on Pennsylvania Avenue and entered the hotel. Nora gave a backward look at the bars covering the underground slave pens Walker had shown her. A few old men sat in the lobby, fanning themselves with folded newspapers, too hot to spare them even a glance.

Kemper's room was yellow with bad lighting and ancient water stains. Once inside, Nora made a show of searching the closet and opening drawers.

"That's very cunning," said Kemper. "Pretending to look for what you already possess."

Nora leaned her hip against the dresser while Kemper sat on rust-stained bed sheets. His cheeks were flushed pink and he was looking at Nora in a way that reminded her of someone, Cavan the baker. This was her cue to show righteous indignation. She thought of all the actresses she'd lately seen in movies, trying to remember who played that well.

"You're saying I have the cup? The one you took from my hand in front of my father, God and the publican? How did I manage that trick?" She didn't need a mirror to know her cheeks had flushed convincingly.

"You managed it by enlisting the help of…let's see, Mr. Neil Gold, William Cutler and a darkie named Walker. How you enlisted their help, I won't speculate." He was back to his high church English again. "That you now know the whereabouts of the cup, I have no doubt."

Nora gave away nothing, her face still as pond water. She dropped her right shoulder and raised both eyebrows like Myrna Loy in *Deception*. But no matter the skill of her performance, she knew Kemper wasn't buying any of it. How had he picked up her trail so easily? And all the names. If her face was calm, her stomach wasn't.

Kemper laughed in an un-merry way. "It was the General who tipped me. Saw the whole thing from beginning to end. The man has witnessed a campaign or two, what? And you waiting on the dock! With that hair? It wasn't very smart but still…." Kemper rose from the bed and came closer. He was huffing some, with beads of sweat on his forehead. "I must say you surprised me. Did better than I expected and by quite a bit. Yes, very resourceful. Which leads me to my offer."

"An offer?"

"Partners. I use my contacts and expertise to sell it. We split the profits exactly in half. And maybe move on to other items."

Nora snorted. "Even if I had the cup, I'd melt it down before letting you profit a penny from its sale. You're wasting my time, Mr. Kemper." She moved past him to the door, but as she reached for the knob he grabbed her from behind and pinned her to the wall. Surprising agility for a man so large, thought Nora, reassured by her own calm. But then why should she be afraid? Wasn't she the undisputed red-haired champion, 2 and 0 against better men than Kemper. He'd be no problem, even if he was, at the moment, squeezing the breath out of her.

"The cup doesn't belong to you. Or to me for that matter," he whispered in her ear. "That cup belongs to people long since dead."

Nora got a foot loose and kicked his shin, but the man's legs were tree trunks. All she got for her effort was a rough scrape of her cheek against the wall.

"I have an interest in redheads," said Kemper. "Did you know that Helen of Troy was a redhead, along with Cleopatra and Aphrodite? In ancient Egypt redheads were sacrificed to the god Osiris, buried alive as a matter of fact. So you see, you were born to be spoiled."

As he spoke, Kemper slid his right arm slowly down her side until it reached her waist. Nora was aware of his arm in the same way she was aware of his words, as unpleasant objects with very little connection to her. That changed when he suddenly reached round her waist and yanked on her pants. What young Rosario had been unable to do with both hands, Kemper accomplished as easily as tearing paper from a roll. The top buttons snapped off and her pants fell halfway down her hips.

"Now this, you think is yours as well," he said, jamming his hand into her underwear and between her legs. Nora gasped with the shock of it, his fingers moving inside her like wild animals. She felt herself go weak and Kemper must have felt it too. He immediately freed his other hand to undo the buttons on his pants.

She needed to convert her fear into anger, but all she could muster was disbelief. This man who couldn't run thirty yards without fainting from the effort was attempting to rape her! And from behind. She took a breath and summoned her brother Brendan, Catholic saints, Celtic heroes and every other spirit she no longer believed in then pushed away from the door with all her might.

If Kemper moved, it was only to press himself more forcefully against her, his head so tight to her own she could feel his pulse against her ear. He was working his pants lower and hers as well, his wet breath on her neck. What could she do? There was nothing to do…except scream.

At the same moment Nora sucked in a breath to do it, Kemper moved to stop her. He gave up on his pants and reached toward her mouth, leaning back just enough to make room for the bend in his elbow. It was no more than an inch or two but gave Nora a chance. She snapped her head back and caught Kemper's eyebrow.

The blow was weak but well-placed and drew a gush of blood. Kemper instinctively leaned back to keep the blood from dripping down his face, which gave Nora room for one more shot. She bent her chin to her breastbone, snapped her head back with a loud grunt and felt the bridge of his nose mash like celery.

Kemper pulled his right hand from Nora's pants and the other from her throat and used both to cover his nose. Nora yanked her pants up and was reaching again for the door when Kemper's soft moan stopped her. She took aim over her shoulder and spun an elbow into his throat. Kemper dropped to his knees, gasping like a cracked steam pipe. Nora moved in front of him, intending to say something so sharp and true, the scar would stay with him forever. She could still feel his hand inside her and was scared to think she might carry that with her, a lasting imprint of evil.

When punishing words wouldn't come, Nora did the next best thing and kicked him between the legs.

Down the stairs, past the desk clerk and the old men with their newspapers, Nora didn't look back until she was safely across the avenue. The sun was long since down but she could still see the shape of the brick pile where her bicycle lay and other shapes as well, probably more bricks but possibly not. Hot as it was, Nora found herself trembling as she stared into the darkness. She could come back for the bicycle tomorrow but by then it would be gone. She was more scared now than when Kemper had her against the door but if she let that fear grow...she vowed not to. She'd get on her bicycle and ride straight away from this place and remove any possibility that what happened tonight would forever change her. Just as soon as her shaking stopped.

TENT SHOW

"WHY ARE you here? Do you really think wealth and happiness are as easy to attain as coming to a tent?" Eric Sevareid had heard Virni deliver this same spiel at the Mighty My Temple, but he sounded different tonight, sitting on a card table with his legs swinging and the light from three oil lamps dancing on the canvas behind him. Last time Virni appeared theatrically calm. Tonight he was genuinely happy, like the good news he brought wasn't from on high but moving up his body. And it tickled.

Sevareid was all the more impressed because without the elevated stage and purple robe, Virni looked young and vulnerable. His only prop tonight was a tin cup holding one ragweed flower.

"I'm here to tell you…that wealth and happiness are not that easy," continued Virni. "If wealth and happiness were as easy as wishing, none of you would be sleeping in the mud or listening to me talk about spiritual beauty beside a trash dump."

About half of the hundred people in the tent laughed at that. The others, at least the ones Sevareid could see, looked confused which he figured was better than being bored.

Virni's tent show was not likely to be a story any newspaper would buy but Sevareid had other reasons to be there, and not only because it was his best bet to find Nora. There was something about Virni that intrigued him. He'd seen him at the Criers Club gambling and smoking cigars and yet, Virni still managed to convey a kind of purity. Not the purity of avoiding things, but a contrary kind of swallowing everything he saw. Sevareid vaguely remembered reading something similar in school, maybe Epicurus, and made a note to look it up.

"Wealth may be no more than an accident. A lucky combination of hard work and good timing. But happiness!" Virni leaned forward and lowered his voice. "That is your birthright. Not everyone can be wealthy, but everyone can be happy. And the key to happiness is not hidden in some temple but inside each of you. I can show you where to find that, isn't it worth a few minutes inside a smelly circus tent?"

Virni hopped off the table. "I'm not talking about religion," he said raising his hands as if anticipating an argument. "Catholicism, Protestantism, Judaism...each is a blossom of the same flower. I am talking about something more basic than religion. Not the flower or the stem but the soil itself."

A man smelling of onions leaned between Sevareid and the woman to his right. "What kind of plant is he talking about?"

"A flower," she answered. "Some kind of flower."

"It is written that God sleeps in the mineral, dreams in the vegetable, wakes to consciousness in the animal, and finally to self-consciousness in the man. We will awake to divine consciousness in the man made perfect."

Someone near the front shouted, "Make something appear."

Virni hesitated before returning to sit on the table. "Making things appear is not so simple as wishing for it to happen. If the windows to the past and future opened that easily, we'd be always falling in and out."

"Bring back the sword," demanded a woman.

"And the rose," yelled another.

They'd either been to the Mighty My Temple or talked to people who had, thought Sevareid, and they wanted the full show.

"You must understand," said Virni, "it takes preparation to do this. Many voices. A powerful energy...."

"It's a fake."

"Prove him wrong."

"Religion is a capitalist plot."

Voices called from every part of the tent. Again he left his table to come closer. "I'm trying to tell you about a happiness within your reach. What good to you are swords and roses?"

"Is it because we don't have money to give you?"

A few people at the back of the tent walked out. The woman who'd demanded that Virni bring back the sword asked again, this time in a pleading voice.

"Okay," said Virni. "We'll try. But I need all of your help. Even if you don't believe, pretend. Like a school play. Take a deep breath and chant with me. *Hoooooooooooo. Hoooooooooooo.*"

Slowly and then with force, the veterans and their wives began hooting like owls.

"There is no present, no future, no past," said Virni above the chanting. "There is only time. And time itself is an illusion."

∽

NORA KNELT outside the tent, her forehead against the canvas and chanted, dropping her voice lower and deeper until her chest vibrated with the sound. She'd arrived just after Virni began speaking and, looking through the flap, saw the back of Eric's head. She wanted to talk with him but not there or then, afraid if he put his arms around her, she'd feel Kemper's, and so she went halfway around the circular tent and bowed her head to Virni's words.

It was good to be alone in the dark and unafraid. This chanting created a tingle of heat across her forehead and down her back. She felt herself sinking deeper into the sound. Abruptly, Nora lifted her head. Some amount of time had passed just now and carried her with it. Not sleep, but something beyond her body. Was this what they called bliss? Before she could enjoy that thought, another came to her.

Nothing was going to drop from the ceiling this night, no sword, parchment or rose.

The chanting continued with fits of coughing like static on a radio. Even outside the tent, the smell of the lamps was harsh in her nose. Slowly she stood and backed away, unwilling to witness Virni's failure.

The night sky was starless and there were few fires to light her way. Dennis Diamond, Tom Halloran and the others who usually kept a small blaze burning, must have been at Virni's tent show. Nora eventually found her pallet and the cup buried in soft dirt beneath it. She wiped it clean with her shirt then sat with it pressed between her legs. It's funny, she thought, all the flirting and hair-combing and iambic pentameter eventually come to this, men wanting to get inside her and she desiring, selectively of course, to let them in. The funny part was not that it came as any surprise, being a farm girl who'd witnessed a few thousand hillside ruttings, but that she'd let herself be surprised in Kemper's room. And why had she waited so long to call for help? Because James Kemper hadn't seemed dangerous until he suddenly was, and because calling for help during a fight was....girlish. Kemper was right, the world was both more and less than she imagined.

She stood and walked. Without intending to, she found herself again at the dark side of the tent. The chanting inside had grown considerably weaker and the coughing had increased. She felt the weight of Virni's failure and the veterans' despair, not figuratively but actually, her cup suddenly heavy as paving stone. A cone of light shone above the tent. It was not the Mighty My's violet oracular flame but only lantern light escaping through the hole where the poles and ropes met. Nora reached her cup toward it and remembered contests with her brother, lofting stones up and into the chimneys of abandoned farm houses. How high could she throw something as heavy as this cup? A purely hypothetical question, because even as she reached her arm back she knew there was no way she'd ever let it go, not with all the magic of finding it and the work of getting it back.

The cup brushed a strand of her hair in passing. She stood with both hands raised, waiting for it to fall back, but the only thing that came to her was an excited shout from inside the tent.

Nora lowered her head to find Walker standing beside her.

"I'm sorry," he said.

"You're four days late for being sorry," said Nora. "Did you at least bring me some food? I could eat a pony."

By the time the tent fire started, Nora and Walker were fifty yards toward home and neither looked back.

ENGAGEMENT

THE MORNING of July 28th began better than any since Eric Severaid arrived in Washington. Eight-thirty in the morning and he's drinking coffee with Max Berga, probably the best reporter in D.C., and Police Superintendent Pelham Glassford, whose face is ten inches from the nipple of a reclining nude in the members' lounge of the National Press Club.

"So this is 'Phryne,'" said Glassford, stepping back for a wider view of the 6-by-4 foot painting. "I swear I've seen her before."

"You have," said Berga. "In nearly every statue and painting of Aphrodite. Phryne was the model."

"And Phryne was...?"

"Athenian courtesan. Fourth Century B.C. The widow of the Brazilian ambassador to the U.S lent the painting to our club last week. It caused quite a stir in Paris twenty years ago, so you can imagine what the reaction here will be when the wrong people get a look at it. She lends a bit of class, don't you gentlemen agree?"

Severaid nodded approvingly and took another sip of coffee. Given how little he knew about art and naked women, he figured it best to withhold comment. He'd been invited to this breakfast as payback for handing Berga the story of Virni's tent fire, quotes and all. There was no way he could write it, knowing what he did about Nora's cup, but it was too good a story to let die. And Berga had done a good job with it, even if he was a little mean in his description of Virni.

**TENT FIRE
AT BONUS CAMP**

By Max Berga
WASHINGTON HERALD

A 16-year-old minister of the Mighty My faith brought down more than religious blessings last night on a tent filled with Bonus Army veterans from Camp Marks (Anacostia). In the rush to touch a silver cup that minister Virni Tabak claimed to have summoned from the ancient past, a kerosene lantern shattered, setting fire to the tent. One hundred and fifty people fled the flames. No serious injuries were reported.

"It was an accident, but no harm done" said Tabak, a self-anointed Elevated Master who usually conducts his "services" at the Mighty My temple on 13th and Upshur Streets, N.W. Last night the 16-year-old erected an old circus tent beside the Navy Yard trash dump, then persuaded a group of veterans to make hooting sounds to help summon objects through a "time window." After 20 minutes of cacophonous concentration, a silver cup fell through the roof of the tent and landed on the table beside Tabak.

Rush To Touch

The appearance of the cup, which was adorned with images of human sacrifice and a pagan fertility goddess, set off a rush to touch which led to the kerosene fire. With no water available, Minister Tabak and the veterans could do nothing but stand aside and watch the flames.

"Something magical happened here tonight," said Tabak, clutching the cup outside the burning tent. "I'm hoping this will be a good omen for the Bonus Expeditionary Force."

Berga didn't ask why Sevareid wasn't writing the story himself. "As long as it's accurate," he said, "I'll give it a good home."

For the last three nights, Sevareid had been bar-hopping with Berga and sleeping in his alley house. Berga knew everyone and everyone knew him, including Will Rogers, who put his arm around Sevareid's shoulders and said in a theatrical whisper, "Son, it's not too late to quit this business and do something useful with your life."

S evareid felt as though he'd passed into journalism's inner sanctum, and had no intention of ever going back.

While Berga and Glassford talked art, Sevareid studied the painting. The woman lay on her back, her right knee raised, naked except for a pair of sandals and a ribbon tied under her breasts. Not exactly his type, except for her dark eyes, which seemed to be watching him, and her commendable lack of clothes. He thought of Nora, and wondered again how she'd disappeared so quickly after tossing her cup into the tent. Or did someone else throw it?

"Mr. Sevareid, you seem to have a real appreciation for this work," said Glassford.

"She reminds me of...something," answered Sevareid.

Berga laughed. "The sweet something. I believe our young friend here has penetrated to the heart of art."

~

AT THE SAME moment Eric Sevareid was judging Phryne's body in the National Press Club, Nora O'Sullivan stood on the sidewalk at Third and Pennsylvania, listening to Walt Waters' bugler blow assembly.

The 300 men, women and children who lived in the Fort, Showroom and Morgue gathered on the dirt lots between buildings, or watched from outside steps and windows. It was already 92 degrees on what would be the hottest day of the year.

"Men, a few days ago I struck a deal with General MacArthur," said Waters, lifting the heels of his black cavalry boots. "As our part of the bargain, we must evacuate these buildings today."

The men knew this was coming. The Treasury feds had not only been threatening to evict them for weeks, but Waters himself leaked the deal to the *Washington Herald*. Their displeasure was close to the surface.

"By God, Waters, have you lost your nerve?"

"What about staying here until 1945?"

"How much did you get for selling out to Hoover?"

Nora felt sorry for Waters. A few weeks ago he seemed so happy, marching around the camp, joking with the soldiers and showing off his new boots and coat. Being Commander-in-Chief didn't look quite so much fun today.

"Damn it men, this is a war just like any other war. We give and we get. If I'd waited, we wouldn't a got a thing. Besides, I gave my word on this."

While the men stood their ground, spitting and kicking at the dirt, the women near Nora started for the buildings to pack. Waters had promised them a barracks in Maryland with hot water and electricity, and that was enough to win over a host of accomplices.

"This is not a surrender," insisted Waters. "And whoever it was that asked about 1945, I'll be here until then. Or until we get the bonus. We've got all day to pack and be ready. The trucks come at 7."

No sooner had he finished than a uniformed messenger arrived and handed him an envelope. Waters read the note then crushed it in his hand.

"Men, you're double-crossed. I'm double-crossed. The Undersecretary of the Treasury, a bastard named Mills, is giving us ten minutes to get out or says we'll be arrested."

The women stopped and began throwing questions at Waters.

"How can we pack that fast? What about our deal?"

Waters' shoulders sagged, his posture very similar to what Nora had seen on the day of the Senate vote. "We pack and wait for the trucks," he said. "My deal was with General MacArthur, not millionaire Mills."

A group from the Fort, the middle building now occupied primarily by the families of bricklayers and other mid-western tradesmen, gathered to one side. Nora was close enough to hear William Hrushka, a 37-year-old Chicago butcher, say there ought to be a vote.

"We're not in the army any more. This is a democracy, ain't it?"

Nora had been told that Hrushka lost fifty pounds in the last two months, but he was still a big man.

"We could make our stand right here," said another veteran.

"Make our stand how?"

Hrushka gave a look toward Waters. "Let's talk inside."

Walt Waters approached Police Captain Rod Largent who was directing his men to place rope barriers around the three buildings.

"Are you trying to keep us in or get us out?"

"We'll just have to wait and see," said Largent.

∼

NORA FOUND Will Cutler on the second-floor landing of the Fort, standing next to his movie camera and cursing his luck.

"Damn it all. I had Waters right there, crumpling the message and throwing it to the ground. He says 'Men you're double-crossed. I'm double-crossed...' Then bang! The film runs out. I shouldn't have shot so much on the stairway but how could I resist? The veterans lined up with the sun on them like a spotlight, talking about stuff that's interesting, even to me, who couldn't answer one question about the war before I started with the camera."

"You can get more film, can't you Will?"

"Sure I can. But not in time. Do you know what's gonna happen now?"

Nora didn't.

"There's going to be police or soldiers or somebody come up here and drag women and children out of the buildings and the Bonus guys are gonna throw rocks and get chased and....damn it Nora. I'm gonna miss it all!"

"I'm sorry, Will. I didn't know this was so important to you."

Will sat on the top step. "This camera. Looking through it, you see things different. Details. Light and shadows. How people's eyes tell a different story than the words they say."

"Maybe this is what you're meant to do," said Nora.

"Maybe." Will pulled the camera across the landing. He was unlatching the carry box when William Hrushka and his men came up the stairs. One of them stopped for an interview. Will didn't tell him there was no more film. Instead he pointed the camera at the veteran, but twisted the recorder to pick up what Hrushka and the others were saying behind him.

"If we don't push back now, when will we?" asked Hrushka.

"What if that's what they want. Give 'em an excuse to wipe us out?"

"At least here we've got the advantage of cover and high ground," said Hrushka. "Not to mention all the little bends and corners in these buildings."

"Mr. Cameraman?" The veteran on the stairs was impatient to start.

"Okay," said Will fiddling with the camera, "but talk real soft. This recording thing won't work if you're too loud."

∼

PELHAM GLASSFORD was surprised to see so many of his men lining Pennsylvania Avenue.

"My orders were to show only a token presence," he told Sevareid who was riding on the back of his motorcycle, a courtesy lift after their morning coffee at the National Press Club. "One thing I've learned since the Bonus Army arrived is that these men do best when trusted to do well."

He parked the motorcycle inside the rope barrier and asked Captain Largent for an explanation.

"The Secretary of the Treasury gave orders for them to leave right now."

"Why in the hell is he dipping his beak in here?"

"I don't know, but these guys aren't moving fast enough to suit me."

"Making you happy is probably not a big concern of theirs," said Glassford, moving away to look for Walt Waters at the Morgue. Sevareid followed close behind.

"Good morning, General." A woman with an infant in her arms and a girl of about four on her knee, spoke to him from the front steps of the building.

"How old is your baby?"

"A few weeks," said Grace Tumulty, offering it for Glassford to hold.

"She looks like you," said Glassford, sniffing the infant's head.

Nora O'Sullivan came out of the building carrying a boy on her back.

"Eric!"

"Nora."

Nora blushed under the curious gaze of both Sevareid and the police superintendent. She turned her attention to Grace Tumulty. "He was wanting to show you these." The little boy handed his mother a pair of wooden chopsticks. "I told him the Chinese eat meatballs with them."

Glassford introduced himself. "I've been meaning to thank you. For the other day at the Capitol."

He was interrupted by a police whistle and shouts from the street. They turned to see spectators on the north side of the avenue pushed forward like water before a big ship. Following in their wake was John Pace, leading a group of men who carried sticks and bricks.

"You should get inside," Glassford told Nora. She immediately hoisted three-year-old Ben onto her back and grabbed his sister Patty by the hand. When Grace had trouble standing, Sevareid took her arm and helped her into the building.

He came out in time to see a brick hit the side of Glassford's head. Glassford didn't fall, just stood perfectly still as Pace's men raced past. One of them reached out and ripped the police badge from his shirt. Sevareid jumped down the steps, his impulse to tackle the thief. He was stopped by an uncomfortable thought—it wasn't his job to take sides.

Sevareid led Glassford to the doorway of the Morgue. "Are you okay?"

"The comic books are right," said Glassford. "You do see stars."

～

ON THE second floor of the Morgue, Nora helped Grace Tumulty and her baby into a dark closet and moved aside to let Patty follow. But when she tried to lift Ben from her neck, he held tight.

"Please," said Grace. "Sit with us for a minute."

Nora had good reasons to refuse. She was extremely anxious about leaving Eric on the battlefield and Will on the second landing of the Fort, where the stick-and-brick men were headed. She was less worried about Walker, who'd told her the Communist Society only wanted veterans to be involved in Bonus Army actions. She should have stayed with him that morning, even though leaving seemed the only thing to do at the time.

"I promised to write a story for Ned Grant," she'd told Walker, who was still in bed and trying to pull her back.

"Write it tomorrow," he said, stroking her wrist.

Nora grabbed the newspaper she'd picked up the night before in Georgetown and put the front page story between them like a shield.

BONUS ARMY CAPITULATES
Special to THE NEW YORK TIMES

Washington, July 27—Capitulation of the bonus expeditionary force to the Treasury in its efforts to evict them from condemned Federal buildings was announced tonight by Walter W. Waters, commander of the veterans.

The decision to evacuate the squatters from the buildings, as fast as the contractors found it necessary to raze them, followed a long conference between President Hoover, Secretaries Hurley and Mills and Ferry K. Heath, Assistant Secretary of the Treasury.

It was reported that if the marchers had persisted in defying the Treasury, it was proposed to call out troops to evict them forcibly and concentrate them in one camp under guard.

Demand for Waters to Resign

An indication that the veterans might not follow Mr. Waters in any evacuation agreement, however, was seen in a story carried in a newsletter distributed throughout the bonus camps, to the effect that the national executive committee of the Bonus Expeditionary Force had formally demanded the resignation of Mr. Waters as commander.

The demand was based on charges that he had "deliberately incited the riot in front of the Capitol Building last week, and then after the men had been aroused to a pitch of excitement and violence, tried to slip out of the mob and run away."

"If I'm going to write the story, I have to do it today," she said and there was truth in that. But the other part of needing to leave she didn't share. They'd spent all but a few hours of the last two days in bed, and not much of that time sleeping. It was wonderful, deliriously exhausting and a little frightening as well. Their love-making had a life of its own, beyond what either she or Walker seemed able to control. It was as if they'd joined forces to steal pleasure, not just from each other but from the world itself, and were now driven by the power of it. At one point during the night, she dreamed she was riding Neil Gold's big horse. She woke to find herself wrapped tightly with Walker in sweat-soaked sheets, and wondered if she'd been dreaming at all. She needed a few hours apart, to figure out where she ended and they began.

But here, inside a closet playing father to a scared family, was not the place for that discovery. Besides, what kind of reporter hid in a closet while a battle raged? Then again, this was the story she'd been commissioned to write—a mother in tears, her terrified children. These buildings were bursting with stories—the seamstress from Tennessee who traced on a map the 2,000 miles she'd walked looking for a job; the Chicago school teacher who taught without pay for a full year and spent the last of her money buying lunches for her students; an eight-year-old boy who watched his father die of tuberculosis at a Hooverville camp in Manhattan's Central Park. Those were the stories she would write.

"Tell us again about the gypsies," asked Grace, taking hold of her wrist.

"Okay, I'll tell you the gypsies, but then I must go outside to see if it's safe. We call them tinkers. They travel the roads in horse-drawn wagons and sing in a language of their own. When I was a girl I wanted to go with the tinkers, to feed the horses and see the world."

"And do they tell fortunes like other gypsies?"

"They do. One tinker wanted to tell my future but I wouldn't let her."

"I wouldn't either," said Patty.

"If I had a horse, I'd ride away from here," said Ben.

His mother laughed. "That's right Ben. We'd all get on the horse and live happily ever after."

Nora didn't laugh. Who was to say her own ideas were any less childish. Kemper was right. The world was not like the movies, where people chose between right and wrong. The real world was a dozen choices and none of them clear.

～

POLICE CAPTAIN LARGENT held his men in check until the brick hit Glassford's head.

"Officers, draw your weapons. They've wounded the Superintendent!"

Only a few of the police withdrew their guns, but many put hands to holsters as Captain Largent led their charge. As he passed Glassford, Largent either didn't hear or chose to ignore the Superintendent's order to halt.

Pelham Glassford pushed himself out the Morgue's doorway and followed Largent to the Fort. Sevareid rushed to join him, nearly colliding with Nora.

"Will's in there," she said in a frightened voice.

They arrived at the Fort just after a shot rang out. Glassford blew through the doorway, past crouched police with guns drawn. Captain Largent was halfway up the stairs, just below a veteran who lay in a pool of blood on the second floor landing. There was another man up there, standing behind something big and black on tall metal legs.

Glassford would later write that in his concussed state, the scene seemed more dreamlike than real. Then Captain Largent fired his gun at the man behind the…camera. But if it was only a camera why was he shooting? As Largent aimed his pistol again, Glassford tried to order him to stop but the words wouldn't come. The gun went off at nearly the same moment that a rock hit Largent on the back of his head. It all seemed to happen in one extended moment: the light shining through the missing wall onto the cameraman as he tumbled down; the rock bouncing off Largent's head.

A red-haired girl bumped past him and climbed over Largent to kneel beside the cameraman. The girl who sang on the Capitol steps. The leather sling he'd noticed in her right hand as they ran toward the Fort was gone. Glassford pictured the rock hitting Capt. Largent. It came not from above but below, from a spot just behind Glassford, where the girl must have stood. He couldn't see her face through the tangle of her hair, but from the way her shoulders shook he guessed she was crying. The blow to his own head, he guessed, would no doubt cause him to forget some of these details in the hours to come.

A dozen veterans started down the stairs with obvious purpose. Glassford ordered his men to holster their guns and asked the veterans to drop their bricks. Both orders were obeyed, but the veterans continued their descent. The first man to fall was a policeman, hit by a punch. The veteran who floored him was knocked down in turn. Glassford stood with his arms folded as men fought around him. The only blow he received was from one of his own officers, who hit him in the act of falling.

"Hey fellas," said Glassford, "that policeman you just knocked down was a Congressional Medal of Honor winner. How's about we stop for lunch." It was just preposterous enough, suggesting lunch in the middle of a pitched battle, that it worked. Both sides lowered their hands and allowed medics to tend to the dead and wounded.

WHISKEY WAR

HERE'S HOW the sting was supposed to work. Fat Carlos and his men would come from one direction at the same time that Jamaican Juan Wilson led his gang from the other. There'd be arguments and fighting and, in the end, three cases of fake whiskey splattered all over Seventh Street. I didn't need Tommy Baker to tell me it was a bad plan.

"What if one of them's late and the other takes home all those bottles of beet water? They gonna drag your ass through Georgetown from the back of a Model A."

"So it's a bad plan, it's the only one I could come up with," I said as we unloaded the pre-cut whiskey bottles from a pony cart and stacked them on a tilted wooden platform, designed after the one I'd built while ferrying customers on the *Edie*.

"How's that white girl doin' you?"

"She's Irish. Her name is Nora."

"Is it good gap?"

"It's not all about that," I said.

"What you talkin' about? Irish or Zulu, it's always about that." Tommy was the only person I knew who could laugh without looking the slightest bit amused. "And it better be damn good for all the risk you're taking. Out here in the high and wide."

"How about you. Anything good goin' on?"

"Me? I got more girls than I got sense. Things are too damn complicated all of a sudden."

"I never thought I'd hear you complain about too many girls."

"You get to be a man and things change." Tommy posed in profile as he said it, which made him look silly and young. His hair was mostly straight now, lying on his head like small waves on a black beach. He still talked in quick, excited bursts.

"Let's make a last check that these cases are stacked right," he said. "Fuck this up and I'll be burying you next to Mr. Luke."

After the successful sting on the Potomac to retrieve Nora's silver cup, I was feeling smart, lucky and more than a little ornery. If the plan didn't work? Tough. I'd spit in Fat Carlos' eye for trying to set me up for Jenny Broom's murder. At least that was my mood the day I started things in motion.

But on the morning Nora left to write her story about the evacuation, I had a change of heart. I was exhausted, the kind of tired no amount sleep can relieve, and the obvious recklessness of the plan made me more tired still. I couldn't care less about the whiskey or the money. The bottles, slit behind the labels and filled with juice, could stay stacked in the locked closet outside Griffith Stadium for a hundred years, until the Senators won another pennant.

Fat Carlos and the Jamaican? I'd deal with them later. Just then I needed to find Tommy and tell him to cancel the plan, which was supposed to be sprung the following day. He'd be happy to hear it.

I found one of his girls on 13th Street, chewing gum and wearing too much lipstick. She told me he'd rushed off about half an hour earlier, said he had business at Griffith Stadium.

I figured he'd be waiting for me at Willie's Tavern, to try once more to talk me out of it. When he wasn't there I didn't worry. It wasn't until I was two blocks from the stadium that I started running. By the time I turned the last corner, I felt the same panic as the day Smoke was shot, so I was exhilarated to see Tommy sitting on the platform with broken whiskey bottles at his feet.

"It worked just like we planned," he said. His head was bent to the side and he had a smile on his face like he'd been smoking weed. "You're home free. Off the hook."

The beet juice stained the pavement in dull, pink puddles everywhere but directly beneath his feet, where it was darker and strangely bright. The stain grew darker still as I watched. Something was wrong.

"Worked just like we planned," he said again, "'cept I got in the way." His head dropped lower, as if he was about to fall asleep.

"Wait here," I told him. "I'm gonna get that donkey cart across the street and take you to the hospital."

He tried to lift his hand to me but couldn't reach. "Don't leave me just yet. I need somethin' to lean on or I'll fall over like a damn wino. Don't let me fall over."

I took off my shirt and tied it round the knife wound at his back. I said "You did good, fooled all those bastards," and kept talking till he was past hearing.

~

AT 4:45 PM, minutes after most of Washington's civil servants had left work, General MacArthur gave the order to advance. Down Pennsylvania Avenue, past trolleys filled with homebound workers, rode the horse soldiers of the 3rd Cavalry with sabers drawn. They were led by Major George Patton who wore pearl-handled pistols and believed himself to be a reincarnated 16th-century Chinese warrior. Behind Patton's mares marched the infantry with bayonets fixed. Taking up the rear was a machine gun unit and six tanks grooving tread marks in the soft asphalt.

Nora joined Pennsylvania Avenue just ahead of Patton's Cavalry, pedaling her bicycle with head down, paying only as much attention to the road as she needed to avoid automobiles, trolleys and fresh piles of horse manure. She was aware of the horses and sabers only in the general way she was aware that the air was hot and her breathing heavy. Her mind was on Will Cutler, and not all of him but only the hole below his right shoulder, the bubble of blood just below the collar bone, his fluttering eyes and fish-white complexion. She saw death hovering there, and not some abstract idea but death itself, like one of her father's moldy spirits. That scared her to tears and scared her still.

She'd followed his ambulance to the hospital, a tea-colored building with black-framed windows like bruised eyes. Twice she tried to sneak into the emergency room and was stopped both times by a nurse with shoulders wide as the doorway.

"There's no use coming back 'til tomorrow morning," she said. "He'll either be alive then or dead."

She reached the Fort ahead of the cavalry, stopping at the stoop to talk with Dorothy, the school teacher from Mississippi. Her red shawl was dotted with what looked like plaster.

"Are you well, Dorothy?"

"Not entirely," she said with a wan smile. Dorothy's brown hair was streaked a very fine silver where it fell against her cheekbones. "I'm well enough. And you?"

"I've come back for my friend's moving picture camera. Have you seen it?"

Dorothy looked slightly away, as though trying to picture what a movie camera might look like. "I haven't, dear. There are policemen inside who might help."

Before Nora entered the building, Dorothy called her back. In a lowered voice she asked, "Have you heard anything about the barracks in Maryland with the beds and hot water? That isn't spoiled, is it?"

"I wouldn't know," said Nora. "But I'll be sure to tell you if I hear."

The three policemen inside were of no help concerning the camera. Nora had never seen them before, but she recognized a change in them all the same. They looked from Nora to the blood stains and back again with flat, emotionless expressions. The building itself was similarly transformed. A few hours earlier it had exploded with bricks and gunfire. Now it might have been the quietest place in the city.

Nora found Grace Tumulty in front of the Showroom, the baby asleep against her chest. As unmoving as they were, they might have been statues. Patty and Ben came running from the street.

"Horsies!" squealed Ben as his sister pointed down the avenue. Nora could hear the clop of hooves. She looked to the street and saw pennants and sabers floating above the heads of the crowd. It seemed an odd time for a parade.

She put her hand on Grace's shoulder. "Are you with us Grace?"

Grace's eyes darted to the street then back to Nora. "We should be ready to leave here. If it comes to that."

～

THE CAVALRY came to a halt between the condemned buildings at 3rd Street and on the other side of the avenue, the New Capitol Hotel, between veterans on one side and spectators on the other. Clearly, this is not a drill, thought Sevareid. No one else seemed particularly worried.

He recognized a U.S. Senator in front of the hotel, Henry Brighton from Delaware, and went to interview him.

"I'm sympathetic to the Bonus Army," said Brighton. "Though I am disturbed by the sight of these veterans and their families—hanging laundry from missing windows, cooking cabbage soup over open fires this close to the Capitol. There must be a more suitable place fo…."

A sudden movement of Major Patton's Cavalry distracted the Senator. The horse soldiers had formed a double line. They sat tall in the saddle, as if waiting for a signal. Sevareid expected them to move into the veterans like cowboys herding cattle, and felt great sympathy for the veterans. But he couldn't deny his excitement as well. He was about to witness and record history being made. It was curious that the horses were facing him and the other spectators rather than the Bonus vets, but he guessed they'd worked on some dramatic whirling maneuver, all of them up on their hind legs. That's what he'd do, rise and whirl, then charge.

When the signal did come, a barked command from Patton himself, the soldiers neither rose nor whirled but only raised their sabers and charged—directly at Sevareid, Senator Brighton and the other spectators standing five deep in front of the hotel. Sevareid immediately sprinted to his left, toward a narrow alley. In the shocked silence he heard Senator Brighton's voice and, without slowing, turned his head to watch.

"Stop this at once!" ordered the Senator, stepping toward the horse soldiers with hands raised. The soldiers never slowed.

Brighton was spun by the flank of a passing horse and hit on the cheek with the flat of a saber blade. Falling to the sidewalk, he rolled to the wall of the hotel against the metal bars of the old slave pens.

~

WHEN THE FIRST tear gas canister hit the ground, Nora grabbed Patty and Ben by the back of their collars and stiff-armed them toward the Capitol. She turned to call for Grace and found her close behind.

Things went well enough until they encountered a crush of people on the sidewalk at 2nd Street. The gas was drifting toward them like a low fog. The children grabbed at their eyes and the baby screamed. Nora yelled to Grace, "Across the street!" and pushed Patty and Ben off the sidewalk. They cleared the street and ran another half-block before Grace stopped, demanding rest.

"I'll count to twenty and then we're off again," said Nora as they slumped below the awning of a real estate office. Taped to the window was a yellowed sketch of a manor house for sale. Two men ran past, only to stop and throw rocks at the soldiers.

"Get up!" ordered Nora. Grace obeyed reluctantly and too late as the cavalry charged from both sides. Their only exit was to follow the rock throwers down an alley. A bad choice, but Nora saw no other and pushed Ben and Patty forward.

By Washington standards it was a short alley, only forty yards to the connecting street. But halfway through, Nora heard the rasping breath of the horses and knew they wouldn't make it. A gap appeared to her right, barely big enough for the few large trash cans there. Nora threw herself sideways, pulling Patty and Ben with her. Grace was only steps away when one of the horses lowered its head and hit her in the back. As she flew onto an overturned can, her baby squirted from her arms into Nora's.

"That was a pretty neat trick, Grace," said Nora after the Cavalry passed. "We've only one more to do."

Grace kicked her feet like a petulant child. "No more. We stay here until it's over."

Nora sniffed the air. "Can you smell it? The wind has changed and the tear gas is coming this way. All we need do is reach that street and we're free."

Grace sobbed, Patty and Ben whimpered at her side. Only the baby gurgled happily. Nora felt absurdly pleased to be holding this little girl, especially since she had no doubt that she'd get them all to safety. "One more run and it's done," she said, handing the baby to her mother. "You see that statue of the horse soldier? In the little square? There's a tunnel there. I know because I've been inside it. Now, let's run and no more stopping."

～

A VETERAN with blood dripping from his chin staggered along the avenue shouting "Shame! Shame!" and "Yellow bastards!" General MacArthur, in his riding pants and boots, ignored him. But when another man, a civilian yelled, "The American flag means nothing to me after this," MacArthur pointed his riding crop at him and issued an order. "Put that man under arrest if he opens his mouth again."

Eric Sevareid had found his way behind the cavalry and now, holding up his notebook so the soldiers could recognize him as a reporter, stayed as close to MacArthur and Eisenhower as possible. The gas grenades left behind a dirty yellow haze that stung his eyes and throat. Sevareid watched a woman on an exposed stairway of the Showroom building, begging for someone to catch the child in her arms. Ignored, she finally carried it down the stairs herself.

The infantry used rifle stocks to push and prod the remaining veterans toward Anacostia's newly named Camp Marks. Even the few who turned to throw bricks and taunt, "Tin soldier! Tin soldier!" retreated quickly. Within minutes, ambulances were moving up and down Pennsylvania picking up the injured.

Sevareid spotted a medic holding a...severed ear between his thumb and forefinger. He wrote it down in his notebook. A Negro man wearing an Army jacket sat in a tree beside Pennsylvania Avenue, waving a small American flag.

"God that gave us this here country, help us now!" he called out. "God that gave us this here country, help us now!"

Sevareid didn't bother to record that. A colored veteran waving a flag from a tree was not quite good enough, not on this day of lethal shootings and cavalry assaults. Already in the notebook were accounts of women pulling children from beneath horses' hooves, and men armed only with rocks going against bayonets and sabers. On this day the bar was set extremely high.

He was still unnerved by the morning's events at the Fort: Will with a bullet wound below his shoulder, carried out on a stretcher while Nora held his hand. Sevareid had apparently been the only one to see her sling the rock at Captain Largent.

"I've got to go with him to the hospital," she said, her eyes red from crying. "I'll find you later."

After she left, Sevareid tried to talk himself out of her. He'd seen prettier girls. Hell, right off the top of his head he could think of two or three back at the university who were nearly as pretty in their own ways. But that was the thing with Nora. In her own way she was like no girl Sevareid had ever met or imagined. Sleeping with Walker? That just proved she wasn't bound by convention. Assaulting a police officer? Look what she was willing to risk to save a friend. Sevareid was reminded of a character Faulkner described in *The Town*:

> It was that there was just too much of what she was for
> any one human female package to contain and hold: too
> much of white, too much of female, too much of maybe just
> glor....

No use denying it, Nora might not be the perfect woman but she was perfect for him. When she and Walker came apart (and the odds of that were overwhelming) he'd be waiting for her.

The colored man was still on his tree limb waving the American flag, when a blue tear gas tin exploded against the trunk. It took abut twenty seconds for the gas to rise and the veteran to tumble onto the sidewalk. Sevareid opened his notebook. Now it was worth writing down.

He went looking for the cavalry, which was still charging madly about the streets, swinging sabers. He heard a shout from the alley off 2nd Street where he'd escaped the first cavalry attack. As he entered the alley, he saw a policeman, his back to Sevareid and his gun drawn. He was talking to someone Sevareid couldn't see.

"Come on out, you bastard. Make it easy on yourself."

Sevareid opened his notebook and moved deliberately down the alley. He was fifteen yards from the cop when he heard a second voice that stopped him in his tracks.

"Answer me one question. Why did you kill her?"

Max Berga! Sevareid couldn't see him but knew he must he behind some trash cans.

"Why I killed that tramp is none of your business," said Officer Tobin. "Why I'm going to kill you is what you should be asking."

If Tobin saw him now he'd be shot as well. But he couldn't just back out of the alley and leave Berga to die. He was still short of a good solution when Tobin turned and spotted him.

"Down here, officers!" shouted Sevareid, gesturing behind him to a posse of invented soldiers. "Down this alley."

Tobin quickly holstered his revolver. But seconds later, with no soldiers in sight, he drew it and aimed at Sevareid.

"Don't be a fool, they'll hear the shot and catch you red-handed," he said. He wanted to turn and run but forced himself to keep his chest and eyes forward. Slowly he began backing up. Only when Tobin closed his left eye to take aim did he dart right, then left. The first bullet whizzed over his head. He rolled to the ground as the next one kicked up dirt a few feet from his shoulder. Just my luck, he thought as he ran hunched low, listening for a third shot. It never came. What he heard instead was a wet thud, like watermelon on brick. He looked over his shoulder and saw Max Berga standing over the prone body of Tobin. In his hands was a metal bar.

"Keep going!" ordered Berga "I'll take care of this."

Sevareid did as he was told, overcome by a feeling in his belly, not fear or regret but a wild joy at being alive.

~

ON THE ANACOSTIA side of the 11th Street Bridge, all fires had been ordered extinguished. Only rumors still burned.

"The Marines wouldn't do it. They flat-out refused to cross into our camp!"

"If we march on the bridge, the soldiers will join us!"

"MacArthur won't let us down."

That last assertion came from Dennis Diamond, who hadn't lost his faith in the General. Faith being the only thing he had left.

Thousands of veterans and their families had already packed and gone but the majority remained. Even after Police Supintendent Glassford visited the camp to warn them it was hopeless.

"I told MacArthur a night invasion was the height of stupidity. But I was outranked," said Glassford. Before he left, he shook hands all around, like an officer in a war movie, sending men on a suicide mission. Nora saw more than a few weeping openly.

"Where else are we gonna go?" asked Joe Angelo, the veteran who buried himself six feet underground. Hopeless or not, and despite the mud and mosquitoes, Camp Marks was home. Besides, said Angelo, when had they given up anything without a fight? "We'll get in our licks at least."

Nora wandered through the camp looking for Walker. Near the stage she found Virni Tabak sitting on a wooden newspaper wagon. Virni jumped up and hugged her.

"You're not mad at me?" she asked. After the tent fire, when Virni was told the cup he'd conjured was actually thrown through the top of the tent by Nora, he tossed it to the ground. Dennis Diamond retrieved it and had returned it to Nora just hours earlier.

"Of course I'm not mad. I was an idiot. I had a vision of something falling from the sky. It happened. How it happened makes no difference. How is Will? I went to see him but the hospital was closed to visitors."

"I don't know. They wouldn't let me in. Catherine is there waiting."

"I will see him," said Virni. "I will tell them I'm his priest."

It hurt Nora's face to laugh. "If anyone can do it, you can."

"Will you come with me?" he asked.

"I can't. I have to find Walker." Nora had other things to do as well. She kissed Virni's cheek. "Tell Will I've said a prayer for him. I still remember a few."

~

ERIC SEVAREID crossed the bridge, knowing soldiers would soon follow. He wasn't sure what kind of greeting awaited them, but he and Max Berga had heard a variety of opinions on the subject from men in the 12th Infantry.

"Them old bastards have a stockpile of weapons, shipped in from Pennsylvania."

"I hear they've been making homemade bombs."

"They stole rifles from that military school."

One of the infantrymen asked Berga what he'd heard.

"I heard the Bonus Army is going out the way it came in," said Berga. "Without a pot to piss in."

Sevareid tried to raise the subject of Officer Tobin with Berga, but the reporter brushed it away. "You don't talk about casualties of war. I know from first-hand experience in Germany. Things happen. You learn to forget them."

"I felt excited today, during the violence, and it worries me," Sevareid confessed. "Was I hoping for it, to enhance my stories?"

"That's not excitement you felt. That's adrenaline. It can save your life. If you don't have that, you better find a job filing papers."

Now, on the Bonus side of the river, with only a dim glow of bridge lights, Sevareid made a vow. He would allow himself to feel whatever there was to feel and not analyze it until later. Not until he'd seen this story through.

Someone was approaching.

"Eric?"

Sevareid let out his breath. "Nora. I should have known you'd be in the thick of things."

Their hug was short and awkward.

"I need to find a reporter from the *Evening Star*," she told him.

"Which reporter?"

"It doesn't matter." She held out her notebook. "This needs to get to Mr. Ned Grant."

"What's in it?"

"A story for the newspaper. About the families that were evicted from those buildings today."

"Do you like what you wrote?"

"I didn't like the way I felt writing it, but I'm feeling better about it now."

A dozen fire trucks started their engines on the far side of the bridge. "So how are you and Walker?"

"We're fine," said Nora.

Sevareid thought to say something like "That's great" but didn't. As much as he liked Walker, and he liked him as well as any friend he'd ever had, Sevareid didn't think Nora should drop herself into that kind of trouble. As for his own self-interest, well, he wasn't going to look too closely at that either.

The fire trucks started across the bridge, their searchlights swinging from side to side. Nora pushed her notebook into Sevareid's chest. "Will you deliver this for me?"

"I'll do my best," he said taking it from her hands. "Right now let's make sure we don't get caught in the crossfire."

⁓

BEHIND THE FIRE TRUCKS marched the infantry, led by General MacArthur. At his side was Major Dwight Eisenhower. As the soldiers reached the other side of the bridge they stepped off to right and left in files of two and moved slowly forward. Behind them were the cavalry and tanks. MacArthur sent scouts to secure the obvious spot for an ambush, a line of trees ahead and to the left.

The fire trucks threw their lights to the outer circle of camp shacks, tents, teepees and chicken coops. A box of lettuce lay in a latrine ditch. A wrecked automobile was filled with hay. Most of the remaining Bonus veterans and their families had pulled back to the stage at the center of camp where kids once tap-danced for pennies. A few waved banners and flags.

With the wind blowing at their backs, the infantry didn't bother to secure masks before tossing the gas bombs. Soldiers on each end of the advancing line set fire to anything that would burn. As the first flames shot into the air, some veterans answered with bricks and rocks. The infantry charged. What had been an orderly advance became a rout. The fires spread quickly—some Bonus veterans helped it along by lighting fires of their own. The flames silhouetted the confusion.

Sevareid watched the advance with veterans near the stage. But after the fires were lit, he came forward with his notebook held high. To his left, three veterans with hands raised, stood at the edge of what looked to be a well-tended vegetable garden. Sevareid guessed they were trying to protect it, but no use. The cavalry trampled the plot, knocking one of the men onto his back.

Dennis Diamond appeared through the smoke waving a white flag. For a moment he appeared invisible to the horse soldiers riding past. Diamond was within a dozen yards of MacArthur, before the General moved away. When Diamond tried to follow, whatever the spell that protected him was broken. Two cavalry pinned him between their horses, knocking Diamond to his knees.

Sevareid's path was blocked by a soldier with a rifle. He held the notebook higher and said, "I'm a reporter. Looking for the General." The soldier came slowly forward. Dark as it was, Sevareid could see the fury in the man's face and it scared him. When he started to speak again the soldier hit the left side of his face with the butt of his rifle.

"The General's back there," he said and moved on.

Sevareid could feel his cheek swelling. He was unsure which way to go, when Major Eisenhower appeared out of the gloom.

"Sevareid. You better get back here with me."

"Thank you Major, I'd appreciate that."

Major George Patton rode past them, chasing a group of flee-ing veterans. A brick to his chest knocked him off his horse. In the circle of men closest to where Patton fell, Sevareid saw Joe Angelo who, fourteen years earlier, earned the Distinguished Service Cross for saving Patton's life. Now, Angelo turned from Patton and ran. Eisenhower ordered two of his men to rescue the Major.

When Eisenhower left MacArthur to inspect the right flank, Sevareid went with him. The whole scene appeared pitiful. "These ragged veterans are no match for MacArthur's troops," said Eisenhower. "And they're certainly no threat to the United States government."

A boy, no more than seven years old, ran past them toward a tent. An infantryman stepped forward to intercept him.

"I forgot my rabbit," said the boy, trying to slip past. The sol-dier shouted, "Get out of here," and blocked his path with his rifle. Whether by design or accident, the bayonet sliced into the boy's thigh.

When Eisenhower and Sevareid reached him, blood was run-ning down his pant leg. He appeared to be in shock, shivering in the 90-degree heat. Eisenhower put his military jacket across the boy's shoulders and called for a medic.

"What's your name?" he asked as he applied pressure to the wound. The boy didn't seem to hear him.

"Son, I need to know your name."

He looked at Eisenhower with dull eyes. "Eugene. Eugene King."

After the medic took over, Eisenhower confronted the soldier who'd stabbed him. "Do you know what you just did?" The infantryman's face showed only surprise. Whether for what he'd done or for the fact that he was being admonished for it, Sevareid couldn't tell.

NORA WAS JUST back to her hut when the first flames lit the sky. Grace Tumulty and her baby were in the process of waking. The other two children still slept.

"There was a colored man here looking for you," said Grace brushing back her hair.

Nora bent her face to Grace's. "We've got to get out of here."

"We're too tired."

Nora pointed to the fires. "Soldiers are coming. They'll throw more gas."

Grace rose slowly, tucked her baby under one arm and grabbed a bag of possessions with the other. "You bring Patty and Ben," she said, starting away.

Nora called for her to wait, but Grace disappeared in the smoke. Nora shook the children. "Come now, time to wake. We're going to a better place." Patty and Ben barely moved. Nora saw the outline of soldiers approaching. She pulled Patty off the leaf mattress and then Ben. Both protested and tried to lie back down. Using a hand for each, she pulled them to their feet. Squatting between the pair, she pressed Patty against her right hip and Ben against her left. But when she tried to stand, the cup in a pouch around her waist prevented it. She tried putting the pouch around her neck but the fabric obscured her vision. The soldiers were close now, kicking and poking with their bayonets. Nora sat Patty and Ben on the ground and once again buried her cup in the soft dirt beneath her pallet. Now the children fit against her hips. They were heavy, but they'd wake soon enough. She set out in the direction their mother had gone, toward the darkest part of the camp and Good Hope Road.

WALKER

The fire spread toward the woods where I waited with a dozen men.

"We draw straws to see who shoots MacArthur," said the man who called himself Detroit Don.

"Why MacArthur?" The question came out of the dark. "Because he'll make a loud sound. And because he sold us out." "I don't like it," said Robbie Adams. Robbie was a young white kid I first met at the New Masses office, an annoyingly friendly type who twice invited me to dinner at his parent's home in Cleveland Park. I declined both times and had avoided his company ever since. Robbie was wearing a hat with earflaps, his face deliberately smeared with mud. "A thing like that could destroy the party. Set everyone against us."

"Listen kid, why don't you go back to college," said Detroit Don.

"He's got a point," said another man. "MacArthur's a hero to people. We kill him and there's a black mark on the party forever."

"A black mark? Who gives a damn? We're fighting a war here. Better a black mark than we starve to death." Don pulled a gun from his waistband. "Forget the straws. I'll do it myself." MacArthur was visible in the light of the fire, maybe fifty yards away.

I didn't have an opinion about whether shooting MacArthur was good strategy or bad. It was risky, but then the Party wasn't winning any popularity contests and a bold strike might have been exactly what it needed. But the part of me that wanted to see Don pull the trigger had no connection to logic. My best friend was dead, my mother had disowned me. It seemed right that somebody be punished besides me.

When Detroit Don moved to the edge of the woods for a better shot, Robbie Adams followed and grabbed his arm. "I won't let you."

The two wrestled for control of the revolver like Laurel and Hardy fighting over a drumstick. If I hadn't been so disgusted I might have found it funny, particularly since MacArthur was at least twenty yards out of pistol range. I moved to where Robbie and Detroit Don were still thrashing around. "Give me the damn gun!" I said. It went off as soon as I wrapped my palm around the barrel. I felt the bullet pass through my grip.

Detroit Don and Robbie Adams fell away, leaving me holding

the revolver. While the concussion still rang in my ears, ten men jumped to their feet and ran through the woods. The only one left with me was Robbie Adams, lying where he fell.

"Get up," I ordered but Robbie didn't answer. He was on his back, his head resting against a rotted log. He looked silly under his hat flaps. His mouth wide open as though he was about to sing. The bullet must have gone through his heart to kill him so quickly and I was grateful for that. I didn't think I could comfort two dying men in one day. I felt a tear roll down my face. I put a finger to my cheek and tasted the salt. The soldiers who'd dropped to their bellies at the sound of the shot were up again. I put the gun in my pants and joined the retreat.

∼

PATTY AND BEN woke when Nora started running. They each took one of her hands and raced beside her. After their experience with the horses in the alley, there was little need to urge them on. They reached Good Hope Road without finding Grace and kept moving, occasionally calling out her name. At a small park a few blocks up, Nora saw women from the Showroom building huddled together. No one had seen Grace or her baby. Nora left Patty and Ben with the women and went back to find them.

Negro families on both sides of the road had opened their doors to women and children, but Nora couldn't knock on every one. Besides, she was sure Grace would not take shelter without Patty and Ben. On the walk back to the Bonus camp she heard airplanes and wondered if they were dropping bombs.

At the edge of the camp she found Neil Gold in a dark suit, a handkerchief covering his mouth and nose.

"You're going the wrong way."

"I need to go back."

Gold put the handkerchief in his pocket. "For Walker?"

"For the mother of two children I brought out. I think she's still in there."

"Let's go then," said Gold.

They moved toward the center of camp, against a flow of retreating veterans. There was little panic now. MacArthur's troops had set up a line across the territory they controlled and were now moving slowly and methodically forward. Nora heard the distant sound of a phonograph playing *Old Black Joe*. Two water pumpers sprayed a fire in a nearby woods.

"When you love someone, it's different," said Gold.

"What's different?"

"The stupidity. You don't notice it so much. Or maybe you just don't care. But now, it's all I can see. The stupidity."

Nora tried to remember who it was that Neil Gold had loved. There was so much she didn't know, about him, about everything. The smoke and tear gas burned her eyes. She thought of the woman on the *Jerseley* whose little boy died, and couldn't remember her name. That saddened her. If she didn't remember, who would?

They found Eric Sevareid beside a burning hut. The left side of his face was bruised and swollen. "It got a little wild back there," he said with a lopsided grin. "A press badge isn't much of a match for a rifle butt."

In the wall of noise ahead, Nora heard a woman's cry and followed the sound to Grace Tumulty. She was slouched on the ground inside a ring of soldiers, clutching her baby to her chest. The soldiers stayed back, as if afraid to go any closer. A medic lifted the infant from Grace's arms.

"This baby needs attention," he told her. "You can ride with her in the ambulance."

The baby wheezed and coughed, her skin ghostly pale in the smoky light. Nora pushed through the soldiers. "Patty and Ben are fine," she told Grace. "You go to the hospital, we'll look after them."

Nora wasn't sure Grace had understood a word she said. She wore the same look as…Deirdre Kelly. That was the name of the mother who lost her little boy on the *Jerseley*.

Nora felt no better for having remembered.

〜

PATHETIC AND DISTRESSING SCENES
MARK EVACUATION OF BONUS VETS

The Washington Times

Straggling over the brow of a hill on their way out of the Anacostia flats last night, the bonus marchers were framed by a crimson sky. Crackling flames and smoke were marking the end of their shanty city.

Some came out in military formation. Others trudged slowly on the sidewalk. A hysterical woman pushed a baby buggy with two small children while another group sang the refrain, "Where Do We Go From Here?"

One colored man remained almost to the last, playing records on a phonograph after he had set fire to his shack.

———————

Newspaper men scurried hither and thither. Press services, out-of-town newspapers and local newspapers had made "arrangements" with residents on Chicago Street, leading out of Camp Marks, and reporters scurried up the hill to the private houses to telephone. An airplane bearing photographers circled the flats time and again. Those on the ground could not see the plane for the dense smoke.

———————

A pretty girl living on 13th Street Southwest watched the burning of a shack until tear gas drove her inside her home. She said:

"Poor fellow. He has been working on his house two months."

———————

Citizens around 11th and M Streets Southeast followed suit of the veterans by picking up tear gas bombs hurled at them by troops and promptly throwing them back. The policeman driver of a patrol wagon was overcome by gas and fell to the pavement, with Superintendent Glassford helping to pick him up. Citizens, some of whom had gone to bed before the gassing started, came into the streets pleading with the police to quit throwing the bombs because their wives and children were suffering in the houses. Crying children could be heard in many of the houses.

A bonus veteran encountered Police Supt. Glassford. As the huts burned around them he said, "Mr. Glassford, you know what the Belgian children used to say? 'They have burned our beds. They have even burned M'sieu Jesu Christ.'"

"Those were Germans," said Glassford.

The veteran shook his head. "The fire is the same."

I lowered the newspaper and looked at Nora, hunched over her notebook.

"Will your story appear in today's *Star*?"

"We'll know in an hour," she said. The story she was writing now had her face furrowed with concentration. There were pictures in her mind that needed exorcising: blood bubbling from below Will Cutler's collar bone; Grace Tumulty bent over her wheezing daughter; terrified children running through the tear gas at night. She had an idea that if she wrote it all down, the pictures would no longer belong to her but to a story.

We were behind a mound of rusting cans and scrap metal, between the Navy Yard dump and the smoking remains of the Bonus Camp. Not hiding exactly, but conveniently hidden from the uniformed soldier sixty yards away who stabbed at the rubble with his bayonet.

We'd come back to retrieve Nora's cup.

"How long?" I asked.

"I don't know. How long are most newspaper articles?"

"No, I mean how long do we wait?"

I had pictures of my own: Tommy dying in my arms and Robbie Adams at my feet. But I wasn't sure I wanted to be rid of them. I felt spent, but at peace after a night of weeping. Once it started I couldn't stop, the sound in my throat and chest like a wild animal's. Twice I threw away the revolver only to retrieve it, for no other reason than it felt good to hold something so cool and hard. Watching Nora write with a stubby brown pencil, a flame of hair over her left ear, I felt content, with no desire except to be with her on the edge of this smoking dump.

She looked up from her notebook. "What do we do after this?"

"Get some sleep."

"No. I mean after that?"

"Take a swim."

"And then?"

"Go fishing."

Nora laughed, a hand at her mouth to suppress it. I watched her eyes dance above the closed fingers, merry green despite all that had happened.

The soldier moved from the area where she'd buried the cup, back toward the center of camp. I took Nora's arm, pulled her close and whispered, "Let's go."

I stood, adjusted the revolver in my waistband and stepped into the open.

ABOUT THE AUTHOR

DENIS COLLINS has been a journalist with the *Washington Post,*
Miami Herald and *San Jose Mercury News* and a freelance writer
in New Zealand, Belgium and the Netherlands. He covered diverse
areas including books, politics, urban and outdoor affairs, and
sports. *Spying: The Secret History of History,* his non-fiction book
was published in 2004. His writing appears in *Smithsonian, FYI
Forbes, Men's Journal* and other publications in the United States
and New Zealand. He received a BA from Fordham University, and
attended Trinity College, Dublin, Ireland, and Talladega College in
Alabama. As a writer and teacher first educated in and again living
in Washington DC, he works as a creative writing teacher and pub-
lisher of the literary journal *The Oracle* for the Sasha Bruce
Youthwork Center.